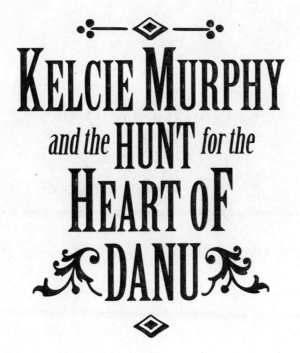

KELCIE MURPHY
and the HUNT for the
HEART OF
DANU

ERIKA LEWIS

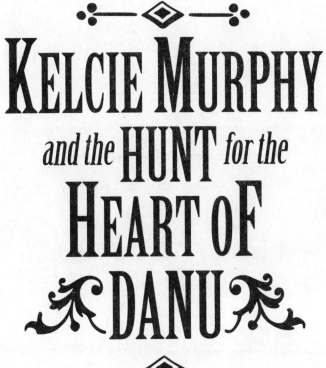

KELCIE MURPHY
and the HUNT for the
HEART OF
DANU

STARSCAPE

TOR PUBLISHING GROUP · NEW YORK

For Jack,
you inspire me every day.

KELCIE MURPHY AND THE HUNT FOR THE HEART OF DANU

Copyright © 2023 by Erika Lewis

A Starscape Book
Published by Tom Doherty Associates / Tor Publishing Group
120 Broadway
New York, NY 10271

www.tor-forge.com

The Library of Congress Cataloging-in-Publication Data is available upon request.

ISBN 978-1-250-20830-9 (hardcover)
ISBN 978-1-250-20829-3 (ebook)

Our books may be purchased in bulk for promotional, educational, or business use. Please contact your local bookseller or the Macmillan Corporate and Premium Sales Department at 1-800-221-7945, extension 5442, or by email at MacmillanSpecialMarkets@macmillan.com.

First Edition: 2023

Printed in the United States of America

0 9 8 7 6 5 4 3 2 1

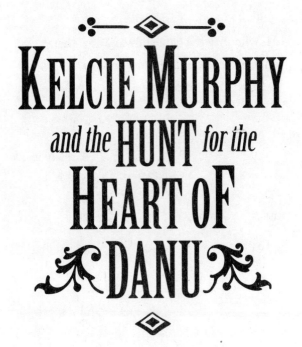

KELCIE MURPHY
and the HUNT for the
HEART OF
DANU

All who play the game of war know that
when the enemy catches you unaware,
the battle is already over.

Already lost.

PROLOGUE

WINTER

A THUNDEROUS RUMBLE WOKE Lexis before dawn. Half-asleep, she stumbled out of bed to the window. During daylight hours, from her room in the Saiga Den at the top of the tallest of the Eternal Peaks, Lexis had a good view of the frozen tundra below, the Dauour Forest to the north, and in the east a sliver of the toxic mist swirling hundreds of feet above the Abyss. But right now it was too dark to see much of anything.

Another rumble, and Lexis shuddered, afraid and confused. Her barefeet planted firmly on the floor sensed it came from the east, from the Abyss. But that was *impossible*. Nothing *ever* came out of the Abyss! The ebony waters that plummeted straight down into a never-ending waterfall were noiseless, the unnatural thing strangling even the water's gurgle before it could make it out. The thing gave Lexis chills every time she looked at it.

As if someone were deliberately trying to confuse her, the next quake came from the north. She glanced at the alarm button at the other end of the room, every instinct telling her to pull it, but hesitated. No one else had stirred.

A tick later, the sun peeked over the mountain, just enough for Lexis to see into the forest's gloomy shadows. Everything *looked* normal.

Maybe it's the drill, Lexis mused, relieved. Aífe, their preceptor, *had* been promising an all-school drill for weeks now.

Petrified trees in the forest uprooted in wide thudding swaths. The vampire owls, normally turning in at this hour, suddenly spirited away, screeching like someone or something was about to eat *them* for a change. Crunching, like the sound of heavy boulders rolling on hard-packed snow, escaped the forest—slow at first, but gaining speed. Raging roars shredded what was left of the easing dawn. Lexis gulped. Whatever it was, it was heading for everyone's favorite escape from school: the small village of Volga.

Okay. This isn't a drill.

This isn't a drill!

"Wake up!" she yelled at the thirty sleeping bodies. She tripped over cot legs, running for the alarm. "Wake up!"

"What is it?"

"What's going on?"

"Will you shut up!"

With determined hands, Lexis yanked the lever beside the door and let the alarm answer for her.

MINUTES LATER SHE boarded a creaky flatbarge along with the rest of the students twelve and over. The vessel, normally used for training exercises, was flown by Aífe's sacred pets, Potham and Wallace, who were strapped to it with harnesses. They were the very last two wyverns left in the Lands of Winter, and the most majestic beasts Lexis had ever seen.

The launch bay door—a granite section of the mountain—retracted. Old and creaky, Wallace's and Potham's enormous hairless wings beat the air fast and furious to achieve enough lift for takeoff. Lexis gripped the railing so hard her knuckles turned white. If she'd only seen what they were facing, then she might have a clue how to fight it, but as it was, they were heading into their first battle blind.

"Listen up!" Aífe said, her long red hair fanning out behind her. She always wore the same black Braverwil uniform as her students because she liked them to see her as a friend as much as a teacher. Like she was one of them, something Lexis really appreciated. Aífe climbed up on the railing, hopping onto Wallace's strap for balance, and raised her flaming spear. "Summer has found a way to do the impossible. *Cewr* have broken into Winter."

Nervous mumbles spread around the deck.

"Giants?" someone called.

"Yes. Giants. How? We have no idea, and no time to ponder. Troops are on their way, but they are engaged in three other locations with them. We will have to do all we can to save Volga! There could be one or there could be ten."

Ten? Lexis's palms broke out in a cold sweat. She was scared. There was no harm in admitting it to herself, but she could never let it show. That was rule number one for fianna leaders. If she was afraid, her fianna would be too. Fear led to mistakes, and mistakes led to injuries, or worse.

Lexis squared her shoulders.

"This is a day for Braverwil cadets to show me what you're made of! Cold hard steel!" Aífe raised her spear. The flatbarge jolted from stomping and cheering, Lexis's among the loudest. "You will not let me down!"

Lexis's powers heated with rising adrenaline. Letting Aífe down was something she never, ever wanted to do, not after all the preceptor had done for her.

Lexis's parents had never wanted her to go to Braverwil. Abbots at the Fomorian temple in Mezron, they were pacifists, and didn't believe in war. Or training for war. Or wielding weapons of any kind except a kitchen knife. They hid Lexis away, never letting her attend any formal school, refusing to let her use her powers at all, but Aífe had found her.

On her tenth birthday, the preceptor showed up on their doorstep with a letter from the Queen demanding to know why the pulse elemental hadn't reported to school. It was the best day of Lexis's life, and the worst. She never saw her parents again. They said if she chose to go, chose to fight, that she was no longer their daughter. She belonged to Aífe. Lexis never looked back.

She turned to say something inspirational to her fianna, but Swappy stretched, farting at the same time.

Lexis chuckled, shaking her head, relishing the tension release. Swappy Toots was small for his age and the youngest in her fianna, still eleven. He was the craftiest of changelings except for one little problem that would always give him away. He fizzled whenever he got excited—or nervous—or sad. Really any emotion could bring on the gas.

"I heard that," Jack growled.

Swappy smirked. "Better than smelling it."

Jack Postal was a legend. He could morph into his saber-toothed tiger familiar first year. His mother was Badb, one of the three Morrígna, and a goddess of vengeance, which was why he never forgave Lexis for choosing Swappy to be in their fianna. She chose Jack for his eyes, so blue they glowed during Selection, so intense they rattled Lexis, and had challenged her ever since.

Behind him, the last member of their fianna ignored them. Pavel was busy, scrutinizing every square inch of his ice armor. He bent his elbow, testing movement, then shaved a millimeter off, only to add it back again. Ever since word came that his aunt was imprisoned in Summer, Pavel had turned into an extreme perfectionist, as if preparing to go and get her back.

Two years Lexis had led them. Two years—they were more than her best friends. They were her family. If anything happened to them, Lexis would never, ever forgive herself.

The transport halted. Earth-shaking crashes were followed by murderous roars and frantic screams. Cadets rushed the railings, Lexis and her fianna included. Her breath caught. The five giants Lexis could see were at least twenty-five feet tall, made entirely of boulders, and storming through the streets in raging fits, pulverizing building after building. The Frosty Cone where they got flavored icicles—gone. The shop of the tailor who fabricated and repaired all of Braverwil's uniforms—reduced to rubble. Then Lexis saw the bookstore she frequented during break when everyone else went home, and her heart stopped beating. There was nothing left. She felt terrible. She never knew the name of the woman who owned it, but she was always nice. Let Lexis borrow books when she didn't have enough money to pay for them. All she could do now was hope she wasn't inside when the walls came crashing down.

"Summer is going to pay for this!" Jack spit.

Her sentiments exactly.

Aife raised her spear at the wyverns, and the transport lowered until it was only ten feet off the ground. "Pick your target! Keep them busy! And don't *die*!"

The older kids leaped off without looking. Most of Lexis's classmates hesitated, choosing a safe spot to start their descent. Lexis was choosing a giant, like Aife had told them to do.

Directly beneath the transport one stood on the crushed remains of an ice house. A fairy, maybe five, still in her pajamas, was trapped under its big toe.

"That one! Pavel, Swaps, see what you can do to move it away from the house," Lexis ordered. "Jack and I will help the girl."

Swappy smacked Pavel's cheek, rousing an annoyed groan from their ice fairy.

As a changeling, Swappy could turn into anyone he wanted, he only had to touch them. In less than a second, his pale, skinny body tanned and grew a foot. His curly green hair shrank until he, like Pavel, was shaved bald. Canines elongated. His eyes went from green to solid white and butterfly wings sprouted.

The giant ripped an electric pole from the ground and hurled it, spearing poor Potham through his wing! Shrieking, Potham dipped, falling, dragging the transport down on one side. Lexis and Jack were close enough to the railing to grab hold. Others weren't so lucky. They plummeted toward frozen ground or worse, the giant's sharp teeth.

Pavel and Swappy jumped, joining the other fairies in the school scooping classmates out of the air.

Potham screeched, struggling against the leather strap that

was tangled around his neck. At the same time the little girl screamed.

"Jack, you've got her!" Lexis ordered. "I'm going to release Potham and I'll be right behind you."

"You better be!" Jack let go of the railing, transforming into his saber-toothed tiger familiar on his way to landing on his feet on the ground beside the pinned girl.

Adrenaline turning her blood cold, Lexis slid down the railing, careening into the steel loop where the taut strap was tied. The giant's fist pounded the flatbarge, causing Wallace to lose precious altitude, moving Potham within its reach.

Lexis was out of time. Holding on with one hand, she made a fist with the other, sparking fire, her favorite and most practiced element. Her blazing dagger burned through the strap with a single hard slice, setting the wyverns free. Potham chicken-ran one way while Wallace, weighed down by the barge, flapped in a wild panic, barely escaping the giant's mad grab.

Lexis jumped off the transport, diving the last eight feet, tucking into a roll when she hit the ground. She lost her bearings, but then found Jack on the other side of the giant. He was still struggling to get the little girl free. His curved, sharp canines bit and scratched the giant's massive foot, but nothing he did got the monster to move.

"Hey! Rocks for brains!" Lexis sprinted around to the front of it, rapid-firing airballs, landing a winner right up its nose. It sneezed so hard it stumbled forward enough for Jack's fangs to pull the little girl out by the back of her pajamas.

The giant was chest-pounding *mad*. Before its two-ton foot landed on Lexis's head, she rolled out and ran, taking cover behind the last remaining wall of a house. But the giant found her. She was barely able to put up an air shield before rubble crashed down on top of her.

When the dust finally cleared, she was relieved to see Jack giving the little girl a piggyback ride, taking her out of the danger zone, and surprised to find two giants grappling across the road.

One was on top of the other, throwing a flurry of punches. The one on the bottom getting beaten to a pulp fumbled two fingers skyward, the signal Lexis had taught Swaps so she could always tell which was him when he was in trouble. And he was in big trouble.

"Swappy!" She panicked. "Ignis!"

The giant turned, unhinging its jaw, and, to Lexis's grave disappointment, ate her massive fireball, swallowing it whole without so much as a flinch. No wincing indigestion followed! Or a stuck-out burnt tongue! The mass of rocks went right back to pummeling poor Swappy.

Lexis needed help. She saw Pavel circling and whipped an airball at him, catching his attention. As he dive-bombed, she tried distracting the giant again.

"Hey! Firebreath!" Lexis nailed it in the back of the head with another fireball. "Try and catch me!"

But she only made things worse for Swaps. He yelped as the giant ground a knee into his rocky chest, chipping off bits to pivot and stretch to reach her. Pavel buzzed its head, blasting ice, smothering the giant's eyes until the fairy's well ran dry. It would take him a few minutes to replenish his power. Until then, he was helpless and Lexis was on her own. The blinded giant flailed, beating the ice with fury, leaving Lexis with mere seconds to help Swappy get out of there.

"Mistral!" Her gust knocked the giant off balance, giving the changeling the advantage he needed. He flipped the giant over his head, then, to Lexis's horror, transformed back into himself.

In a mad dash, Lexis ran to him, throwing up an air shield inches before the giant's foot would've landed on Swappy's head. She strained under the pressure, her knees shaking, when she heard the rising sound of a thousand buzzing ice-fairy wings, giving her a tiny snowflake of hope.

The reinforcements from Winter's armies had finally arrived. If she could just hold on a little longer . . .

Blue hail-flumes shot down with precision in a single

coordinated *whoosh*. The frozen giant toppled over on its side. Shoulders sagging with relief, Lexis helped Swappy stand up, which wasn't easy. He was frantically waving at the squadron flying overhead, who weren't looking back. There was another giant, and another after that, but still Swaps waved his gratitude, and burped a loud, "Thank you!"

HOURS LATER, LEXIS walked with her fianna around the frozen giants, somberly taking in the heavy damage to the village as they looked for Aífe. Lexis found a book in the middle of the street and picked it up, thinking she should hold it for safekeeping for the shop owner.

"It's lucky that so many heard the giants before they got here, and were able to escape into the Woods," Jack commented.

"They can rebuild," Swappy offered, ever the beacon of hope.

But how could anyone begin to rebuild after suffering so much loss? Lexis touched the book's torn leather binding. "Why would Summer want to destroy this little town? Hurt innocent people?"

"It wasn't just here," Jack answered. "You heard Aífe on the transport. They hit several towns."

"Summer is turning up the heat on this war, and if something isn't done soon, Winter is going to be in real trouble. And I for one am not going to stand by and let it happen!" Pavel yelled, firing off an ice dagger at a frozen giant's head. "First you take my aunt, and now this?"

"How do you even get something the size of a giant into a Sidral?" Swappy asked, shrugging.

"I don't know," Lexis fumed. "But Pavel is right. They're going to pay." She hurled the book at the giant.

A few minutes later, she spotted Aífe at the end of the road, stitching Potham's wing. "There she is."

As they approached, the wyvern's long snout tucked beneath his body. His barbed tail coiled and he growled. This was the closest any of them had ever been to him. His leather skin flaked, and it was obvious this was not the first time his wing had been injured. There were several other long scars. Lexis really hoped he was going to be okay.

"Quiet," Aífe stressed to him, tying off the last stitch. He nipped at her as she rolled the extra copper wire around her hand. "Yes, I've had enough of you too." Holding the bloody foot-long needle straight up, she slid off him.

"Don't come closer. He's in a bad mood. Not that I blame him. He's going to have to walk back to school." She set the needle and thread down and padded over to speak with them. "You four will ride back to school with me."

Lexis saw Aífe's horse-drawn chariot parked a few feet away. Her stomach tightened. "Did we do something wrong?"

"Quite the contrary." Aífe gave Lexis a confidence-building half smile. "The Queen has asked me for the best fianna in your class for a mission, and that would be you four."

"Yes!" Pavel high-fived Jack.

Swappy nervously twitched. "Like, a real mission?"

Pride swelled, only to be dampened by apprehension. Third-year cadets, only twelve years old . . . "What kind of mission, ma'am?"

"Top secret. I know very little except that I was asked for you to arrive tonight."

WITH THE SUN setting, they were given no time to change. Aífe put them directly into the Sidral at Braverwil.

It was the last time Lexis or any of them would see her or their school for months. Had she known, Lexis probably would've chosen a better thing to say than, "I really need to use the bathroom."

A SINGLE GUARD DRESSED in a blue-and-black tabard escorted them through a tunnel beneath the Boreal Citadel, Queen Kefyra's impenetrable sapphire fortress.

Pavel sweat profusely. His ice armor flaked off, leaving a trail of puddles in his wake. But that wasn't nearly as bad as Swappy letting a loud ripper go. Jack growled, morphing a hand, ready to take a swipe at Swaps, but Lexis caught his wrist and shook her head. The guard's gag from the smell was bad enough. If they started fighting in the hallway, they would lose this mission before they even found out what it was.

A door at the end of the dank tunnel was ajar. Once all four had crossed the threshold, the guard closed it behind them.

Queen Kefyra looked up from an empty gray table with no chairs. Lexis had never seen her in person before. *Imposing* was the only word that came to mind. She was at least eight feet tall, with folded wings that brushed the ceiling, a bob of white hair, and skin so pale it was the color of fresh snow. She wore the same uniform as all Winter soldiers: a plain white unitard. The one striking difference was the diamond diadem resting effortlessly on her forehead.

Two soldiers flanked the Queen. Lexis only had a second to look at them. With so many silver snowflakes stitched into their collars, they must be the two Advisors Pavel's aunt had mentioned before. Their identities were always kept as secret as the missions they doled out—only their matching ice-blue eyes were visible behind their expressionless, polished silver face masks.

Bowing along with her fianna mates, Lexis strained to keep her knees from knocking.

"Stand up."

The Queen narrowed blazing yellow eyes on Lexis, then on each of her fianna as they folded in behind her to a single-file line.

"What are you, ten?" She sounded annoyed.

"Twelve, Your Majesty," Lexis answered. "Except our changeling, he's eleven."

"I was hoping for the best of your class, and Aífe sends me . . ." She snapped her fingers and one of the Advisors pulled a piece of paper out his sleeve, then gestured to Jack.

"A foundling arrested in Galanta for stealing, who chose Braverwil over the workhouse," he read disapprovingly.

Jack brazenly morphed to his full sabertoothed form, growling at the insult. Lexis rolled her eyes and pressed her heel on his paw, silencing him.

Queen Kefyra wrinkled her strong nose, pointing a long, sharp nail at Swappy.

The Advisor lifted the paper again. "A clown, an embarrassment to his noble family."

Swappy lowered his head. Pavel felt the sting next. "An orphan raised by a disgraced aunt who now sits caged in Summer's prison."

Lexis braced for her turn.

"And the daughter of shirkers who hide their cowardice behind a shield of benevolence."

The Queen leaned over Lexis. "Are you a coward too?"

"No, ma'am!" Lexis was nothing like her parents, especially after today. She would do whatever it took to protect the Lands of Winter.

The Queen stepped back while the Advisor folded the piece of paper until it was so small he could swallow it, and did. Lexis cringed.

"You witnessed firsthand what Summer is now capable of. Volga has been sacked, but also Bushmills and Noir." She held up a bit of fabric with writing on it. "But in all that chaos, something miraculous happened as well. News from Summer that gives us a chance to stop this from *ever* happening again. In order to take it, you four will have to go deep undercover in Summer. The mission wouldn't be easy for a fianna with years of experience."

Swappy, Jack, and Pavel twitched excitedly. Lexis's stomach cinched. Deep undercover? For how long? Nausea rising, she asked, "What do you want us to do, Your Majesty?"

"To steal the *Croí na Bandia*."

"What's that?" Pavel asked.

Lexis's jaw dropped as she remembered an unforgettable story her father had told her about that very thing when she was little. "Danu's Heart."

Queen Kefyra gave Lexis a calculating grin.

"Aífe was right. You are the right fianna for the job. You will go and bring it back to me. We will bring Summer to its knees, and end this war once and for all."

1

A STRIKING WELCOME
TO CHAWELL WOODS

THREE WEEKS LATER . . .

KELCIE MURPHY NEVER intended to die her first day in Chawell Woods, but from the start, it seemed inevitable.

The guardhouse, the only way to enter the Woods, was made of shiny silver metal that reflected the scenes around it, blending it seamlessly into the wall that kept Fomorians locked inside. The only reason they found it was because of a sign posted above a burly soldier's head that said *No Visitors Allowed.*

That meant Kelcie's cousin Brona wasn't allowed to stay with her.

"I'll write you every day!" Kelcie hugged Brona hard. Saying goodbye to her hurt.

"You better!" Brona's fingers dug into Kelcie's braided hair as she loosed a tiny cry.

Kelcie never remembered anything about her life in the Otherworld when she was little, not until she touched the obsidian sword her mother had left for her at the Academy for the Unbreakable Arts. A sword Kelcie used last year to destroy King Balor's evil eye once and for all.

Before that day, Kelcie and Brona didn't know they were cousins. They had grown into friends though, good friends, and vowed never to be separated again. For most of break they had gotten their wish. Kelcie hated the idea of not being with Brona all day, every day, but her grandmother was in Chawell Woods, waiting for Kelcie on the other side of the camouflaged guardhouse, and there was only a week left of break.

It was Kelcie's last chance to see her grandmother. Her last chance to put pieces of her past together. And to find out if something bad had happened to her father. It had been seven weeks of writing letters to him every day without a single one answered.

Tao Lee, Brona's father, joined in on the farewell hug, squishing the life out of both of them. "Kelcie, tell your doyen hello for me."

"I will."

"She'll be so excited when she sees you in your dress uniform," Brona added.

Kelcie wasn't so sure, but the yellow Saiga cloak and white pants were the only clean clothes she had left.

Striker jumped up on Kelcie's back, yowling, impatient to get inside.

"Okay! Okay!" She shooed him off, wiping embarrassing tears.

Kelcie fumbled the strap of her duffel bag as she turned toward the guard, who was opening the door. She wasn't nervous about seeing her grandmother. She was apprehensive about what she might find on the other side of that door.

Fomorians are all registered, Tao had reminded her as she packed up on the ship.

Kelcie accepted the inevitability, but what exactly this registration entailed was a mystery, and sent Kelcie's imagination into all kinds of tortuous directions. Was she simply going to have her picture taken and her name put into a computer system, or was there hair-pulling, or worse, needles involved?

Needles.

Elliott Blizzard, her social services caseworker, had often

made the mistake of telling Kelcie ahead of time when she was going to need shots at her annual checkups. It had been much harder for Elliott to find her when the time came for those appointments.

After a nervous wave goodbye to her cousin, Kelcie followed Striker across the threshold into the guardhouse.

"Murphy, we've been expecting you." Deirdre Crane threw the bolt, locking her inside.

Oh joy . . . Deirdre Crane, Kelcie's tormenter from school last year, had apparently been assigned to Chawell Woods. She should've been expecting this, considering the first time she saw Crane, she was boasting about registering Fomorians in the Woods.

Kelcie recognized the faces of Deirdre's fianna as they closed in around her, but she couldn't remember their names. It didn't help that their uniforms were no longer color-coded. Active-duty uniforms consisted of brown pants and tunics. The only thing distinguishing Deirdre from the rest of her fianna and marking her as Charger were the suns on her lapels.

The reception room wasn't very welcoming. It was completely empty. There were no chairs to sit down. No information desk where someone could ask questions. Only three doors on the wall in front of her, bleakly labeled *In, Out,* and *High Command Personnel Only.*

A yellow light flashed above the door branded *In.*

Ignoring it, Crane frowned at Striker. "Didn't you see the sign? No visitors are allowed in Chawell Woods."

"What?" Kelcie's heart skittered. He'd been by her side the whole time she'd been on break.

Striker growled, baring teeth.

High Command's door jerked open. Another soldier, older, with a scraggly yellow beard and bushy silver eyebrows, poked his head out, glaring at Crane.

"What are you waiting for? A bloody invitation? Didn't you see the light?"

Deirdre started. "Sorry, sir! But the cú sith—"

"I knew you were going to be a pebble in my shoe the minute your father insisted I give you this assignment! That cú sith slips through the magical barrier this time every year. His kind are the only ones who can!" he barked. "There's no stopping him because he'll only go around! How many times do I have to tell you that?"

"You didn't, sir," Crane answered contritely.

"I didn't what?"

"You didn't tell me that, sir."

"Well, I did now. Move it before you all go on report!"

The door slammed shut.

Flustered, Deirdre shoved Kelcie through the *In* door, into a room that looked like a bank. On the other side of a glass partition, Yellow Beard sat on a stool behind a counter while a futuristic-looking machine scanned a girl's face with a thick red beam, leaving a three-dimensional image of her hovering.

When it was finished, he pressed a button and her image pixelated and vanished. That was it? No needles, just a picture? Relieved, Kelcie let out the breath she'd been holding.

"Done. Wait for this one." He pointed at Kelcie. "You can go out together. Been trained at AUA. You'll want her with you."

The girl nodded solemnly and went to stand by the door marked *Exit*.

Yellow Beard waved Kelcie over. "Step up to the glass where I can get a look at you."

"I'm here to see my grandmother."

Yellow Beard coughed a laugh. "Oof, I know who *you* are, Kelcie Murphy. Daughter of Draummorc."

Kelcie frowned. What did that mean? She glanced at Deirdre who winked, smirking. Were they not going to let her out? As he adjusted the scanner down to match Kelcie's height, she blurted, "I have to be back at school in a week."

His lack of response left her worried. What if Roswen didn't come? What if this was some kind of trap?

Striker leaped up on the counter, barking and whining while Kelcie's tense image materialized in red, then faded.

"Go on." Yellow Beard waggled a finger dismissively. "Don't want to be dawdling tonight."

As she approached the other new addition to the Woods, she felt like she should say something, at least introduce herself.

"Hey, I'm Kelcie."

"Lexis." Her expression softened a little as she looked down at Kelcie.

Lexis was taller by several inches. She had russet skin and long, curly dark brown hair pulled into a tight ponytail. Her eyes were two-colored like all Fomorians', only hers were a much more saturated aqua green and richer ruby brown than Kelcie had ever seen before. Her oversized gray T-shirt was tied off at her midriff by a rope belt holding up too-big black pants that looked like they belonged to someone else. She clasped her hands, threading her fingers together, twisting them into a knot. She was nervous. Kelcie was too. Neither had no idea what to expect on the other side of the door.

"Give 'em the spiel quickly, Crane. Getting darker by the minute," Yellow Beard grunted.

Crane rushed over. "As part of the welcome, I'm obliged to offer a few warnings. One, stay on the paths, day *and* night. Two, don't pet anything, even if it looks cute and cuddly."

Striker yipped in agreement.

"And lastly," Deirdre's voice lowered to just above a whisper, "it's a new moon. Dullahan rides tonight."

"The headless horseman . . ." Lexis uttered, gasping.

"Headless horseman?" Kelcie gaped at Crane. "You're kidding, right?"

A honking horn blared. An orange light above the door flashed, and it popped open.

"Get a move on. Night is falling fast!" Yellow Beard shouted.

Striker bolted. Lexis hesitated, tossing Kelcie an anxious glance. Kelcie obliged and went first. She stepped into a courtyard surrounded by dense woods on three sides. Behind them, the door slammed shut.

A lonely light on the corner of the guardhouse flickered on, casting everything in muted yellow shadows. Manicured colorful flowers broke up a cobblestone patio. There were topiary bushes shaped into suns and a twenty-foot gold statue of Queen Eislyn in the center. It was an eerily perfect likeness. Hair woven into a braided work of art, the mantle she'd worn around her neck, the unitard smothered by the long, dragging cape—she looked exactly as Kelcie remembered her, right down to the smug smile. Her arms were raised waist high, palms *down*. Kelcie interpreted it as *I am your overlord, bow down before me.*

"That's weird, right?" Lexis grimaced beside her.

"Very."

Striker paid homage to the Queen by lifting his leg and peeing all over her boot.

"Good boy," Lexis hummed.

Kelcie laughed, then sobered quickly, seeing Lexis scan the trees anxiously. The delicious scent of pine needles did nothing to calm her racing pulse.

"This Dullahan." Kelcie's voice quivered. "Is he real? And like all headless horsemen? Wanting to chop other people's heads off?"

"From what I read . . ." Lexis warbled back.

Two flickering torches emerged from the trees. Striker barked, spinning in excited circles. A strangled cry escaped from Kelcie when she saw who carried the first torch. Her grandmother's smock was tattered. Her gray hair was so much longer, down to the middle of her back, and the torc necklace made from Kelcie's grandfather's horns was exactly where Kelcie last saw it, around her doyen's neck.

The other torch was held by someone else with a familiar face, this one with a goofy grin and freshly buzzed hair that showed off his burgeoning horns.

"Doyen! Ollie!"

Kelcie tackled her grandmother first, noting she smelled exactly the same, like mint tea.

"No time for reunions. Let's go!" Ollie declared.

Striker's whimpering slipped into a harsh growl as his head jerked toward the trees across the courtyard from them. Kelcie heard galloping horse hooves, soft at first, sounding like the light patter drizzle makes on leaves, but getting louder by the second. She looked back, about to tell Lexis to go with them, but she was gone.

"Lexis?" Kelcie called, worried.

"Bug, we have to go!" Doyen insisted.

"Lexis!"

Kelcie hated to leave her, but her grandmother didn't give her a choice.

She grabbed Kelcie's hand, tugging her along, chasing after Ollie, who had sprinted ahead. Very quickly though, Doyen started to fall behind. She couldn't keep up with Kelcie, so Kelcie slowed down, matching her pace, fixating on Ollie's bobbing torchlight leading the way.

Alongside them, Striker snarled and growled as the hoofbeats grew louder and louder, getting closer and closer. Then Kelcie saw him, the headless rider on his gigantic black horse, galloping parallel to the path. Dullahan's long black cloak and clapping leather armor were outlined in a crackling red energy. If that wasn't bad enough, fire shot from the horse's nostrils, cutting across the path.

"Doyen!" Kelcie cried.

"I see him!"

Doyen's torch dipped lower, giving Kelcie an unwanted better look at the severed heads tied to his saddle, all covered in wrinkled, hardening flesh. Their hollowed eye sockets shot on, glowing a piercing white, and they smiled at her. Kelcie shrieked.

"What does that mean, Doyen?"

"You don't want to know! Run! Just keep running!"

Kelcie clutched her grandmother's hand tighter, pulling her. "Faster, Doyen!"

"My legs only go so fast these days!"

The horse jumped onto the path and reared, whinnying. Dullahan's hand lifted his axe back to strike.

Kelcie was raising her arms, about to spark an air shield, but Doyen was way ahead of her. Doyen's bracelet melted down into the palm of her hand, forming a sharp pick that she threw so hard it impaled Dullahan's axe hand through his glove. It was the most awesome thing Kelcie had ever seen!

The axe landed at Ollie's feet as he came flying out of the darkness, hurling a confident water bomb that—combined with a desperate airball from Kelcie—was enough to knock the headless horseman off his horse. Striker joined in, snatching the string of decomposing heads off the saddle and sprinted into the Woods. Screaming a neigh, the horse reared again, spewing fire toward the sky, then raced after him.

Ollie raised his fist, crying, "Caenum!" The rain came down in sweeping gusts, soaking everything, including Kelcie and Doyen. "That'll help Striker with the Red Caps."

Kelcie cringed. "Red Caps? What is that?"

"Who! And you'll find out soon enough!" Doyen pushed Kelcie from behind. "Run! Now, Kelcie!"

Around the next bend in the path, a lit cave appeared. Doyen and Ollie sprinted inside, but Kelcie hesitated at the entrance, worried about her cú sith.

"Striker!" she called. "STRIKER!"

If anything happened to him, Kelcie would never forgive herself. Having once belonged to her father, Striker was her responsibility now.

She started to go after him, but Ollie held her back. "You can't!"

"But—"

A green streak shot past her into the cave.

While Striker shook, showering Kelcie in raindrops, Ollie secured the heavy metal door.

Panting to catch her breath, Doyen shrugged off the blanket over her shoulders.

"I'm getting too old for this."

CLANK! Metal struck metal, and Kelcie knew right away it was Dullahan slamming his axe against the door, trying to break in.

Kelcie raised her hands, ready to spark, but her doyen pulled them down and gave her a warm smile. "You're safe here, Bug. I smelted that door myself out of metal from bits and pieces of the guardhouse. Juggernaut is indestructible."

From the way the walls shook, dropping dust on their heads with every strike, the metal might be indestructible, but the cave wasn't. It was only then Kelcie had a second to think about the poor girl who came through the registration with her. Lexis. That was her name. Why did she vanish like that?

Any thought of going after her vanished when another murderous thud struck the door. Ollie's breath caught audibly. Striker pressed into a downward dog and put his paws over his ears.

Doyen was the only one who seemed immune to the racket. She leaned over and patted Kelcie's cheek. "It's late. We should eat and get ready for bed."

"Bed?" There was no way Kelcie was going to sleep with a headless horseman knocking on the door.

"He'll be gone soon enough. He too has things that stalk him in Chawell Woods." She turned to Ollie. "You will stay here to-night." It wasn't a question.

Ollie nodded, wide-eyed. "Most definitely!"

Though it made her feel guilty, Kelcie wished she was alone with Doyen. It was her first night with her grandmother. One of only seven, and she really wanted to ask about her father. But it would have to wait until tomorrow. She didn't want to talk about it in front of Ollie.

Doyen took Kelcie's duffel bag from her and set it beside a bed that looked like it was made of folded blankets.

Kelcie sat down, getting a whiff of lilac. The scent jogged her memory. Doyen always dribbled oils infused with lilac on their bedsheets when she was little. Her grandmother had probably brought the bedding from the little cottage where Kelcie had once lived with her father, Draummorc. If so, though, it seemed like it was all she'd brought; not that there was room for much more.

The tiny cave barely had enough space for the bed, the wooden table and chair, and the small firepit that served as a stove beside it.

As they ate some of her grandmother's delicious stew, Dullahan gave up, giving them a few moments of peace. After, they got ready for bed. Ollie passed out on the floor with Striker curled up beside him, and they were trading snores by the time Doyen blew out the candles. Someone rapped the door.

Bang. Bang. Bang. Bang . . .

A steady beat that sounded like a human hand. What if it was Lexis? Her grandmother made no move to open the door.

Kelcie bolted upright. "Should I answer that, Doyen?"

"No." Doyen yawned. "Cauchemar. Nasty things that feed off your dreams, turning them into nightmares over and over again until you lose your mind. It's the same every night. Just ignore them."

BANG! BANG! BANG!

"Just ignore them? How?"

Her doyen dragged her back down and pulled her closer. "Don't worry."

But all Kelcie could do was worry. Her doyen's breathing evened out and Kelcie knew she was already asleep.

Kelcie was too angry to sleep. Chawell Woods was a kind of hell. Monsters everywhere. Nowhere safe to sleep except in caves on top of unforgiving rock. Her doyen deserved better. She deserved to be in her own home. If her father saw this . . .

No. Kelcie sighed at the bitter truth. Her father was the *reason* her grandmother was forced to live like this. He'd given in to King Balor's evil eye, allowing it to control him, to force him to burn down Summer City, the capital of the Lands of Summer, a fire that took the life of Kelcie's best friend Niall's father. But it was Niall's mother, Queen Eislyn, who was responsible for punishing the Fomorian folk for Draummorc's actions, locking them in this dreadful place. *Two wrongs don't make a right.* This was wrong, very wrong.

Clutching her grandmother's hand, and closing her eyes, she silently cast a wish on the moonless night, hoping it could get past the cauchemar and the headless horseman, and rise out of the gloomy forest, into the Otherworldly stars. A wish for Doyen and for her to find a way to go home.

2

WHO ARE YOU, KELCIE MURPHY?

THE CAUCHEMAR DIDN'T go away until sunrise slid under the door. Kelcie woke up when Doyen let Striker out, but didn't open her eyes. It felt like she had only just fallen asleep.

She heard Ollie stretch and yawn beside her.

"Kelcie . . ." He shook her shoulder.

She placated him with a "What?" so he'd stop.

"I'll be back in fifteen minutes. Get dressed." Ollie's footsteps padded for the door. "We have somewhere to be."

"Where?" she called after him, but he was gone.

Alone with her grandmother for the first time since she arrived, Kelcie hurried to get dressed. Fifteen minutes was not a lot of time to talk. She rifled through her duffel bag quickly, pulling out her tattered sweats. Her shirt was ripped in three places, fortunately near the bottom. Her pants were a mess, with holes in the knees so large they were more like shorts. Brona's father had promised to take her shopping for some new clothes, but they never got the chance.

Tao sailed them all over the Emerald Sea, combing remote, uncharted islands, searching for a stash of frost bombs hidden in a cave by the Winter fianna who had attacked the school last year. By the time he found what he was looking for, there was only one week left before school started, and she wasn't going to trade a minute of the time she had left to see her grandmother for a new wardrobe.

By the time Kelcie was dressed, her grandmother set out breakfast on the table. Kelcie grabbed an empty crate so her grandmother could have the only chair. Steam wafted from Kelcie's too-hot tea. She cradled it, blowing, unsure how to start the conversation with her grandmother. After a night of reunion, morning brought a strangled strangeness between them. After so many years apart, Kelcie supposed it was a loss of familiarity. Whatever it was, it felt heavy on her chest.

"I—"

"I—"

Kelcie started talking at the same time her grandmother did. Doyen gave a little laugh.

"You go first," Kelcie said, hoping a few extra minutes would help calm her nerves.

"Okay." Doyen spread a conservative smudge of jam on a piece of flat bread. "I want to ask you about your time in the human world, Anuyen, but you don't have to tell me if you don't want to."

Kelcie smiled as her brain auto-translated the word *anuyen*. The Fomorian word for granddaughter, but also apple. The kind of apples that were used to make Zinger, magical and healing. It was a good word.

"I don't mind."

As quickly as she could, Kelcie told her about her life in Massachusetts. About Elliott Blizzard, her social services caseworker who moved her around a lot (leaving out the parts she thought would upset her grandmother too much), and about how Elliott turned out to be a spy for the Lands of Winter. She explained how Elliott and the other ice fairy forced her to start the battle against Draummorc for control over the evil eye, which led to her finding the Academy for the Unbreakable Arts. Then how she and her fianna were able to defeat the eye and get rid of it forever.

"I'm so very proud of you, Kelcie. Though, I did curse your mother's name when I finally remembered you," Doyen said, sucking in a sharp breath. "Which might have been a bad idea in retrospect. Wouldn't want it to happen again."

Kelcie laughed. "Me either."

"But she did see more than I could ever have. She knew you had to be the one to free our family from that torment, to end the eye."

Her mother must have seen. On the night she took Kelcie to the human world, she also left her the sword enchanted with Kelcie's memories, the sword she plunged into Balor's evil eye. But there were a thousand other ways her mother could've accomplished the same thing. She could've taken Kelcie home with her, trained her, then brought her to the Academy when she was old enough to test. But she didn't. Kelcie never saw her mother again, and wasn't sure what she would say to her if she ever did. She tapped her finger on her teacup, steeling herself, working up the courage to ask about Draummorc.

"My father helped me, you know." Starting with a positive felt like the right way to begin the conversation.

Her grandmother set her tea down, wincing, like the mention of his name hurt.

Kelcie hesitated. She didn't want to cause her grandmother more pain, but her grandmother was the only person she could ask. A deep breath later, she blurted, "Doyen, have you heard from him?"

Her grandmother's frail hand squeezed the torc around her neck. "Not in many, many years. And you shouldn't expect to hear from him either."

Doyen's anger unexpected, Kelcie wrestled over saying anything else. This was not going the way she'd seen it playing out in her head. Of all people, Kelcie thought it would've been okay to talk about her father to her grandmother, but it wasn't. He really was public enemy number one.

"Kelcie!" Ollie sang, barging in. A duffel bag slung over his shoulder, Ollie too had changed into his Saiga-yellow T-shirt and sweatpants. "We have to go."

"What are you two doing today?" Doyen asked.

Ollie's face lit up as he sang, "Training."

"Oh." Kelcie should've seen that coming. Ollie and Killian, Ollie's older brother, had told Kelcie a lot about their grandfather last year. She was hoping he might be able to help her finally figure out why her powers were so—confusing. She'd only had luck controlling air so far (with her cousin Brona's help). As a pulse elemental, she should be able to control all four elements. But water ignored her. Fire was too combustible. She almost burned down the stables at school. And the one time she tried to manipulate the bonds of a hunk of metal, it got so hot it burned a hole in the floor of the training den. She jumped up, excited. This was going to be a new beginning for her, and she couldn't wait to get started too.

"Take this," Doyen said, pressing her toast into Kelcie's hand. "Stay on the path, and as soon as the sun touches the tops of the redwoods, I want you inside this cave, Bug."

"Yes, ma'am!" Kelcie called, running after Ollie.

The piece of bread was so small she ate it in two bites on her way out, then felt guilty for eating her grandmother's breakfast.

Ollie walked swiftly down a snaking path to another that snuggled tightly to a river, never veering off. Running along both sides of the paths, delineating them from the Woods and the river, were long, thin, tubular colorless crystals.

Ollie caught Kelcie staring at them. "Selenite. Littlefolk hate the high vibrations coming off it. Keeps the paths clear."

"Littlefolk?"

"Yeah. They live in the trees, and think the Woods belong to them, and that everyone else are trespassers to be dealt with." Ollie slid a finger across his neck.

"How charming."

Kelcie kept a constant lookout, panning the sea of giant redwood trees that stretched as far as the eye could see. Freakishly large, the trunks spanned forty feet in diameter, and the tops reached for the heavens, dwarfing every other living thing in the forest.

The branches were weighted down by an impossible number of crows, their beady black eyes tracking Kelcie's and Ollie's every move. A chill ran up her spine. Crows were her mother's familiar. The war goddess even had long black feathered wings just like the birds. If Kelcie didn't know better, she would've thought her mother was checking up on her.

But Nemain wasn't exactly mother of the year, promising her daughter a motherless life right before she abandoned her in Boston Harbor in the middle of winter. Kelcie shook her head dismissively. The crows couldn't have anything to do with her mother. The world would have to be ending for Kelcie to ever see *her* again.

Striker's high-pitched screeching stopped Kelcie in her tracks. A hundred yards away, pint-sized axes sliced into trunks barely missing his whirling green streak. Striker pulled a U-turn, barreling toward her with a herd of ankle-high people dressed all in red hot on his tail. Two more dropped from branches, latching on to his tail with their oversized sharp teeth. Striker yelped and spun in circles, trying to get them off. The rest caught up to him and pounced. Heart racing, all Kelcie could see was red.

"Striker!" She started to leave the path, but Ollie grabbed her arm.

"Red Caps. He'll be fine. *You* won't be. Remember what your grandmother said? Stay on the path!"

"How can you say he'll be fine? They're all over him!" Kelcie held her breath as Striker spun faster and faster, until screaming red spots flew in all directions. As he slowed and appeared Red Cap free, Kelcie wasn't taking any more chances.

"Striker!" Kelcie called, waving furiously at him. "Get over here! Now!"

He raced toward her while she fired off rounds of airballs, blasting everything red. Two got by her, latching on to his hind legs. The selenite glowed as he leaped on the path, and the little menaces fell off. Striker growled, ready for more fun, but Kelcie grabbed the scruff of his neck, keeping him from leaving her side.

"Enough! You stay!" she ordered.

He whimpered, trotting after Kelcie, straining to lick the bleeding teeth marks on his side.

"You'd think once would be enough for Striker to learn to leave them alone, but every break he does the exact same thing," Ollie explained. "All day. Every day. Chases them with glee, and then is surprised when he gets bitten."

He bent dodging a tiny axe spiraling a hairsbreadth from his ear. Two more struck trees on the other side of the lake after buzzing Kelcie's elbow. Unrelenting, toothpick-sized knives bounced off Kelcie's air shield. This was getting ridiculous.

"Whatever you do, don't leave the path and if you do for some stupid reason, don't let them bite you." Ollie used his powers to lift water from a pouch on his belt and spin it into an umbrella shield, dipping it sideways, fending off the next round of Red Cap attacks. "Several of the clan lost legs to single bites when we first moved here."

Kelcie halted, grabbing hold of Striker's neck to check the wounds. "You sure he's going to be okay?"

Ollie shrugged. "Always has been before."

That wasn't reassuring. Striker licked her hand as if saying he'd be fine.

Her thoughts drifted to the girl she had seen last night at the guardhouse. What if Lexis was bitten by a Red Cap? What if she was out there somewhere and needed help? Chawell Woods was a nightmare. She couldn't just leave her alone out there. If Lexis didn't turn up soon, Kelcie was going to have to risk it and go looking for her.

After another five minutes of Red Cap torture, the menaces gave up and vanished inside hollowed-out trees. Kelcie shrank her air shield, but only a little.

"We've been walking forever. Where exactly does your grandfather live?" she asked Ollie.

"About that . . ." Ollie gave her a fleeting, uncomfortable glance over his shoulder, letting the water from his shield fall to the ground. "He said there was no way he's training Draummorc's daughter."

"Oh," she said, trying to mask her disappointment. "But then where are we going?"

"Well, first off, I have *huge* news! Killian and his fianna got assigned to the Bountiful Plains!" Ollie said it like Killian had landed a million-dollar-a-year job on Wall Street.

"Yay, Killian?" Kelcie half-cheered, confused. "He gets to watch crops grow with Zephyr's parents."

"You don't understand. High Command could've assigned them here, to Chawell Woods, making it so Killian could never leave, like the rest of us. But they didn't. He's free, Kelcie. Free! And he thinks it's all because of the eye being gone. He believes that what happened last year was a defining moment. The beginning of the end of our captivity. He thinks the Queen is going to change her mind."

Gone was the goofy Ollie that Kelcie had met on her first day at the Academy who loved to tease her all year. What Kelcie was seeing was the birth of a new Alpha, a leader of the Saiga Den, taking over where his brother left off. He was good at it too. Inspiring. Hesitant hope ticked Kelcie's pulse up a notch, but only one.

Kelcie had met Queen Eislyn at the end of the school year. The word *heartless* came to mind. She treated Niall, her own son, like he didn't exist all because he was limb different, born with one hand rather than two. The Queen also wanted to send Kelcie back to the human world for break, and would have if Niall hadn't stepped in. She listened to him though—Kelcie was granted permission to stay in the Lands of Summer—but she wouldn't let Kelcie visit her father in prison, and right now, with her father not answering her letters, she wondered if it was the Queen's doing, like she was keeping Kelcie's letters from getting to Draummorc. Kelcie didn't trust the Queen, not one bit. She loved the idea of hope, but didn't want Ollie to put too much stock in Killian's optimism.

"Queen Eislyn probably has other motivations for stationing your brother there."

Ollie made a point of frowning at her. "With thinking like that we'll never get out of here. Killian said that now is the time to recruit. Get as many as we can to test for the Academy. Fill every first-year fianna with one of us. And your training is how we're going to start. I've enlisted support, called on the most gifted of testing age in the Woods to help you. One from each discipline, except water, which you have me for."

Kelcie bit her bottom lip to keep from reminding him he hadn't been very successful as a teacher for her at school. It wasn't Ollie's fault. There was something inside Kelcie still broken or chained, something she couldn't figure out.

"We're going to attack your issues the way we should've been able to at the Academy if there were more of us, together. Teaching each other, the way Scáthach has all the other Dens. And while they're helping you, you will be convincing them to test. Only one problem."

"Let me guess. They don't want to teach me, either." Despair seeped into Kelcie's mouth, tasting a bit like moldy cake.

"They're skeptical, but after they heard you destroyed King Balor's evil eye, they're willing to meet you and listen."

"And you think my stunning personality will win them over?" She batted her eyelashes at him, teasing, but Ollie was a guy on a mission—all business.

"You can win anyone over if you put your mind to it. You won me over." Ollie walked on without waiting for an answer, adding, "And Killian."

She hadn't won them over. They accepted her last year, immediately and without judgment. Ollie's challenge dropped her stomach into her shoes. Public speaking terrified her. When she had to give an oral report on the life cycle of a caterpillar in the fourth grade, Kelcie vomited all over her shoebox with the poor caterpillar in its chrysalis phase. Needless to say, neither her speech nor her butterfly ever emerged from the box.

Around the next bend, Kelcie saw two kids leaning on tree trunks. A girl with light brown skin and short black hair, yo-yoing a mini-tornado, and a big guy who looked much older than twelve, the testing age for the Academy. He had deeply tanned skin and black hair like the girl's, only his was past his shoulders and tied in a ponytail at the base of his neck. His pale-yellow and golden-brown eyes darted to Kelcie, then quickly shifted to his palm, which was cupped, cradling fire as if it were a raw egg.

Neither made a move to say hello, in fact, they were looking everywhere but at her. But the third kid enthusiastically hopped up from where he was sitting crisscrossed in the middle of the path.

On the smaller side, and ghostly pale like Kelcie, he had a flat, runny nose, bucked front teeth, and sandy-red hair that hung in his garnet and brown eyes. He stumbled toward her and tripped down on one knee.

"I'm Dollin." His bottom lip tucked under his buck teeth as he grinned up at her.

The girl nailed him on the back of his head with a marble-sized airball. "Are you bowing to the jerk's daughter?"

"My father's not a jerk! He made a mistake!" Kelcie snapped. "And I prefer Kelcie or Murphy if you don't mind."

"So you're half and half like Lynch then?" She sniffed at Ollie. Kelcie was confused. "Half and half?"

Ollie rolled his eyes. "Payton, Kelcie grew up in the human world."

"Really?" Dollin swooned, beaming at her. "Wow . . . that is so—"

"Stop idolizing her before I brainball you!" Payton hissed. Her steely blue and brown gaze bore down on Kelcie. "Human world or not, that doesn't change the fact that she's Draummorc's daughter."

"That's not what I mean!" Ollie shouted, frustration dropping his ears. "Kelcie doesn't have any idea what you're talking about." He turned to Kelcie. "Fomorians don't have family names. My father is Summerfolk, my mother Fomorian. In the Woods, I'm just Ollie."

"Oh." This was news to Kelcie, and suddenly she understood why Elliott Blizzard gave her the last name Murphy. It wasn't because she couldn't remember what it was, it was because she had never had one. And everyone had at least three names in the human world. In the fourth grade she once met a boy with six: John David Michael Stephen Buxomly Lindenberg the Third. They all called him Trip for short, because really, who needs that many names.

Murphy had no real meaning to Kelcie, but she had been a Murphy since she was five. Letting go of the name felt like more than just a simple name change. It felt like she would be letting go of her past, and Kelcie wasn't sure she was ready to do that.

"You're just Ollie in the Woods, because half and half or not, it doesn't matter. Our clan is united. It comes first," Payton explained sternly. "Surnames were never adopted like with the Summerfolk because it would divide us, putting family first. The clan is everything. And your father *is* a jerk because he didn't put the clan first. He betrayed Summer, and we were all punished for his actions."

Fire-guy clapped, snuffing his ball. "You get now why I said this was never going to work, Ollie? Her father is so despised that his very name incites so much rage in ignis-born we rarely speak it for fear of burning down the forest. Our families lost—"

"Everything! So did mine!" Kelcie glared at Ollie for putting her through this torture. He had the grace to look sheepish. He wanted her to smooth-talk them into helping her? And then get them to come to the Academy to test? They hated her guts.

Ollie's eyes widened, imploring her to say something. She took a deep breath, trying to calm down. "I get it. You hate my father. He's my father. I can't change that. But I'm not him! I'm here because I am Fomorian. I'm a part of this clan too, and I need your help."

"A Fomorian who knows nothing about us," Payton countered. "Right, Markkus?"

Fire-guy nodded.

"But one who wants to learn," Kelcie argued, stepping closer to Payton.

Dollin bravely slipped between them. "See. She wants to learn! I think we should give her a chance." He smiled at Kelcie. She gave him a small smile back.

Markkus shifted his jaw forward, mulling, then crossed his arms over his chest. He one-shoulder-shrugged at Payton. When he started talking, Kelcie took that as a good sign. "Well, one thing that every Fomorian knows, or at least should know, is that it was our ancestors, Chaos and Order, who built the foundations."

"Foundations? Of what?" Kelcie asked, intrigued.

Dollin held his spindly arms wide. "Everything," he enthused. "They established the building blocks of everything around us, and our own fundamental beginnings."

Dollin sounded an awful lot like Niall when he explained things. She really missed him, really wished he was here. He would know what to say to get them to help her. He always knew the right thing to say.

"It's how we connect to our element. Theran." The bracelet on Dollin's wrist melted into his palm, coming out the other end a blade, much like she'd seen her doyen do last night.

Excitement brewed in Kelcie's chest. "Will you teach me how to do that?"

Markkus arched a sleek distrusting brow. "First you should show us what you've learned so far."

"Start with air," Ollie instructed for obvious reasons.

Kelcie raised a confident hand.

"Mistral!" She sparked a four-inch tornado on her palm. Before it could dance off, she smashed it with a hard clap. When she separated her hands, the flattened air spun into a circle that grew into a shield. She held it up for them all to see, winking at Ollie. "Brona's arrows never got past me."

"Basic stuff." Payton shrugged, unimpressed. "My turn."

She uttered the sparking word and produced two airballs, one in each hand, sending them flying at poor Dollin. His backside slammed into a groove of a wide trunk and Kelcie heard his trousers rip. But Payton wasn't done torturing him. With a synchronized whip of her hands, the airballs thinned into a tightening air rope that wound around the trunk, pinning him against the tree.

"Not funny, Payton!" Dollin struggled.

Markkus sniggered. "It's a little funny."

Kelcie hated to admit it, but she was awestruck.

"Nil mistral," Payton sang, fisting her hands.

The air dispersed with a taunting hiss.

"Wow," Kelcie gushed. "Payton, you should really test for the Academy."

Her narrowed eyes rolled. "They don't want us there."

"Didn't," Ollie corrected. "Something changed after Kelcie and her fianna saved the school. I'm telling you, we need to use it to our advantage. We need to keep that momentum going. Ride the wave of acceptance and rebuild."

Dollin grinned, nodding at Payton and Markkus, but they looked less convinced.

"I don't—" Payton started, but Markkus interrupted.

"We'll think about it," Markkus said. "Right, Payton?"

She huffed her pursed lips.

Markkus's expression turned evil. "Now, let's see what the pulse can do with fire."

Kelcie cringed. Fire was so dangerous, especially in her hands.

What if she accidentally hurt one of them? "Okay. But you should stand back, way back."

Payton sniggered, taking a step toward her, sparking an air shield. "Give me your best shot."

Ignoring Payton, Kelcie aimed her fists straight up.

"Ignis!" The word was her favorite. The flood of fire and fury that raced through her veins, rushing down her arms was the most exhilarating thing she ever felt, and the most terrifying.

Flames launched from her thrusting fists—like water through a fire hose—shooting into the sky. The pressure was so strong, Kelcie couldn't control it. The streams tilted, striking two huge trees directly above them.

"Nil ignis!" Kelcie yelled. "Nil ignis! NIL IGNIS!"

The fire tap inside her shut off. But the flames in the trees spread to another and another. "Ollie! Help!"

"Caenum!" Ollie cried.

A raincloud materialized above the burning branches and let go a huge downpour. Kelcie felt Markkus staring at her.

Waiting for him to criticize her performance, when he just kept staring, she growled, "What?"

He smirked. "You're on fire."

A tickling warmth ran up Kelcie's sleeves, turning quickly into blistering pain. She beat her arms on the ground, putting it out, but still smelled rotten eggs burning. She glimpsed a flame over her shoulder, and screamed.

"Uh-oh!" Ollie threw his arms out, dousing her back with freezing river water.

When it was finally out, her arms were blistering and red, and six inches of her hair lay in a pile of ashes at her feet.

Kelcie wanted to cry. "Maybe we should quit for today."

"Oh no." Ollie waggled his bushy eyebrows. "We're just getting started."

3

OLLIPHÉIST! GOD BLESS YOU!

KELCIE TRIED HER hand at manipulating earth next. Dollin set one of his metal bracelets on the ground. But as soon as the sparking word was out of her mouth, the ore melted clean through the rocky ground, leaving a hole so deep Kelcie couldn't see the bottom.

Dollin gasped, "Impressive!"

"Not so much," Payton countered. "She has absolutely no control."

"Oh yeah? Try water, Kelcie," Dollin encouraged.

Kelcie tried to raise a drop of water from the rushing river. Per usual, the element ignored her entirely. Her shoulders slumped. "I'm hopeless."

Striker yipped in agreement, and went off to foolishly chase Red Caps before Kelcie could stop him. She waited for the others to send her packing but instead the four of them huddled, dissecting her issues like a batch of middle-aged Fomorian therapists.

"It's like her impulses are all confused," Dollin commented.

"Kind of like her name issue," Payton added, nodding.

"It's not surprising since she grew up in the human world, so far away from her own people," Markkus surmised, exchanging a glance with Ollie. "She doesn't know who she is."

"Wrong," Dollin exclaimed. "She just hasn't accepted it yet."

"Accepted she's Fomorian? Sniffles is probably right. She thinks she's too good for us," Payton spit.

Kelcie took offense to that. "I do not!"

"No! That's not it, Payton," Ollie argued, turning to Kelcie. "You still think you're human."

"What? That's the most ridiculous . . ."

Catching a glimpse of her rippling reflection on the river, Kelcie's protest faltered. She didn't recognize her own face. Her fingers lifted to the singed ends of her much shorter hair, but that wasn't what shocked her the most. She'd filled out. Her cheeks fuller, her arms less skinny, she was stronger, fitter, healthier. She had twice as many freckles from the hot sun overhead all day, every day. And two different-colored eyes staring back at her. She looked like a completely different person, someone she didn't know how to be.

Mesmerized, Kelcie stood, her shoes sinking into the soft ground while Ollie spoke in hushed, disconcerting tones behind her. When she looked back at him, she realized she was surrounded by the four of them and Ollie was holding a coiled rope of thick vines.

"Kelcie, you're still afraid of water," Ollie said matter-of-factly.

"No—"

"That was rhetorical," he interrupted. "You are most definitely still afraid of water."

"I was afraid of water. I'm not anymore. Not really. I mean, I'll get in."

She removed her shoes and socks, and took a step backward into the river up to her ankles. "See."

"Go under," Payton instructed.

Kelcie wrinkled her nose. "I don't want to get my hair wet."

"Why not? It might help the smell," Markkus said, wrinkling *his* nose.

Kelcie glowered at him.

"I know you still have nightmares about nearly drowning." Ollie inched closer with those unsettling vines.

Kelcie raised her hands, ready to literally blow him away. "How—?"

"I lived with you all last year. You're afraid of the water," Ollie repeated in a condescending tone.

"Well, you—you snore!" she stammered.

"You can breathe underwater, can't you?" Payton asked.

"Yes, but I couldn't then."

"Then?" Markkus asked. He looked at Ollie who shook his head, confused.

"If you don't tell us what happened, we can't help you," Dollin said with pleading eyes.

Reluctantly, Kelcie swallowed what was left of her pride and told them about the dismal night she was abandoned. About how Kelcie's mother brought her out of the Otherworld, into the human world, and cursed her to lose her memories and suppressed her powers right before she'd dropped her into the frigid, deep waters of Boston Harbor. Kelcie would've drowned if it hadn't been for the navy sailors on the USS *Constitution*.

Kelcie finished by saying, "So, the *then* was before . . ."

"Before you were a pulse elemental?" Dollin asked, scratching his head.

"Before the curse was lifted by the spriggans at the school," Kelcie explained.

Payton stepped closer, invading Kelcie's personal space. "Even if your mother suppressed your powers somehow, she couldn't change who and what you are. You are Fomorian. You're not human."

A breeze whipped between them without sparking. It was as if Kelcie's mistral powers were mixing with Payton's, agreeing with her.

"What does that mean?" Kelcie asked.

"Stupid simple." Markkus inched closer. "You're a pulse. You can't drown. It's a biological fact." The air between them heated. A single bead of sweat trickled down Kelcie's cheek.

"But I did!" Kelcie insisted. "Didn't I?"

"I bet you were just scared. I would be," Dollin answered.

"Let's find out." Ollie nodded at Payton who smiled in a terrifying way.

The next thing Kelcie knew, air whips lassoed her arms and legs, pinning them together. Ollie worked quickly, tying Kelcie's ankles together with the vines.

"What are you doing?" Kelcie struggled, but Payton was too strong.

"Let me go!"

Striker must've heard Kelcie in trouble because he came out of nowhere, taking a flying leap at Markkus, but never reached him. He slammed into Payton's air shield. Scratching and leaping, the cú sith never gave up as Ollie secured the vines. He wrapped them tight around her waist and looped them crosswise over her shoulders so there was no way Kelcie was going to be able to slip out.

"We need something to weight her down," Markkus said, spying a heavy rock. He heaved it over and secured it to her feet. "That'll sink her all the way to the bottom."

Kelcie begged, "No! Ollie, please! Don't!"

"He's doing this for your own good," Dollin smiled. "Trust me."

"I don't trust you! I don't trust any of you!" Kelcie yelled.

"You can do this" was the last thing Ollie said before raising a wave of river water, and in one fell swoop dragging her into the deepest part of the river.

Kelcie sank straight down, cursing at Ollie—fully aware he couldn't hear her. The tethered rock sank into the murky bottom, leaving her well and truly stuck. She tried to undo the knot in the middle of her back, but it was tied so tight she couldn't get it to budge. The vine straps bit into her shoulders with every twist and turn. Short of dislocating a joint, there was no way to get out of this!

"Caenum!" Kelcie gurgled, willing the water to lift her out, but it ignored her pleas. As the last bits of her frantically gulped breath escaped, bubbling to the surface, she sighed, settling in to the fact that she was going to be down here for a long, long time.

At least the lung strain vanished much quicker than it had when she was held under Morrow Lake last year at school.

The water was unexpectedly warm and tasted strangely like lox. She bent backward, trying to reach the dagger in her shoe only to remember she stupidly left her shoes on the riverbank.

Five blurry shadows peered down at her from the surface— not moving, not diving in to rescue her—probably placing bets on how long it would take her to get out of here . . . if she ever did.

Her hair swept forward, a curtain of red with charcoal-black ends, blocking her vision. She jerked her head into the opposite direction of the current, letting it move her hair off her face so she could see and wished she hadn't. A school of large pink fish laboriously swimming upstream on the far side of the river performed a synchronized pivot, heading straight for her.

Black eyes blinked. Their tails and fins worked triple time against the current to stay in one place to gape at her. Mouths fell open in unison only to split into amused big-toothed grins. It was unnerving, but not as unnerving as hearing them *speak*!

"You're all tied up!" one said, swimming close enough for her to smell fish breath.

"Tell me something I don't know."

"You have dirt on your face," another added with glee.

"Those are freckles!"

You're talking to fish . . . Kelcie didn't need her subconscious to tell her how ridiculous that was! A painful ringing started in her ears. She cringed, which the fish took offensively, gasping in unison.

"She scowls!" one exclaimed.

"No! Worse! She scoffs!" another barked.

"Much worse! She thinks we smell!"

That comment earned a round of huffed discontentment. Kelcie tried to speak but the ringing grew louder, making her wince even more.

"That is enough!" the largest fish bleated. "How dare you make that face in our presence! We are descendants of *the* Salmon of Knowledge!"

When Kelcie didn't respond, the bleater sadly moved closer so that he could properly scold her in her face.

"Our ancestor ate nine, not eight, but *nine* hazelnuts that had fallen into the Well of Wisdom, and from then on, he knew everything about everything."

"Yes!" his tiny sidekick with abnormally bugged eyes (even for a fish) exclaimed.

"Hear! Hear!" another said.

"Or is it here? Here?" yet another pondered.

"Both, for she must hear and we are here!"

"Hear what?" Kelcie couldn't hear anything over the ringing!

Bug Eyes flittered closer, pushing the bleating leader out of the way until the fish was mouth-to-nose with her. Unblinking, he looked deep into her eyes, the edges of his lips turning down. "Why are you so afraid?"

Night fell suddenly, leaving Kelcie a wheezing mess. "What's happening?"

The bottom fell away and suddenly she was floating on the surface of water so cold that her limbs instantly numbed. She heard the sound of flapping wings and looked up, seeing her mother flying in the night sky, a small figure cocooned against her chest. No! Behind Kelcie, the lights of Boston left a trail on the water. Confused at first, to her horror Kelcie realized that she was floating in Boston Harbor, on the coldest of wintry nights, about to witness the worst moment of her life!

Kelcie thrashed but the vines were still there, somehow holding her even in the nightmare. Something in the magical talking fish's gaze must have unlocked the unwanted memory that had plagued Kelcie for so many years, only with the perspective changed. She was about to watch herself *fall*!

Thunder cracked. Lightning flashed. Her mother let go like she always did, and her small self plummeted. She heard her own terrified scream for help, but saw her small hands reach down, not up. Down . . . to the water.

A surge of power rattled the vines.

Water lifted high into the air, catching her, easing Kelcie's fall. But how? Her ability to wield the elements was snuffed by her mother's curse *before* she let her go. How was this possible?

It wasn't.

But then why was Kelcie seeing it this way now? Water thrummed in her ears—a bell tolling—an awakening to the truth. Her fear of the water was misplaced. It was her mother who'd dropped her. Her mother who'd cursed her. The water had caught her, protected her, and as it slowly started churning around her head, a strong and unbreakable show of force, she felt like it was trying to tell her that it would always be there.

The physical impact of what had happened to her wasn't holding her back. The emotional scars were. The confusion of not knowing who she was, followed by the sheer terror of not knowing where she was, of being lost and alone.

But she never was alone. She was in trouble, and the water was there for her. Dollin was right. Her powers were an inseparable part of her that, even if she was cursed to forget the connection existed, the elements never forgot.

The answer was so obvious now. She only needed to believe in them and to believe in herself.

The darkness lifted and Kelcie was shocked to see her own reflection staring back at her. The blue and brown in her eyes swam, a current in a small pool. The river was holding up a mirror, saying, *This is who you are. This is where you belong. Why are you so afraid?*

A part of her soul that had been adrift for the past eight years felt like it slipped into place.

"Thank you," Kelcie said to Bug Eyes who gurgled next to her ear.

Fishtails whipped, clapping.

"*Olliphéist!*" a salmon sneezed from the back of the class.

"Bless you," Kelcie answered, settling into the slow-motion, hypnotic pace of the current, and the silence on the bottom of the river. No wonder Ollie loved to sit in the deep end of the pool in the Saiga Den. It was very peaceful. Or at least it was until the Salmon of Knowledge shrieked.

"Hark! The sea monster cometh!"

And cometh it did! An all-consuming shadow crossed above her head. A ten-foot-long serpent skated past on webbed fins, heading downstream. Staying as still as possible, she hoped it wouldn't notice her, but the blabbering salmon made that impossible.

"A bad way to die!" one trumpeted.

"A very bad way to die!" another seized.

To Kelcie's horror, the serpent pulled an illegal U-turn! The current shuddered from its loud screech.

"Olliphéist looks hungry! Swim for your lives!"

Now Kelcie understood. The fish weren't sneezing. The monster was named Olliphéist! Not that it made the situation any better . . .

School dismissed. Fish scattered. But sadly for the descendants of the Salmon of Knowledge there was no escape. Gawped jaws filled with razor-sharp teeth plowed through the back of the class, chowing down on enough fresh salmon sushi for twenty people.

The feast was over in seconds, but the monster didn't leave. From fifty feet away, she saw his big gray eyes narrow directly on her. Olliphéist charged.

Kelcie screamed, "Help!"

Shadows on the surface of the water shifted, but none of them dove in to help. Anger choked her. If it were anyone in her fianna up there, they would never have stood by and watched!

Didn't Payton say the clan comes first? Kelcie was a part of the clan too, wasn't she?

Kelcie pushed off the bottom, going absolutely terrifyingly nowhere. Webbed fins worked in tandem with the triangular tip of his tail, quickly carving through the river's current like a knife in soft butter. A low rumble started in the back of Olliphéist's throat, sending chills up her spine.

Movement across the surface gave Kelcie hope that the others were finally coming to help. But it was only Striker who plunged into the depths, spastically doggy-paddling toward her. Unlike on land where his speed made him practically uncatchable, underwater, Striker moved slower than the salmon, and Kelcie couldn't bear the thought of Olliphéist having the cù sith for dessert!

Sure enough, Olliphéist banked a few feet from Kelcie, heading straight for Striker.

"No!" Kelcie yelled. "Eat me!"

Distraught, she had to do something! *The water and I are one. Connected. It is as much a part of me as my beating heart.* Kelcie could do this. She had to do this!

"Caenum!" She swept her hands, pushing against the current and vines as hard as she could, refusing to take no for an answer. Her fingers tingled. Something in her stomach popped. An underwater wave surged, driving Olliphéist off course.

Kelcie's squeals of success were cut off as the sea monster somersaulted for another pass.

"Go!" Kelcie bellowed at Striker, but the cú sith refused to listen. He doggy-dove in her direction, his cheeks puffing with his last bit of breath.

Yelling the sparking word, Kelcie thrust her arms at Striker. A spinning current launched, carrying him straight up and out of the water.

Olliphéist bore down on Kelcie. There was no way she was going to get the vines off in time to save herself. Unsure of the right moves, she stretched her arms over her head as far as possible, hoping the water would be as intuitive with her as it was the night she was abandoned. *We're in this together, and always have been.*

"Caenum!"

Olliphéist's fangs scraped her abdomen as she shot past. Being catapulted out of the water wasn't as gentle as being caught by it. Landing hard on her back, the wind knocked out of her, she rolled back and forth, clutching her stinging stomach. Panting from exhaustion, Striker sank into the mud beside her.

"You did it!" Ollie exclaimed, pressing a bottle of Zinger into her hand.

Dollin whooped, dancing a jig too. "I knew it! I knew it!"

Markkus's heated hands slid under Kelcie's armpits, jockeying her to standing as if she couldn't get up on her own. "And you doubted our methods!" He chuckled in her ear.

"That thing almost ATE ME!" Kelcie fumed.

Dollin launched an imperious finger into the air. "But—"

"But nothing. Not a single one of you came to help! It almost ate Striker!"

Ollie went to untie Kelcie's ankles but she shewed him away.

"I don't need your help now! Mistral!" Air spun into a saw blade and cut the vines off her legs. The rest fell off. Her shoulders sagged with relief.

"Sorry about Striker." Ollie winced. "Hadn't counted on him being dumb enough to try and save you. But I knew Olliphéist wouldn't eat you. He hates the taste of Fomorian blood."

Kelcie flicked her muddy hands in his face. "That's reassuring!"

Payton hadn't said a word. She stood there, glaring at Kelcie, arms crossed over her chest, as if Kelcie had done something wrong.

"What?" Kelcie spat.

"I can't believe you. You're so ungrateful. You just commanded water!"

"Yup," Dollin said, with a reluctant shrug. "That's what I was trying to tell you."

Markkus leaned over her, huffing, "The words you're looking for are *thank you*."

"Well, that's not the . . ." Kelcie's fury fizzled. "I—Wait." Maybe they had a point. "I did." She lifted a hand off the cut on her stomach and stared at her bloody, pruned fingers. "I really did."

Kelcie had broken through the last bit of her mother's curse. Her days of being a confused, lost kid in Massachusetts felt over. Because she knew who she was, Draummorc and Nemain's daughter, and what she was, a pulse elemental, but as she glanced at the smiling, nodding, cocky grins of her clansmen surrounding her, catching the stern confidence in their mismatch-colored eyes, for the first time in her life Kelcie actually *felt* Fomorian.

These were her people, and she was part of this clan just like she was part of her fianna at school. Their tactics in breaking through to her Caenum powers were ruthless, but she supposed it was no different than Brona nearly turning her into a pincushion with her bow and arrow trying to get her to control air. Kelcie really wished Brona were here to see what she did. She would tell her as soon as they were back at school. No! She would show her.

With only six days left before she returned, Kelcie wanted to learn more. She wanted to learn everything they could teach her.

"I'm sorry. Ollie, I am your humble student, oh mighty Alpha of the Saiga Den." She donned a wicked smile, arching a challenging brow at the others. "What's next?"

4

DRAUMMORC

HOURS LATER, WITH three-quarters of the orange sun dipping beneath the treeline, Kelcie hustled along the path, praying she would make it into the cave before sundown. Ollie and the others lived in caves too, but on the other side of the hill. She jogged alone, except for Striker. Holding on to the scruff of his neck to keep him by her side, she hurried, eyes scanning for anything that might jump out at her, but also for Lexis.

As Kelcie started away from the river, following the path she and Ollie came down this morning, she was hit by the delicious smell of warm bread coming from her grandmother's cave. Striker whined and broke free, sprinting so fast for home dirt smacked Kelcie in the face.

"Striker!" she grumbled, spitting a pebble.

Something dashed across the path behind her, but by the time Kelcie turned around it was gone.

"Hello? Is someone there? Lexis? Is that you?"

Lexis was out there somewhere, alone, and probably scared. The sun lingered enough to see anything coming. Why not try and find her?

A noble idea, but as soon as Kelcie stepped over the selenite, into the tall ferns covering every inch of ground, the hair on the back of her neck spiked. No wildflowers grew in this forest. The only colors were variations of green from the different kinds of leaves, pine needles, and brush, the stone-brown bark clinging to the enormous trunks marked by vertical streaks of blood, likely from the Red Caps. A foreboding wind gave her chills.

"Lexis?" she called.

She felt something rustle against her boots, then, to her distressed shock, tighten over her ankles. Kelcie surged forward, trying to run, only to fall flat on her face, feeling thorns dig into her Achilles.

"Ow!"

Ferns stretched, lassoing her waist, spines scratching her sides through the many holes in her T-shirt. The forest was trying to kidnap her!

She wrestled her hand farther into the prickly ropes wound around her legs, doing her best to ignore the burning pain crawling up her arm, straining to reach the dagger in her boot. The pain all the way to her shoulder, she ripped the knife out, slicing fern along the way. As soon as she was free, she ran for the path, twisting her left ankle, forcing her to slow to a distressed skip-step.

Ferns rustled behind her. Taking a flying leap over the selenite, she felt the sting of thorns whip across her exposed calf skin where there used to be fabric, before bellyflopping on the path. Catching her breath, she listened carefully, hearing high-pitched squeals and shuffling. Red Caps! A barrage of four-inch spears soared straight for her. She rolled and rolled. Most struck the ground. But she didn't get away fast enough. As Kelcie sprinted for the safety of her grandmother's cave, two stabbed the back of her thigh.

She slammed and bolted the door, then took a second to yank the spears out, muttering in defeat. The Woods were too dangerous. Even if she wanted to, there was no way to leave the path and look for Lexis. There was nothing she could do. Lexis would have to find her if she needed help.

Limping to her duffel bag, Kelcie pulled out a bottle of Zinger, grateful Roswen made them pack a half dozen. The pain in her leg eased and the new wounds scabbed over after only downing half. She decided to save the rest. Judging by day one, she was going to need to ration it to survive the next six days.

Her grandmother had been busy while Kelcie was gone. In addition to the boiling pot of stew Kelcie saw hanging over the hearth, her laundry had been washed, and was strung on a line a foot from the ceiling, taking advantage of the heat from the fire. A basket of warm bread and a bowl of fruit compote were on the table, along with two place settings. Huddled over his food bowl, Striker hadn't bothered to wait for them to eat.

"I was getting worried." Doyen padded from the rear of the cave and dropped her teacup at the sight of her. "Are you bleeding?" She ignored the spill and rushed to Kelcie, lifting what was left of her shirt. "What happened to your clothes? And your hair!"

Any explanation would only make things worse. "I'm fine, Doyen. Training was good today actually."

"Good, huh?" Her grandmother spun her around, sniffing her head. "Oof, your beautiful hair. Oh, well. Nothing to be done now except trim it even."

Kelcie's stomach sank, not from the thought of losing more hair, but at the sight of an envelope in the middle of the bed with Kelcie's name on it written in ALL CAPS.

Niall's signature handwriting.

Her grandmother squeezed her shoulder. "That was here when I returned from the river."

Kelcie hurried to pick it up. Her hands shaking, she skimmed a finger over the perfect printing. *Finally!*

Kelcie had asked him to see what he could find out about her father, but that was two weeks ago, and Niall had never taken more than two days to answer her letters before. She'd given up hope, which was dumb because Niall was the one person in her life who never let her down. She should never have doubted him.

Anxious, and inexplicably self-concious, Kelcie set the letter down, and changed into an old T-shirt of Brona's and her Saiga pajama bottoms before sitting cross-legged on the bed to read it. She noticed the flap was open. A quick glance at her grandmother who had her back to Kelcie while she stirred the stew, and Kelcie knew she'd read it. She was too anxious to see what Niall had said to worry about that right now.

Kelcie held her breath, lifting out the piece of paper, and started reading.

> HI KELCIE, MY MOTHER HAS BEEN OTHERWISE OCCUPIED AS OF LATE. AS YOU KNOW, SHE LEFT TO TOUR THE TERRITORIES AND HAVE MEETINGS WITH THE CHANCELLORS. SINCE HER RETURN, SHE'S BEEN VERY BUSY. THE ASCENSION CERE-MONY WILL BE THIS YEAR. ALL THIS IS TO SAY I HA-VEN'T HAD AN OPPORTUNITY TO ASK HER ABOUT THE SITUATION WITH YOUR FATHER AND DOUBT I WILL BEFORE WE RETURN TO SCHOOL.

Ascension ceremony? She didn't know what that was, but how could a ceremony be more important than Kelcie's father? And why did he sound so formal? Did he not understand how important this was to her?

Sensing her frustration, Striker crawled up on the bed beside her, laying his head on her lap.

Kelcie stared down at Niall's note, fuming. But who was she mad at? Niall or her father?

Kelcie knew when she wrote asking for Niall's help that it was unfair to put him in that position, but what choice did she have? She had no one else to turn to.

Kelcie's lower lip trembled. Tears threatened. Why was she crying? She couldn't even remember her father, not very well. Yet here she was, a stupid, blubbering mess because he won't write her back.

"Kelcie." Her doyen sat down beside her. She took the letter from her hand, pretending to read it for the first time. When she was finished, she folded it and passed it back to her.

"This Niall is in your fianna?" Doyen asked.

Kelcie nodded.

"He speaks of a mother in council meetings. He's Queen Eislyn's son, isn't he?"

Kelcie wasn't supposed to talk about his identity, but wasn't going to lie to her doyen.

"Yes."

"I worry that by bringing up your father's name to him, to anyone," she wrapped a weary arm over Kelcie's shoulders, "that you risk losing all that you have gained."

Her grandmother had a point. Kelcie glanced around the claustrophobic cave they now called home.

The night before Kelcie was due to leave Tao's ship for Chawell Woods, she had asked him why the Queen had ordered the Fomorians arrested when they had nothing to do with Draummorc's crime. Tao claimed it was for their own protection. That Summerfolk turned on Fomorians in their communities, pillaging their homes, burning them to the ground, or worse. That no matter the edicts she dispensed, Summerfolk took their retribution.

Whatever the reason, Kelcie didn't want to make things worse for her grandmother, or lose Niall's friendship because of this.

Doyen squeezed her. "Your father can never be a part of your life."

Kelcie crushed the paper, holding it to her broken heart. "It wasn't his fault, Doyen. You know the Queen sent him to get the eye. He was obeying her orders."

"I do, and I begged him not to go, but he went. He followed her orders, and many died because of it." Doyen let out a long breath. "You, my beautiful anuyen, you had the courage to do what he could not; you fought against that evil. It will never plague another of Balor's heirs or anyone in the Lands of Summer ever again, but it makes my son no less a villain in the eyes of the people of Summer, our own clan included. The others in the Woods have shunned me, Kelcie."

"Is that why you live so far away from them?"

She let go of Kelcie to give Striker a pet like Kelcie did when she was upset and needing comfort. "Yes. I've turned into a living ghost because of your father's actions." Her voice cracked on the word *father*. Her hand stilled. "Do you understand what I'm saying?"

"You want me to forget him," Kelcie said, looking down and fingering the silver bracelet on her doyen's wrist.

"No. Never." Her grandmother removed both of her bracelets and placed them on Kelcie's wrists. Doyen's hands lingered as she used her power to shrink them to fit Kelcie's thinner frame. "These were your father's. I kept them all this time and now I want you to have them. You see we will never forget him, Anuyen."

Kelcie clutched the simple silver bands tarnished with age and use. "But you need them."

"You need them more." Doyen cupped Kelcie's chin and forced her to look at her. "But you have to let him go."

How could she let her father go? A piece of her was missing, a piece made up of warmth and love because that's what she remembered about him. Even if she didn't need him, she needed to know he was okay. But what else could she do? Hope ended with Niall.

Doyen kissed Kelcie's hair and got up slowly. "Let's eat before the stew gets cold."

Kelcie wasn't hungry anymore but knew she would eat. Her grandmother went to so much trouble to cook for her. But first, Kelcie smoothed out the letter to read the last sentence.

LOOKING FORWARD TO SEEING YOU SOON. NIALL

She puffed at the dismissal. All Niall's other letters ended with *write back soon*. With six days left, he sounded like he didn't want to hear from her anymore. Her grandmother was right. Bringing up her father was a bad idea. She didn't have to let him go, but she had to stop talking about him.

"Doyen, want to see what I learned today?"

Her grandmother looked over her shoulder, her ashen cheeks warming slightly. "Of course."

"Ignis," she whispered.

A tiny flame sprang to life on the tip of her index finger. She lit Niall's letter, watching the fire consume the bad news.

"Careful, or you'll be returning to school bald."

Flustered, Kelcie tossed the rest into the firepit and quickly blew out her finger.

5

AN UNEXPECTED FRIEND

KELCIE KEPT A lookout for Lexis whenever she left the cave, but the week had flown by without so much as a sighting of her. Doyen tried to alleviate Kelcie's fears by telling her that she probably had family in the Woods who met her at the same time Ollie and her grandmother came for her at the guardhouse. That in all the rush to escape the headless horseman, they must have missed them. Kelcie hoped she was right, but if she was wrong . . . Chawell Woods was barely survivable in the daytime, and Lexis had been out there for six nights alone.

"Kelcie!" her grandmother shouted, startling her. "Come!"

Kelcie ran out of the cave with Striker on her heels and found Doyen kneeling a few feet from the entrance.

"Are you okay?" Kelcie sank down beside her.

"I'm fine. Look!"

She gestured to a handful of flowers, each about the size of a dandelion, with long white petals and bulbous lavender centers, that had sprouted between gaps in the rocks.

"They grew overnight. They're called diema."

"Diema," Kelcie repeated. "They're beautiful."

"They're a sign of good luck, a blessing from the earth. Tomorrow morning, I will cut some for you to take to school. That way the luck will be with you until you return to me."

Kelcie hated the idea of leaving her grandmother, especially knowing how lonely she would be after Kelcie was gone. No one ever came to visit her. The last eight years must've been the worst of Doyen's life. But Kelcie refused to get upset about leaving, at least until tomorrow morning. Today was going to be hard enough.

"Can I take one of them with me now?" Kelcie asked.

"You need luck to train? I thought you were making progress with your powers."

"This is for something else," Kelcie answered, earning a furrowed brow from Doyen.

Doyen carefully picked one and placed it in Kelcie's palm. It was heavier than Kelcie expected.

Her grandmother cupped the bottom of her hand holding the flower with her own, and asked, "What is it for, Bug?"

Today she had to convince Payton, Markkus, and Dollin to test for the Academy. None of them had said a word about it since that first day when Kelcie and Ollie brought it up. She had to find a way to convince them, but had no clue how.

"For our future, Doyen."

EVERY DAY KELCIE had worked, switching disciplines and instructors. She traded air blows with Payton, swapped flames with Markkus, and whipped water ropes at Ollie. Today, it was Dollin's turn.

"You're late," Dollin declared, pacing circles as Kelcie met him at the riverbank. His strawberry blond hair stuck out in all directions like he'd been raking it with impatience. "It's your last day and you're wasting it!"

Striker jogged to Ollie who was beside the river, using the water as ammunition for target practice, lobbing water bombs at an X marked on the opposite bank. Markkus and Payton were nowhere to be found which meant they weren't coming tomorrow. Ollie tossed Kelcie a disappointed frown.

"Sorry, oh master of the Theran arts." Kelcie bowed ridiculously, trying for a laugh, but Dollin only scowled deeper. "My grandmother gave me these bracelets." She held up her wrists to show him.

"And maybe, one day, you'll be able to do this!" Liquid silver snaked down Dollin's wrist and into his palm, coming out a honed dagger. "But not yet. Right now, they're pretty bangles, not weapons. And you're leaving tomorrow!" The blade vanished up his sleeve.

It wasn't lost on Kelcie that he said *you're* leaving tomorrow. She had to do something, but what? Before Kelcie could say another word, Dollin put her to work. For all his blustering, he was a surprisingly good teacher, and Theran was so much more interesting and useful than Kelcie had ever expected.

"As a discipline, Theran breaks down solids, but can also reconnect those bonds. Metals, crystals, gems, anything you can sense the complex structure of can be broken apart and put back together," he explained.

It wasn't easy. Only in the last hour did Kelcie have any success. She manipulated small, square bits of iron into coin-size circles. It wasn't a weapon, but it was a start.

As they were packing up, Markkus and Payton made a sudden appearance, whispering tersely with one another, arguing. Ollie walked over, and the five of them stood in a tense circle.

"We came to say goodbye," Payton explained, refusing to make eye contact.

Kelcie inferred from that that it was Markkus who was reluctant to go, and one thing Kelcie learned over the past several days is that Payton and Markkus never did anything without each other.

"No." Kelcie squeezed the flower in her pocket, hoping that sticky goop oozing out really brought good luck, otherwise she had ruined her last pair of sweatpants for no reason. "Look. Roswen will be waiting at the gatehouse to escort Ollie and me to school. Just come and talk to her."

"You'll have to do better than that with these two," Dollin

snorted, shooting two fingers at Markkus and Payton. He smiled imperiously. "I already told my parents I'm testing. Maya is packing extra underwear just in case I get in."

Kelcie could've hugged him. Ollie swatted him on the back so hard Dollin fell into Markkus, who tossed him off.

"Traitor!"

"Hey!" Kelcie snapped. "He's not a traitor and neither are we! Come on. You two are so good. There's no way you won't get in, especially if we tell you tricks to get over the Bridge of Leaping." She waggled her eyebrows at Payton. The corners of Payton's mouth curled, letting Kelcie know she was tempted. "What is it, Markkus? Are you scared?"

He scoffed. "I don't want to go to a school where I'm going to have to pledge to protect the Lands of Summer when the Summerfolk turned on us."

"I understand," Kelcie offered, because it was true. "More than anyone." Ollie looked heartsick. His plans were all falling apart. But what could she say to convince them? They had a valid point. There was one thing that came to mind, the reason she couldn't wait to get back to school, her fianna. "But I found something very unexpected at the Academy. Loyalty."

Markkus rolled his eyes, but Payton's remained fixed on Kelcie so she spoke to her.

"Sure, there were bullies who told me every day I wasn't good enough, who called me a demon, but it's the ones who didn't that gave me hope."

Ollie picked up on where Kelcie was going with this and took over. "My fianna has my back always. Just as much as my clan. And if there are more of us there, I know we can be a force for change!"

Markkus stepped forward, standing over Kelcie. "What do we say to the ones who don't want us to test? Who don't want us training and fighting beside them?"

"That the Lands of Summer is our home too, and no matter what they say, we're not going anywhere," Kelcie answered.

Payton smirked, shrugging at Markkus. "Come on. Let's just test."

Markkus rolled his eyes at her, but his long relenting sigh let Kelcie know she and Ollie had won. "Fine. But when this ends up a disaster, I'm going to tell you I told you so."

Striker barked, leaping up on him celebrating.

Ollie unleashed his toothiest grin ever. "You won't be sorry! Let's walk back together so Kelcie and I can tell you what to expect tomorrow."

THE HIGH-PITCHED WHOOP of the Littlefolk's axe was barely audible. Lexis ducked too late. The blade lopped off three inches of her ponytail before thunking into a tree. This place was barbaric! Being miserably hot and sweaty, Lexis counted on. But Chawell Woods was a hell all on its own.

Another tiny blade scraped her leg. Warm blood leaked into her shoe.

Gah!

Needing to catch her breath, she let her selenite hoop drop, keeping the evil Littlefolk from getting too close. She'd smithed it from the barriers on the paths. It was the only way to get a second's peace off the dedicated trails. When another axe nicked the top of her ear before she could get an air shield up, Lexis sent a roaring wind in the direction it came, taking great satisfaction in the flying red spectacle that yelped, bouncing off a trunk.

"Serves you right!" she shouted.

Lexis hoped no one noticed the missing selenite bars. Her orders were to stay away from everyone until the day of the test to get into the Academy for the Unbreakable Arts. From what the Queen's Advisors knew, a teacher would come to the court-yard outside the gatehouse in Chawell Woods to escort testers to the school. It was the only way to get out of the Woods and to the Academy.

For the past week, she'd done a full recon of the forest, then escaped the tormenting Littlefolk by climbing to the top of the Moaning Mountains. She was both startled and panicked when she discovered that they weren't mountains in the traditional sense at all. They were sleeping *giants*, the exact same kind that had demolished Volga. After a small meltdown the first time their eyes opened, she quickly realized these giants were much more docile. In fact, they only woke when Lexis stumbled on a particular sensitive part. And then went right back to sleep.

But tomorrow she would be leaving for the Academy, and today was her final check-in with Swappy—the only member of her fianna who could sneak in and out of Chawell Woods—and she was late.

Groaning, Lexis picked up the hoop, sliding it over her shoulder, and started running again. She only made it a hundred yards before another sharp edge cut into her other calf. Yanking it out, she kept going. She should stop and tie it off, at least stuff it with the antiseptic moss she found when the headless horseman sliced the back of her arm her first night here. But it would have to wait. She was almost there and couldn't take a risk that she might miss him, or worse, that he'd get caught.

She zigged, then heard spears and axes thump ground and trunks a second after she zagged. Hurdling bulbous roots, she tripped into the copse, her destination, falling over in a graceless manner. She rolled over, panting, finding the amused red eyes of a circling hawk. The bird swooped down, stopping to chase away Red Caps, then landed at Lexis's feet.

Swappy shimmied, transforming back to his usual self, only he looked miserable. Sweat glued his shaggy green hair to his forehead. He wore shorts that showed off his bony knees, and a white T-shirt complete with pit stains. Sandals showed off blistering red sunburnt feet.

"This place is horrible!"

He stomped at a snapping pink armadillo who had scampered into the copse.

"Tell me something I don't know." Lexis wiped off the blood on her legs, then noticed a bald spot on the side of his head.

"What happened?"

"Ravens . . ." he growled. He rubbed the spot with one hand, and passed her a small package in the other. "It's what you asked for. I stole it out of a High Command arsenal. I didn't realize those shifters would try and eat me! And by me, I mean a stink-rat. They have worse gas than me. I thought it would be the perfect cover. Boy, was I wrong!"

Lexis couldn't help herself. She hugged Swappy, laughing. This week had been the loneliest of her life. "How are Jack and Pavel?" she asked, letting him go.

"The hideout is cramped. Pavel's wings are an issue. The glamourie we have isn't very good. It only works for about an hour. Then he mopes the rest of the time. Jack is moody and constantly griping at me, but that's nothing new. He really needs something to do though or I might not make it back to Winter alive."

The Queen's Advisors told her to parse out assignments one step at a time. Everything was very need-to-know so that what they didn't know couldn't be used against Winter if they were caught. It sounded so cold when they said it, and didn't sound any better replaying it in her mind now. But the good news for Swappy was that it was time for step two.

"Tell him I said to go smooth-talk someone in the nearest town, like a seamstress. They'll be getting orders for new clothes for the Ascension. The date should be finalized by now. Then, once he finds out when it is, all of you should go to Moon Bay, to the empty house I told you about. Wait for me there."

"Yes, ma'am!" Swappy saluted. "I have something else for you. Technically, I'm supposed to tell you it's from Jack."

Jack sent her a present? Lexis felt an undignified blush coming on. She sank her upper lip into her bottom teeth to stop it. They weren't like that. Not that Lexis didn't find him the most handsome boy she'd ever met, but she was his leader. Crushes weren't allowed. She gave the orders, and if she thought of him as anything but her favorite saber-toothed contrarian, she might not be able to do that. It was hard enough to calm her fluttering heart every time he said her name.

Swappy lifted out a piece of paper from his pocket and passed it to her. "It was delivered to him for you, but I don't see how that makes it from Jack."

Lexis turned it over. Her name was written across the back in elegant, swooping letters. "That's not Jack's handwriting."

"No. It's from the Queen!"

Overwhelmed with pride, she pressed it to her chest. *Queen Kefyra sent me a letter?*

"Oh, look! I want to try it!"

Before Lexis could stop him, Swappy touched a creepy-crawler on the trunk beside him and shrank into a four-legged bug with a square thorax and spiked pincers, then started turning in circles, wide-eyed. He never noticed the pink armadillo return, or it's super-long orange tongue snap in his direction.

Lexis snatched it by the hind legs and hurled it up and over the hedges.

Swappy enlarged, hyperventilating. "Great spider-troll balls! That was close!"

"What do I always tell you about changing into bugs?" Lexis shook her head.

"Did you see that!" a familiar and practically on-top-of-them voice exclaimed.

Heart thundering, Lexis ducked, dragging Swappy with her, tucking closer to the bushes for cover.

"I didn't see anything," another voice answered.

"Is that you, Lexis?"

"It's her. Kelcie!" Lexis whispered. "This is perfect."

"The girl the Advisors told you about?" Ever curious, Swappy started to peek out. Lexis shoved him back down and mouthed the word *Go*.

A second later, a squirrel scrambled halfway up a tree. Swappy gave her a sad salute, eyes glistening with tears, then took off in the direction of the guardhouse.

This was the second time Lexis had to say goodbye to her fianna, and she hated it, but it wouldn't be for long.

No. They'd be back together before the Ascension, so long as everything went according to plan.

"You are obsessed," another girl exclaimed. "She was probably a ghost," she said in all seriousness. "We're going ahead. We have to deliver the news to our parents."

"And pack," another voice chimed.

"See you tomorrow," Kelcie said.

Footsteps shuffled off, but Lexis knew Kelcie remained. She could hear her steps coming closer.

Lexis's stomach twisted into an impossible knot as she steeled for what came next. She didn't know what time the teacher from the school was coming. The pinched-faced soldier at the guardhouse refused to tell her. She'd watched Kelcie return to her grandmother's cave one evening, almost got caught that time too, and had planned on showing up there first thing in the morning tomorrow to see when she left to meet the teacher. But this was destiny taking a hand. She wasn't supposed to spend any extraneous time with Kelcie, but even the Advisors wouldn't pass up an opportunity like this.

The corners of her mouth ticked into a devilish smirk. This is what Lexis trained for, and she was going to put on the performance of a lifetime.

Lexis heard Kelcie start walking away. She stuffed the precious note from the Queen in her pocket to read later, took a deep breath for courage, and exited the glen.

"Hey! Kelcie! Wait for me!"

6

YEAR TWO

ELCIE STOPPED, RELIEVED to see Lexis. "I was so worried about you! Are you okay?"

Lexis was out of breath by the time she caught up, and held up a finger before answering. She wore the exact same clothes as she did the night in the guardhouse, the gray T-shirt and black pants that were much too big for her, only now they were torn and bloodstained. Kelcie's grandmother had been wrong. Lexis had been fighting for survival for the past six days.

"I, um . . ." Lexis gasped. "Um . . . no. I'm not." Her eyes glossed over with tears. "I don't know what to do. I can't be here anymore! This place is too hard! I thought I could take care of myself, but I can't do this." Her tears turned to sobs.

Kelcie set a hand on Lexis's shoulder, trying to comfort her. "Come home with me. My grandmother won't mind."

"Are you sure?"

"Absolutely. She'll love the company. And I have something that can help with those cuts."

Lexis's brows knitted. She wiped her cheeks with what was left of her sleeve. "Thank you."

It wasn't until after dinner that Kelcie worked up the courage to ask Lexis how she ended up in Chawell Woods. She had a feeling it wasn't a very pleasant story, and it turned out she was right.

"We were hiding." Lexis spoke in hushed tones, giving Kelcie the impression she was embarrassed. "My parents and me. We didn't want to move to Chawell Woods. We wanted to stay in our home. But the soldiers were coming. So we left and hid. The sewers were . . . not good. Every year, they got sicker and sicker."

"You lived in sewers for *years*?" Kelcie cringed.

She shrugged. "I don't know why I didn't get sick like they did, but when I lost them last year, I didn't want to stay there, not by myself."

Lexis was alone, and Kelcie understood how that felt better than anyone. Forever lost even if you knew your surroundings, there was always a sinking feeling in the pit of your stomach, an ache to belong that refused to go away.

Lexis continued speaking softly. "As soon as I came out, the soldiers brought me here." She knotted her fingers. "But I don't think I can stay."

Striker bumped Lexis's leg. She stiffened, looking wide-eyed and afraid.

"He does that when he likes someone. He won't hurt you," Doyen explained.

Lexis pet his back tentatively. "He's really soft."

"My cave is very small, but you are always welcome to stay here." Doyen smiled warmly. "Although Striker will be going with Kelcie tomorrow to the Academy for the Unbreakable Arts."

"Whoa! Really? You go there?" Lexis asked.

Kelcie nodded. And couldn't believe she hadn't thought of it before. It was the perfect solution. "And you know what? You should test tomorrow for the Academy!"

"That is a marvelous idea, Kelcie." Her grandmother winked at her.

Lexis gaped at Kelcie with intrigued apprehension. "I'm supposed to be a Caenum, but when my parents saw me trying to use those powers, they told me to stop and refused to teach me anything. Said it was too dangerous. I hardly feel them anymore. It's like they withered from lack of use."

"The spriggan's zap will take care of that," Kelcie figured. "Strong stuff. Broke my mother's curse."

Confusion washed over Lexis's face. "Curse?"

"It's a long story and we have to be up early tomorrow, if you want to come, that is."

Doyen patted her shoulder. "Go, Lexis. You children must bring a better future for us all, and you can't do that locked in Chawell Woods."

Nodding, Lexis smiled for the first time since Kelcie met her, then turned deadly serious. "Tell me, what exactly is on the test?"

THE NEXT MORNING, Ollie brought Lexis the set of black clothes Kelcie had sent him a note about last night so she would have something to wear to the test. All he said in response was "Glad she wasn't a ghost. And yay! We've got another tester!"

But his exuberant enthusiasm was gone by morning, replaced by impatient, irritating nagging. He paced outside the cave, bellowing every five seconds while Lexis changed.

"What's taking so long?"

"Roswen is probably already in the courtyard!"

"Do I need to come in there?"

"No! She's hurrying!" Kelcie shouted. Lexis was nervous enough. The last thing she needed was Ollie barking at her.

Striker jumped up on Doyen, his way of saying goodbye, and bolted out of the cave with a spring in his step. Kelcie suspected he was as excited as she was to be returning to school. For all its vast space, there was no freedom in Chawell Woods.

Kelcie slung her duffel bag over her shoulder, then went to work on a futile attempt to close the clasp on her cloak. Her grandmother brushed her fingers aside and did it for her.

"You have thick fingers like your father." She pressed the Saiga's horns flat, and cupped Kelcie's cheek. "There. You're perfect."

"Except my hair." Kelcie frowned, sweeping it behind her ears. It was too short for a ponytail.

"Bah. Hair. There are much more important things to worry about. And I like it. Lets your freckles take a starring role on your face." She poked Kelcie's nose.

Kelcie hated her freckles, but loved her grandmother so she kept that to herself. She hugged her. "I'll see you next break." She swallowed hard, pushing the lump down. It was one thing to say goodbye to Brona for a week, but leaving her grandmother alone in her tiny cave was the hardest thing she'd ever had to do.

Doyen let go first, her ruby and brown eyes glistening with tears. "I'll understand if you don't want to come back, Kelcie. This is not a home."

Kelcie shook her head. "Wherever you are is *our* home."

Doyen pulled her in for another hug. *"To nammasa."*

Kelcie's heart nearly burst. "I love you too."

Lexis walked out from the back of the cave where she was changing. "This okay?"

Her curly brown hair was pulled off her face into a high pony-tail and Ollie's black T-shirt and shorts fit her perfectly.

Hearing Lexis, Ollie poked his head inside and chimed without looking, "You look fabulous! Let's go!"

"Thank you!" Lexis waved at Doyen, jogging after him.

"Wait, Bug!" Doyen caught Kelcie's arm before she could leave. "You need to take the diema with you! Get the scissors."

By the time Kelcie got there with the scissors, the flowers had turned to ash.

"They're dead. All of them." Her grandmother's haunted tone gave Kelcie goose bumps.

"What does this mean, Doyen?"

Her expression grim, Doyen scanned the surroundings. "That a powerful ill wish has crossed this threshold, a sign of bad things to come."

Crow caws raked the morning calm. A single black bird launched into the sky, wings beating furiously, lifting higher and higher as if it were on its way to sound an alarm, but to who? Her mother? Was another curse about to fall? What exactly was the difference between an ill wish and a curse anyway? There was no time to ask. If she missed Roswen, she would never get out of the Woods and back to school!

Doyen gave Kelcie another squeeze, harder than the last. "Be on your guard, Kelcie. Something dark looms and you must be ready for it."

A SEA OF CHAOS greeted Kelcie in the courtyard. She fisted the strap on her duffel bag, fear tightening a new corkscrew in her stomach several rungs, not at her parting words with her grandmother, *Something dark looms and you must be ready for it*, although they were unsettling. But at the crow, her mother's familiar, racing away, squawking as if life depended on it.

Striker spirited here and there, diving between the testers who were all vying for Roswen's attention. Roswen's pink hair was in a high ponytail similar to Lexis's, her white bodysuit pristine, and she was uncharacteristically heavily armed with two swords crossed on her back, daggers sticking out of her boots and a silky white pouch hanging from her belt, the contents of which glowed blue, red, and yellow.

"I'm Payton," Payton was explaining to Roswen. "That's *P-a-y-t-o-n* and there's no second name, and this is Markkus, with two *k*s. He doesn't have a second name either."

"Does Markkus speak?" Roswen asked, twirling her axe-pen between her fingers. "It's not mandatory, but it would be good to know."

"Only when I have to," Markkus said.

Roswen laughed under her breath. "I think I'm gonna like you."

Payton shot a thumb over her shoulder. "And that's Dollin."

Dollin stomped his foot. "I wanted to tell her!"

Ollie watched, a prideful look on his face while Lexis stared up at the statue of Niall's mother, brows furrowed. She looked angry. The dreaded words *ill wish* rolled around Kelcie's mind, and as uncharitable as it was, she couldn't help but wonder if the flowers dying had something to do with Lexis. Those flowers were alive last night when she brought Lexis to her grandmother's cave.

"Hey," Payton grunted, jerking her chin at Lexis. "Is this ghost-girl? The mysterious Lexis?"

"Yes," Ollie answered, walking Lexis over to Roswen. "And she wants to test."

Lexis nervously chewed her fingernails.

"Well done," Roswen said to him, her axe-pen busy on her clipboard, logging Lexis's name.

Lexis gave her nails a break, moving on to her lip. "What happens if we don't get in?"

Roswen stopped writing. "I bring you back here."

Lexis looked crushed. "Do you have to? Would anyone even know—"

Ollie bumped her shoulder. "Don't think about that."

"It's all I can think about," Lexis sighed.

Markkus leaned over to whisper in Kelcie's ear. "Why are you looking at *her* like that? What's wrong?"

She wanted to tell Markkus about her suspicions, but how many times in the past had Kelcie been accused of things she'd never done because people didn't know her and assumed the worst? Ashamed for even thinking it, Kelcie shook her head.

"No reason."

"Kelcie Murphy." Roswen spun her around. "You've done something different with your hair."

"Not on purpose."

Ollie snuck up behind her, popping Kelcie on the back of the head. "What will O'Shea say?" He batted his eyelashes.

"Who cares what he says?" Kelcie answered, knowing full well *she* did.

"Who's O'Shea? He your boyfriend? Is he cute?" Lexis asked, sounding way too intrigued.

"Oh, Niall's dreamy," Ollie teased. "Dark hair, big purple eyes. Only one hand. And oh so in love with Kelcie."

Cheeks burning, Kelcie shoved him. "I will get you for this, Ollie!"

Roswen pinned Ollie with a stern stare. "You're Alpha, Lynch! Start acting like one."

"Yes, ma'am," Ollie said, winking at Kelcie.

The door to the guardhouse cracked open. A ripple of jovial anticipation spread around the courtyard as the burly yellow-bearded soldier Kelcie met on the way into the Woods poked his head out.

"That's our cue," Roswen exclaimed. "Follow me. Next stop, the Academy for the Unbreakable Arts!"

STUDENTS SPILLED OUT of the Sidral. Kelcie stood far enough away to not get trampled, but close enough to see who exited. She played with the upside-down clasp on her cloak, using her peripheral vision to see, trying to look inconspicuous.

A big dimpled smile came rushing toward her. "Nice haircut!" Zephyr scooped her into a big hug, lifting her off the ground.

"Did you grow another foot?" she asked, laughing.

"You know it!" He dropped her.

"Will you stop?" Brona pushed Striker off of her. "I've missed you too but you're getting muddy pawprints all over my dress uniform! We have inspection!"

"Doyen told him to give you a hug!" Kelcie tackled her. "I've missed you!"

"I missed you more! You are never going back to those woods, not without me!" Brona frowned at someone over Kelcie's shoulder. "Hey . . . who's the pretty girl staring at us?"

Kelcie glanced back, seeing Lexis who quickly looked away. "That's Lexis. She's testing."

"That's great! You've been busy!" Zephyr exclaimed, flexing.

"I have too. Look at that." He ran a hand over his bulging bicep. "Hauling rocks out of the old pasture all break."

"That sounds miserable," Brona commented.

"No worse than being trapped on a ship searching for buried treasure," Zephyr countered, then reconsidered. "Never mind. That sounds way better than hauling rocks."

"Yeah, it was one big adventure after another." Brona hissed a laugh, winking at Kelcie. Brona always did like to keep secrets, that secret being it would've been miserably dull if they hadn't been together.

Kelcie was going to give the testers from the Woods another pep talk, but they had disappeared into the masses making their way to Hawthorne Field. Striker licked Kelcie's hand, then ran off, likely to the Shadow, their preceptor Scáthach's office and home where he lived during Kelcie's missing years.

"We should get to the field," Brona said.

"Shouldn't we wait for Niall?" Kelcie asked.

Brona rolled her eyes, hooking her elbow, and dragged Kelcie away from the Sidral. "I'm sure he's already there."

By the time they got to the field, the Dens were lining up behind their Alphas. Kelcie walked slowly toward Ollie, scanning the pit of Adders. Niall wasn't there. He was with the testers, talking to Lexis. She was holding his silver bough, her expression filled with awe as she examined its many branches and gemstone leaves. It was so much bigger than Kelcie's. A full-grown tree. Kelcie suspected Niall had access to every Sidral in the Lands of Summer. Being the Queen's son had its privileges.

Tucking his bough under his green cloak, he laughed at something Lexis said. He was probably just being nice, she rationalized. Niall was the first person Kelcie met last year, and she never would've made it through the test without him. His Alpha called Niall to line up. Still looking over his shoulder at Lexis, he stumbled, turning bright red, and didn't even notice Kelcie waving as he passed by.

Jealousy tore through Kelcie.

A single water droplet fell on the tip of her nose as she peeked up and gasped, surprised. A basketball-size storm cloud hovered directly over Kelcie's head. Thinking this was Ollie's doing, she went to say something, but he was standing at attention, eyes fixed on Roswen on the platform.

Before Kelcie could stop it, the cloud let go, rain pouring down, soaking her from head to toe. Ollie hopped forward, out of the line of fire, calling for it to stop.

The line of Cats beside her witnessed the debacle and were still laughing when Kelcie worked up the courage to speak.

"Ollie, how can my powers spark without the words?"

"I don't know. Never happened to me before. Maybe you needed cooling off." He chuckled, then sobered as Roswen stormed down the steps, heading straight for her. "I hate to tell you this, but you're never going to pass inspection."

7

BAD OMENS

KELCIE EARNED TWENTY laps around the field for failing inspection before being summarily dismissed by Roswen. Students stacked up waiting to get through their Den doorways under the archway at Haven Hall. Like last year, the Chargers went first, stampeding their way to the front. Kelcie felt a pang of loss when Brona morphed and flew into the Raven Den surrounded by Den mates. It was only until dinner, but she'd hardly been able to talk to her cousin and she had so much to tell her—about Niall's last letter, about her training, about the crows and the ill wish. As Alpha, Ollie stayed for the testing. Kelcie stood off to the side, the lone yellow cloak. She saw Niall with his back to her, and waded over.

Tugging on his cloak, she blurted a mortifying, overzealous, "Hey."

"Hey," he said, turning to face her. His brow creased. His big lavender eyes studied her. When his lips parted, and nothing came out, Kelcie lost all confidence and decided that whatever he was going to say could wait.

"I'll, um, see you at dinner!"

Kelcie shouldered to the front, casting a blistering gale that shoved several hissing tabby cats out of her way.

"Sorry! It's an emergency!"

She pressed her bough to the wall under the arch. The bronze Saiga door materialized. The white antelope shook his over-sized head, flapping the sides of his droopy nose as if waking up from a long nap.

"Hurry up! Open the door! Please!" she begged in a whisper.

He let out a nasally roar, offended, but lowered his thick, ringed horns. As soon as the door opened, she leaped on the fireman's pole.

For the next few hours she settled in, unpacking the few things in her duffel bag, most of which went straight into the laundry chute in the back of her locker. Then she took a long, hot shower, something she'd missed being on the ship and in Chawell Woods during break.

Back at her locker, she found an entirely new set of clothes had been provided. She put on a pristine dress uniform for din-ner, then plopped down in her desk chair and glanced at her new schedule, noting it hadn't changed much from last year, although the textbooks took a much darker turn. In one called *The Unexpected Interloper*, the first chapter was about Vampires in Winter. Unlike the legends in the human world, vampirism was a part of many species in the Lands of Winter: goblins, owls, and ten pages dedicated to the most revered of them all, Vampire-Trolls. As if vampires alone weren't dangerous enough. In the Otherworld, they had to start breeding.

Kelcie closed the book and checked the chalkboard on the back of the door for important announcements.

Welcome Back, Murphy. Striker is Not Allowed in the Den, But you can Come Visit Him at the Shadow Whenever you Like.

That was disappointing. After spending all of break with him by her side, it was going to be very lonely without him. The door banged against the wall so hard it made Kelcie jump.

"Hi, roomie!" Payton strided in.

Kelcie flew out of her chair. "You made it!"

Kelcie rushed over. Hanging around Payton's neck was a

shiny new silver bough half as long as Kelcie's with a tiny yellow crystal leaf on the end of it.

Then Lexis walked through the door.

"Me too!" She danced in with popping jazz hands. She elbowed Payton and with complete sincerity said, "Thank you. I wouldn't have made it over the Bridge of Leaping—"

Payton shushed her. "We stick together. Our clan is one."

Lexis nodded, an unmistakable hint of sadness in her eyes. "That's what my father used to always say."

Markkus strutted into their room, his black hair wet and slicked back, looking dapper in his new Saiga cloak. "Admit it. I wear yellow well."

It was true, but Kelcie would never admit it.

"Not as well as I do!" Dollin chased after him. Chin down, crushing his buck teeth into his chin, his little fingers dusting the antelope's ringed horns stitched into his lapel. "I love her. I'm going to call her Nesra."

Kelcie's heart grew three sizes. They'd all made it. Every Fomorian tester. "I never thought to name mine before."

Ollie strutted into the room, a blooming grin easing his big ears backward. "Now this is what I'm talking about. We have a Den!" The board on the back of Kelcie's door made a scratching sound. Ollie tugged it forward. The welcome for Kelcie erased. It said, *Congratulations to the New First Years! Schedules have Now Been Sent to Your Desks. The Banquet will Begin in Five Minutes.*

Two *swoops* led to two loud *dings* from inside previously unused desk drawers announcing Payton's and Lexis's schedules had arrived. But before they could get to them, Ollie clapped. "Who's hungry?"

Every hand went up.

Four tries later, first years finally got up the fireman's pole, but by then they were all late to dinner. Kelcie rushed to the second-year table, taking the empty seat beside Brona, across from Zephyr and Niall.

"Hey," Kelcie said, her heart thundering for no apparent reason.

Niall stared at her like he did earlier, as if he didn't recognize her, then quirked a shy grin. It was the hair. Kelcie's shoulders lifted, dipping the ends beneath her cloak's collar. The always-graceful Cat, Delilah Quick, laid delicate fingers over Niall's wrist.

"Sorry," Niall said to Delilah, like they'd been in a deep conversation before Kelcie had arrived.

With his attention fixed on the Cat, Kelcie allowed herself a peek at him. Gone was the shaggy brown mop that always hung in his eyes. His hair was cropped short. A new pair of black-rimmed glasses perched on his nose in the perfect spot, no longer too big for his face. Niall looked older, more distinguished, and he still hadn't said more than two words to her. It was depressing, but she refused to let it ruin her first day back.

Kelcie started eating like there was no tomorrow. Roswen had added some strange food to the banquet this year. There was a yellow vegetable that tasted like candied asparagus and crunchy black flowers that tasted like sour sawdust—both weird, but not entirely disgusting.

She listened as her classmates talked about vacations they took during break to places Kelcie had never heard of with glorious names like Languid Falls and the Dorrga Verge Hot Springs.

"What did you do?" Marta Louisa, the tallest girl in their class, and one of the nicer ones, asked Kelcie.

Brona answered for her. "Kelcie and I were assigned to my father's ship, helping him search for a stash of Winter munitions, until she had to go, that is."

Kelcie laughed. *Assigned* was Brona's glamorous way of saying they were put to work mopping the deck, catching fish, and cleaning up after every meal. They were never allowed to leave the ship. Tao had refused every time they asked to disembark, claiming Brona couldn't be trusted if they found the stash of

Winter weapons not to try them out. Kelcie couldn't argue with that logic.

Nosy Willow Hawkins, Brona's roommate in the Raven Den, turned to look at Kelcie. "Where did you have to go?"

"Chawell Woods," Tad Fagan bellowed as if speaking through a megaphone. He scowled at the first-year table. "And now there's more of them."

"You say that like it's a bad thing," Zephyr scoffed. "If I recall, our fianna kicked your butt last year, taking Queen of the Hill."

"How was it?" Willow asked Kelcie, determined to extract as much information as she could, likely to use against her. "Is it as awful as they say?" Her tone softened; genuine curiosity mixed with a heavy dose of concern.

Niall shifted in his seat to look at Kelcie, his gaze narrowing, wary. Kelcie thought about telling them of the dangers, of having to live one day at a time. How little time they had to forage for food, gathering just enough to survive before barely escaping being axed or bitten. Then there were the nightmares banging on the door all night long, and the decapitating headless horseman and his fire-breathing steed who rode once a month—all creatures hell-bent on keeping Fomorians in their places—on the path, at the river, and locked in their caves at night. But those images weren't as fresh in her mind as the day in the river with the sea serpent, Olliphéist, and the training with her Fab Four teachers, who she now called Den mates.

Kelcie smiled at Tad. "It was fruitful. Caenum."

The water from the pitcher raised along with her fist, then slid over his head, churning, waiting for her command, except for a few insubordinate droplets that ski-jumped off the back of his mullet.

"Don't you dare!" Tad dove under the table.

Her classmates were still laughing when she put the water back in the pitcher.

"You did it!" Brona whooped. "This year is going to be so great."

"Saiga!" Zephyr cheered.

"What else can you do?" Marta Louisa prodded.

Kelcie shrugged. She set her cupped palm upright on the table and drew a slow, calming breath, before whispering, "Ignis."

A little flame burst to life, flickering and snapping, tangling with the breeze.

Her classmates' adulations left Kelcie a blushing mess. They used words like *incredible* and *amazing*, words they never used to describe anything Kelcie had done before.

But Tad Fagan couldn't let Kelcie be happy, not for a second. He slapped the table, demanding everyone's attention, then pointed at her. "So, that's what happened to your *hair*!" He cackled along with David Dunn, the Adder in his fianna who also took great joy in tormenting Kelcie last year.

Humilated, Kelcie raised another pitcher of water, intending to soak them both, but caught sight of her reflection on the churning surface, and froze, fixated on all the bits and pieces of her that looked so much like her father. Her eyes, yes, but the biggest connection, the most visible, was her red hair, most of which was gone now. All those years in the human world, she'd never cared about her hair. Short, long, it made no difference because she didn't know then that it had come from her father. And now that it was gone, it was like losing a part of him.

She was supposed to let him go. But Kelcie couldn't. Not ever. He'd helped her last year. He told her he loved her. But why then wouldn't he write her back?

What's the matter?

Niall's concern only made her more upset. He knew what was wrong.

The water fell on the dessert tray, drenching the delicious-looking elderberry tarts.

Her classmates collectively moaned, except for Niall, who was staring at her.

Kelcie?

Chest tightening, Kelcie got up from the table, refusing to let them see her cry. She left a brisk wind in her wake and didn't look back to see whose Zinger bottle she accidentally spilled, but from all the high-pitched meowing, it sounded like Delilah's.

"Kelcie, wait!" Brona called.

But Kelcie didn't wait. She ran as hard as she could to the Shadow, finding Striker sleeping upside-down in the knee-high grass outside the curtain wall. Showered in orange from the setting sun, his bright green fur looked almond brown. Stirring when she sat down beside him, he rolled to set his nose in her lap.

"Maybe I should sleep up here with you."

"I didn't think I'd be seeing you here this soon," Scáthach said, startling Kelcie.

Her preceptor was coming across the Bridge of Leaping toward her. In her black armored bodysuit, Scáthach's swords crossed on her back, beaded sweat drying on her brow, she looked like she'd been working out.

Kelcie stood up, stiffening to attention, but relaxed to a heavy-hearted slouch when Scáthach held a hand up. "No need for that. School doesn't officially start for me until tomorrow. But this is a genuine surprise. I would've thought that with so many coming with you from Chawell Woods, all of whom made it through testing, this would be an evening of celebration. Why are you here all alone?"

Kelcie sat down, examining Striker's sprawled belly, unable to look Scáthach in the eye when she lied. "I was worried about Striker."

Footsteps pattered on the Bridge of Leaping. Kelcie glanced over, and saw Brona leading Payton and Lexis across. Brona plopped down on the other side of Striker.

"The boys wanted to come, but I told them no."

Lexis kneeled and tentatively brushed Striker's snout. "He's so soft. Can he sleep in the Den?"

"Does he look like he wants to sleep in the Den?" Scáthach asked, pulling her foot behind her, stretching her hamstring.

Lexis didn't answer her. She stared at Scáthach, mouth hanging open, as if she were too intimidated to speak.

"No, ma'am," Payton chimed in with conviction. "Pets should be kept outside."

"Cú siths are not pets," Scáthach corrected, switching legs. "They are eternal spirits, reborn with every lifetime. Striker has chosen Kelcie's family to be a part of this time around. But, all cú sith must be free to roam. They must soak up sun during the day and bathe in moonlight at night."

"Why?" Kelcie asked.

"Because they're not of this world, a little like your mother, and Brona's."

"Your mothers?" Lexis asked, intrigued.

Brona explained about their mothers being Nemain and Macha, two of the Three Morrígna. Kelcie clocked the deep crease that formed in Lexis's forehead. Her intense scrutiny shifted from Brona to Kelcie and back again, like she was looking for something—resemblance maybe? They looked nothing alike. Brona had black hair and silver eyes, like their mothers.

"So you're cousins?" Payton asked, sounding incredulous.

Brona pulled Kelcie to standing and threw an arm over her shoulder. "Yes." She jerked her chin at the sun, which had dipped beneath the Shadow's wall. "And it's almost curfew."

"Yes, it is. Dens. Run along," Scáthach shooed. "Striker and I have some catching up to do."

Kelcie crossed the bridge walking backward, gobsmacked at seeing Striker and Scáthach doing wind sprints, moving so fast that neither the preceptor's nor the cú sith's feet rustled the grass.

On the way to Haven Hall, they cut through the forest. Spriggans hung from the first tree Kelcie passed, dangling on linked arms like a barrel of monkeys. The one on the bottom whistled and waved.

Kelcie waved back. "I think that's the one who fell into the Abyss water last year."

"What do you mean?" Lexis asked, curious as ever. "Water from the Abyss was here, on campus? And how can he be here if he fell in?"

"I fell into it too, but here I am. It's a long story." Kelcie shrugged, not sure she had the energy to tell it right now.

"I'd really like to hear. Please?" Lexis pleaded.

Brona saw as much in Kelcie's long face and put Lexis off, at least for a little while. "You can tell her all about how you heroically saved the Academy for the Unbreakable Arts by destroying the eye tonight." Brona skipped ahead to walk with Payton. Over her shoulder in a veiled haunting tone, she added, "It will make a wonderful bedtime story."

"*We* destroyed the eye. Not me," Kelcie corrected.

"What eye?" Lexis pressed.

"Do you know what King Balor's evil eye is?"

Lexis's jaw dropped. "Yes. It was here at the school? How did it get here and how did you destroy it?"

Payton spun around, walking backward, to ask, "*How* could you not know this story? Even I heard it in Chawell Woods."

Lexis didn't answer. Kelcie knew the reason why, but Lexis's life before Chawell Woods wasn't Kelcie's story to tell.

"Not everyone hears everything," Kelcie answered for her. "It's a long story, Lexis. I promise I'll tell you later."

"It's so nice to be able to walk through woods and not expect to be killed," Kelcie heard Payton say to Brona.

"I walk everywhere thinking I'm about to be killed. Keeps my senses sharp," Brona replied.

Out of nowhere, a crow and a raven appeared on the path near Kelcie's feet, then proceeded to get into an argument, cawing and croaking, snapping beaks at each other, black feathers flying off with every disgusted swipe.

"Jeez!" Kelcie hopped sideways to get out of the line of fire, but they followed her, mimicking her move.

"What's wrong?" Lexis asked, nearly bumping into her.

Brona came flying back in her raven form, landing between the birds. She croaked excitedly at the raven, and it responded ruthlessly, snapping its beak.

"That's so cool!" Payton gushed. "Does she morph like that all the time?"

"You're talking about Brona, right?" Kelcie asked. "Or the other raven?"

"What other raven?" Payton and Lexis asked at the same time.

Kelcie wildly gesticulated. "You two don't see them?" she squeaked in a high-pitched, completely undignified tone.

Scowling incredulously, Payton crossed her arms, huffing. "Oh please. We're not falling for that."

"We know upperclassman always play tricks on the first years." Lexis smirked a head shake at Payton. "Kelcie's good. I almost believed her."

Brona transformed, and started pushing Lexis and Payton down the path. "You're both right. Wow. You found us out so quickly. And here we wanted to make you late for curfew on your first day. Run along."

"Won't you two be late for curfew?" Lexis asked, sensing something was up.

"Take the hint, roomie. The cousins want to be alone," Payton explained.

As soon as they were out of sight, the crow squawked at the raven. After an overt eyeroll, the raven hopped out of the way, letting the crow take center stage between Kelcie and Brona. It stabbed its left claw into the packed dirt, dragging it round and rounds, carving—a spiral.

Letting out a sharp, mission-accomplished *CACK*, the raven hopped forward, joining the crow. In a synchronized move, their wings slapped together over their heads. The subsequent explosion sent Kelcie screaming for an air shield while tackling Brona to keep the residual twinkling stardust from getting near either one of them. When the smoke cleared, every sign of the birds had vanished, even the feathers lost during their squabble. Only the mysterious spiral remained.

Last year, Kelcie would've been elated to see this kind of magic, but not anymore. It was troubling enough seeing crows in Chawell Woods, but now a raven and a crow together, at school? That magically vanish? This was not a coincidence. This had something to do with their mothers.

Brona knelt, running her finger over the grooves. Kelcie's whole body started shaking. Her mother wasn't supposed to be in her life. That was the deal. She tugged on her cloak's tightening collar, wheezing oxygen past the tension in her neck.

"What's wrong? You're turning green. Are you going to vomit?" Brona looked horrified. "You know how much I hate vomit!"

Kelcie learned that the first time she got seasick on Brona's father's ship, and since they shared a cabin, Brona made her sleep on deck for a full week just in case it happened again. But Kelcie wasn't seasick right now. She was worry-sick.

She sat down beside the crow's crude carving, putting her head between her knees.

"Why are you freaking out? This is from our mothers!" Brona squealed, excited.

"I figured that out, but why do you say that like it's a good thing? The last time they decided to pay us an unexpected visit we were torn apart, separated by worlds, and my mother cursed me!"

"It's not a curse. It's just a message."

"That could end up with us all cursed!"

"Not if we figure out what it means." Brona looked at Kelcie expectantly.

"What?"

"Your mother's familiar drew it. What does it mean?"

"How should I know?"

Brona huffed a sigh. "Well, it looks like a mark of some kind."

Not taking any chances, Kelcie backed away from the spiral.

"We need to talk to Niall. I bet he'll know what it is. He always does."

The sea eagles traded shifts overhead. Two stopped on branches next to them, steely gazes shifting from Kelcie to Brona.

"We have to get to the Dens. I'll send him a note," Kelcie volunteered. At least she had a reason to write to him now.

"No. Don't put anything in writing. There could be another changeling at the school," Brona insisted as they started walking. "We'll talk to him and Zephyr tomorrow."

Kelcie's legs stiffened with fear as she dropped into the Saiga Den. First the flowers outside her grandmother's cave, then her aunt's and mother's familiars deliver a cryptic message.

No, not a message. An omen.

Knowing those two, likely a very, very *bad* omen. Something dreadful *was* going to happen, but what?

8

AVALANCHE!

L OOK!"

"Did you see the size of *that* one?"

For a full hour, Payton cried out every time another planet drove across the night's sky pictured in the sea-glass ceiling.

"I can't believe I get to live here all year!"

Lexis didn't see it. She couldn't think about the Den. Her mind was too busy reeling from the story Kelcie told her. Pavel's aunt, Achila Grimes, and her fianna had been plotting for most of Kelcie's life to use her to wield King Balor's evil eye to destroy the Academy for the Unbreakable Arts. Achila was in prison, along with the rest of them, which Lexis knew. They'd been captured after the whole mission fell apart when Kelcie removed that cursed eye from having any future role in recorded history; at least that's how Lexis's father would've described it.

Lexis wanted to believe Kelcie was lying, but, in the retelling, Kelcie told her that her father, Draummorc, was the reason the Fomorians were "relocated to Chawell Woods." It was a polite way of saying *imprisoned*. She admitted to Lexis that her father was a traitor to Summer, and had done bad things with the eye, really bad things.

Incredulous the whole conversation, Payton didn't understand how Lexis didn't know who Kelcie's father was or what he had done. He was the most infamous person in all of the Lands of Summer. Lexis came up with an excuse quickly, saying she was too young at the time she went on the run with her parents to remember any of that, which she was pretty sure Kelcie and Payton bought, but still . . . Why didn't the Advisors tell her? Was it because they were afraid that if Lexis knew that Winter tried to hurt a school that she might not go on this mission? It was a terrible thing to do. But she fought Summer's giants, saw Volga turned into rubble with her own eyes. That attack on Winter was unforgivable. So many innocent Winterfolk lost everything they had, including their lives.

As the lights turned off, Lexis began counting the seconds, waiting for Payton and Kelcie to fall asleep. Sweat soaked the lumpy mattress. Everywhere in Summer was too hot! She kicked off the covers, missing her Den at Braverwil, missing the window she opened all the time to look out over the tundra, missing the sound of the steady cold wind carving a path through the mountain peaks.

She glanced at her cubby, at the new yellow cloak with the fancy Saiga antelope stitched into the lapel. This Den was so different. Colorful and rather empty with only five students—or rather six, including her. But honestly, Lexis was surprised that there were that many.

Strange. That was Lexis's first thought when she heard Payton, Markkus, and Dollin agreeing to pledge loyalty to Summer by joining the Summer army in exchange for attending the Academy for the Unbreakable Arts.

Why would any Fomorian ever do that?

Summer's Queen had locked all Fomorians in those miserable woods for the past nine years. And now that Lexis knew why, she was even more confused. Why would they want to fight for Summer?

Lexis yawned, eyelids threatening to close. The bottle of Zinger the traitor gave her after she passed the test was on her bedside table. Picking it up, she cracked the top off underneath the blankets to make as little noise as possible. She was grateful the Advisors had warned her that Roswen would be at the school. Although all missions are confidential, they told her the entire story of Roswen's and her fianna's botched mission to save the last wyvern eggs that had been stolen from the crypt in the Queen's citadel. She was their Tol, their leader, and during the confrontation with the Summer soldiers who had the eggs, Roswen had run and left her fianna behind to pay the price. They all died. She was the only one to return, and was banished for it. Then, to make her betrayal complete, she went back to Summer, to the soldiers who killed her fianna, and now trains soldiers for them, probably telling them all of Winter's secrets.

The Advisors left out the part where Roswen's wings were clipped. Lexis was surprised by the backplate. No, not simply surprised. Shocked and horrified. Maybe the Advisors didn't know. Summer probably did that to all fairies when they caught them. Lexis thought of Pavel's aunt sitting in a Summer prison, and her stomach turned with worry. When they find Achila, would her wings be clipped like that? No matter how prickly Lexis thought Pavel's aunt was, she would never wish that on any fairy. Clip their wings and their powers vanish. Clip their wings and they can't run or fly. Clip their wings and no self-respecting fairy would ever befriend them. For Winterfolk, it was like being sentenced to a living death.

Queen Kefyra would never punish someone like *that*. Niall O'Shea's mother, Summer's Queen, was a monster. No matter how pleasant he seemed today, she would hate him, always and forever. He was the enemy. They all were, and Lexis had to remind herself of that every day.

Kelcie's and Payton's breathing softened, evening out. They were finally asleep. But as Lexis set her feet on the cool floor, Kelcie mumbled.

"Not again . . ."

She had been moody when she returned from walking back with her cousin. *Jack's* cousins. How bizarre was that? Two of his cousins were at this school. One born from each of the Mor-rígna. Lexis's father would have called that noteworthy, and make sure to write it down. To Lexis, it sounded ominous. But it was strange. Jack had no family he knew of in Winter, and yet *in Summer* he had two first cousins.

Lexis settled on the corner of her bed as Kelcie continued murmuring. She wondered what Brona's Raven Den was like, imagining nests for beds and special combs for tail feathers. The Cats slept in prides, curled up together from what another first year told her, very much like the Tiger Den in Winter. She wanted to see all the Dens, but asking her classmates to take her might raise suspicion. She already found her mark and saw the asset she was there to acquire. All she needed to do now was put the plan in motion, keep a low profile, and bide her time.

Kelcie fell silent. Lexis eased off the bed and tiptoed out of the room, pulling the door almost closed. Latching it would make too much noise. Then she padded into the pool room, stopping to listen by the boys' door, making sure there were no sounds of movement. There weren't, but how the three slept with all that snoring was beyond Lexis.

From the second Swappy had put the Queen's note in her hands, Lexis had been surrounded by people. First in Chawell Woods at Kelcie's grandmother's cave, and then here at the school, where there was absolutely no privacy. Braverwil was the same, but she'd never received a letter as important as this and no matter how much she needed sleep, she couldn't wait any longer to read it!

She sat on the edge of the pool, dipping her feet in the cool water, contemplating sleeping on the bottom. She was supposed to be a Caenum. With green and brown eyes, it was the only choice. But it was a good one. Lexis always saw it as the weak-est of the Fomorian elements, the least threatening. She didn't want to be perceived as any kind of real threat, not until it was too late.

The rough parchment was sealed with the Queen's unbroken crystalline snowflake seal.

Her skiddish thumb slid over the center of the snowflake. Crackling energy pricked the pad sharply, causing her to bite back a hiss, wincing. A tiny drop of her red blood filled the snowflake's valleys turning it purple. The Queen's Advisors had taken a sample from everyone in her fianna's blood before they left to use in sealing spells, a way to ensure any communications sent were only opened by the intended recipient.

The seal melted, falling into the pool before Lexis could catch it. She would've gone to get it, but time was of the essence. If she was caught by any of the others in the Den with this letter, the jig was up. Lexis moved swiftly, bending open the creases, smoothing out the letter. Her stark red print soaked into the fibers as she started reading.

On the eve of your greatest test, I send word so that you know I believe in you. You will not let us down; of that I am certain. I am certain because your success will earn you a place in the books your parents hold so dearly. A place only the truest of warriors are immortalized. What will be written will be nothing short of the greatest achievement of our time. The only one that has ever mattered. The end of the Never-Ending War. Our people will be saved, all by your hand.

Lexis paused reading to let that sink in. Her name would appear in history books, immortalized for all time. A true hero for Winter. What would her parents have to say then? Would they apologize for trying to keep her from Braverwil? Would they love her for who she is, a courageous warrior who helped end the war once and for all? She was to steal the Heart of Danu and deliver it to Queen Kefyra. The Queen, the Advisors, all claimed the war would be over as soon as it was in Winter, that it was that important to the Lands of Summer. Lexis didn't really know what Danu's Heart did for Summer. She didn't really care. If it was going to end the war, that was a good enough reason to steal. She didn't know what it was when Queen Kefyra brought it up. Her father told her an old parable about it when she was little. What she remembered was the name: *Croí na Bandia*, and what the words meant. Luckily, that was enough to get her fianna the mission.

Brimming with renewed confidence, she returned to the letter.

Don't be foolishly misguided into thinking that this is all some-how your destiny, that ending this war was your future from the day you were born. It wasn't. Destinies are made. We are all personally responsible for making them happen. So I leave you with one last thought. Something you should recite every dawn of a new day in Summer, and at the end of every night before you rest.

Missions end one of two ways, in success or failure. Failure is not acceptable. If the prize is not brought to Winter on the day of the Ascension, the consequences will be severe.

Lexis's heart, so filled with joy a minute before, tried to jump out of her chest and drown itself.

No! Her queen would never threaten her, would she?

She reread the letter from top to bottom, this time not stopping, and felt sickened. She *was* threatening her. What about her fianna? Would they suffer severe consequences if she failed too? What did that even mean? Would they be kicked out of Braverwil, or worse? Could there be anything worse than losing their place at school? Roswen's clipped wings flashed unbidden through her mind. No. Summer did that. No fairy, Queen or not, would ever do that to one of their own. But then why send this letter at all? Especially now?

Was it because Queen Kefyra knew this place was so similar to Braverwil? The Dens, fiannas. Scáthach too, Aífe's twin in every way. Lexis had been unprepared for how much they looked alike. It was a shock. She stopped blinking when Scáthach rode out of the Shadow's gate on her immortal horse to welcome the passing testers to the school. But that changed nothing. *Did Queen Kefyra really think I wouldn't see them all for what they are—the enemy?*

Did the Queen believe for a second Lexis would forget who she was?

I am a daughter of Winter. Now and always.

Lexis *was* the lynchpin to the operation. She gripped the letter so hard her finger stopped bleeding. Then it dawned on her. The Queen likely had no faith in Lexis because too many had failed her in the past, like Pavel's aunt.

. . . the consequences will be severe.

"Ignis."

Lexis dipped the parchment in the flaming ball on her trembling hand, setting it ablaze, ensuring that no one would ever read it.

Failure is not acceptable.

Tomorrow she would attend classes, learn the terrain, watch her mark, and begin gathering what she needed for the next step.

Failure is not acceptable!

That's what Lexis would repeat morning, noon, and night. She would never let her fianna down, never let her realm down, or her queen.

Not ever.

The door to the girls' room opened wide. Lexis's heart jumped into her throat as Kelcie padded out and sat down beside her, plunking her feet in the water.

"Can't sleep?" Kelcie asked, sounding as if she were genuinely concerned. But what if she saw the letter? What if she saw Lexis wielding fire? How could she have been so stupid? Her heartbeat thundered in her ears.

"No. Day keeps swirling through my mind."

"Yeah. I remember that happened to me last year. I saw you met Niall earlier."

At dinner Lexis noticed that they didn't sit next to each other, hardly looked at each other. Lexis loosed a cross breath. Kelcie didn't get out of bed to check on Lexis out of concern or suspicion, but because she wanted to pump her for information about her crush. "Well, he met me actually. He stopped to talk to me. Just a pep talk kind of thing. I thought you sent him over." That would drive a helpful wedge between them.

Kelcie shook her head, clearly jealous.

"It's fine."

It was working like a charm. "Really. It was nothing, Kelcie," Lexis pressed. "He was only being nice. I'm sure that's all it was."

"It doesn't matter," Kelcie lied.

But it did. It was written all over her sullen face.

"Big day tomorrow. We should get some sleep."

Lexis hopped to her feet, racing to get to bed before Kelcie asked any more questions. She was halfway to the door when Kelcie sniffed audibly.

"Do you smell smoke?"

Lexis stopped, taking a long, deep sniff, and shook her head. "I don't smell anything."

9

ASCENSION

WHAT IS GOING on with them?" Kelcie griped at Brona.

Kelcie had showed up at breakfast early to meet her cousin, leaving plenty of time to speak to Niall and Zephyr about the mysterious symbol before unit training, but from the looks of things, they weren't going to get a chance.

After a fitful night's sleep, Kelcie was glad to have something else to focus on beside Niall's disheartening lack of communication. A message from Nemain and Macha was way more important. And it was the icebreaker she and Niall needed too. He could never resist the lure of deciphering a cryptic message from angry goddesses. It was like dangling a piece of bacon in front of a dog. And they would solve the mystery of the spiral together, as a fianna, just like they did last year. If only she and Brona could physically get to them. Niall and Zephyr were surrounded by a mob. Most of the second-year class vied for their attention, and some of the third years too. It was bizarre, unsettling, and annoying.

"Are they . . ." Kelcie choked on the word. ". . . popular?"

Delilah Quick giggled her way through eating five pieces of jam-filled tarts (yes, Kelcie kept count), pausing between bites to right Niall's crooked glasses for him, or set another tart on his plate, as if he couldn't feed himself.

"Here." Brona passed a commiseratory tart to Kelcie. "It's because of all the press."

"Wha' . . . pre'?" Kelcie mumbled between bites.

"Being stuck on the ship, we missed all the hubbub over break. Willow showed me the chronicles last night. The whole story of what happened at the end of the school year was front page news."

Kelcie was aghast. "Then why aren't we more popular?"

"Our winning personalities?" Brona said sarcastically, batting her long, black eyelashes. "Seriously though. Careful what you wish for." Her cousin rolled a bottle of Zinger between her palms. "As I found out last year, being popular only puts a target on your back. Come on. We'll talk to them later."

Scáthach began class where she left off last year, with no review and no consideration for falling out of shape during break, which was no problem for Kelcie. Between Brona's forced laps on the ship and all the training in Chawell Woods, Kelcie was in the best shape of her life, and she wasn't alone.

On the obstacle course, Niall showed off what he'd been doing during his time away by climbing the rope wall in three leaping grabs, stunning the entire class. In the next part, Zephyr cleared their blocked path of the many boulders of unusual size by tossing them out of the way like they weighed no more than a basketball. Topping that, during Queen of the Hill, fianna three put on a masterful show. Brona awed the class by transforming her bottom half from tail and claws to legs and pointed boots midair to kick Tad Fagan off the hilltop before he could declare himself queen. Once fianna one's charger had been dethroned, Niall used the scream while Kelcie spun windshields and hurled air bombs keeping the rest of Fagan's fianna far enough away for Zephyr to charge up the hill and declare fianna three the winners.

Scáthach noticed as well. "Fianna three, your times are remarkable. Keep up the good work." She clapped and fiannas scrambled to line up in number order before the platform. "I have a few announcements. This is a very special year in the

Lands of Summer. Queen Eislyn has declared this year a Year of Ascension."

Audible gasps rang out, which clued Kelcie in to the fact that this was a big deal, and not just a ceremony as Niall indicated in his letter. She tapped him on the shoulder.

"What exactly is Ascension?"

Shhh . . . he shushed, waving her off like she was nothing more than an irritating fly.

Scáthach paced slowly. "The Regent will be revealed to the Lands of Summer, and begin duties to take over the throne."

Gasps morphed to whispers and speculation of who the heir to the throne might be. For some reason, several of her classmates thought Willow's father was a contender, but they were wrong. Regan O'Shea was Regent.

Kelcie had found out last year, along with Brona, Brona's father Tao, and Zephyr. Scáthach had likely known for much longer. They had all been sworn to secrecy. For the safety of the realm, no one could know. Niall and Regan were the Queen's children. What Kelcie didn't understand was, why now? Was it because of the baby being born? Niall's little brother came halfway through break. She knew that much from his letters.

"Niall . . ." she whispered. "Is this because—"

Be quiet! I don't want to get in trouble for talking!

Since when did that ever bother Niall before? He was acting really weird. That was it, then. He didn't like Kelcie like that anymore. He didn't seem to like her at all, even as a friend. Or maybe he was afraid to be her friend any longer because of her father. Because of what she'd ask him to do. She should never have brought Draummorc up to Niall. It was her problem, not his. She made a vow right then and there to never say her father's name to Niall O'Shea again.

Scáthach spoke louder, her voice climbing above the chatter. "As part of the fanfare, High Command puts on a military tattoo, which some of you will be participating in."

Cheers erupted from all sides.

Kelcie frowned. "What's a military tattoo?" she asked Brona.

Brona groaned, whispering in terse bursts in her ear. "If you would just listen, I'm sure Scáthach will tell you everything you need to know."

Zephyr looked at the two of them, waggling a finger in warning.

Why were they all so amped up over a military tattoo? Kelcie imagined the four of them lining up with a bunch of burly soldiers to get a tattoo on their shoulders of the blazing sun, which might be cool, or the Queen's face, which would be an utter nightmare.

"For those of you who don't know, a military tattoo is a procession, a parade of sorts. This one will take place through the streets of Summer City, at the end of which the High Guard will present a ceremonial scepter to the Regent that symbolizes the declaration of loyalty by Summer's armies," Scáthach explained.

That made a lot more sense.

"While all will be attending, one fianna from each class will be a part of the parade, and from what I'm seeing . . ." Scáthach jerked her chin at Zephyr, ". . . fianna three has a head start in this class for being chosen."

Fagan elbowed Dunn. "Not for long."

Brona passed a confident smile through their line. Zephyr and Niall exchanged fist bumps. Kelcie's pulse skyrocketed, not because of the parade. She didn't care about the tattoo or the Ascension. Scáthach said *all* would be attending!

ALL!

Kelcie was going to Summer City. She was going to be in the same place as her father. Her chest filled with excitement that quickly plummeted into her shoes. What good did that do? It wasn't like she could wander into the prison and ask to see him, could she?

You can't. Niall's voice answered her unasked question, sternly, gratingly.

Kelcie turned away from him. It wasn't his choice to make.

"We leave in eight weeks and will be in Summer City for two days. The day after we arrive, the Ascension ceremony will take place. The temple where it is housed, Rilios, will be opened and the Stone of Destiny inside will sing for the rightful Regent."

Fagan laughed heartily, rubbing his hands together in anticipation.

Kelcie raised her hand.

"Murphy."

"You mean it's not the Queen's oldest who is automatically the heir?"

"Correct. The heir is a mystery until the Ascension when they touch the Stone of Destiny and it sings only for the next in line to the throne. For all of you, it will be a truly once-in-a-lifetime event. I, on the other hand, have endured more of this fanfare than anyone should have to in one immortal lifetime."

Still confused, Kelcie raised her hand again.

"Murphy."

"Are you saying that anyone can touch the stone, anyone could be the next heir then?"

"You think the gods would favor a demon over their own kind?" Fagan hissed. "The next Regent—"

"Will definitely not be you, Fagan," Marta Louisa bellowed.

A parade of laughter swept through the ranks, showing no signs of stopping.

"Enough!" Scáthach pinched the bridge of her nose until everyone silenced. "Fagan, fianna one has earned an extra twenty laps when class is over."

Tad glared at Kelcie like it was her fault that Marta Louisa saw him for the buffoon he was.

"Yes, Murphy," Scáthach continued. "The heir can come from anywhere, and Summerfolk will come from all over the Lands of Summer to touch the stone."

Why did the Queen make such a big deal out of Regan being Regent if it could be anyone? Could she have subverted the rules (something that wouldn't surprise Kelcie in the least) and snuck

Regan inside the temple to touch the stone already? Or was it wishful thinking and there was a chance she was wrong?

"Now, the part I have been dreading." Scáthach's tone dipped on the word *dreading*. "The night we arrive, there will be a ball."

Most of the class convulsed with barely contained excitement. Kelcie felt sick. "A ball?"

She'd never been to a dance in her life, let alone a ball.

Visions of white gloves and tiaras, high-heel shoes and fancy dresses waltzed through her mind. She owned none of those things. She didn't even know how to dance. *Gah!* Did someone have to ask her to go? Her breath caught. Like a *date*?

She risked a peek at Niall and found him staring at her. His frown deepened and he spun around to face Scáthach.

Even if Niall wanted to take her, which he obviously didn't, the daughter of the greatest traitor Summer had ever known could never walk into a ball with the Queen's son. Queen Eislyn would never allow it.

Kelcie sighed, resolved. The risk of mortification was way too high; there was only one possible solution. She would fake a stomach flu and miss the event entirely. Simple. The end.

"Dress uniforms are perfectly acceptable, but not required. Write your parents now if you wish other attire."

The girls in the class broke into a whirlwind of chatter, engaging in a *what are you going to wear?* sound-off.

"We need to be in that tattoo," Niall declared, offering a high-five to Zephyr then Brona.

Kelcie scoffed. Suddenly it was okay for them to be talking because Niall deemed it so?

"Shhh! You don't want to get in trouble with Scáthach!" she whispered harshly.

"Listen up!" Scáthach stomped on the wooden platform, calling everyone back to attention. "The tattoo will follow the Ascension ceremony, and then we will return to the school. Students will be housed for the night in the soldiers' barracks. It will give you all a chance to see what your future will be like. I shouldn't need to tell second years that best behavior is the only acceptable behavior." The chatter started again, but Scáthach wasn't having it. "But it seems I DO!"

Everyone froze.

"*Don't lose focus!* This is a big year, students. With the end of year two, all of you are eligible to be called to active duty should the need arise. And the need may be sooner than we think." Her formidable stare fell on fianna three. "The infiltration at the school last year was only the beginning. Tensions are rising. We must all be on high alert. Is that understood?"

The class cried, "Yes, ma'am."

"Do your best. Work your hardest. Everything you learn this year could be the reason you survive in battle, and what you fail to accomplish could be the reason you don't. Class dismissed."

10

SHILLELAGHINS

EVEN WITH SCÁTHACH's warning to stay focused, the ball took center stage in everyone's conversation on the way to combat training. Kelcie stuck closely to Brona, scooting around the girls whispering about possible dates while pretending they weren't sneaking glances at the boys, who were in fact doing the exact same thing.

Brona looped arms with Zephyr and Niall, trying to pull them from the pack of huddled mewing boys.

"Kelcie and I need to speak with you."

"Not now," Zephyr ordered, yanking his arm away.

Niall trotted after him.

"It's like they've lost their minds, over what? A stupid ball?" Kelcie asked. "We could be talking about a seriously bad you-know-what!" She mouthed the word *omen*.

"We'll corner them after class," Brona reassured her.

Double doors on the brand-new Nether Tower creaked, sliding apart. The structure was still round, but the similarities to the old structure ended there. Roswen and the old troll architect, Rapshider, had outdone themselves. After the fire last year, the trolls had bulldozed most everything. When the students had left for the break, all that remained was the bottom floor with the arena (and perhaps the dungeons lying beneath, although Kelcie had only ever heard about those).

The building was made of a familiar silver metal, the same as the guardhouse at Chawell Woods.

Coach Blackwell greeted them with a full dark beard, and a walking stick with a smoothed gray gem set in the handle resting on his shoulder. "A new year begins! And today, you lot are moving to the second floor. Follow me . . ."

Anticipation built with each step up the winding staircase that clung to the building's sides. At the top, Coach Blackwell unlocked the door, allowing the students to go in first.

The space looked like it was designed for practicing Cirque du Soleil if they did a *Lord of the Rings* show. Ropes and poles dropped from scaffolding that crisscrossed the high ceiling. Midway down, tightropes and balance beams stretched across.

Closer to the floor, shields ringed the room like wainscoting. There were racks of swords, bows and arrows, spears, axes, daggers, and a single pair of twin curved swords on their own special mount. Pistols hung on the wall by their abnormally large cylinders that resembled Ferris wheels. Beneath them were baskets filled with marble-shaped ammunition, separated by colors that spanned the rainbow and then some: maroon, cherry red, orange red, pastel orange, burnt orange, bright yellow, mustard, and so on and so on.

Sidewinders, Niall explained in Kelcie's head. *And each of the different-colored jinxes—that's what the ammunition is called—does something different. The many reds vary by degrees of heat. Yellows shock. Bright orange stings. Rusts are throttle jinxes. They're really dangerous and only to be used as a last resort. Greens are for ground assaults, stopping wood goblins and such, doing things like causing them to grow roots where they stand. Blacks cause sleep. They're called nighty-nights. Oh, and dark blue is interesting. It liquifies, turning anything or anyone temporarily into water.* He pointed at a basket of purple ones. *These are sobbers, for crying fits. And lastly, the pinks work best on ice fairies.*

Kelcie cracked a smile. This was the most Niall had said to her since she got to school. *Why?* she mouthed.

Instantaneous, on-the-floor, uncontrollable laughing fits. Nothing a person with ice in their veins hates more than laughing.

Kelcie picked up a few of the black ones and considered slipping them into her pocket. Nighty-night jinxes would be useful on guards in Summer City if she did try to break into the prison to see her father. As she lowered her clenched fist toward her pocket the jinxes were ripped out of her hand by an invisible force and plopped into the basket. She glared at Niall.

It won't work, Kelcie. You won't be able to see him and you'll only get caught.

"Why don't you let me worry about that?"

"Something you two need help with?" Coach Blackwell asked, an irritated eyebrow arching.

"No, sir," Niall quipped.

Blackwell addressed the rest of the class. "Cubbies, house belts, holsters, and scabbards by Dens. Cat and Raven have their own sections, while Adders, Saiga, and Chargers are lumped together."

He yanked a lever on the floor. To the class's delight, the circular ceiling slid back in pie-shaped sections, letting the outside in.

"All this new hooha," he grunted, pointing to the ceiling, "was redesigned to allow you to show off your wings and claws, strength, telepathy, and of course, elemental powers."

A thrill ran through Kelcie.

Brona squealed, bursting with excitement.

"The walls are made of an unbreakable metal called juggernaut. You see, this second year is about incorporating your powers into your combat skills, and this metal can withstand whatever any of you can dish out." He tilted his bald head at Kelcie. "Even you, Murphy."

Coach Blackwell grabbed hold of the pole. From his elbow down, his arm transformed into smooth black fur. Fingernails grew to sharp claws. The whole class collectively inhaled.

Marta Louisa grinned like she'd found her long-lost cousin. "He's a Cat!"

"I am indeed a Cat shifter." He tapped his claws on the pole, a held-back smirk creasing the jagged scar that ran from his forehead down his neck, trying to hide his enjoyment at their surprise. "My job at the Academy is to teach you how to use every weapon, not only inside our arsenals," he gestured around the room, "but anything at your disposal." He dropped the stick on his shoulder and leaned on it, using it like a cane.

"I can and will impart what I know about how each of them has been used in the past with your abilities, but every soldier is different. Unique. With a Cat, I could be a small lynx."

Coach Blackwell shrank to a small, black-spotted golden cat, tiny black tufts sprouting from the tips of his ears and long whiskers from his furry cheeks. A mew later, he scuffed his paws on the ground, then leaped, transforming midstride into a larger cat, striped like a tiger, and as big as a male lion. He roared much louder this time, making everyone jump.

He transformed back to his human form. "Or a desert lion, the largest, meanest cat in Summer." He smoothed his dark beard, twisting the tip. "One small and nimble, the other heavy, immovable, strong."

He picked up the walking stick and aimed it at Kelcie. "A weak stance or grip, I can correct. But in this class, we learn from each other. I will show you the weapon of choice for the day, how to use it, and you will then spar, incorporating your powers.

"With all things, we are not trying to hurt each other. The blades are sharp, and it is on you to hold back. Anyone, and I mean anyone, who hurts their partner on purpose will be sent to the Shadow and kicked out of school. We are soldiers of Summer, on the same side. Last year was a firm reminder that the stakes are too high for foolishness."

He stared sternly at Tad Fagan, who gave a single contrite nod.

"Today, we tackle the shillelagh." Coach Blackwell held his

stick high for all to see. Pronounced *shil-le-lee*, the stick reminded Kelcie of the practice sword they had to use last year. All that work to earn a real sword, and Coach Blackwell was demoting them back to playing with sticks. "I can tell by the long faces that you were hoping to pick up a sidewinder."

"Not me." Yuri Petrov, the strong-nosed Raven from fianna four, sucked sharply through his gapped front teeth. "I want those twin swords."

Only to be challenged by Mellis Gear, fianna five's petite Charger. "Have to fight me for them."

Kelcie followed their lust-filled gazes, and completely understood why they looked like that. Otherwordly in design, the dual swords had blades made of a blue metal and curved slightly at the tip. The silver pommels were wrapped in matching thick black cords.

Kelcie drooled.

Coach Blackwell slammed the shillelagh's shaft down, demanding everyone's attention.

"All in due time. Don't underestimate the shillelagh. This weapon can take on any in this room. This is not just any stick. It is made from the rarest wood in existence, blunt eucanite. Not even the sharpest blade or wing can cut through it."

"Wing? Like a fairy's wing?" Kelcie asked.

"Armored or not." Coach Blackwell winked. "Nothing will make it brittle. Not freezing or burning. Unlike metal or steel, it is flexible and lighter in weight, and the jewel on the top just makes it all the more useful."

He swung at Brona. She transformed into her Raven familiar, flew over Coach Blackwell's head, and in one smooth, morphing move returned to her human form while simultaneously snatching a shield off the wall. She easily blocked his second strike.

Clapping rang out.

"Good move . . ." Coach Blackwell smiled wryly at Brona. "But I'm not finished."

He faked a jab, drawing Brona's shield, then made like he was sweeping her legs. When Brona leaped, Blackwell jabbed again instead. The gray gem barely touched Brona's arm, but it was enough. She hit the floor, her entire body ramrod stiff, twitching uncontrollably, like she'd been tased.

"Brona!" Kelcie rushed to help her.

"She'll be fine in a minute, Murphy," Blackwell offered, like that would help.

"So much for those godly powers," Fagan sniggered.

Coach Blackwell slapped Fagan on the thigh with the shillelagh. The Charger fell over, his tree-trunk leg jittering as if he stepped on a high-voltage wire, making it impossible for him to stand up no matter how many ways he tried.

"G-g-gah! M-m-make it-t-t st-st-op!"

"Quit whining, Charger. I barely tapped you. Full-blown whack would've left you and the Raven like that for the better part of ten minutes. Now, unless you're asking a question, no one speaks in this class except me right now. Is that understood?"

A chorus of "Yes, sir" rang out as Kelcie helped Brona up.

Blackwell stomped. A floorboard popped, revealing storage beneath, filled with shillelaghs.

"All of you, grab a shillelagh and a shield, and partner up. Spread out. Use the whole room, and the scaffold if you dare."

Within less than a minute, the Nether Tower erupted into a fighting extravaganza.

As Kelcie reached for a shillelagh, Niall tapped her shoulder with the side of his. "Want to spar?"

Kelcie was confused, deeply confused. First he talked to her at length about jinxes, and now he wanted to spar with her? He was up to something, but what? Still, she said, "Sure."

As Niall and Kelcie went stick for stick in the middle of the room, Gabby Arnold, the waifish Cat from fianna five, fell from the rafters. She morphed into a tabby cat on her way down and used Kelcie's back as a scratching post to soften what would've otherwise been a hard landing.

"Gabby!" Kelcie cried.

Niall took full advantage of her distraction, raising his shillelagh to strike. But Kelcie sensed the wind from his overzealous upswing and spun out. With both hands on the stick, she blocked his attack, pushing him off, then jabbed.

Niall's shield slapped away her advance, and he lunged. Kelcie thought to drive her back. She held her ground for too long, and his shillelagh hooked hers. A hard yank and her weapon clanked uselessly to the floor.

Why aren't you using your powers? Or is that tiny flame in the palm of your hand all you can muster?

Oh, he sounded angry. Was he just baiting her? Didn't matter to Kelcie. If he wanted her to use her powers, she was more than happy to. Her wind blast slammed him into a pole, airstreams keeping him there as she advanced, cocking her shillelagh.

He cringed, shifting his shoulders in a futile attempt to break free.

"Why aren't you using your powers?"

Her shillelagh ripped from her hands and jackknifed into her own stomach. The air hissed off Niall. His annoying smirk appeared over her as she lay there twitching.

She would've suffered the humiliation without complaint, not risking a sparking word in this state to set his eyebrows on fire because she might miss and hit something much more vital, but Niall took a congratulatory handshake from Fagan, and Kelcie saw red. Fighting through the shock waves, she leaped on top of Niall's back, knocking him to the ground. He managed to roll over, trying to swing, but her weight pressed down on his shillelagh, grinding the shaft against his rib cage with her own, trying to get the orange ball on the handle to touch his chin.

Oh no you don't! he yelled, vibrating her brain.

The split second Kelcie lost focus was more than enough time for Niall to shift his legs under the shaft. He pushed with his knees, rolling them over.

But before he could pin her, Kelcie kneed the bar out of his grasp. He fell off her, scrambling for his shillelagh at the same time she went for hers. As soon as her weapon was in her hand Kelcie swung but so did Niall. Their sticks locked knobs, leaving them in a game of tug-of-war.

Still crushed over his handshake with Fagan, Kelcie lowered her voice to be barely audible.

"Did you enjoy stuffing your face at glorious banquets while my grandmother and I foraged for every meal, fending off lawn gnomes dressed like Little Red Riding Hood with razor-sharp teeth and an unending supply of axes?"

Niall glanced around the room, worried someone heard her.

But Kelcie didn't care if they did. Staring into Niall's perfect face, the son of the Queen, she choked on anger. "All I asked was to know if my father was okay. To know why he wasn't answering my letters. And you were too busy to ask?"

Niall let go of the stick, giving Kelcie the win.

"Kelcie . . ."

"So don't tell me I can't try and see him. It's all I can think about. Not the omen we got yesterday that you and Zephyr don't have time to hear about. Not the amazing fact that the Saiga Den is buzzing with life this year." She cast her shillelagh to the floor, and clutched the silver bracelets on her wrists, her father's cuffs that she would never take off. "He's all I can think about."

Wait . . . omen? What omen!

"Murphy! O'Shea! Barking, grunting, taunting each other I will tolerate, but you two chattering on in hushed tones like gossiping swans, I won't have it!" Coach Blackwell's normally pink bald head turned irritated red. "Chike! Fianna three gets ten laps. Go! Now!"

"Seriously?" Brona griped from the highest scaffold where she'd been whaling on Marta Louisa.

She swooped over Zephyr's head, startling him so much he lost his stick to Fagan's uppercut.

Fagan laughed at him. "When will you learn, Murphy is bad

luck. She will always be the cause of everything that goes wrong for you, Chike."

"Move it, fianna three!" Zephyr ordered. Snagging his fighting stick on the way out, he dragged it behind him, catching Fagan's ankle. The Charger dropped like a sack of potatoes. He still hadn't gotten up when Kelcie padded out last.

Outside the Nether Tower, no one started running.

"What is wrong with you two?" Zephyr shouted. "Didn't we just talk about being on our best behavior to get into the tattoo?"

Niall held up a finger in Zephyr's face. "Hold that thought!" He turned to talk to Kelcie, pressing his glasses up his nose for no apparent reason other than he was vexed, which was fine because Kelcie was peeved at him too! "What omen?"

"You told him?" Brona gasped at Kelcie. "Without me?"

"No! Will you all be QUIET!" Kelcie screamed in frustration.

"You can't try to see your father, Kelcie!" Niall declared.

As if that would stop her. "Niall, you don't understand! I need to know that my father isn't suffering in some horrible way because he helped me destroy the eye. I know I shouldn't have asked you to ask your mother. It wasn't fair to you, but I did, and you didn't. So I don't have a choice."

"I did."

"What?" Kelcie advanced on him. "You said you were too busy."

"Technically, I said my mother was too busy."

"Really, O'Shea?" Brona glowered at him. "It was hard enough for her to write that letter, you know. All the groveling . . ."

"Groveling? What letter?" Zephyr's head flipped from Brona to Kelcie to Niall. "What are you people talking about?"

Brona leaned on Zephyr's shoulder. "Kelcie sent a note to Niall during break, asking him to check on her father. Draummorc hasn't answered a single letter she sent him, and she was freaked. Apparently, still is, because Niall did nothing to find out why."

"That's terrible," Zephyr said.

"Which part?" Brona asked. "The part where her father isn't answering Saiga's letters or the part where she asked Niall, whose mother is the Queen that put Draummorc in jail for life, to go see him and find out why?"

"The first part," Zephyr said, then frowned. "And the second."

Niall stared at Kelcie, brow creased, but why Kelcie didn't know. *I lied.*

"About what?" Kelcie asked. His lips pressed together into a hard line. "Lied about what, Niall? Tell me!"

"In the letter, okay?" Niall admitted.

He slumped down on the grass. Kelcie sat down cross-legged beside him.

"I told you my mother was too busy to see me, but she did see me." Niall ripped a blade of grass and began tearing it into teeny-tiny pieces.

"I take it it wasn't a pleasant conversation," Brona surmised, plopping next Kelcie.

"None of them are. Worst of all, she was in the High Guard's office. Hologram map of Winter on his desk. They were in deep conversation about a city with a big *X* over it."

"What does that mean?" Zephyr asked with concern.

"We attacked it," Brona answered bluntly. "Retribution for the attack on the school, I'm sure. We can't sit idly by and allow something like that to go unanswered."

Kelcie refused to let Niall get distracted. "What happened when you talked to her, Niall?"

He threw grass bits that caught the wind and landed in his hair. "She was mad that I interrupted."

Zephyr kneeled next to Niall. "I can imagine."

"But I asked, and I got an answer." Niall's expression was enough to tell her she wasn't going to like it. But still, she needed to know.

"What did she say?"

It must've been horrible because Niall's face contorted about a hundred times before he sighed, resigned to tell her. "She said, and I quote, 'No one is permitted to see him. I won't make any exceptions. But, I will tell you that if he's not answering her letters . . .'" He paused to meet Kelcie's stare, his amethyst gaze filled with sympathy. "'. . . it has nothing to do with me. He doesn't want to speak with her.' I'm so sorry, Kelcie."

"Then why didn't you . . . ?" A growing lump in Kelcie's throat made it hard to talk.

Niall answered her unasked question. *I was trying to keep you from feeling like me, like your only parent wants nothing to do with you.* "She was so mad at me for asking." He raked his hand through his hair, parting it in five places. "We had a big argument."

"How big?" Brona asked.

"We didn't speak after."

Kelcie felt terrible. "I should never have asked you to do that for me. I'm so sorry."

Niall's sympathetic frown deepened. "But I think now I understand why he's not answering your letters. He's afraid you'll try and see him. Try and find a way to have him in your life when—"

"I can't." Her grandmother was right. She had to let her father go.

After a short moment of silence, Brona couldn't take it anymore. "And in other news . . ." She yanked a dagger from her boot and used the tip to draw the carving the crow made in the dirt. "O'Shea, what do you think this means?"

"It looks like something my baby sister would scribble," Zephyr commented. "She draws those swirlies on everything. Over and over . . ."

"Haw-haw. Last night this message was delivered by a raven *and* a crow. Together," Brona said in a very conspiratorial tone. "We think it's from our mothers."

"Why?" Zephyr squeaked.

"Because they exploded into dust rather than flying off like normal birds," Kelcie answered.

"What?" Zephyr squeaked again, this time scooting backward several inches, away from the spiral.

Niall leaned over it. "It could be a mark from ancient times. Generally, though, there are three, and they're connected. Each symbolizing one aspect of the circle of life. Life, death, and rebirth."

"Which one is this? Please don't say death . . ." Zephyr pleaded.

Niall shrugged. "Don't know. They all look alike. And as I said, they're normally connected."

"I know!" Zephyr exclaimed. "Maybe your mothers knew Kelcie's father wasn't writing her back and wanted to send her something. A nice gesture. A symbol of life, a way of telling you that you should keep on living it."

"Very moving, but my mother is a goddess of fury. She doesn't do nice gestures." Kelcie scratched out the mark with her heel. "Any other ideas?"

Niall shrugged while Zephyr seemed ready to dismiss the whole thing outright. "We have to get to class."

"But what about this omen?" Brona roared. "The Lands of Summer could be in grave danger and you're just going to dismiss it?"

Zephyr rolled his eyes. "Yes, because if it represents life, great, rebirth, great, and if it means death, then we can't do anything about it because that's not enough to go on! But we can do something about class and us not getting in trouble for missing the rest of it!"

The obstinate Charger faced Kelcie and Niall with a look of fierce determination.

"But first, O'Shea, Murphy, I'm going old-fashioned. As my mother always makes me and my twin do, shake hands and promise no more fighting."

Niall held his hand out to Kelcie, a sudden shy smile blooming. "Truce?"

Kelcie felt an intense blush coming on. It radiated down her forearm. She shook his hand. "Truce."

Niall let go quickly, wincing. "Eesh! Your hand is really hot!"

"Saiga!" Zephyr flicked the back of her head. "He only has one of those, you know."

Kelcie looked aghast at her glowing-red palm. "It was an accident! I'm so sorry!"

"Be grateful, Adder. *You* still have your hair," Brona chimed, jogging backward.

Kelcie paced slower than the others. She should've felt lighter. The fight with Niall was over. She had the answer to the question bothering her all break long, only the answer wasn't at all what she was expecting. Left in a coma from the battle over the eye, no pen or paper because the Queen took them away—the first would have been horrible, the latter not good either—but hearing her father wanted nothing to do with her hurt worse than not knowing who he was all her life.

11

SAIGA

THE CHATTER AT the lunch tables was twice as loud as normal. Kelcie moped behind her fianna, trying to smile, but her heart wasn't in it.

As she passed by the first-year table, she saw Dollin showing off, melting his cuffs into utensils, stabbing a vegetable off the plate of the girl next to him and feeding it to her.

"Do something else!" Kelcie heard her say.

"I'll do something else." Markkus grabbed Dollin in a head-lock and used the tiny flame on the end of his finger to set poor Dollin's nose hairs on fire. Kelcie had never heard such a ruckus of laughter.

A Raven dressed in black swung her arms over Payton's and Lexis's shoulders. "I'll get my mother to send a box of dresses we can all choose from!"

Payton gave a rare smile. "Thanks. That would be really nice."

Lexis set her fork down. "I'm okay. I'll just wear the uniform."

"Oh, no! No offense, yellow is not your color. You will shine in blue. Like, I'm thinking pale blue. I have one in my closet that will fit you perfectly! You'll see!"

Ollie stopped beside Kelcie to stare at the first-year table, looking immensely pleased. "It's just like Killian hoped." He turned to her. "This is because of you, Kelcie. You inspired them to come."

"Nah. That was all you. You're a really great Alpha, Ollie."

Two large shadows fell over them. Kelcie glanced up and was surprised to see Scáthach and Coach Blackwell. Teachers never came to lunch with the students.

"You two did a good thing here," Coach Blackwell said.

"And I was just informed that the military tattoo will be broadcast to all of the Lands of Summer. Just think if all of Summer saw Saigas from the Academy marching in the tattoo? What a catalyst for change that could be," Scáthach added.

Chills raised the hairs on Kelcie's arms.

"Just think . . ." Ollie answered, a gleam in his eyes—challenge accepted.

Starving and still depressed about her father, Kelcie needed fuel if she was going to make it through the afternoon. She sat down at the second-year table, snagging the last piece of a Roswen masterpiece that looked like chicken pot pie.

A hunk of the flaky crust was on its way into her mouth when something soft bumped Kelcie's leg underneath the table. She peeked under, expecting Striker—but it wasn't Striker. As if her day hadn't been bad enough so far, a black cat with warm, bright yellow eyes spit in her lap.

"Ew!" Kelcie jumped out of her seat.

A soggy piece of paper toppled on the ground. She scanned the table, finding the Cat sitting in the chair beside Delilah Quick at the other end of the table. Delilah gave Kelcie an apprehensive stare.

"It's a note," Willow informed her, pointing to the folded piece of paper.

"Oh." Kelcie picked it up with her thumb and index finger.

The Cat transformed back into bashful Gabby Arnold, who looked everywhere but at Kelcie.

"Delilah makes Gabby do all her dirty work," Willow added. "What's it say? Not that I can't guess." Willow's giggle was enough to tell Kelcie whatever it said, Kelcie wasn't going to like it.

Keeping the note below the table so no one could see it, Kelcie unfolded the note by the dryer corners, revealing delicate cursive that could only belong to someone as perfect as Delilah Quick.

Would you be angry if I asked
Niall O'Shea to the ball?

Kelcie's stomach fell into her shoes. Would she be angry if the most beautiful girl in their class asked Niall to the ball? Dejected, humiliated, distraught, bitterly alone, yes. But angry?

"What's it say?" Willow probed.

"None of your business," a familiar voice answered from behind Kelcie. Willow went back to her lunch.

Brown curls fell over Kelcie's shoulder as Lexis bent over to whisper in Kelcie's ear, "I thought *you* and Niall were an item?"

Kelcie glanced at Niall, catching him staring at her. He immediately shifted his focus to a very uninteresting piece of crust on his plate. Did he want to go with Delilah? Did he know what was in the note and was checking what her reaction would be?

She hated the idea of Niall and Delilah at the ball together, but it wasn't like he was going to ask Kelcie. The fact that he was speaking to her now, that the ice had thawed a little between them, that was enough. And, more than anyone, Niall deserved to be happy.

"Niall and I are just friends, Lexis."

"Then why do you sound like that?"

Kelcie cleared her throat. "Like, what?"

"You know like what. Ask him now. Beat her to the punch. A good soldier knows timing is everything."

A good soldier? That was a strange thing to say considering Lexis had only been a soldier for twenty-four hours. Kelcie turned around but Lexis was already walking back to the first-year table. She glanced at Delilah's note. Lexis didn't understand. After what happened with Niall's mother, Kelcie needed to be a better friend to him, to put his happiness above her own. Even if it hurt.

Kelcie folded up the note and tucked it into the top of her sweatpants. After she finished eating, she would muster up enough courage to tell Delilah it was fine.

A FTERNOON CLASS WAS in the brand-new Den practice facility, and unlike the Nether Tower that was completely rebuilt from top to bottom, this building didn't look all that different. The exterior was the same, flat, square, the size of a football field, and showed no signs of being upgraded to the indestructible juggernaut. In fact, there was only one glaring difference.

Brona and Kelcie stared at the fancy gold nameplate that said *RAPSHIDER HALL* for way longer than necessary, mostly to let the flock of bubbly first years enter ahead of them. The building never had an official name. It was simply called the Den training facility.

"I suppose we should go into *Rapshider Hall*," Brona said, flicking the *R*. "I don't know why Puce insisted I come today. I never had to be here last year." She wrinkled her nose in disgust. "What if he wants me to help train the first years? It was bad enough having to sort out your problems last year."

More than slightly offended, Kelcie meant to give Brona a piece of her mind but a Raven landed between her and Brona, bumping them apart, and morphed. Gavin Puce's mohawk lifted a full foot above his skinny head. The Raven Alpha leaned on the building, stretching a still-taloned foot way over his head, and used his kneecap as a pillow. It was like his ligaments were made of rubber bands.

"You're here because I have something special for you to work on today, Lee," he crowed. "Birdbraining."

Brona waved her hand dismissively. "That's not a real thing."

Tad Fagan burst out of the double doors, clucking like a chicken.

"What is the matter with you?" Zephyr jogged after him, trying to pull him upright.

Tad shook him off. His hulking form pecked the ground, burying his nose into the gravel path over and over again, crying, "Ow-ow-ow."

"What's the matter with him?" Kelcie laughed.

"Birdbrained?" Brona asked Gavin with great intrigue.

He twirled the front piece of his mohawk, leaving a springing curl dangling down his long forehead. "Not my best work. Won't last too long, but still . . ." He blew on his talons and rubbed them on his chest.

"Will you stop?" Zephyr cried. "You're going to make us late! Roswen is already at the stables."

When Tad refused to move, Zephyr threw his hands in the air and ran off.

Tad slammed his nose down on a rock and bolted upright. Blood leaked from his nostril. "What? How? Where am I?"

"You're on your way to the stables," Kelcie explained.

He glowered at her, like this was her doing, then at Gavin. Gavin winked, and blew him a kiss. Tad stormed off, with a look that promised payback.

Gavin chuckled at Brona. "The ancient art of mind manipulation. Only the most gifted Raven can do it. But, if you still don't believe me . . ."

He started to strut away, only to be halted by Brona's firm, taloned grip. "You have to teach me!"

He smiled too sweetly at Kelcie. "You busy right now?"

Gavin's *cock-a-doodle-doo* trumpeted Kelcie's mad dash into the building as she got away from the twisted Raven as fast as she could.

FEELING OUT OF sorts, Lexis stood behind the other Saigas outside the new Saiga space in Rapshider Hall, waiting for Roswen to open the door. The threatening letter from Queen

Kefyra kept coming back to her all day at the worst possible times, leaving her distracted and agitated, two states that led to novice mistakes. She stupidly used the phrase *good soldier* with Kelcie. Even from the side, Lexis caught the suspicious look on Kelcie's face, and hotfooted it back to her table before she said anything else incriminating. The Summer version of Lexis wasn't a good soldier, and would never use that term.

And it was a good thing Coach Blackwell was using rudimentary wooden practice swords for the first class or she might've been skewered by the Cat in her new Summer fianna. Lexis couldn't remember her name. She tried. Ran through every letter of the alphabet, trying out different names in her head, hoping to stumble on it. But it was gone.

In unit training, she had also made the mistake of calling the Raven in her fianna a Crow, and the girl was so mad she nearly pecked Lexis's eye out. Lexis had purposely forgotten her name.

But then again, that happened to her at Braverwil too. When she was ten and started school there, it was the first time she got to be around kids from other cultures. Fairies, changelings, and shifters rarely visited the Fomorian temple where she lived with her parents. It was hard those first few days. She stepped on the ends of Pavel's wings all the time and pet Jack every time he'd morph, something shifters hate. But this was different. The stakes were too high. Everything depended on Lexis and her success, and failure was not acceptable, not to Queen Kefyra or to Lexis.

She needed to focus all that nervous energy on the next phase of the plan, secretly gathering the things she needed, one of which was hopefully inside the Saiga training space. Payton tapped her fingers on the wall, impatient to get in. "How much longer are we going to wait for Kelcie?"

Roswen scooted around Lexis to get to the front, giving Lexis an unwanted look at the plate on the fairy's back where her wings had been clipped. Yesterday, she found it shocking, today it was much more intimidating. She was surrounded by the enemy, and this is what Summer did to the enemy. Lexis took a sizable step back, landing on Markkus's foot, earning her a low growl from him.

"Kelcie?" Ollie bellowed down the hallway.

Kelcie rushed down the hallway toward them. "Sorry!"

Holding the brass knob on the door, Roswen turned to face them. "Ollie, when your grandfather taught combat training here, he would always tell me that Fomorians are elementals, and should not be caged in a room with four walls. Water should be readily available for training, and not from a pump. Therans' feet need to be able to touch the earth so they can sense the vibrations and on and on. Until Murphy blew off the exterior wall, Scáthach wouldn't let me have the funds to change it. So you can thank her for this."

Dollin gave Kelcie a big bucktoothed grin. "Thank you."

The door whisked open.

Before them was a large space, much larger than Lexis expected from the outside. The exterior wall was only waist high, leaving a large portion open. Fresh air poured in, along with sunshine that reflected off of Roswen's white unitard—the same as Winter soldiers wore. Lexis was stumped and irritated by her choice of wardrobe. A traitor to Winter had no right wearing that.

There was no floor. The exposed ground was layered with smooth pavers. In the middle, a pond gurgled and burped.

Payton tugged on the ends of Kelcie's hair. "Aren't you glad we threw you in the river now?"

Her wide-eyed gaze darting from one section to another, Kelcie looked too awestruck by everything to answer. Lexis was too. She'd never seen anything like it. The training space for Dens at Braverwil was in their lodgings. Ill-equipped with only a thin stream that trickled down natural rock walls that were charred and blistered from fire and smelting, Lexis never bothered using it after her first fews months at school. She spent as much time as she could outside, climbing the mountain or on the tundra, working with the elements. This space was well thought out with expansive sections for every element, incorporating the outside within, filling it with nature's charge.

"Underground fed," Roswen said, gesturing to the pond. "And the walls and ceiling are made from juggernaut like the Nether Tower. It can stand up to fire or extreme wind."

Lexis made a mental note to take a piece of that metal with her when she left. It wasn't something she had ever seen in Winter before. Payton whooped, stepping into a maze built for honing air skills. There were tall and short spinning obstacles to be slalomed by stong gales. Beyond that, hoops hung from the ceiling, spinning vertically and others horizontally for airball target practice, and on the far side loose obstacles sat pinioned on tees—all to work on control, agility, and precision. It looked like so much fun Lexis wished her eye were blue and she could've pretended to be a Mistral.

Markkus strutted into the Ignis area. Similar to the Mistral in size, the challenges were different. There were circles mounted on poles of varying circumferences and lengths to focus on accuracy and flame size control. Bending fire was impossible—at least for an Ignis. Lexis smirked. Not for a pulse, though. She could combine air and fire, a recent trick she learned last year all on her own.

Dollin picked up a silver metal bar from the many stacked in a corner of the Theran section, catching the full weight of Lexis's attention. It was a very close match in color to Lexis's new bough. Elated at how easy this was going to be, she deflated after a second glance, and summarily dismissed the idea. That was brumal glaze, and was too dangerous a metal to work with. She would have to find time to go through the Theran area alone to find something more suitable. And sadly she had time; too much time.

When Scáthach said it would be nearly eight weeks before they left for Summer City, Lexis had a panic attack. Hyperventilating and nauseous, she had backed into tree cover to keep from being sick all over her fianna. That was a *long* time to be living with the enemy.

"Dollin . . ." Lexis started to warn him about the brumal glaze, but fortunately caught herself before making another costly mistake. How would a girl who was supposed to be living in hiding in a sewer have any idea what that was? "Never mind."

Dollin turned the bar over in his hand. He should've noticed the obvious small green spots in the silver that glinted, catching sun. He held it to his ear, then sniffed the odorless stone. The clues were all there, but still he asked, "What is this?" The little fool didn't wait for Roswen's answer before sparking, "Theran . . ."

Lexis watched, stiff lipped to keep from cringing, as the bar melted in his hand. Yelping his fool head off, he tried to pry it off, but his skin was stuck to it like a steaming tongue to a frozen pole. Roswen dunked his arm into the pond up to his elbow. The metal slipped off, leaving a large blue venomous stain on his hand.

"Pure brumal glaze, mined in from the caverns beneath the Eternal Peaks in Winter," Roswen explained, handing him a bottle of Zinger. "Drink this."

"Why?" Dollin's hand was already turning green around the fingertips. "It doesn't hurt."

"Because if that spreads, you'll lose that hand."

He downed the bottle in three gulps.

Payton laughed.

Roswen's eyes narrowed at her.

"Sorry."

"That won't be the only dangerous element you come across in here," she said to Dollin, then waved Kelcie over. "You two need to research before you touch anything. Those books detail the name of every metal in that stack. I suggest you evaluate what each one is before trying to smelt." Lexis scanned the pile and noticed several she didn't recognize. Finding the right material was going to be a challenge, and require time here, alone. Roswen jerked her chin at a metal case beside the door. "There's a stash of Zinger and a med kit in that cabinet. I'll replenish it daily."

An ear-piercing scream rocketed overhead, drawing everyone's attention. Necks craned as a first-year Raven arced across the skies, losing tail feathers on the way to a bone-crushing crash landing. She bounced twice more, barreling into a tree trunk.

Lexis and Kelcie leaped out the open part of the wall, reaching her at the same time. Kelcie flinched at the sight of her. Lexis didn't blame her. She was breathing, but her leg was bent in a way that it shouldn't be.

"Whoops," Gavin cackled from the roof.

"Gavin Puce!" Roswen yelled, storming beside Lexis to look up at him.

"What? Gotta fly sometime. Am I right?"

"He is right," Lexis commented, earning a sharp stare from Roswen. Lexis wanted to roll her eyes at her. The traitor knew perfectly well that all ice fairies learned to fly the exact same way.

"Don't encourage him."

Puce didn't need any encouragement from her. The other first years were clamoring for position on the roof, all pleading, "My turn!"

"That Alpha will be the end of me!" Roswen muttered, pulling out three bottles of Zinger. The girl still hadn't moved. "I've got her. You two go back to practice."

Hours of listening to Ollie pontificate on the best way to spark a simple water whip left Lexis bored out of her skull. It was her own fault. She kept looking over at Roswen tending the injured girl, fixating on that backplate. When Ollie caught her, he repeated everything she missed five times.

Finally, after the others were long gone, he smiled—a teacher proud of his student—as Lexis snapped a perfect water whip dousing one of Markkus's residual flames. "Good work. We're done for today."

"Thanks." Lexis let the water fall into the pond and was about to walk out the door when he added, "Oh, and since we're the last out, you're on cleanup." He waggled his bushy eyebrows. "It's good to be Alpha." Then the Alpha strutted out without so much as looking back.

Lexis couldn't believe her luck. Ollie had left her alone, and Kelcie and Dollin made a huge mess of the Theran corner. Blocks and books scattered all over the place. She rubbed her palms together. Could there be a more opportune moment?

She picked up a piece of pompous mold and promptly sneezed. She was so allergic to it. It looked different in the heat of Summer, more brown than black, but the effect was the same. She sneezed again.

"That stuff gave me fits in the Dauour Forest when I was at Braverwil . . ." Roswen said, climbing over the short wall into the room, giving Lexis a heart attack. She dropped the block. "Sorry. Didn't meant to startle you. Ollie left you to clean up, I take it?"

"Yes, ma'am." Lexis's chest tightened. Why would she bring up Braverwil to her?

Her frantic pulse made it difficult to concentrate on what Roswen was saying. It was something about a person named Killian . . .

"Yes, ma'am." *Please go away . . . please go away . . .*

"I'll help you."

Roswen bent to pick up a block, giving Lexis a full view of the plate on her back yet again, and a harrowing thought went through her mind. What if it wasn't Summer's Queen who did that. What if it was Queen Kefyra who ordered that done?

Failure is not acceptable. The consequences will be severe.

Roswen had failed her mission.

Could she ask Roswen? That was a stupid question. Of course not. If she did, it would completely give her away.

Roswen tossed a block to her. It was a piece of something labeled *dobrum sway*—an exact match in color to Lexis's new bough. Lexis made a mental note to look it up as she set it down with others like it and returned.

Roswen held out a common ocral stone next, but didn't let

go. Terror tidal-waved over her as Lexis glanced back at Roswen, seeing her softening expression. "I understand that you're new to Chawell Woods."

Lexis let go of the stone, turning away, hoping that Roswen's clipped wings meant that she couldn't hear Lexis's heart hammering against her chest the way other nimble fairies would have. Their hearing was normally so sensitive they could hear a diddle bug crawl across their path from a hundred yards away.

"Kelcie told you about my parents?" Lexis asked, feigning humiliation.

"I made inquiries. After the fiasco with Murphy last year, Scáthach got on me about my background checks. Apparently, I made some false assumptions."

Roswen's head tilted ever so slightly. She was listening. Lexis inched away from her, trying not to give in to the overwhelming urge to run. *Stick with your story. Your parents died. You were taken to Chawell Woods.* What was the name of the town? The one she was hiding in?

Gads!

It was a port town. With sewers . . .

"You mean you thought it was safe to have her at the school, and it wasn't? Are you asking me something or accusing me of something? I don't have a secret past, if that's what you're asking."

Please don't ask me anything else . . . But then Lexis realized Roswen had yet to ask her a question. She was just blabbering on like a fool, offering information that could be used against her. She bit her lip, hard.

Roswen stood up, raising her hands. "I know that the Woods are rough. And I've lost people close to me too. Everyone I ever cared about, in fact. I had to keep moving forward and start over. That's all I wanted to say. That, and if you ever wanted to talk . . ."

Lexis tried not to blench as Roswen set a hand on her shoulder.

"I'm here." Roswen's warm smile was the final nail in the coffin. By *I'm here,* she really meant, *I'll be watching you.*

12

STICKY FINGERS

A WEEK LATER, THE good news was there had been no other encounters with anything resembling a crow or raven. Kelcie wanted to believe their appearance meant nothing, but combined with the wilted diema flowers outside her grandmother's cave, the facts made it difficult to let go. Doyen believed it was an ill wish that caused the flowers to die, a sign that something bad was going to happen, and Kelcie knew that the spiral Nemain's familiar had carved into the ground was yet another warning.

Not surprisingly, Brona agreed.

The best way to find out about anything ancient was to ask Scáthach since she was thousands of years old. Kelcie insisted they not tell the preceptor that it was their mothers' familiars who had delivered the cryptic message because after last year, if Scáthach sensed the school was in danger again, she might ask them both to leave. Brona explained to the preceptor that it was something they saw over break, on an island, and were curious what it was—a lie that left Scáthach pursing her lips in disbelief, but she didn't push for more information.

Scáthach only confirmed what Niall said, that the spiral was a common symbol, and did generally come in threes. She allowed them to search through the many stacks of textbooks in her office (so long as they organized them), a task that took over five hours and provided no new information other than the fact that the spirals were chiseled into places connected to the gods and goddesses, leaving little doubt that this one was a message from their mothers.

After that, Kelcie and Brona spent their free time after lunch checking the school's campus, examining every building, the stone circle, anywhere that could possibly have been marked with a spiral, and found not a single one on campus anywhere. Kelcie hoped that meant Zephyr was right all along, their mothers were simply saying hi. Only, neither Kelcie's nor Brona's mother had ever sent them a message before, not ever.

On her way to the lunch table, Kelcie laughed as another group of Chargers making an illicit run into Befelts Garden were chased out before getting to the first bend by Roswen and her axe-pen.

Since the announcement of the ball, her classmates suddenly cared about what they looked like and how they smelled. They emerged every morning artfully groomed. Hair always sculpted with oil, spiked, or braided. Peach fuzz shaved. Eyebrows and nose hairs plucked. Teeth blindingly white. Stranger still, the boys showered—multiple times a day.

Roswen had cordoned off the Sow Pretty section of Befelts Garden with a thick line of zapping powder when she caught the acerbic Adder Alpha, Arabel Wasp, pilfering from the lemon balm section to make perfume. She was sentenced to three straight days of detention in the stables. But the loss of a few zapped feathers or the threat of shoveling manure wasn't enough to deter Gavin Puce from diving beak first into a life of crime. His illegal stealth raids in the middle of the night were legendary, and he drove a hard bargain for his ill-gotten booty. He sold the most popular items like lavender, rose, and peppermint to the highest bidder. Kelcie overheard Tad Fagan give up two stolen jinxes from the Nether Tower for a bag of rosemary sprigs. From that day on, he showed up to every class smelling like roasted chicken.

If that wasn't bad enough, a countdown list circulated

tracking which of the second years were still unasked to the ball. Kelcie caught a glimpse of it under Willow's elbow on the lunch table as she sat down at lunch. Four weeks until the actual event and most everyone's name was crossed off, including Niall's. Depressed, she finished eating quickly, and decided to use the rest of the free time to work on homework.

Kelcie lay on her belly underneath the shade of the Sidral's leafy canopy. Textbook standing on edge and open to the page about woolly flatworms, her pen was perched on her paper, ready to write her second of two essays due this week in Madame Le Deux's Sword & Sorcery class. The teacher was making up for lost time, and unlike the changeling who had posed as her last year, the real Madame Le Deux didn't play favorites, and lateness, be it to class or turning in an assignment, was not tolerated under any circustances.

Kelcie couldn't blame her. The whole miserable story of what happened to her last year came out their first day in class, when Fagan broke the lock on Direwood Keep's door so it wouldn't open. The entire class besides his fianna showed up fifteen minutes late.

"Lahteness will naht be tahlerahted fahr ahnytheeng!" she barked as they filed in.

It didn't help that Zephyr made a point of whacking Fagan on the back of the head on the way to fianna three's table, earning him a stern glare from their teacher.

"Ahnd now weeth ze Ahscension? We'll nevair cahtch up! Zat chahngeleeng went cahmpletely off syllahbus lahst year!"

"I think that was on purpose, ma'am," Brona had chimed.

"Mahny sings were on purpahse lahst year, Raven. Zat dahstardly chahngeleeng brahke eento my fahvahrite hair sahlahn," she cried. "Pahsed ahs hees pretty ahsseestahnt, ahnd set a jeenx on Ahlberto's chair right undair hees nahse! BOOM."

"What did she say?" Brona had whispered to Kelcie.

The real Le Deux's French accent was even harder to understand than the changeling's fake one.

"Something about a pretty assistant and an explosion . . . I think . . ."

"My neck blew up. I could naht breathe. I hahd to remahve my bough. But I ahm ahlways prepahred. I hahd ze pahtion to sahve myself een my purse."

But the story sadly didn't end there. It took a much, much darker turn. When Le Deux went into the bathroom to drink the potion, someone hit her with a glamourie. She came in as a tall woman and walked out a gargoyle. Police chased her through the streets as she raced to get to Île de la Cité, to Notre Dame, where she planned to pretend to be a statue on the roof with other gargoyles until she changed back. Cell phones galore captured her mortifying takedown on a bridge crossing the Seine River.

She turned her ire on Kelcie at that point. "You lived een ze humahn wahrld."

The whole class gaped at Kelcie with surprise. Only her fianna knew about that, and Kelcie had hoped to keep it that way.

"You know whaht zey're like! Heleecahpters, cahmerahs; ze zoo keepair mahn kept showeeng me ze footahge unteel I ahte hees phone."

Enduring countless research doctors poking and prodding her for months was nothing compared to the horror of being fed raw meat day after day that was not steak tartare! The glamourie lasted the entire school year. After she finally changed back, without a bough to return to the Lands of Summer, she stalked a *loup-garou* that lives in the catacombs in Paris for four straight weeks, finding him on the worst night, the full moon, when their size triples. The long scars on her forearms a permanent reminder of the struggle to the Sidral that took nine bottles of Zinger to heal.

And just to make things even worse, Madame Le Deux's stolen bough was never found. A gift passed down through her family, the teacher's bough was gone for good. She could no longer spend her breaks in the human world. Hearing this,

Kelcie had clutched her bough, her key to the human world. Her mother's only gift to her. In the back of her mind, escaping to the human world was always a possibility, a place to run if things ever got too much. She understood why Madame Le Deux was so angry.

When she finished telling the tragic story, all Kelcie could think to do was apologize, although she wasn't entirely sure what she was apologizing for.

"I'm sorry?"

"I dahn't wahnt your ahpahlogy! None of you cahn be lahte fahr clahss! Zere ees too much you hahve ahll meessed!" Le Deux trembled from head to toe. "Weentair ees ruthless! Zey will stahp aht nahtheeng to ween ziss wahr!"

Heated stares on Tad Fagan, the entire class pledged never to be late again.

As Kelcie started reading, Brona leaned around the Sidral's breathing trunk. "We have more important things to do."

"What could possibly be more important than Le Deux's essay?"

"Escaping all this ball stuff!" Brona slammed Kelcie's book shut and held it hostage against her chest.

"I was escaping into the life cycle of the woolly flatworm." Kelcie got up and tried to take it back, but Brona moved it behind her back.

"News flash, they die. Like all things at the end of their life cycle."

"You're full of sunshine today," Kelcie laughed.

"I'll be better after a little physical therapy and so will you!"

"What does that mean?" Brona started jogging, dragging Kelcie with her. "Where are we going?"

"Where else would we be going? To hit something, of course."

The Nether Tower was open when Kelcie and Brona arrived. Coach Blackwell and Scáthach were in the arena on the first floor, embroiled in an epic duel. Scáthach with two swords, Blackwell with a sword and shield, every clank or crash struck with such force the rafters shook. Unlike with his students, Coach Blackwell wasn't holding back. Grunting and groaning, ducking under his shield, their coach worked the right side, then left, but Scáthach was way too fast. He retreated time and time again, Scáthach nearly cracking his head open when she caught him peeking out like a frightened turtle from its shell.

Scáthach's feet moved so impossibly fast that she left a dusty trail in her wake. When she flipped her swords, Coach Blackwell used the split second of advantage, lowering his shield, and went on the attack. Only Scáthach had done that on purpose.

The muscles in her forearms tensed as her crossed swords captured Coach's blade. He front-kicked, but Scáthach was long gone, and he missed badly. By the time he realized his sword was out of his hand, the goddess of teaching was behind him, the tips of her swords pressing against his shoulder blades.

Kelcie stared in awe. She had never seen anyone fight like Scáthach.

Brona clapped, catching their attention. "That was a thing of beauty to behold!"

Scáthach raised a sword in salute. "Extra practice?"

"Yes, ma'am!" Brona bellowed.

A glint of approval flickered across the preceptor's face. Scáthach put away her swords, swinging the scabbard belts over her shoulder. "I'll be off, then."

"Oh, no." Coach Blackwell heaved a chuckle. "I think you should stay and humiliate me a little more in front of my students."

After a conciliatory wink at him, she was gone. Coach Blackwell exchanged his shield for a rag to wipe off the sweat dripping down his shiny head into his eyes. "Let's go up to the second floor."

Grinning from ear to ear, the first thing Brona did was pick up a wide-mouthed sidewinder.

"Is there a target set up?"

Blackwell pulled a lever on the far side of the room. A fairy-shaped wooden cutout dropped from the ceiling.

Jinxes clinked as they were loaded. Brona spun the wheel, then took aim at the fairy's nose.

Meanwhile, Kelcie went straight for the twin swords. She didn't care that the blades were chipped and their leather grips worn. She wanted to learn how to use them.

"Are you sure? Those will be hard for you to use even with complete control of your elemental powers, Murphy. They take dedication and patience."

"I can do it, if you give me the chance. I promise I won't use my powers at all, not at all until I've mastered them. Until I can disarm you the way Scáthach did. And I'll be here every day practicing for as long as you let me."

Arms crossed over his chest, he gave a curt nod. "I'll get my broadswords, and we'll get started."

L EXIS SHOULD BE at lunch with her fianna, but based on the last three days of watching Madame Le Deux, she knew it was the only time of the day when the teacher wouldn't be in her classroom. She needed crystals from the trays on the shelves behind the teacher's desk. She'd waited as long as she could to get them, but with only four weeks left until the Ascension, she couldn't wait any longer. A dead ringer for the leaves on Niall's bough, once fitted to the branches she'd made out of the dobrum sway, her little art project would look like an exact replica.

She hid in a storage closet outside the classroom, listening to Madame Le Deux's lunchtime routine, which was always the same. She left precisely ten minutes after the first years' class ended, and then returned forty-five minutes later; plenty of time for Lexis to get what she needed.

And today was no different.

She heard the teacher's footsteps on the stairs, and the door to Direwood Keep slam shut. Lexis held her breath and peeked out, finding the coast clear, then tiptoed to the door and cranked the knob—but it was locked.

Lexis groaned. What kind of a teacher doesn't trust her students? The kind whose life was hijacked by a changeling, she supposed. This was going to be harder than she thought. She would have to melt the lock and then try and smith it back together. As long as Le Deux didn't return early, Lexis could do that with forty-five minutes, but she would have to hurry.

With a quick stretch of her dexterous fingers, she gripped the knob with both hands.

"Theran . . ."

The metal softened, dipping ever so slightly on either side, then broke in the center, exactly where Lexis had intended. The inside and outside knobs clanked, hitting the floor on either side of the door. Just like that, she was in.

Heading for the shelves behind the teacher's desk, she was overtaken by a smell worse than the inside of her shoes after sweating through unit training. It was coming from a pot Le Deux had left brewing in the cauldron at the very back of the room. Holding her breath, Lexis brought out the first three trays of crystals and set them on the clean desktop. Her lips curled into a triumphant smile. Rummaging through the tray, she pocketed only what she needed. There were so many, Le Deux would never notice any were missing.

She confidently scooped a last handful of greens, but froze hearing multiple sets of fast-moving footsteps pounding on the stairs. Lexis sneaked a peek through the empty knob hole, and swallowed a yelp seeing two boys a few steps from the landing. Lexis dashed to the bottles of glamourie potions, rifling through them at a frenzied pace, making way too much noise, desperate to find the only one that would save her. Keys jingled outside the door at the same time her hands fell on the one she needed.

"What happened to the knob?" one of them asked.

The door clunked against the broken knob. Lexis popped the

cork from the bottle and poured it over her head. Her arms vanished at the same time a shoulder plowed into the door. Holding her breath, she shook the last drops of the glamourie on her still visible shoes as the door gave way for a bulky Charger. He was a second year, the Fomorian-hater, Tad Fagan, and he wasn't alone. An Adder was with him.

"Madame Le Deux has had a break-in!" Tad exclaimed, sounding way too happy about it. He picked up the busted knob. "And this looks melted."

Wearing a sinister smile, the blond Adder puzzled out with frustrating accuracy how it happened. "Had to be someone with earth powers. Which means it was either Murphy or that first-year redhead, the one with the huge, protruding front teeth."

"No. It wasn't him. It was Kelcie, Dunn. We *saw* her leaving." Fagan's laugh was low and sinister. "Quick! Get the potion Le Deux asked for and let's go get her!"

"Brilliant, Fagan! There is no chance they'll get picked for the tattoo now." Dunn hefted the smelly cauldron off the hook, and hurried with it out the door.

A pang of guilt beat steadily against Lexis's chest. She hadn't even thought about Kelcie or Dollin getting the blame for this. Why should she care? Her palms started sweating. They are the enemy and failure is unacceptable. But then, there was another problem too. If Kelcie or Dollin were implicated, the Saiga Den would be searched and Lexis couldn't afford for that to happen. And she needed to get to lunch or she would be missed. This was a disaster! She would have to find another way to replicate Niall's bough's leaves.

Lexis tossed the crystals back on the trays, dumped them on the shelves, then she started working on repairing the knob.

She was only halfway done when she heard footsteps coming up the stairs. There was nothing she could do about the broken interworkings of the locking mechanism, so she left it angled, like it had been bent, possibly by someone superstrong.

Smirking, she didn't make it into the closet before they rounded the top of the stairs. None of them seemed to notice her standing perfectly still only a few inches from them. The glamourie was still working, but for how much longer?

"Wait! What happened to the lock?" Tad cried.

Madame Le Deux's extremely pale cheeks burned red with anger. "Yes! Look aht eet! Eet looks like you brahke eet!"

The teacher rushed through the door. Tad stumbled after her, pleading his case.

"But it wasn't me! I'm telling you it wasn't like that a minute ago, ma'am! Tell her, Dunn!"

But the Adder didn't follow him. He stayed on the landing, leaning in Lexis's direction, coming within an inch of her nose with his own, and sniffed. Lexis didn't move. Or breathe. When he raised his hand and his eyes narrowed, she braced for what would come next. Adders were legendary for their scream. They could drop an opponent to their knees, writhing in pain, just by looking at them.

But the pain never came, and Lexis realized that it was because he couldn't *see* her.

"Dunn! Get in here!" Fagan called.

A reluctant snarl skittering across his face, the Adder went into the classroom. Still shaking with fear, Lexis grasped the railing to keep from falling over, and walked down the stairs as quickly and as silently as possible.

Outside the keep, it dawned on her that she couldn't be around her classmates, or anyone when the glamourie wore off, or they would know she'd been in Madame Le Deux's classroom. One Charger or Adder would talk to another, and those two knuckleheads would figure out who really broke the doorknob. She needed to find someplace to hide for a while and fast!

Directly behind Direwood Keep was the Fringe. By order of Scáthach on the first day of school, it was off limits to students. Once the glamourie wore off, Lexis would have to sneak back out of the Woods, but at least she wasn't at risk of running into anyone until then. She sprinted into the Woods, sticking to the remnants of an old trail, craning her neck, taking in the intricately woven green canopy formed by weeping branches of tall trees bent by age. There was no forest in Winter that looked like this. No place that felt so alive. Unlike on the main part of campus where few birds or animals dared to tread around Scáthach's sea eagles, these woods were brimming with life. White spotted brown birds no larger than Lexis's hand sang a sweet warbling tune. Red jays stayed closed to nests on higher branches, feeding their young fresh meal-worms plucked off the backs of nearby leaves.

Leaving the trail to wander thoroughly, she spotted an owl and stopped short, but relaxed when she saw it didn't have fangs. She forgot all about the glamourie until rodents scampered across her invisible shoes, making her laugh.

Lexis spun, not wanting to miss any of the beauty around her. It was still too hot, but Summer was a wonderland of its own.

A high-pitched screech shattered the peace. Frightened birds filled the skies, fleeing. But Lexis wasn't about to run away. She moved toward it. There was something familiar about that screech, something that made her entire body tremble, this time with excitement. When she reached the top of the hill, she couldn't believe her eyes. A bright blue wyvern, no larger than Potham's or Wallace's tail, sat on a nest made of hay, wailing like a hungry baby. Golden-yellow eyes locked on her as if it could see through the glamourie, and the wyvern cried harder.

Giving in to foolish temptation, she came down the hill slowly, carefully, the wyvern's unblinking stare following her every step of the way. It *could* see her. A maddening thought furrowed her brow. There were no reported wyverns in Summer. That was why they stole eggs from Winter. This baby wyvern must have been hatched from one of those stolen eggs that Roswen and her fianna left behind! That meant this little one belongs to Winter! As soon as she was home, she would report this to the Advisors, and they would make plans to somehow bring it home!

Lexis couldn't keep her legs from moving toward it if she

wanted to, which she didn't. Unlike Aífe's wyverns who were unfriendly, the closer Lexis got, the calmer this one became. It whined in her direction, lowering its head all the way to the ground. Lexis tentatively touched the tiny horn on its brow, and it rolled over on its side, giving her full access to its belly.

Rubbing its stomach, Lexis gave a gleeful giggle. She was petting a wyvern! When it started purring, tears brimmed in her eyes. If only her fianna were here!

"Ah, nice to see you've learned patience!" Roswen called, cresting the hill. She pushed a wheelbarrow filled with leafy green plants Lexis didn't recognize.

The wyvern forgot all about Lexis, food taking precedent, and sat up immediately, its three-foot-long tail sweeping back and forth.

"Here you go, girl." Before Roswen dumped the contents of the wheelbarrow in front of her, the wyvern was already eating. "Good to see you got your appetite back. I told them that it was only a flu bug, but you know how those keepers panic. Well, I guess you don't, but you will when you go back."

Lexis's smile fell at a strange tingling sensation tearing through her pinkie. Her rough nail materialized. Then her finger up to her knuckle. The glamourie was wearing off. Getting away was going to have to be done slowly, methodically, and quietly, which her head understood, but her pounding heart refused to accept. Lexis inched backward. The wyvern's head jerked suddenly in her direction, mewing and thrashing, tugging at Lexis's heartstrings. The poor thing was probably too hot all the time because wyverns belonged in Winter! Lexis would give anything to stay, but there was no staying. No returning for another visit. It was too dangerous.

The wyvern's infernal whining covered her tracks. Lexis made it to the top of the hill in three long strides before Roswen sensed something was wrong.

"What's the matter?" Roswen asked, walking around the wyvern.

There was nothing else to do, but run. Halfway through the Woods, to her horror, the rest of Lexis turned visible. She glanced over her shoulder every few seconds, but thankfully didn't see Roswen coming after her. Still, she didn't slow down, not until she exited the Fringe looking backward. Bowling over someone, she crashed to the ground.

"Ow!" That *ow* belonged to Niall. "In a hurry, huh?" He got up and politely reached his hand down to help her.

Grimacing at the pain in her side from her elbow on the way down, Lexis took it, sneaking another peek at his bough that had fallen out of his shirt during the collision. "I'm sorry, for running into you."

"The Fringe can be kind of scary." He grinned warmly. Too warmly. Maybe it was an act. The son of Summer's Queen could never be a good person . . . could he? "But you should know it's off-limits. Scáthach told us at the start of the year."

"I didn't realize that was the Fringe." The lies were coming easier now. "I just needed a little time to myself."

"Don't worry. I won't say anything. But I'd stay out of there," he continued, adding, "I'm rooting for your fianna to be in the tattoo, and if you're caught it would count against you." The wall of anger she kept up around Niall thinned. But no matter how nice he was, it changed nothing.

When the time came, Lexis would do what needed to be done for the mission to succeed, even if it meant hurting Niall O'Shea.

13

DETENTION

O VER THE NEXT several weeks leading up to the trip to Summer City, Kelcie poured all her energy into her classes, hoping that it would be enough for her fianna to earn a place in the military tattoo. Ollie gave a pep talk every morning these days, rallying the Den. He truly believed that it was the key to their families being released from Chawell Woods, and his enthusiasm was infectious.

Assignments piled up in Madame Le Deux's Sword & Sorcery class because Kelcie spent so much time with Coach Blackwell and her favorite swords. But she refused to turn anything in late. She'd stayed up half the night writing an essay on *bodachs*. Trudging into the class exhausted and blurry-eyed, she carefully placed her paper with everyone else's on the top of the stack on the corner of Le Deux's desk. Their teacher was on the other side of the room, counting bottles of glamourie as she did at the beginning and end of every class since one had gone missing a few weeks ago.

"Someone put out our fire," Niall commented as Kelcie sat down at their table.

They'd been brewing an antifreeze spray to counter frost bombs for the past week. It was a request from High Command. All the classes were brewing them to replenish supplies that had been blown up in a raid a month prior.

"Three guesses who that was . . ." Brona glared at fianna one's table, where Fagan was looking everywhere *but* at them.

As Kelcie relit it, the chalkboard with the list of ingredients for Madame Le Deux's proprietary formula for the antifreeze spray dropped down from the ceiling, and started to slowly turn. When they'd begun working on this for Summer's armies, Le Deux was very specific about the secrecy of what they were about to embark on.

"You will naht find eet een a textbook. You may naht sell eet to a publeeshair, eithair! Eet ees top secret!" According to Niall, by top secret she meant she supplemented her teaching income by charging High Command a fortune for it, not that he blamed her. Scáthach was notoriously cheap.

"We added the dried hockings root, splintered yarrow seeds, and hexonite blood drawn under a full moon. Brewed for a week . . . yep," Zephyr rattled off, craning his neck to keep up with the spinning board. "What does that last ingredient say? That should be it."

Brona walked around the table. "Ground waterhorse baby teeth."

"I've got it," Niall said, carrying a small bowl with blue powder toward them.

"Murphy! Lee! Where ahre your ahssignments?" Madame Le Deux questioned, standing over the stack that she'd moved from the corner to the middle of her desk.

Brona walked toward her. "I turned mine in when I came into class."

"Me too," Kelcie said, following her.

"Zen why ahre zey naht here?"

Brona had flipped through the paper stack three times searching for them by the time Kelcie got there.

"They're gone."

Kelcie rifled through the stack just in case Brona missed hers. "I don't understand. I put it on the top."

"You both get zeroes."

"You know I don't ever miss an assignment, ma'am!" Brona insisted.

"Ahnd how would I know zat?" Le Deux retorted.

"Well, you wouldn't," Brona backtracked, "but, if you were here last year, you would know I never miss assignments!"

The fire beneath fianna one's cauldron flared. Out of the corner of her eye, Kelcie saw Fagan shredding a piece of paper with her handwriting on it and tossing it into their fireplace.

"Tad stole our papers!" Kelcie exclaimed, shooting an accusatory finger at him.

"I have no idea what you're talking about." Fagan slipped his hands behind his back, flashing Le Deux an arrogant smile. "I would never touch another person's work."

"But he did! You can see the edge of the paper burning! Caenum!" Kelcie lifted fianna one's potion out of the cauldron to use to douse the fire.

"No!" Le Deux cautioned—too late.

The resulting explosion blew out the window and part of the wall behind the fireplace. Tad Fagan was blasted across the room, where he crashed into the shelves, knocking off hundreds of empty glass viles that broke all over the floor. If that wasn't bad enough, the bundles of dried herbs hanging near Madame Le Deux's desk went up in flames along with the teacher's ruffled sleeve.

"Mon dieux!"

Students scrambled to put it out. Burning lavender was hurled out the window, along with several smoking books from the teacher's desk. When it was all over, the damage to the classroom was luckily minimal. But Madame Le Deux was livid.

"Zat's eet! Clahss ees deesmeessed fahr ze day! Fianna one will remain ahnd clean up ziss mess!"

"What?" Tad protested.

Zephyr laughed.

"Ahnd fianna three, detention!"

"No!" Zephyr gasped a plea.

Fagan leaned over to Zephyr, wearing a gloating smile.

"Yes . . . And with the teachers voting tomorrow, I'm pretty sure that detention means you lose."

With all the confidence of a boy prince about to lose his crown, Niall rushed to Madame Le Deux's desk. "Ma'am! How can you give us detention when they stole their papers?"

"Fahr setteeng me on fire!" Madame Le Deux ended the conversation with a stern warning. "Naht ahnahthair wahrd or eet will be two detentions!"

This was a crushing blow. If Tad was right, and they were voting tomorrow, then they were doomed. Their fianna would be the only one in their class to have earned a detention this whole year, and it was all Kelcie's fault.

MADAME LE DEUX delivered swift punishments too. That very afternoon, Kelcie returned from her workout with Coach Blackwell to find a note on the chalkboard on the back of her door from Roswen:

Report to the stables. NOW.

When she climbed between slats in the paddock's fence, she found Niall, Brona, and Zephyr with shovels in hand and scowls on their faces.

Roswen's pink head poked out the stable door. "'Bout time, Murphy. Come on then. Right this way. Oh!" She gestured to a pile of manure the size of a baseball mound. "Pick that up first."

Zephyr held one of his two grungy shovels out to Kelcie. "For arriving last, I grant you the honor of lugging that steaming wad into the wheelbarrow in the barn."

This felt like cruel and unusual punishment considering she wasn't late on purpose. She didn't even know she was supposed to be here, but the detention was because of her actions, so she scooped the poop without complaint, and carefully shuttled it into the barn. She added it to the half-filled wheelbarrow before gagging a breath, and taking in her surroundings. Like the rest of the campus, the barn was a mixture of rustic and mystical.

There were thirty occupied wooden stalls, fifteen to a side, each gate made from a solid piece of yellow crystal.

Dimitri whinnied loudly from the first stall.

"Hey, girl." Zephyr padded over to stroke her cheek.

"There is another wheelbarrow at the end of the stalls to use when this one is full. When you're done, bring them to Befelts Garden. We'll give the grindylows a tasty treat."

Brona wrinkled her pert nose. "That's disgusting."

"To them, it's dessert." Roswen gave Zephyr a stiff pat on the arm. "All set?"

Zephyr nodded, giving a stiff proffered smile. "Yes, ma'am."

"Good. Chike, send me a note through the tubes from the desk in the back before you leave for the garden, and I'll meet you there."

As soon as Roswen was gone, a pony in the stall beside Dimitri bit Zephyr's horse on the backside. Dimitri's infuriated neigh slid into a high-pitched yelp. The pony flared gums, flashing teeth.

"Hey!" Zephyr snapped at the biter.

The transluscent yellow gate cast a citrine shadow over the stall as Zephyr threw it open and stormed inside. He maneuvered to Dimitri's rump, wiping a hand over raised red bite marks.

"Ponies are the worst." He aimed the tongs of a pitchfork at the pony. "Stop biting her, Cheeky, or I'll report this to Roswen!"

Cheeky turned around, lifting his tail, and farted.

Brona guffawed. "I guess he told you who's boss."

The four of them laughed so hard, they had to lean on the stall to keep from falling over.

"I guess we better get to work," Niall said, sobering.

A hiss rocketed from below. Gates clinking against the locks, the entire barn shook all the way to the rafters for three long, harrowing seconds. Kelcie latched on to the handle of Niall's shovel while he used his arm to keep his glasses from falling off into a pile of manure. Brona and Zephyr grabbed the side of the stall, leaving their fingers in the perfect spot for Cheeky to bite them too.

"Ow!" Zephyr swatted him. "Go away!"

As soon as it stopped, Brona was the first to ask, "What was that?"

"It came from underneath the barn," Niall said.

"Is there a basement, Zephyr?" Brona asked.

"Yeah. Sort of. But we're not allowed down there. It's where Glinnadrian, Scáthach's horse, has his quarters."

"Quarters? Is he royal?" Kelcie asked.

"He's immortal, like Scáthach," Zephyr explained.

Glinnadrian's frantic neigh rose through cracks in the floorboards. Pounding hoofbeats raced from one end of the barn to the other, the hissing speeding after him as if whatever was down there with him was equally as fast. The horses in the stalls whinnied and began kicking their gates, sounding the alarm.

"Something's down there with him and it's after him!" Kelcie exclaimed.

"That's not good!" Zephyr gulped. "We're already in trouble. We should get help, but—"

"No buts. Getting help is the right course of action!" Niall insisted.

"There's no time! Where's the entrance?" Brona demanded.

"First things first . . ." Zephyr let his pitchfork fall against the gate on his way to hefting aside a blanket on the floor of Dimitri's stall. Expecting a cellar door, Kelcie was surprised to see a weapons stash. Bow and arrows. A sidewinder and bag of jinxes. A sword and shield, and shillelaghs.

"Emergency weapons kits. They're in every stall. You know, Chargers always have to be prepared."

"Listen! We're already on thin ground because of this detention! What if we're wrong? What if this is just another of Fagan's tricks? Being a Charger, he has access to the barn! Are we really willing to risk our spot marching in the tattoo? Brona can fly and get help," Niall pleaded.

Brona answered by trading the shovel for her favorites, the bow and arrows. Zephyr went for his sword and shield. By the distraught look on his face, Kelcie half-expected Niall to leave. Instead, he snagged the sidewinder before Kelcie could get it. She ended up with the shillelagh, but took comfort when the stone at the top snapped a sizzle bumping into the gate on their way out of the stall.

Zephyr lifted the tip of his sword, pointing deeper into the barn. "This way!" He led them out of Dimitri's stall, around the poop wheelbarrow, skating through loose hay on the way to the last gate on Dimitri's side, which, unlike the others, was made of smoky quartz. The last gate. As Zephyr shouldered through, it shattered into a million tiny pieces.

"That's not good. The crystal should keep everyone but Scáthach out. No one is allowed in there. Not even Roswen. Not ever," Zephyr exclaimed.

Kelcie reached for a leather handle on the wooden floor that she suspected opened a hatch.

But Niall grabbed her wrist, stopping her. "Are we sure? Fagan would know we would have detention."

Glinnadrian's frantic squeals started again, turning over and over, his cry rising in pitch and frequency. It sounded like it was coming from everywhere, but then, all of a sudden, Kelcie swore she heard him galloping directly under their feet.

"Never mind!" Niall let go of Kelcie and used his telekinesis to pull the handle. The hatch slid back, opening a three-foot hole in the floor. Twenty feet below, Kelcie saw tall orange grasses growing in shallow water—a marsh—and heard a slow, burping croak that sounded like a frog had swallowed a tuba.

Zephyr went first, then Brona, who morphed before she hit the water. Niall next. Going last, and in a rush not to be left behind, Kelcie leaped through without looking down, losing her footing on the slippery marsh bottom and nearly falling, but something caught her. She looked up to see Niall staring at her, his brow creased, concentrating. His powers growing astonishingly stronger since last year, he set her on her feet with what felt like invisible hands clutching her shoulders.

"Thanks," Kelcie said, then raised an air shield just in case. "Where is Glinnadrian?"

"Brona's scouting," Zephyr answered for him in hushed tones. "I want eyes in every direction! And let's keep the talking to a minimum. Scáthach likely has other defenses protecting her horse. Who knows what's lurking down here . . ."

Kelcie swallowed, tasting mud and salt. Her nose itched, the air eerily heavy with magic. Beyond the end of the marsh some fifty feet ahead was a grove of hawthorn trees with prickly branches and yellow bark and purple leaves.

"Is this Scáthach's magic?" Kelcie whispered to Niall.

Yes. I think so. Like last year's overnight.

Last year, on their overnight, Scáthach's magic had manifested all kinds of tortures. Things like selkies with poisoned blow darts, and rhinoceros-sized white boars with tusks as long as Kelcie's arm. Nearly trampled to death by those terrifying monsters, she really didn't want to see either of those again.

Trudging through the soppy muck, Kelcie glanced over her shoulder, watching their backs, while Niall's head flipped back and forth. In the lead, Zephyr looked up, searching for Brona's signal.

Twenty feet from dry ground, there was still no sign of Brona, which means she didn't find anything, and Glinnadrian and the hissing had gone quiet. What if Niall was right and this was Fagan playing a trick on them? Scáthach would not forgive an intrusion like this.

Worry slowing her pace, Kelcie was about to suggest turning back when the grass patches around them started shaking.

"Guys . . . I think we've got company."

"What? Where?" Zephyr asked.

Three-eyed frogs launched out of the tall grasses at Zephyr.

Splayed sucker-feet landed on his sweatpants. Abnormally large mouths opened, revealing toothpick-sized teeth that sank into his leg.

"Uh! Gads! Bumper frogs!" he cried. "Get 'em off me!"

Niall raised his arm. Invisible hands tugged on their hind legs, trying to pull them off, but like a rubber band, they stretched and stretched, the suction cups on their front feet refusing to let go.

"Batter up!"

Kelcie did her best Ted Williams impersonation with her shillelagh, swinging for the fences. The bumper frog twitched on contact, its eyes rolling up into the back of its head, and fell off. With every at bat, another fell. But relief dipped to disbelief, because for every fallen frog another five launched—this time at Kelcie and Niall.

She raised her air shield, batting them away, but there were just too many of them. A snapping tongue broke through her defenses, stinging her shillelagh-wielding arm. Her weapon sank to the bottom of the marsh.

Niall had better luck levitating a huge piece of driftwood. The bumper frogs missed him and ended up dangling by their teeth from the soggy log. He hurled it as far as he could. Grabbing Kelcie's wrist, he dragged her along as he raced for dry land.

We're almost out of this!

Whatever was chasing Scáthach's horse hissed. Shock waves rippled the marsh water. Glinnadrian roared so loud the bumper frog hanging from Kelcie's arm shivered.

Brona soared over the grove a few feet ahead, croaking her fool head off—telling them to hurry!

Splashing through the last bit of soggy earth, Kelcie stumbled into the copse. The frog fell off at the edge of the marsh as if that was as far as it was allowed to go. But the bite immediately swelled and started itching.

"That way!" Kelcie scratched with one hand and pointed with the other to where she could see Brona, circling about a hundred feet ahead.

On the other side of the copse was a pasture of red grass that ended at a wide, gurgling river where they found Glinnadrian.

Kelcie had seen Scáthach's horse before, but only from a distance when she would ride him around campus. He was the biggest horse she'd ever seen.

His black hair reflected the sun rather than absorbing it, bouncing light that glistened in waves of magic. Agitated, Glinnadrian stomped his hooves and thrashed his head, snorting madly. He had matching bite wounds on his sides and legs, but not in a semicircular pattern like the frog left on Kelcie's arm. These marks were two evenly spaced puncture wounds, like fangs.

"Whoa, boy," Niall tried coaxing.

Glinnadrian reared, kicking at him, driving him back, keeping him away from him, and the water.

Zephyr reached for his mane, but Glinnadrian wasn't having it. Head flipping, flaring heated nostrils, he exhaled with so much force it left deep grooves in the dirt around him.

A dark spot no larger than a quarter sprang to the surface in the middle of the white-capped river.

Kelcie inhaled sharply. "Is that Abyss water?"

Zephyr peered more closely. "No," he dismissed, "it's silt from the bottom working its way up to the top . . . which means whatever bit Glinnadrian is in the river!"

The current dipped all at once, spinning into a whirlpool. A giant eel with a head the size of a car tire launched out of the river.

Kelcie shuffled back a step unable to believe her eyes! During the Ta Erfin trials last year, Balor's spirit had somehow released a grappler eel in Morrow Lake. He sent it to attack her fianna mates while they were in the water, far out of Kelcie's reach, to force Kelcie to go in after them or helplessly watch them drown. It was the only creature Balor released that wasn't captured, killed, or sent back into the Abyss waters where they came. All this time, Kelcie never gave it a second thought. In the aftermath, it had vanished, but apparently not for good.

Kelcie recoiled, expecting Balor's eel to come for her, but was horrified when its gaping jaws wrapped around Glinnadrian's midsection, then began dragging him backward, toward the river. Glinnadrian fought, stiffening his legs, his muscles tensing like a body builder attempting to haul a refrigerator, but the grappler eel was too strong. Scáthach's horse gave a foot, his back hooves skating into the churning water.

Kelcie blasted fire at its back, but her flame stream bounced off the eel's slippery skin as if it were coated in some kind of flame retardant. Brona scraped her talons along its neck. With a hard jerk, the eel flicked her off. Her cousin crash-landed next to Kelcie, and quickly morphed.

"I hate these things!" she trilled, ignoring a bleeding cut on her knee, and loaded her bough.

Zephyr charged, taking a flying leap, punching the side of the eel's head. Teeth cracked, falling into the churning waters, but the eel had plenty more in its head and easily hung on. The horse strained, pounding its front hooves into the ground, digging in, a last-ditch effort at the tipping point of a losing game of tug-of-war before the eel pulled Glinnadrian halfway into the water.

"It's going to eat him!" Brona fired off one frustrated arrow after arrow, striking the eel's back, barely getting a flinch out of it.

Kelcie whipped the water into a rope, taking a wild throw, and somehow managed to lasso the eel's gawped jaws. Niall frantically unloaded jinxes from his sidewinder that sent shockwaves through the eel. Smoke escaped through tiny cracks between its teeth. Its grip loosened, but it wasn't enough. Legs flailing, Glinnadrian was on the edge of the whirlpool, his hindquarters lifting into the violent spinning torrent.

"No!" Zephyr called a split second before taking a flying leap onto the horse's back.

Fangs cut into Zephyr's hands but he growled through the pain, prying open its jaws enough for Glinnadrian to escape.

"Go, boy!" Zephyr yelled, jumping off the horse.

Glinnadrian rushed out of the river. The eel lunged for Zephyr, and would've had him, but Zephyr somersaulted on his way into the water, giving Kelcie an opening to help.

"Caenum!"

Her water-whip lasso snagged the eel's neck, keeping it from getting to Zephyr but she wasn't going to be able to hold it for long. Niall grabbed Kelcie's waist, adding his weight to anchor her. Brona joined in, but it wasn't enough.

"Zephyr, get out of there!" Brona snapped.

But Zephyr had something else in mind, something both incredibly heroic and monumentally stupid. He landed on the eel's back as it slid backward, into the whirlpool. Kelcie's feet landed into the water, but still she held on to the water rope with everything she had left. Zephyr pulled his sword and, without a second to spare, drove the blade straight down. The eel let out a long hiss, like a deflating tire, and its fight lessened, but the current in the whirlpool was too much and Kelcie had to let go or they were all going to be dragged in.

"Zephyr!" Kelcie growled.

The Charger jumped off at the same time Kelcie's whip dissolved into the river. The eel collapsed, falling backward into the spinning pool, disappearing right before their eyes.

The dark waters drained, the whirlpool smoothing. The current returned to normal as if the eel was never there.

"I hate to ask, but do we think that is the same grappler eel that tried to kill us last year?" Niall panted.

"That would be a big fat YES!" Zephyr shouted, equally out of breath.

"Yeah. In hindsight, we probably should've killed it when we had the chance, but as I recall the Nether Tower was on fire," Brona surmised. "Well, we got it this time!"

Did they? Were these incidents really over? Kelcie got a very bad feeling in the pit of her stomach. "Are we sure that wasn't Abyss water?"

"No! Stop trying to make this something more than it is! It's like that little swirl your mother sent you. That wasn't Abyss water! It was just silt!" Zephyr let out a frustrated huff. He slid a gentle hand along the horse's cheek. They both visibly calmed. "You're okay now. No one is going to hurt you anymore."

Glinnadrian nuzzled into Zephyr's touch.

"Chike! What is your fianna doing down here?" Scáthach's voice boomed as she exited the copse. "All Chargers know this stall is off-limits!"

Striker was tagging along behind her. Kelcie cringed as he bit a bumper frog off his leg, tossed it in the air, and ate it in three chomps. That cú sith had an iron stomach.

Glinnadrian neighed at Scáthach, tossing his head back and forth. Their preceptor rushed to him, her gray eyes flaring at the bite marks on his side.

"There was a grappler eel trying to eat Glinnadrian," Zephyr explained. "We heard him in trouble through the floor in the barn. That's why we came down here."

"There was no time for us to get help!" Niall added, probably still worrying about the tattoo, but Kelcie was pretty sure that possibility was long gone with their detention.

Scáthach pulled her long sword from her back scabbard. "Where is this grappler eel now?"

"Zephyr killed it," Niall offered. "It's in the river."

Striker ran into the water, likely hoping to eat the eel too! Kelcie ran in after him.

"Striker! Come back here!"

But halfway across, Kelcie was surprised to find the water level was still below her knees. She padded across and back, finding the entire river only inches deep, and the eel nowhere to be found. "It's gone."

"But—" Brona frowned, shaking her head. "None of this makes sense. There was a giant whirlpool! And then it sank when the eel shrank."

"Maybe the eel's body washed downriver?" Zephyr suggested, shrugging.

"Possibly, but my worry is it's still here." Scáthach sheathed her sword, frustrated.

Kelcie didn't bring up the Abyss water. Zephyr's anxious reaction to her just saying the word *Abyss* was the same way people reacted every time she brought up her father's name. The Abyss, like Draummorc, was too taboo to mention.

"Do you think Winter left it here on purpose? Maybe they're going to attack again! Maybe they wanted your horse out of the way," Brona reasoned.

Scáthach's expression dipped into a concerned frown. "Well, if that is the case, Winter has failed again, thanks to your fianna." The preceptor gave Glinnadrian a once-over and returned, worry still creasing her brow. "You four are to be commended."

"Does that mean we can skip the rest of detention?" Kelcie begged, scratching her bumper frog bites.

"No. Afraid not. But don't worry. Fagan's fianna will be running extra laps for the stunt he pulled in Le Deux's class. Lopez and Hawkins may be in his fianna, but they have no interest in winning a place in the tattoo by cheating."

Kelcie couldn't believe her ears. "Wow. Now if only they would be forced to rewrite my paper for me."

Scáthach crossed her arms. "On day one I said you four were the fianna to beat for year two's spot, and I meant it. But know this." She looked down at Kelcie. "Maturity must be on display as much as talent. Rise above it. Rewrite the paper tonight."

"Tonight?" Brona fretted. "But—"

"They'll do it, ma'am," Zephyr interjected. "And deliver them to Madame Le Deux before lights out!"

That night, much to her roommates' annoyance, Kelcie kept the lights on until almost midnight rewriting her essay. When she finally climbed into bed, she was so tired all she wanted was to sleep. But it wasn't meant to be.

Fury had other plans in mind . . .

14

A HARBINGER OF DOOM

THE INCESSANT CAWING started at midnight. Through an exhausted haze Kelcie saw stars twinkle and Mars play tag with Venus. It was very normal for the planets to put on a nightly show, but what wasn't normal was for a shadow to speed by, blotting out half of the full moon—a shadow with wings.

"Payton?" Kelcie whisper-hollered.

Payton groaned, half-asleep, mumbling something Kelcie couldn't hear. Grating coos pealed from above, keeping a steady beat as Kelcie military-crawled across the floor. She stopped beside Payton's arm hanging over the side of the bed and tugged on her sleeve.

"Payton . . ."

"What?" She yanked her hand away, rolling over like she was going back to sleep.

"Do you hear that?" Kelcie looked up, and gasped at the shadow crossing again. "There! Did you see that bird, on the sea glass?"

An exasperated huff later, Payton rubbed her eyes and stared up at the ceiling. "No. I don't hear or see anything." She turned over, dragging the pillow over her head.

She could try Lexis, but she was on her stomach, arms splayed at her sides, eyes firmly shut.

Ignore it. Go back to bed was her first thought, and a good one. She walked backward, intending to do just that, when the bird, which turned out to be an abnormally large crow, halted above Kelcie, treading air. A shake of its wings, and black feathers fell off, passing right through the glass, transforming into a glinting smoke trail that stretched from Kelcie's bare feet to the other end of the room, under the door. She slapped her hands over her mouth to keep from screaming and scrambled into the bathroom. A high-pitched screech demanded Kelcie's attention. Wishing she hadn't, Kelcie glanced up and saw talons scraping the glass.

But neither of her roommates stirred.

There was no question in Kelcie's mind that this was her mother's doing.

Riddled with abject terror and a pinch of curiosity, she made her way to her cubby to get her robe.

Why now?

And why not just fly down and knock on the Haven Hall door? Why all this drama? *Why drop you in the bay when she could've simply set you down on the dock?* Excellent questions, and a good reason to not go. She stared at her bed, tempted.

The impatient crow tapped the glass with its beak, ticking off the seconds. This was how it would be if her mother didn't get what she wanted. Ticking and ticking, all night long, and probably the day after that, and the day after that.

Rushing toward the door, Kelcie tied off her robe ready to get this epic confrontation over with, stumbling on Lexis's boots at the foot of her bed. Kelcie froze and risked a glance. Lexis didn't wake up. She didn't stir at all. She must have been really tired. Kelcie silently set the boots by Lexis's locker, then tiptoed out the door.

Riding the pole, Kelcie got stuck at the top, waiting for the Saiga door open. It was taking forever. When it finally did, her arms ached from holding on for so long that she jumped out without looking and crashed into Brona, landing on her foot.

"Careful!" Brona exclaimed.

In her black pajamas, her cousin had left in such a hurry she forgot to put on shoes. Her hair was loose and matted on one side, but that wasn't why Brona told her to be careful. Perched on her shoulder was a scowling raven. It croaked at Kelcie as if to say, *What took you so long?*

"They're baaack," Brona sang.

A crow landed at Kelcie's feet and gave her an elongated, displeased squawk.

The raven lifted off of Brona's shoulder at the same time the crow launched off the ground into the night air. They flew around the side of Haven Hall and out of sight.

"What do we do?" Kelcie whispered.

Brona waggled her eyebrows, smirking. "Follow them, of course."

"I knew you were going to say that."

Brona took the lead, slinking between overgrown bushes a foot taller than either of them—the perfect cover. It was so dark it was impossible to see much of anything. Kelcie was tempted to light a small flame, but it was too dangerous. They were out after curfew. Way after curfew. As it was every time she accidentally snapped a branch wiggling through the bushes, she held her breath, expecting a sea eagle to appear and sound the alarm. For some strange reason not a single one had yet.

They'd gotten lucky so far, but as they emerged from the cover of the bushes, Kelcie didn't think that luck was going to last, especially when she heard a warbled screech coming from behind them—in the Fringe. It was the strangest cry Kelcie had ever heard, but there was no time to dwell or investigate. The raven and the crow arched overhead, guiding them, indicating they should stay close to the dormitory.

From the looks of the overgrown ivy and waist-high grasses, no one had been behind Haven Hall for a long time.

Moonlight cast a haunting spell over the asymmetrical rooflines. Like the front of the building, the rear boasted tall, rectangular windows with diamond-shaped panes, but unlike the front, the bottom half of the dormitory was consumed by overgrown ivy. The raven and crow plummeted, disappearing into the thick vines.

"You're going to say to follow them, aren't you?" Kelcie asked rhetorically.

Snatching Kelcie's wrist, Brona dove in after the birds, dragging Kelcie along with her, at least at first. The growth so thick, it took both of them pulling and stretching the vines out of the way to keep moving, that is until they came to something hard and immovable. Kelcie spun the air into a circular saw, and cut away enough to reveal a wall of solid stone covered in the same spirals the crow drew their first day at school.

"Our mothers are on the other side of this. I know it," Brona whispered. Her cousin sounded less confident than she did moments ago. Maybe she was having second thoughts about wanting to see them too.

Kelcie's stomach backflipped as she sidestepped closer and pressed her hand to a spiral, hoping something would happen, but nothing did.

"What now?"

"I have an idea."

Brona morphed. Using her beak like a hummingbird searching for nectar in flowers, she shifted up and down the stone slab, poking the dead center of the spirals. When that didn't work, she tried another pattern, skipping every other one. Then reversed it. She let out a loud, irritated croak and returned to her human form, disappointed, and sporting a budding bruise on the end of her nose.

"Melt it," was Brona's next big idea.

Kelcie flattened her palms against the cold stone, and sparked. "Theran . . ."

Steam hissed. She sensed a little give in the stone, but when Kelcie lowered her hands the only thing she'd managed to do was leave indents of her fingerprints that were already fading.

"I thought you mastered that," Brona quipped.

"I did!" Kelcie set her hand back on a spirals and *listened*.

Most kinds of metal and stone hummed a single tone, something Dollin taught her recently, but there was no hum, no sounds at all. It was quiet.

Dead quiet. They were never going to get through.

"I've had enough. Scáthach is going to find us out here after curfew!" Kelcie grabbed Brona's hand, fully prepared to haul her cousin back to the front of Haven Hall and shove her into the Raven Den door if that's what it took. But their joined hands twinkled as if they had been dipped in stars.

Eyes wide, Brona asked, "Are you seeing this?"

Kelcie nodded, raising their clasped hands higher. Tiny lights swarmed like fireflies. On instinct, she pressed their hands to the stone. The tiny lights drifted upward—like smoke climbing a chimney—casting shimmering dust over the spirals.

The crow landed on Kelcie's shoulder and the raven on Brona's. Rock scraped rock as the stone slab shifted a foot, just enough room for them to slip inside. When Kelcie didn't move, talons dug into her shoulder.

"Okay! Not so hard. I'm going."

The stone closed behind them, plunging them into stale air and unblemished darkness.

"Ignis." Kelcie sparked a small ball of fire.

Brona's shadowed face grinned with relief beside her. "I am so glad you figured out how to do that without blowing us up."

The space was only five feet across. Made from crystal or gemstone, the rounded walls multiplied and refracted their confused reflections. Every time she caught a glimpse of the two of them with the raven and crow perched on their shoulders, chills ran down her spine. As if the crow sensed her unease, it jumped off, and the raven joined it on the ground.

Kelcie turned around slowly. "What is this place?"

Brona took a few crunching steps, then stopped. She used Kelcie's shoulder for balance and wiped off her bare feet.

"I think it's a crypt."

Horrified, Kelcie stepped backward toward the wall, hearing a sharp snap, and cringed. "That would mean—"

"Yeah." Brona wrinkled her nose. "You just broke a dead guy's femur, but think of it this way. He doesn't need it anymore."

Kelcie's palms started to sweat, dimming her fire. She took a deep breath, willing the flames to grow higher, and they listened. A shot of pride brought a small smile while her shoulders lifted protectively, waiting for what was next.

"Look!" Brona pointed at the ground, to the shadows of the raven and crow, shadows that were not birds, but winged women. In a glistening display of transformative magic, the shadows whisked to standing. Two women, both dark-haired and silver-eyed like Brona, stood before them. Their bodies were cocooned and camouflaged in silky black feathers. Their wings were so long they dragged on the floor as they approached, only they made no noise. Stopping a few inches before them, Kelcie stared at her mother, and saw her own haunted reflection on the rear wall behind her, and realized they weren't actually here at all.

But still Kelcie's chest grew unbearably tight at the sight of her mother's face, with its strong cheekbones, matching freckles to hers, and chiseled jaw. The last time Kelcie saw her mother's, face she was staring down at Kelcie that night in Boston Harbor so long ago, when she dropped her into the deep, frigid water, powerless and alone.

When Kelcie was little, Doyen said Nemain and Macha never returned out of fear for their daughters, that for war goddesses to have children meant only bad things for their children. And it had only meant bad things.

The memory of Brona and Kelcie's last time seeing each other when they were little, when they were torn apart by their mothers, flashed through Kelcie's mind. Anger fought with joy, a raging grapple for Kelcie's state of mind. Anger won. In a big, bad way. She was the daughter of a goddess of fury, after all. But instead of acting impulsively, lashing out, she stepped closer to her cousin. Their pinkies touched, and Brona hooked Kelcie's.

"Are you ghosts?" Kelcie asked.

Nemain's bewildered gaze fixed on Kelcie for so long it made her shrink back a step. A slight grin flickered on her mother's face, then vanished. "Not the first question I expected from my daughter, but no. We are not dead. We cannot breach the Academy's isle. We've been trying, but this is the best we can do. Our spirit forms traveled through this old burial mound that Scáthach saw fit to leave undisturbed when she built the school."

"Fascinating," Brona offered, still clinging to Kelcie's pinky.

"What do you want?" Kelcie asked, trying and failing to hide the bitterness in her voice.

"Oh, Fury's daughter has a temper of her own," Macha goaded.

"Is that any way to greet your mother?" Nemain bristled. "You were a lot sweeter when you were younger."

Kelcie lifted her flames higher. "Before you cursed and abandoned me? I lost everything because of you, and I'm not willing to let that happen again. So if that's what you're here for, if you're going to try and take our memories from us again—"

"We're not going to let you," Brona finished, her enthusiasm from outside the crypt gone.

Maybe she felt it too, like they were standing before two women who weren't looking at them with a mother's warmth, but rather as formidable enemies.

"We're not here to do you any harm," Macha said.

"Then why are you here?" Brona asked. "Why the theatrics with the crow and raven before? Why not—"

"A test to see if we could break through Scáthach's defenses," Macha explained. Her eyes crinkled with sudden understanding. "I know what this is, Nemain. They're teenagers now!" She cackled. "Isn't that right? You two are thirteen! I've heard about this phenomenon, sister. It's all the hormones raging inside of them. Makes them arrogant and snotty."

"And always blaming their parents for everything wrong in their lives it seems," Nemain added.

Kelcie's shoulders lowered, anger straightening her spine. "Funnily enough, everything wrong in my life *is* because of you and my father."

Macha arched an annoyed brow. "I don't remember ever feeling that way. I'm not sure I can even remember our parents."

"That's because you haven't been thirteen in thousands of years!" Brona retorted. Her head shook with deep disappointment. "Is there a reason you're here, or did you just come to tell us we're bad daughters and get us in trouble for being out after curfew?"

"You said you were never coming back," Kelcie uttered to Nemain.

"I thought that was true when I said it, Kelcie, but it seems fate has chosen another course."

Macha's lips curled. "We bring an omen of death."

Kelcie groaned. *Of course.* Was it too much to ask that they bring a good omen? Something like, *hey, just flew in on the spirit express to let you two know that Niall was going to ask you to the ball, or your fianna will have a place in the tattoo, or the Queen will free the Fomorians and your grandmother will be home in Moon Bay by the next break.* But NO.

First time around, the misery her mother foresaw was all destined for Kelcie. Now it seemed she wasn't the only one being included. Brona was here too.

"Excellent." Brona bristled, but smiled at the challenge. "Nothing but the best for your daughters."

Kelcie yanked Brona back by her pinkie. "Have you lost your mind? I don't want to die!"

"It is not your death we come to show you." Nemain's eyes glossed over. Moving images too small to see materialized on her mother's corneas. Nemain snapped her fingers, and the faceted walls came to life, projecting what her mother was seeing.

A bird's-eye view skimming burgeoning wheat fields.

"That's the Bountiful Plains," Brona explained to Kelcie.

Soaring over mer people sunning their scales on lake shores, then on to a bustling port with a ship Kelcie recognized.

Brona frowned, and sounded apprehensive as she said, "That's the Lakelands, and Binary Gulch where Dah docks the Greedy Lark."

The view rose above a dense forest, dipping beneath the tree line, flying over Kelcie's grandmother and other Fomorians at the riverbank, washing clothes.

Kelcie touched the image. "Chawell Woods . . ."

And then came a glorious city perched on top of an elevated island, streets filled with bustling crowds.

"Summer City," Brona declared. "But what's wrong? It all looks perfectly normal. Why are you showing this to us?"

Macha answered. "Because a devastating change is going to occur . . ."

The silver in Nemain's eyes dimmed drastically.

A sky view of the same places flashed on and off with wild abandon, all in the process of being smothered in grim darkness. Whatever the darkness touched died. Grains wilted in frostbite. Fish and mer people froze beneath the surface of the lake. Ships were cemented in unyielding ice. The dark never broke. It was all-encompassing, impenetrable, like in the human world when the electricity goes out in the middle of the night.

The last image materialized beside Kelcie. A man in filthy gray rags huddled in the corner of a bleak cell, shivering. Lips cracked. Icicles in his red hair. Arms and legs bound in black chains.

"Is that my father? Is that him in prison? Are those obsidian chains on him?" Kelcie's knees weakened, but her flame tripled in size, feeding off her fear and anger. "How cold will it get in that cell? If those are obsidian chains . . . He'll die if he can't spark fire! And my grandmother! I have to warn her, warn all the Fomorians in Chawell Woods. Foraging in the dark is impossible. They'll starve to death!"

"I'm afraid your father will die whether he can or can't spark. All of them will . . ." Nemain's voice trailed off.

"The diema flowers that wilted outside Doyen's cave," Kelcie breathed. "She said it was a sign of bad things to come."

"Yes," Nemain said as if she'd seen them too.

Cold dread seeped into Kelcie's veins, dimming her flames.

"When is this going to happen?" Kelcie choked out.

Nemain sighed. "We don't know precisely. But it will come to pass."

Brona scraped a rigid finger over the ice between the ships stuck at sea like she was trying to crack it. "What causes this to happen?"

"We don't know that either," Macha said.

Brona stifled a frustrated laugh. "Well, that's entirely unhelpful."

Kelcie felt like she had last year in Morrow Lake, the second after her last breath and before she realized she could breathe underwater, only this time she was drowning in a sea of unknowns. "Why tell us?"

"Because we can only communicate with you, and not for much longer, I fear." Nemain's gaze dashed to something Kelcie couldn't see, then quickly returned. "You and your fianna *must* stop it, Kelcie. Everyone's lives depend on it."

Nausea rising, Kelcie stepped closer. "Why can't you stop it?"

"We can no longer pass into your world. The Sidrals are closed to us all." Her mother looked down at Kelcie with something in her eye that looked like regret.

"Are you not in this world?" Brona asked, confused. "The Isle of Eternal Youth—"

"Is no longer here," Macha answered.

"Because of what happened last year?" Kelcie worried.

"No." Nemain half smiled. "Because of what happened nine years ago, when I left you in the human world. There is no time for detailed explanations right now."

"No time?" Kelcie was fuming mad. "Haven't Brona and I been through enough?"

"I understand your anger, daughter." Nemain moved toward

her. "Anger and rage come to us naturally, but my love for you will never cease, not in this lifetime or the next."

Kelcie had heard her mother say those words to her once before, right before she cursed and abandoned her. Nemain's ghostly aura twinkled like the Milky Way above her as she made to kiss the top of Kelcie's head. Kelcie backed away from her, afraid of what that kiss would do.

Nemain gave her a sad, understanding smile. "May you claim victory in battle, for I fear this is only another of many to come."

Her aura exploded, stars shooting through the air into the faceted walls, not returning. Just like that, Kelcie's mother was gone.

"What's that supposed to mean?" Kelcie asked Macha.

"I don't know. We see different things." Macha reached out toward Brona. "You can do this, Brona. You have the mind and strength to save them all. I believe in you."

Brona's bravado faded with her mother's image. "Wait!" She let go of Kelcie's pinkie, trampling on bones and who knows what else, waving her arms through the dimming lights around her mother until the woman vanished completely.

"They're gone," Brona uttered, sounding disappointed.

Kelcie's emotions swung like a pendulum starting out with sadness, arcing through fear, and ending with bitter-tasting anger. "Only another of many to come? How could my mother say something like that and leave without explaining what she meant? Are our entire lives going to be fighting off one bad omen after another?"

Brona let out a resigned sigh, throwing an arm over Kelcie's shoulders. "I don't know. But at least we're in this together. We can do this."

"We have to do this." Kelcie touched the wall, unable to stop seeing her father freezing in his cell. "If what my mother showed us is really going to happen, we have to stop it! If we don't . . ."

Brona said what Kelcie couldn't. "Everyone in the Lands of Summer is going to die . . ."

15

LAUGHINGSTOCK

SOMETHING WALLOPED THE stone door with such force the walls splintered. Dust fell into Kelcie's eyes, making them sting. Another loud crack, and the massive stone drove forward, slamming into Kelcie and Brona.

"Mistral!" Kelcie screamed, throwing her arms out. *Please work!*

The scraping halted. A cushion of air pulsed between the faceted wall and the stone slab, keeping Kelcie and her cousin from being crushed to death.

Brona exhaled audibly.

Kelcie heard Scáthach yell in a terrifying booming voice, "Who dare—?"

Kelcie and Brona peeked out from behind the stone. The blinding light from their preceptor's flaming spear hit them squarely in the eyes.

"Murphy? Lee?" She lowered the spear. "How did you get in here?"

Overzealous sea eagles on Scáthach's shoulders yipped, frustrating the preceptor even more. She let out a short whistle and they flew off her shoulders, disappearing into the night.

Scáthach was in her nightclothes—oversized red flannel pajamas—and was sopping wet. She came farther into the crypt and looked around as if she had never been in here before. Their preceptor lifted a tentative hand toward the crystal wall, but stopped, as if she were afraid to touch it. She raised her spear high, illuminating the whole space.

"Do you know what this place is?"

"Judging from all the bones, a grave?" Kelcie answered.

"Not exactly. The bones are of those who have tried to pass between the worlds without invitation." She tilted her head like she was listening to something. "It is a gate between this world and the next. Here long before the school, and it has never opened, not even for me." She spun to face them. "How did you do this?"

"Wasn't hard, actually. We just touched it," Brona said.

"Well, that is most curious." By her expression, Scáthach wasn't pleased by that explanation. "Why are you out after curfew? And how did you even know this was here?"

Striker rushed to Kelcie's side and shook, sending water droplets flying in all directions. It was only then Kelcie heard the sound of drizzling rain. The Lands of Summer were ecologically perfectly balanced. It rained when it was necessary, feeding saplings, replenishing rivers, lakes, and oceans, with never too much or too little water. By morning, the rain always stopped, and the sun rose, warming without threat of cloud cover. That's the way it had been since Kelcie arrived. Never a single gray sky. At school, on the Emerald Sea on Brona's father's ship, in Chawell Woods with her grandmother. It was as if the weather in the Lands of Summer were on some kind of perfect weather timer, that was about to be turned off permanently—somehow.

"Our mothers decided to pay us a visit, sort of," Kelcie said. "Their familiars led us here. It's hard to explain."

Scáthach sighed. "I know I'm going to regret asking you this, but what is it they wanted?"

"They came to deliver an omen. A really bad one," Kelcie said.

"Something else going to attack the school?" the preceptor asked, sounding displeased.

"No. It wasn't about the school. The Lands of Summer are going to turn cold and everyone is going to die, unless *we* can stop it," Brona blurted with gusto. "This is so much bigger than King Balor's stupid evil eye."

"Turn cold." Scáthach's gaze narrowed. "How?"

Kelcie shrugged. "They don't know."

"When?"

"We asked that too. Same answer. It's a mystery," Brona mused.

"So, your mothers came to tell you the Lands of Summer are going to turn cold and everyone is going to die—"

"Unless our fianna stops it. Yup. That's what they said," Brona boasted. "Isn't that great? I mean, not the dying part. Of course, that's horrible, but they asked us to stop it! We've been given a mission from our mothers!"

Her cousin's excitement made Kelcie very nervous, and frankly, sick to her stomach. It didn't help that they were still standing on the bones of dead people.

Scáthach simply said, "I see."

"See what?" Kelcie asked, confused. "Do you know how this could happen?"

Striker trotted around the crypt, sniffing like a dog tracking a scent, until he ended up where he started, by the exit, and ran out of the crypt.

"No. But come." Scáthach glanced around uneasy, gesturing for them to follow. "Let's discuss this outside."

As soon as Kelcie and Brona were out, the stone slab flew across the crypt, settling back into place, the carved spirals turning 360 degrees like a vault locking.

Scáthach paused to look back at it, but then parted the vines, stepping out into the rain.

Once under the cover of the archway entrance to Haven Hall, Kelcie asked Scáthach, "Should we tell someone? Like Queen Eislyn?"

"I'll report it to High Command, but . . ." Scáthach leaned on the shaft of her flaming spear that was undampened by the rain. Her stern stare shifted between Kelcie and Brona. ". . . in my experience with omens, no matter how much you fight against them, try to out-fox them, or change the outcome in any way, they ultimately still happen. Look at King Balor."

"What do you mean?" Kelcie asked.

Brona scoffed. "Don't you remember what we talked about last year in Scáthach's office, about how he was a Fomorian king? That his eyeball was his only one because he was a cyclops?"

"I think I blocked that out."

"I don't blame you." Scáthach smirked. "That particular part is irrelevant to my point however. When he was king, he received an omen that his grandson would one day kill him. So he locked his only child, a daughter, in a tower where she was to remain alone and untouched, never to marry. But the man who would one day claim her heart broke into the tower. Three grandsons were born. Two Balor found, and ended their lives first."

"That's the saddest thing I've ever heard," Kelcie said. "King Balor was a horrible man."

"Cyclops," Brona corrected.

Scáthach continued, "But one grandchild slipped through his grasp."

"Lugh," Brona said with a knowing smile. "He was like you, Kelcie. Half Fomorian, half a godly Child of Danu."

"Yes, and he fulfilled the prophecy," Scáthach explained. "He killed his grandfather in battle and claimed his throne."

Kelcie looked up at Scáthach, still confused. "Oh. So you're saying . . . no. I don't get it. What are you saying?"

"The events may have to play out in order for you to have a chance at saving Summer."

Kelcie didn't like the sound of that at all.

She and Brona took turns giving Striker a hug goodnight, then watched him trot after Scáthach down the path, returning to the Shadow.

"We have to tell Niall and Zephyr right away!" Brona insisted, her eyes narrowing. Her fingers dove into her hair, and squeezed. "But what if they don't believe us again? No! They have to believe us! Our mothers gave us a mission, Kelcie! We can't let them down!"

Kelcie had never seen her cousin so frazzled. "I'm less worried about letting them down since they're not here in this world anymore, and more worried about the people who are. Look, it's after midnight. Let's talk to the boys in the morning. And if they don't believe us then we'll take them down to the crypt and lock them inside until they do."

Kelcie crept through the pool room and tiptoed into her bedroom, tripping over a pair of boots next to Lexis's bed. She stopped in her tracks, hoping she didn't wake her. Kelcie was picking them up to set them by Lexis's locker when she remembered that she'd tripped over these same shoes on her way out, and set them by the locker once already, before she left.

She turned them over, finding wet mud caked into the soles. Kelcie could see Lexis was in bed, in the same position: on her belly, arms out, like she was paddling a surfboard. *Did she follow me? Why would she do that? Unless . . . she was spying on me!* Once again, suspicion fell over Kelcie. Only this time it felt like a wet blanket, hard to shake off. Could Lexis be a Winter spy? Kelcie stared at her roommate's sleeping form. Maybe she was just curious why Kelcie was leaving in the middle of the night. But then, why not catch up to her and ask?

An ill wish crossed this threshold. That's what Doyen had said when she saw the wilted diema. And now she was following her? It didn't prove anything, not conclusively, but she would keep an eye on Lexis, just in case. Kelcie yawned, exhausted and tired of thinking, but sleep would have to wait.

Kelcie set the shoes back down in the same place she found them, by Lexis's bed, and padded softly to her desk, where she wrote two letters. One to her grandmother and one to her father, warning them about what Nemain and Macha had showed her and Brona. Her father would likely never even read it, but at least Kelcie would know she tried.

By the time she climbed into bed, she could barely keep her

eyes open, but every time they shut, she saw her father shivering in his cell. As her eyes drooped, caving in to utter exhaustion, she turned on her side and could've sworn she saw Lexis staring at her.

The next morning, Kelcie woke up so late, the room was empty. Lexis and Payton were already at breakfast. She threw on her clothes and hurried to meet Brona, finding her pacing angrily at the edge of Befelts Garden.

"Of all days to sleep late!"

No amount of apologizing was going to help the mood Brona was in. If she was an elemental, she would've spontaneously combusted. There were only a handful of students left at breakfast, but fortunately that included Niall and Zephyr. As she and her cousin approached the second-year table, Kelcie saw that their usual seats across from their fianna mates were taken by Delilah and Willow.

Brona shook the back of Delilah's chair. "Out. We have important fianna business."

Kelcie was mortified. "Sorry. We just need to talk to them for a minute."

"It's no problem." Delilah relinquished her seat in a hurry, but made no move to leave.

Willow scooted over one, giving her chair to Brona, but turned to listen in too. The last thing Kelcie wanted was an audience, but Brona didn't seem to care.

"We have a serious problem," her cousin began.

Zephyr slammed his bottle of Zinger down on the table, garnering the attention of the rest of the table. "You didn't rewrite your paper, did you?"

Niall leaned forward, panic turning his face red. *Please tell me you both turned it in! Scáthach was very—*

"Will you stop worrying about a stupid paper! Our mothers paid us a visit last night to tell us we're all going to die!" Brona yelled so loud that the foxtails in the greenhouse on the far side of the garden heard and started barking. Everyone still at the table fell silent.

Zephyr spilled Zinger all over himself. "Why did you have to say it like that?"

"Like what? You want her to sugarcoat it?" Kelcie asked.

"Die?" Delilah yowled. "The mothers who are part of the Morrígna?"

"You're a lot smarter than you look," Brona commented. "I officially like you. You can stay."

"I want to stay too!" Willow passed Zephyr a handful of napkins. "This sounds serious."

Niall gaped at Kelcie. "You found the link with the spiral! You didn't come get us."

"Because it never happened." Fagan dragged a chair over, flipping it around, and plopped down beside Niall.

"Fagan, this doesn't involve you," Zephyr said.

Brona's fist gaveled the table. "But it does involve him." Kelcie wanted to die as Brona stood up on her chair. She tried to stop her, tugging on her elbow, but from the look Brona gave her, Kelcie knew that, in her cousin's eyes, this mission had already begun—and maybe she was right. She coned her hands around her mouth and megaphoned, "It involves all of us! Listen up! Last night our mothers came to the school and showed us an omen that the Lands of Summer are going to freeze over!"

Kelcie saw Lexis stand up from the first-year table, shushing those around her.

Gabby Arnold lifted a timid hand. "Um, why exactly?"

Brona gestured to Kelcie, wanting her to field the next question, which Kelcie did not want to do. But what choice did she have? She climbed up on her chair, seeing Fagan's challenging glare fall on her knocking knees. She really hated public speaking!

"We, um, don't know," Kelcie answered.

"Of course you don't." Dunn's blond head bobbed from hearty laughter.

"And when is this temperature drop supposed to happen? I'll

need to buy some proper clothes," someone from the fourth-year table jested.

"We don't know that either," Kelcie admitted.

Fagan chuckled, smoothing his wavy brown hair. "Why do you keep doing this, Lee?"

"Doing what?"

Dunn answered for him. "Lying about your mother."

"Mothers! And she's not lying! I was there!" Kelcie argued.

Tad got up, tossing a gloating smile at Kelcie. "It's pathetic. Trotting out your infamous mothers to save your spot in the tattoo. I bet you told Scáthach already, didn't you?!"

Kelcie's face fell.

"Look at Murphy! They did tell her!" Dunn howled with laughter.

Roswen stormed over to the table, took one look at the crowd around Kelcie and Brona, and shouted, "Class time! Now!"

Startled students hopped to attention. As everyone filed out, Kelcie saw mixed reactions on their faces. Some smirked. Others laughed. But a handful looked concerned. Lexis, however, was gone.

Her shoulders slumped, Brona refused to get down until the tables were empty. She stormed over to Kelcie who was waiting with Zephyr and Niall a few steps away.

"That didn't go as well as I'd hoped for."

"You can't just tell people they're going to die like that! There needs to be a buildup to something that catastrophic, and proof!" Zephyr gassed. "Can we just keep these conversations to our fianna for now?"

"Is that really all your mothers said?" Niall asked.

"Afraid so," Kelcie said.

He groaned a worried sigh. "Tell us what happened from the very beginning."

Brona jerked her chin at Kelcie, indicating she'd done enough talking this morning already. As they started walking to class, Kelcie told them everything. The late-night summons from the familiars, the spirals on the backside of Haven Hall, how it opened at a touch from their joined hands, and then what happened inside.

By the time Kelcie finished the whole story, they'd reached the end of the path through the woods and could see their classmates lining up in front of the platform for unit training.

"Scáthach said she would report it to High Command, but . . ." her stomach twisting, Kelcie took a deep breath before finishing, ". . . but that the events may have to play out for us to have a chance at saving Summer."

"She referenced the omen about Balor being killed by his grandson," Brona offered by way of explanation. "Basically, that omen—"

"Happened regardless of Balor's actions," Niall finished, jumping to the right conclusion, as always. He rubbed his chin. "But it also took decades to play out."

"That's good!" Zephyr exclaimed. "I like that! Decades! Because we have nothing to go on!"

"I'm not so sure," Kelcie began. "I think Lexis followed me last night."

Brona gasped. "Are you sure?"

Kelcie nodded. "Pretty sure."

"What if she's a Winter spy? What if she's the harbinger of doom who will send the Lands of Summer into the foretold cataclysmic event, extinguishing life as we know it?" Brona asked. "Should we report her to Scáthach?"

"You got all that from her following you? Maybe she was just curious where you were going? Sneaking out in the middle of the night, I'd be curious. Do you have any real proof of that?" Zephyr pressed.

"There was the ill wish," Kelcie said, keeping her voice low. She explained what happened in Chawell Woods.

"Wilted flowers?" Zephyr sounded incredulous. "What else?"

"I saw her coming out of the Fringe," Niall commented, his brow creased with worry.

"When?" Brona asked.

"The same day the glamourie potion went missing in Madame

Le Deux's class," Niall said warily. "What if she went into Le Deux's classroom to steal something, and got caught, used the glamourie potion to hide, then had to lay low in the Woods until it wore off?"

"We can't go to Scáthach with a bunch of speculation and circumstantial evidence," Zephyr groused, suddenly sounding like a lawyer. "We keep an eye on her."

Brona moved on. "How are we going to figure out what the omen means?"

"What about Roswen?" Zephyr whispered. "She is from Winter after all."

"That's a good place to start." Niall looked at Kelcie.

"What?" Kelcie frowned at him, knowing full well where this was going.

"Roswen likes you best."

"She does not!"

"Line up!" Scáthach bellowed from the platform officially ending their discussion.

T HAT AFTERNOON, FORAGING Class was in the Herbaceous Horrors section of Befelts Garden, inside the greenhouse that was kept colder than a freezer, where all sorts of Wintry plants grew. The first class Kelcie attended in here, she was startled by how much noise the frosty flora made. It was impossible to hear Roswen's lectures. Today was no exception.

Trellises of whimpering wisteria wailed when the doors opened, waking the foxglove in the middle of the raised beds. For most of the hour, the foxglove refused to stop barking until Roswen relented, and moved them to the window so they could exchange rumbles with their new Summer friends, the wolfsbane planted outside.

By then, Roswen was angry because there wasn't much time left. She thrust her axe-pen forward. "For the last few minutes of class, I have something to show you. A new bloom awaits."

When they stopped, Kelcie lifted the hood on her Saiga sweat-shirt to keep her ears from freezing and falling off, and stood on her tippy-toes to see over Niall's shoulder. He sidestepped, making room for her.

"Thanks."

You're welcome.

This was what they were now, awkwardly polite to each other. Kelcie never said too much or too little to him to keep from saying the wrong thing. Maybe he was doing the same thing. It felt like there was an insurmountable wall between them, and she hated it. She missed the old days when she could say anything to him and not worry about it. Missed Niall's notes he always sent her last year before they went to bed. Missed his laugh when she said or did something ridiculous, even if he was mad at her.

She missed his friendship.

Roswen leaned over the last bin in the greenhouse.

"Chike, what is this?"

"Frothing eranthis."

"And what does it do?"

"A tiny dollop of the excretions from the pistil will eat the flesh off your entire hand," Fagan blurted, sniffing in Zephyr's direction.

Roswen rolled her eyes at Tad. "Is your name Chike?"

"No, ma'am."

"I didn't think so." She shook her head. "Now, next time I'll expect you to be able to identify which flower in here is the antidote for it."

"Yes, ma'am," the class responded.

"Dismissed!"

As the class filed out of the greenhouse, Niall slowed his pace, keeping Kelcie from leaving.

Ask her. Now.

Kelcie caught Niall's determined stare. Brona and Zephyr glanced back nodding at her. She threw her head back, dreading this conversation. If Kelcie was really her favorite, she wouldn't be for long.

Kelcie waited to speak to Roswen until everyone else was gone.

Besides Kelcie's fianna, no one knew Roswen was from Winter. Roswen never spoke of it, not since Kelcie and her fianna found out last year. Secrets were sacred as far as Kelcie was concerned, and her fianna agreed. Neither Kelcie nor anyone in her fianna would ever divulge Roswen's secret because it wasn't theirs to tell.

"Need something, Murphy?" Roswen asked, seeing she was still there.

"Yes, ma'am. Can I ask you—?"

"About your mother's vision?" She smiled at Kelcie's shock. "I was at breakfast too this morning."

The wolfsbane licked the outside of the greenhouse, their tongues screeching like windshield wipers on dry glass. The foxglove jiggled their bell-shaped blooms in response, adding yip-chimes to the noise.

"Tell me what the Morrígna showed you and speak loud enough so I can hear over that racket!" Roswen bellowed in frustration at the flowers.

Kelcie told her about the omen, but Roswen didn't seem surprised.

"You knew? Scáthach told you?"

Roswen emptied a bucket of berries into the foxglove's bin. The dinging ceased, only to be replaced by slurping and chomping. "She asked me the same thing you're about to ask me. If I knew of a weapon Winter had that could cause that kind of catastrophe."

Kelcie followed Roswen to the snapdragons. She tossed them pieces of meat from another bucket. "I'll tell you what I told her. No. Not that I'm aware of. There was never a frost bomb big enough to turn the Lands of Summer that kind of cold. If there was when I was there, Queen Kefyra would've used it."

"Oh." That was disappointing, and frightening.

"Hey, since it's just the two of us, tell me." She lobbed another piece of meat at a whining snapdragon. "How is Lexis doing?"

Her question startled Kelcie. Had she noticed something strange about her behavior too? "Why do you ask?"

"She seems to be struggling. Always off by herself. Never

with her classmates, not even her Den mates. I tried to talk to her, offered her a sympathetic ear, but she wasn't having it. Maybe check in on her for me?"

"Sure." Now Kelcie had an excuse to snoop. "I'll do it today."

Later that afternoon, Kelcie went looking for Lexis, but couldn't find her. She did find one of her fianna mates leaving Hawthorne Field, but the Cat didn't know where she was. He said she only trained with them after class if their Charger insisted, and that wasn't very often, even though they trained every day, hoping to get in to the tattoo. The overexcited Charger tried to defend his leadership, saying something about Lexis being difficult, but Kelcie couldn't hear him over that little voice inside her head that had started screaming. If Lexis wasn't with her fianna every afternoon, then where was she?

The Saiga Den was quiet.

"Anybody here?" Kelcie called from the pool room. "Lexis?"

She walked into their shared bedroom, but it was empty.

"Lexis?" she called, then checked the bathroom.

Finding it empty too, she stared suspiciously at Lexis's locker, abandoned all reason, and closed the door to the bedroom. She would just take a quick peek, she reasoned, to alleviate her fears. Pangs of conscience slowed her pace. *This is so wrong.* Kelcie hated it when people went through her things, which, as a foster kid moving from home to home, they did often, and always when Kelcie wasn't around to stop them from taking anything they wanted. But this was different, Kelcie rationalized. *This is war, and Lexis could be a Winter spy.*

Kelcie combed through her neatly stacked clothes, finding nothing, and then moved to her desk. Opening the drawer, she found the stack of paper provided by Scáthach still tied together, and her pen, meant for writing letters to send through the magical tubes that ran all over the Lands of Summer, still in the box. That wasn't surprising. With her parents dead, she had no one to write letters to. But what if none of that was true? What if Lexis made the whole story up?

Lexis's bed was next. Kelcie checked under her pillows and between her mattress, finding nothing but lint and a dirty sock, and chucked a laugh, feeling all kinds of stupid. This was ridiculous. Lexis was no more a spy than Payton. She was about to leave to practice with her favorite twin swords when she caught sight of a stuffed doll peeking out from underneath Payton's pillow. A picture of Payton's parents was taped to her locker cubby.

And it dawned on Kelcie. There were no personal items of Lexis's in her locker or her desk or on her bed. She didn't have a single thing from her life before. Nothing at all that connected her to her past. No pictures. No books. No keepsake notes from her mother or father. No old clothes except the ones she had on the first day Kelcie met her when they were registered, the same ones she had on when she found Kelcie again the night before she was due to return to the Academy.

That was a big coincidence too, wasn't it?

Worry twisting her stomach, Kelcie decided to check one more time. She sat down on Lexis's bed, intending to recheck everything starting with squeezing the life out of her pillow, and heard a clank. She bent over, looking underneath, and saw a small bowl had been dislodged from wherever it had been hidden. Flat on the floor, Kelcie wiggled under, stretching as far as she could, trying to reach it when she heard the door open.

Kelcie started, banging her head on the box springs.

"What are you doing under my bed?"

Kelcie crab-crawled out and found Lexis glaring down at her with a bottle of Zinger in hand. Her eyes were wider than an angry cat caught off guard by a dog—a small dog from the fearless and feral way they narrowed on Kelcie.

"I dropped my pen and thought it rolled under here, but I can't find it." It was the worst excuse, and by the extremely cynical glower Lexis was giving her, she didn't believe a word of it.

Flustered, Kelcie went to her locker and started to change her shirt. "I would've thought you'd be on the field with your fianna training. That's where they are now, right? I saw them. I just needed to change." Kelcie was rambling like a fool. There was no way Lexis didn't see through her every word. She knew Kelcie was spying on her, suspecting something. And that would leave Lexis on her guard, making it much harder to find out the truth.

Lexis set the Zinger on her desk. "I like to have a little time to myself after class. Is that too much to ask for?"

"No." Kelcie's pulse raced. "It's just that Roswen mentioned to me that she is worried about you."

Lexis's entire demeanor shut down. "So? I'm not here for Roswen."

Kelcie smoothed her clean shirt, and moved close enough that she could look Lexis in the eye. "What exactly are you here for, Lexis?"

"The same as you. To fight for my home. And I don't need to make a lot of friends to do that." Lexis sat down at her desk, and picked up a book off the top of her stack. Her hands were shaking with anger or fear, Kelcie wasn't sure which. "I've got studying to do, unless you plan on interrogating me some more."

"No. Sorry."

But Kelcie wasn't sorry. She walked out of the room, but didn't leave. She crouched in the shadows of the door that she'd left ajar on purpose. Kelcie expected Lexis to look through her things and make sure Kelcie hadn't stolen anything. That's what Kelcie would have done. But Lexis sat in her desk chair, her back to Kelcie, and lifted something out of her pocket—a folded piece of cloth.

Whatever Lexis had in her hands was so important she carried it around with her all the time. Lexis set it on her desk and started to unfold it. Kelcie leaned in to get a better look. This was it, the proof she needed . . .

Lexis's arm raised. A brisk breeze slammed the door shut.

Kelcie's jaw dropped. Either Scáthach had installed an over-zealous air-conditioner since Kelcie left for classes this morning, or Lexis sparked that wind.

16

A WARRIOR'S WEAPONS

THE NEXT DAY, Kelcie and her fianna had little time to trade theories about Lexis. News spread like wildfire that the final decision about the tattoo was going to be announced at a special lunch (special because the teachers were coming), making everyone jittery during morning classes. Kelcie half-expected them to be canceled, but they went on as if it were like any other normal day. And like any other day, Tad Fagan did something to torture Kelcie. Today he opted for a well-placed outstretched shoe that tripped her to beat Kelcie to combat class to get to her favorite swords first.

Those swords had become like second hands to Kelcie. At the beginning, Coach Blackwell had started her on forms and drilled her on technique. When she'd mastered those, they moved into a kind of mirrored sparring, a ballet dance of clanking metal that echoed off the juggernaut walls, blending into a synchronized song that was blissful music to Kelcie's ears. She was good at it, better at it than anything else she'd ever taken up. Each day after practice she hated leaving them behind.

Worse, when Coach Blackwell let them start choosing weapons during class, she was forced to endure Tad Fagan using them.

By the time Kelcie got there today, the mounts were empty, and Fagan had the swords in his grubby hands, spinning them as she came through the door. He faked a jab at her face with the pommel of one and retreated, laughing.

Zephyr poked Kelcie's shoulder. "It's time. You need to cream him."

Kelcie couldn't believe her ears.

Niall nodded, smirking. *Zephyr's right. It won't matter for the tattoo, not anymore.*

Niall was right. The picks were already in. But still, if Kelcie was going to do this, it had to be about her sword skills, not her powers. She only wished there was another pair of those twin blades.

Kelcie snagged a broadsword, and jerked her chin at Fagan. "How about we spar today?"

He flicked a smirk. "So you can set me on fire? I don't think so."

"Oh no. No powers. Just swords. If I knock you flat, you let me use those swords for the rest of the year."

"And what do I get if I knock *you* flat?"

"What do you want?"

He shrugged. "For you to leave school. Along with the rest of your Den."

"Saiga, I have a better solution for you," Coach Blackwell interjected, coming between them. He pulled out another pair of twin swords from behind his back. The blades were slightly curved, like the ones Kelcie had been using, but they were made from a material that was black as the darkest night.

Obsidian.

And there wasn't a nick on them. They looked brand new. The hilts were made of steel, the grips wrapped in black straps, and round red gems were set in the pommels. They were the coolest swords Kelcie had ever seen, next to the one her mother left at the school for her, a sword she hadn't seen since last year when she used it to stab the eye.

Coach Blackwell held them out to her. "Why don't you try these today?"

"Lucky!" she heard from the rafters.

"No luck," Blackwell said dismissively. "Murphy has been training on these while the rest of you lot prance about worrying over a ball."

The swords' size and weight were perfect for her. Kelcie crossed them, tossing Fagan a cocky grin.

"Well? You want a go? No powers."

He hissed a laugh, raising his swords. "Your funeral."

He thrust, but anticipated her counter, leaping backward as the class fanned out in a circle around them.

Kelcie's wrists snapped, the blades spinning at her sides, forming a double flower, a move that had taken her weeks to master.

"Saiga! Saiga! Saiga!" Brona chanted.

Zephyr joined in. Others did too.

"Oh, please," Fagan scoffed at them.

He advanced on her, throwing a combination fake jab and a hard chop. Kelcie faded from the jab, bringing a spinning blade forward on the chop, making contact, sending the sword crashing against the wall.

"Whoops!" Zephyr laughed.

Fagan's shocked face was reward enough. Rattled, he lunged with a two-handed strike, putting all of his weight behind the thrust. Kelcie sidestepped out of the way, and pushed him from behind, letting his off-balance momentum carry him across the room. He slammed into the unforgiving juggernaut so hard the tip of the old sword chipped off.

"Keep a leash on it, Fagan!" Blackwell barked. "What are you? A first year? Get your stance back."

Kelcie let Tad recover before she advanced. Working her swords in tandem, she moved fast, sliding them across her body. He batted her first strike, but the second stopped just short of his heart.

Her lips curled into a victorious smile. "Trick or treat."

He roared, stepping toward her and the tip of her sword.

"What are you doing?" Kelcie retreated, not wanting to hurt him.

"Enough, Fagan. Take your loss with dignity," Coach Blackwell ordered.

Clearly Tad had no dignity. With fire in his eyes, he tried to grab Kelcie in a raging bear hug. She barely ducked in time, tucking into an escape somersault, and came up, calling the sparking word.

"Mistral!"

An airball sent him careening into a row of shields. He slumped, clutching his chest, the wind knocked out of him. "You-you . . . said you weren't . . ." Fagan gasped, trying to force air back into his lungs. ". . . going . . . to use . . . your powers."

As the others gathered around, Tad turned bright red from embarrassment. Kelcie could've easily made him look even more like a fool, but something Coach Blackwell said on the first day of class came back to torment her. As much as she hated to admit it, they were on the same side, and this was her chance to prove it. "Yeah. Sorry about that, but when you get all angry like that, you're pretty scary, big guy. Good match, though. I really enjoyed it. Let's do it again next class, okay?"

He stared at her like she'd grown three heads. "Yeah. Okay. Good match." He rolled over and crawled toward the sword he'd lost.

Admiring classmates swarmed Kelcie, clapping and patting her on the back. Brona raised Kelcie's arm over her head, declaring her the winner. Mortified, Kelcie's cheeks burned. She never liked being the center of attention because it normally led to bad things happening, but this kind of attention, it felt pretty good. Like her classmates actually liked her.

Coach Blackwell retrieved his own twin swords. "Come, Murphy. Let's put on a little show."

"Okay."

They sped through the forms, then moved into sparring while her classmates watched, their mouths hanging open. All of a sudden, Coach Blackwell jumped at Kelcie—a double-strike offensive thrust. With a synchronized move across her body, Kelcie broke them apart. One blocked his strike, lifting his blades out of the way while dipping the tip of her other into position. She raised it beneath his chin for the win.

He laughed, a deep belly laugh that shook the floor. "Well done, you. Well done."

After class, Coach Blackwell called Kelcie to the front of the class, forcing her to wait there while he left the training room. He returned with a kind of scabbard she'd never seen before.

"Those blades are now officially yours."

Her fianna started a humbling round of applause that spread, and took turns touching the shiny black leather harness.

Dismissing class, he helped her adjust the backpack straps, balancing the side-by-side hangers on an angle between her shoulder blades. Kelcie wished her father could see her with these on. She wanted to write him and tell him. The last thing she wrote to him about her training was that she still had no control over her powers and struggled to earn a real sword last year. So much had changed in the past few months, none of which she'd told him. And tomorrow she was going to Summer City, where her father was imprisoned. Not that she would ask to see him. She had resolved to let him go, as her grandmother asked, but it didn't keep her from hoping that one day, she would hear his voice again the way she did last year, before she destroyed the one thing connecting them, King Balor's evil eye.

"Where did these come from?" Kelcie angled the curved blades, sliding them into the scabbards easily, as if this harness had been designed for her.

"From the sword in Scáthach's office. She said it would belong to you when you were strong enough to wield it. I smithed it into two blades because you are strong enough. That other sword was clunky and a waste of good material."

She didn't know what to say. She'd never had a teacher like Coach Blackwell before.

"Thank you, Coach. For everything."

"There is no greater joy for a combat teacher than to get beaten by your student. Hard work pays off, not only in the classroom but in life, Murphy. Now . . ." He picked a stray red jinx off the floor, setting it gingerly on the pile in the basket. "I'm going to be busy for the rest of the afternoon with final preparations for the trip to Summer City tomorrow. But when we return to school, we start again, only this time we'll be incorporating powers. It's time." He grunted a smile, his finger tapping the juggernaut walls. "Good thing Roswen put these up."

Kelcie nodded, an exuberant squeal sneaking out that made Coach Blackwell laugh.

She dashed out of the room, barreling down the stairs, taking them three at a time, and burst through the door, excited for the big lunch. Not looking down, Kelcie stepped on something. Her ankle rolled, twisting painfully, and she crashed to the ground. The points of her new scabbard dug into her back. Kelcie sat up and found she'd tripped on a familiar-looking empty bowl. The one that had been under Lexis's bed. Discarded beside it was the cloth Lexis had taken out of her pocket.

Kelcie's stomach sank. This was too much of a coincidence. Lexis left this here on purpose. And Kelcie could think of only one reason why she would do that. It was Lexis's way of telling Kelcie that she was up to something, and that she knew Kelcie was watching her and didn't care because she was one step ahead of her. And she was right.

17

A WINTER'S TALE

SCÁTHACH ABRUPTLY CANCELED the first years' unit training class. Lexis suspected it had something to do with the travel arrangements, or the choosing of the fiannas for the military tattoo. The school was leaving for Summer City, for the Ascension, tomorrow morning.

Hiding in Rapshider Hall, in the Saiga training space, Lexis drew a long column of water from the pond. She didn't feel like having another run-in with Kelcie. Her time at the Academy for the Unbreakable Arts was at an end.

One more insufferable lunch, and then she would never have to see any of them again. Not that she wouldn't miss some of them. Not Kelcie. Not anymore. But then it was Lexis's own fault Kelcie became so suspicious of her. She accidentally left her boots out for Kelcie to trip on the other night when she returned in a hurry, trying to beat Kelcie back after following her. She'd been so startled at what she'd heard Kelcie and Brona tell their preceptor, about the visit from their mothers, and what they saw happening to the Lands of Summer.

That night, Lexis thought she might have misheard. Crouching in the vines a few feet from the tomb, she only got every other word. But then the next day, Kelcie and Brona repeated the story at breakfast, confirming what she's heard. Now, Lexis couldn't stop thinking about it, and if it had something to do with the Heart of Danu. She wished she'd listened more to her father when he told her the story about the *Croí na Bandia*. The Advisors told her that it was nothing more than an old artifact vital for choosing the next Regent of Summer. Queen Kefyra wanted to steal it to use to bargain with Summer to stop the attacks. Was it possible they were lying?

Because the more Lexis thought about it, it made no sense that Summer's Queen would care enough about an artifact to end the war unless Summer needed it to *survive*.

The water column fell, soaking her.

The door flew open. Roswen stood like a statue staring at the space with her clipboard and axe-pen in hand. "Inspection, and I have to say this will not pass."

"Oh . . ." Lexis broke from her unsettling thoughts, and hurried to the mess of stinky okril stones Dollin had left scattered all over the ground in the Theran space. He really was a pig. "Can I have a sec to clean it up? Please?"

To her dismay, as Lexis started picking up the heavy rocks, Roswen came into the room and knelt down to help her. "I shouldn't be doing this. In fact, I'm not. This is not me . . . ," she hefted a large one, struggling as she shuffled toward her, ". . . piling these blocks. It's all . . ." She heaved it on the pile. ". . . you."

Lexis laughed.

The last piece was on the other side of the room. As Roswen walked toward it, Lexis saw that frightening backplate and panic set in. Was Roswen here and helping her because she was suspicious too? Did Kelcie say something to her?

Lexis rubbed her ankle against the "gift" her changeling, Swappy, had brought her in Chawell Woods and the now finished replica of Niall's bough, both tucked into her sock. After the debacle in Madame Le Deux's classroom, Lexis settled for quartz that she found around Morrow Lake, dying it with berries she snuck from Roswen's garden. They weren't nearly as good a match for the leaves as the crystals would've been, but it was the best Lexis could do.

Carting the last okril stone across the room, Roswen looked at Lexis with a disconcerting, soft expression. "You know I can feel you staring at my backplate whenever I turn around."

Lexis's breath caught. "I, well, I—"

"It's okay. I suppose after last year I should have known students would be gossiping about me. Please don't tell me who told you. I don't like to hold grudges."

Lexis had no idea what she was talking about. No one had said a word to her about Roswen. No one seemed to know she was from Winter originally.

"Can I ask you . . . you know . . . what happened?"

Roswen set the stone down, and turned to face her. "Well, you did in fact just ask me. Will I tell you what happened? I will. It's not something I've talked about here. I don't know why. Maybe because it presents Winter in such a horrible light."

Winter? Her wings being clipped had something to do with Winter? Roswen was lying. No one in Winter would ever clip a fairy's wings. Roswen sat down beside the pond and patted the grass. Lexis joined her, the water's peaceful bubbling pond doing little to calm her nerves.

"Winter isn't horrible, not the people, but their queen . . ." Roswen shook her head. "She's something else. Not that Eislyn is much better. What is it with regency who prefer to live in a constant state of war? Never seeking peace?" She blew out a peeved breath. "Anyway, I don't want it repeated all over the school, but I'll tell you because I trust you."

Lexis swallowed the bitter taste of guilt rising in the back of her throat. "I promise. I won't repeat it."

"See, I have a thing for creatures. Plants, too. I'm a nimble fairy, or at least I was before my wings were clipped. I was a soldier in the Winter armies, not a very good one though. My heart wasn't in it. My real talents lie with animals. I scored a great assignment at Braverwil Academy, a school that is very much like this one, where I cared for the last two surviving wyverns in Winter."

"Wyverns? Wow! What do they look like?" Lexis brimmed with excitement, pretending she'd never seen one before. It had taken every ounce of her willpower to keep from visiting the baby wyvern Roswen had hidden in the Fringe again.

"Beautiful mystical creatures, large featherless wings, dragon-like snouts. They say that there were once two kinds of wyverns, those that breathed fire and those that breathed ice. But the two remaining had no such skill, not anymore."

Lexis knew all this from the libraries at the temple she grew up in.

"I went to the temple in Mezron to read about them in the great libraries." Lexis went still at the coincidence. Roswen didn't seem to notice. She continued, "Once the Abyss was formed, the wyvern population dwindled. One in fifty born survived. Then one in a hundred. And so on until there were only two wyverns left."

"Why?"

"That's what I wanted to know. And so did the Queen. Queen Kefyra was obsessed with the skies being full of wyverns again. I wanted so much to make that happen. I studied and watched the two at the school, tested different food sources, trying to improve their health. It worked a little. They laid eggs."

"They did?" Lexis never knew Potham and Wallace had any babies.

"Yep, but none of the eggs hatched. The shells started turning from blue to gray. They were dying. Then, I got lucky. A pair of the eggs were stolen by a Summer fianna."

"That's lucky?" Lexis laughed.

"Getting there." Roswen winked. "The Queen sent my fianna to retrieve them. We found them, but they were no longer eggs."

"They hatched!" Lexis smiled. That explained the baby wyvern in the Fringe.

"Yes. Both!"

Where was the other one, Lexis wondered, but asked a more pressing question, "Why didn't they hatch in Winter?"

"Getting there too. The two babies were feeding off tall grasses on the shores of the Boline Islands. And they were thriving. Growing bigger and stronger by the day. I saw them take their first flights, and it seemed to me that is where the wyverns were meant to be. And if we took them back to Winter—"

"They would die. You left them in Summer, then?"

"I did, and now the Boline Islands boasts twenty already. They were never going to survive as a species in Winter. I suspect the wyverns once migrated back and forth between Summer and Winter, taking what they needed, when they needed it. The Abyss changed all that. Turns out the eggs needed the warmth of the sun in Summer to hatch, and the grasses in Boline to eat, and they don't grow anywhere in Winter that I know of."

"So you stayed in Summer with them?"

"No. I wasn't a traitor. I loved Winter. I still do. The snow-flakes tickling my nose in a heavy fall. Speed-skating on frozen lakes, when I could speed-skate. But I miss the people most of all." She sighed. "My family is in Winter, and I miss them every day. But when we returned and tried to explain to the Queen what happened, she refused to listen."

Lexis stared at the pond, her chest growing tighter with worry by the second. Roswen said the word *we*. She didn't leave her fianna to die in Summer. The Advisors had lied. But why? The only reason that came to mind made her feel even worse. Because they wanted Lexis to stay away from Roswen. They didn't want her to find out the truth, which led her to the next heartbreaking question. What else did they lie to her about?

"Queen Kefyra promised severe punishments for not retriev-ing the eggs when we left." Roswen reached over her shoulder to touch the plate. "She kept her word. I lost my wings and was banished out of the Lands of Winter for good."

Roswen must've seen the sudden fear grip Lexis, and mis-taken it for pity.

"Oh, don't feel sorry for us. We knew the consequences. We

made the decision together, as a fianna. I can't run anymore like I once did, but Scáthach took me in. Gave me a home here."

"And your fianna?"

"That's the hardest part. I don't know. Queen Kefyra told everyone that they died trying to keep Summer from hurting the eggs, or so I heard. Anything to keep this stupid war going. With the Abyss between us, there are no conversations, no talks to bring peace. Summer acts, Winter reacts. And on, and on. It's a viscous cycle. Too many people have been hurt in this never-ending war."

Lexis frowned at her. "I thought you were training soldiers for Summer here?"

"I am, but it doesn't keep me from hoping that one day the war will end, and I can go home and see my family in Winter."

"I hope so too."

But that hope dwindled. Lexis knew that if she failed, if her fianna failed their mission, Queen Kefyra's threat would be carried out. It didn't matter what the Advisors lied about. Nothing else mattered but the mission. Lexis would never risk her fianna being punished, risk Pavel losing his wings, or Jack and Swappy being banished.

The time had come.

The Ascension was tomorrow, and Lexis was a child of Winter, and always would be.

18

BETRAYED

WHEN SCÁTHACH, COACH Blackwell, and Madame Le Deux sat down at a small private table Roswen had set up only a few steps from the second years, Zephyr's knees started a nervous beat that felt like an earthquake. A pitcher toppled. A plate of roasted meat slipped out of Willow's hand, bouncing off the table, and landed upside down on the grass.

Willow gave Zephyr a harsh glare that sent the Charger on a mission to pilfer the first years. Niall hadn't touched his food. He stared at the teachers' table like he was willing them to get started.

It was weird seeing the teachers sitting and eating. Kelcie never saw them doing either. They had to eat, of course, but the teachers at the Academy always seemed to disappear at sunset and reappear at first period. Except for Roswen, who was a part of the staff, but she always felt like one of them.

Full, Kelcie leaned back in her chair and used Brona's extra quivers under the table as a footrest. Sure the omen would begin when they least expected it, her cousin wasn't going to be caught unprepared. Her bows hung on the back of her chair. Beneath her black sweats was an entire arsenal of daggers and pouches of stolen jinxes. Kelcie didn't see a sidewinder on their walk over, but she was positive she had one of those too.

Kelcie glanced at Lexis every few minutes, keeping a keen eye on her, but she never looked up from her food.

"How long does it take Scáthach to chew a carrot?" Fagan bleated.

"They're doing this to torture us," Dunn figured.

"Not everyone polishes a plate off in five seconds like Chargers. Maybe they don't want to get indigestion," Gabby surmised.

"Who cares about the tattoo. I can't believe the ball is tomorrow!" Delilah gushed.

"I do," Kelcie admitted.

"Me too." Niall grimaced, stressing.

For Kelcie, getting to walk in the tattoo was about helping her clan, about seeing them freed, but it was much more personal for Niall. He was always trying to prove he was as good as everyone else, but what he didn't realize was that he was better. And all of Kelcie's classmates had seen it too, wanting to be his friend. But it wasn't them he wanted to impress. It was his mother. Last year, when Kelcie met Queen Eislyn, she ignored Niall, like he wasn't a part of her family. And then Kelcie had to go and ask him to talk to his mother about Draummorc, making things worse for him at home. If their fianna were chosen, Niall would be marching with the best, and maybe his mother would stop looking at him as if he weren't worthy of her attention.

A constant, irritating clank started from the third-year table. It was Ollie, his fork tapping impatiently and annoyingly on his plate. A second later, the fork flew into Arabel Wasp's outstretched hand.

Striker polished off the meat from the toppled platter, then snuck under the table, setting his nose on Kelcie's thigh, begging for more. The cù sith was a bottomless pit.

"Oh, shoot." A portleberry mini-pie "accidentally" fell off Kelcie's plate, under the table. Striker ate it in a single gulp but still wasn't satisfied. Before she knew what he was doing, he climbed at light speed into her lap, set his front paws on the table, and scarfed down the entire platter of dessert until only one remained because he couldn't reach it.

"Hey!" Zephyr tried to take the last tart, but Striker growled. Zephyr raised his hands. "Never mind. It's all yours."

"Oh no, you don't!" Marta Louisa morphed into a sleek black panther. She jumped on the table, pawing and chuffing to scare him off, but Striker was so hopped up on sugar he tackled her, thinking it was playtime.

Kelcie laughed as a subtle hum began in Befelts Garden. From where Kelcie was sitting, she could see bright yellow monkey flowers waving in the gentle breeze, grunting a lullaby at the afternoon sun. They were horribly off-key, if they had a key, but that didn't matter.

What are you thinking about?

In the soft orange dusk, Niall's purple eyes were lighter than Kelcie had ever seen them before.

"How beautiful Summer is. I hope that my mother's omen doesn't fall on it anytime soon."

She felt his hand bump hers on the table.

Your hair's grown out.

Kelcie tugged on the ends, a little embarrassed. "Yeah, I guess it has."

It looks nice. But I liked it shorter too. The fact that you burnt it off learning to use your powers makes it a memorable length, don't you think?

The butterflies she'd felt all last year around Niall returned with a vengeance, only they were different. Less spastic.

Kelcie smiled. "I think you're right."

As Scáthach stood up, Tad Fagan sounded like he'd sprung a leak.

"Shshshshshshsh! It's time! Finally . . ."

Chairs collectively shifted to face Scáthach.

"Students, as you know, five fiannas will be marching in the tattoo. You didn't make it easy to choose. I have never seen so much hard work and dedication. Perhaps I will suggest to the new Regent, whoever that may be, that they hold a tattoo every year. Let me also say that any amount of arguing over the choices would be unwise. You are all talented. All gifted and all capable, but I could only choose one fianna from each class. Please stand as I call your numbers.

"From the first-year class, fianna two."

Cheers rose at the far end of the first-year table. Payton, Markkus, and Dollin were clapping and swatting a surprised Lexis on the back as she tried to stand up along with the other three in her fianna. Striker rushed over to her, dancing with excitement.

"From the second-year class." Scáthach paused. In that lull, Kelcie noticed Lexis sit down, her chin dipping as she returned to her seat, all the while holding a hand to her pants pocket. Whatever had been wrapped in that cloth was in there. It was the proof Kelcie needed.

Her mind flooding with ways to find out what it could be, she never heard Scáthach say, "Fianna three . . ."

Kelcie, she just called us! Why are you sitting there? Niall exclaimed, jumping up.

"What? Really?" Kelcie ran around the table to give him a hug. "Us?"

"Me too!"

Brona joined in and suddenly they were huddled in a group hug beside the table, except Zephyr. Rising out of his chair, Zephyr dusted off his fingernails on his T-shirt. "Oh yeah! Fianna three! That's us!"

Most of the table was genuinely happy for them.

Fagan groused. "You have to be kidding—!"

Willow stuffed a piece of bread in his mouth to shut him up.

When Ollie's fianna was chosen too, reality hit home. Three Fomorians would be walking in the tattoo, the maximum possible. Three would be taking part in the ceremony swearing allegiance to the new Regent. Her heart swelling with pride, Kelcie thought of her doyen, how happy she would be, and how she would agree with Ollie that it was a sign of the start of a new day for Fomorians in the Lands of Summer.

"Look at how happy she is," Niall said, lifting his chin at the first-year table. Lexis beamed a smile at them. "Maybe she's not a spy, Kelcie. Maybe we've blown all this way out of proportion."

Kelcie's gaze lowered to the bulge in Lexis's pocket. "I really hope you're right."

In the dark right before dawn, Lexis put on the oversized gray clothes she'd stolen her first day in that seaside port she was supposed to be from, Binary Gulch. They would cause less attention in Moon Bay than the bright Saiga colors. She left everything else behind. It belonged to the Academy for the Unbreakable Arts, a school she was never supposed to attend to begin with—a place she never really belonged.

She lifted a bit of lavender she'd picked yesterday from Roswen's garden to her nose for a last sniff. The school was beautiful, colorful, filled with scents Lexis had never smelled before, from flowers and plants that only bloomed in Summer. Lexis hadn't let herself dwell for a second on the omen Kelcie's and Brona's mothers delivered, but holding this Summer bloom, and knowing she was leaving, she couldn't help it. If the Morrígna's omen came to true, the lavender plants that make these beautiful flowers would likely die in the first frost, wouldn't they? And Striker too. Scáthach said he needed to wander under the sun and moon, didn't she? In total darkness, there would be no sun. And what of the baby wyvern? What would happen to the grasses that he ate? And how would more eggs hatch if it turned too cold? What if the Heart of Danu was somehow connected to the omen? Then Lexis would be responsible for what happened to the wyverns and Striker and the flowers, and all of Summer. Lexis sniffed the lavender, the calming scent having the opposite effect as second thoughts lingered.

Failure is not acceptable.

The Queen's warning returned with a vengeance. She dropped the lavender on Kelcie's desk. Whatever the repercussions of stealing the *Croí na Bandia,* there was no way out of this. Not for her, or her fianna. They were waiting for her, and without her, the mission would fail.

I am a daughter of Winter.

Her roommates sleeping peacefully, she leaned over Kelcie's desk. Sweat dripped from her brow, smudging the ink on the paper. Her pulse racing, Lexis pulled out another piece from the drawer.

Using samples from Kelcie's wastebasket, Lexis had practiced her handwriting for the past few weeks. But she was nervous. Terrified, in fact. The time had come to write *the note* to Niall O'Shea, and her hands wouldn't stop shaking.

Nine words. That's all she needed to lure Niall out of his Adder Den. She needed to hurry, or she would never make it out before the sunrise. She took a deep breath and set the pen against the paper. The ink smeared in two places, which actually added authenticity, and Lexis made sure to leave one of the two *t*s uncrossed too.

I found the answer! Have to show you NOW!

She set it in the drawer and closed it as quickly and as quietly as possible. But as the suction carried the letter away, Payton stirred. Kelcie flipped over, mumbling.

Lexis ran out of the room on her toes to be as quiet as possible, focusing only on what was next. Lexis had one shot with the glacial flakes before Niall would use the scream on her, and if he did, it was over.

"Lexis!" Kelcie called.

How had she woken up so fast? Was she watching her? If she was, she would've stopped her from sending the letter. Unless Lexis was walking into a trap. Her knees weakend, but she kept going. *Don't look back.* Lexis lifted the glacial flakes out of her pocket and grabbed the spinning pole.

Five.

She started the count. Five turns and she would be at the top. She cocked her clenched fist.

Four.

She held her breath.

Three.

She felt Kelcie leap on the pole. "Whatever you're doing, don't! Please, Lexis!"

Eyes fixed on the top, she refused to look down.

Two.

Lexis's fianna was waiting for her. If she showed up without the reason she was at the Academy . . . they would be punished.

ONE.

Time slowed to a monumental halt as the door opened and the sound of the Saiga's nasally roar trumpeted her arrival. Niall's head cocked, surprised to see Lexis leap off the pole instead of Kelcie. He'd stopped to wet his hair in a futile attempt to smooth his bedhead that stuck up in the back, splayed like a peacock's tail feathers. Through his glasses, Lexis saw his inquisitive gaze fall on her clutched fist as she landed right in front of him. But by then, it was too late.

Glacial flakes cracked and popped all around his head, his neck already beginning to swell. At the same time her air rope snagged him, making it impossible for him to get away.

Niall fell over, gasping and coughing, his throat growing to three times its normal size, her air rope pinning his arms and legs behind his back. Careful to stay out of his sight line, Lexis freed his fighting hand, forcing his fingers around the unbreakable chain keeping his bough locked around his neck, then she pulled his wrist with all her might.

The snap echoed in the tunnel. Relief lasted for only a second because Lexis was hit with an airball, bowling her off of Niall—ironically in the direction she needed to go.

"Lexis! Stop!" Kelcie raced after her.

The wolfsbane in Befelts Garden howled, declaring it half past five, as she rounded the last turn. Kelcie's fire sailed over Lexis's head, singeing a loose piece of hair. Her desperate rain poured down next, making the ground to the Sidral slippery.

By the time Niall's bough sank into the bark and the trunk split open, Lexis was covered in mud up skidding on her knees, and Kelcie was only a few feet behind her. Lexis forward-flipped into the tree. Kelcie's water whip on its way, Lexis extended a hand, crying, "Caenum," claiming the other end for her own.

Before Kelcie realized what Lexis was doing, the water tightened around Kelcie's upper body, pinning her arms.

Lexis saw Striker's green streak speeding toward them, and heard the sea eagles whistle, sounding the alarm. It was time to go. Her days at the Academy for the Unbreakable Arts were officially over.

All Lexis could think to say to Kelcie as the tree zipped shut was, "I'm sorry."

19

UNTRACEABLE

SHE'S GONE, ISN'T she?"

Out of breath, Kelcie looked back at Scáthach, nodding. But then, she remembered . . .

"Niall!"

The sprint to Haven Hall felt like it took so much longer than the way to the Sidral, every second an out-of-body experience. *He has to be okay! Please! Last she'd seen him . . .*

A strangled cry broke from Kelcie. Her peripheral vision clocked Striker running beside her. She heard Coach Blackwell's voice too, but whatever he said sounded muffled, like she was listening underwater.

The only thing that registered was the sight of Roswen and Madame Le Deux helping Niall to sit up. Kelcie threw her arms around him, knocking his glasses off.

"I thought—!"

Kelcie choked up, refusing to think about a world where Niall didn't exist anymore.

Roswen held up an uncorked bottle no larger than a thimble. "Lexis left the antidote."

Her anger at Lexis waned, but only a little.

Roswen and Scáthach were dressed already, both in armored unitards. They must've gotten up super early. By contrast, Coach

Blackwell was in pin-striped pajamas and Madame Le Deux in a paisley nightgown.

Whimpering, Striker plunked down at Niall's side, on his way to licking Niall's arm.

"I'm okay," Niall reassured Kelcie, or maybe he was talking to Striker. Once upright, Niall leaned on Kelcie's shoulder for support.

"I don't understand. What just happened?"

Kelcie frowned at the red mark on the side of his neck. Whatever Lexis used on Niall had made him forget what she'd taken from him. "She stole your bough, Niall."

Niall's hand flew to his chest, then neck, frantically searching for the unbreakable chain that Lexis had figured out how to break. His fingers brushed the raw red line, and he winced, his fist clenching with fury.

"We need to speak to High Command right away!"

"High Command? About a stolen bough?" Coach Blackwell picked up Niall's glasses and casually handed them to him. "This makes no sense. Why would Lexis do that? She was in the tattoo. It wasn't as if her fianna were at risk for losing their place here. Not to mention, boughs are traceable. She won't get—"

"My bough is *untraceable*!" Niall shouted. "She can now go anywhere in the Lands of Summer through the tubes without being tracked! Kelcie has been right all along. She's a Winter spy!"

"This is it then." Kelcie locked eyes with Niall, and without words saw he was thinking the same thing she was. The beginning of the omen. Kelcie's chest tightening, she looked back, glad to be blinded by the rising sun, a sign that there was still time to stop this.

"Please let me into my Den!" Niall pleaded.

"You can go to mine! Use my desk to send a letter." Kelcie felt a stern hand fall on her shoulder, holding her back.

"If he has any chance of them heeding his warning, it must

be on his stationery." Scáthach stormed under the archway and pressed her hand on the door. The Adder's cobra didn't hiss at her the way it did the students. He coiled and immediately opened the emerald door. "O'Shea, get a letter off to Thorn! Be brief! Enough to get the soldiers stationed at the Sidrals to know who to look out for. Let him know our report will follow momentarily."

"Yes, ma'am." Niall vanished over the wooden bridge beyond the door, running faster than Kelcie had ever seen him run in his life.

Madame Le Deux snapped her fingers, and Roswen, looking annoyed, handed over the mostly empty bottle of the antidote Lexis left behind. The Swords & Sorcery teacher sniffed the contents and ran a finger over the remnants of the red powder clinging to the sides. A thin blond eyebrow arched high, then fell, dipping, like she didn't have a clue what it was.

"Do you have any real proof she's a spy?" Scáthach asked Kelcie. "It would help to give Thorn every bit of evidence we have in order to convince him of the truth. She's only twelve years old."

Before Kelcie could answer, Roswen interjected, looking crestfallen.

"Madame Le Deux is holding it." Roswen tapped a pink nail on the bottle in Le Deux's hand. "I'm reasonably sure that when Styora tests this, she won't be able to identify it. I recognize the gristly texture and spicy minty smell. Ground entropine root. The antidote for glacial flakes, a choking poison, both only found in Winter." She threaded her tense fingers, clasping her hands, wringing them like she was squeezing out a wet towel. "It's not an excuse, but my guess is that Lexis was left with little option."

"Option or not, I don't care!" Kelcie bristled, fury racing through her veins, spinning her powers like a washing machine on the spin cycle. They were ready for action, and so was she.

But after such a dismal performance against Lexis moments ago, doubt slipped in.

Befuddled, Coach Blackwell rubbed his bald head so hard he left red stripes across it. "Why is Niall's bough untraceable?"

"All the members of the royal family have untraceable boughs," Scáthach explained.

"O'Shea? Royal family? He's Queen Eislyn's son? And his sister too, then?"

Scáthach nodded.

Madame Le Deux looked down at her paisley nightgown aghast. "Royal fahmeely? You should've tahld us, Scáthach!"

"No. I shouldn't have. You weren't you last year, were you? Then a Winter spy would have that information."

"Seems they found out anyway," Kelcie blurted.

The preceptor pursed her lips. "We cannot dawdle. Kelcie, I may have been wrong about how much time you and your fianna have."

Kelcie nodded at Scáthach. "Yes, ma'am."

Coach Blackwell frowned. "Timeline, for what? What's going to happen? If this is anything like last year . . ."

"I dahn't like ze sound of zat aht ahll!" Madame Le Deux agreed.

Scáthach ignored the teachers, speaking to Kelcie. "Hope for the best, but *plan* for the worst." She gave Kelcie a confident nod.

Kelcie grimaced. "I think I should go wake up Zephyr and Brona."

"Wise idea. You're dismissed."

Kelcie pressed her bough to the entrance to Haven Hall, listening to Scáthach doling out orders to the teachers while she waited for the Saiga door.

"Roswen, you're with me. We will get the report off to High Command right away. Thomas, Styora, change and be in my office in ten minutes. We have preparations to make before we leave campus, just in case."

Le Deux scoffed, "Ten meenutes? I cahnnaht be ready een ten meenutes."

"Preparations, for what?" Coach Blackwell asked.

Scáthach turned a weary gaze on the rising sun.

"Unending night."

20

SECOND THOUGHTS

"STAY DOWN! AND beeeeee quiiiiiet!"

Swappy's voice sounding like a mer woman was disconcerting enough, but the sheer joy in his eyes when he rubbed the scales on his arms was too much.

Pinched between Jack and Pavel, Lexis shook with laugher.

"Stop laughing!" Jack griped, his face turning beet red. "What is that banging?"

"Lexis is bonking my wings into the side!" Pavel inched closer to Lexis.

Togetherness was one thing, but this bordered on claustrophobic. And the smell! The tarp they were hiding under was smothered with fifty pounds of fish her fianna had caught in Moon Bay this morning.

While Lexis was at the Academy, Jack legally acquired a fishing boat and illegally procured the Lakelands' chancellor's seal. Pavel retrieved the hidden weapons stash. And Swappy went to Summer City to do reconnaissance and returned with tourist maps he used to pinpoint the two most important locations they needed to get to: Mount Joy, the prison where Pavel's aunt Achila Grimes and her fianna were being held, and the Darling Palace, Queen Eislyn's home, and Niall's.

Jack and Pavel then spent their time poring over the map, calculating how long it would take to get from one place to another, backing into the exact time they would need to leave Moon Bay to begin the final phase.

Everything was going according to the Advisors' plan except for one thing: Lexis's overwhelming guilt. Niall's silver bough weighed heavy on her chest, a constant reminder of him and what she'd done to him. What if they didn't find the antidote? He was the enemy. She did what she had to do! She blew out a breath, refusing to dwell on it a second longer, and lifted his bough out from under her shirt to stare down at her prize. A delicate green leaf for his Den at the Academy was only one of seven. There was a leaf for every kingdom's Sidral in the realm, and another for the Sidral at the Darling Palace—exclusive to the royal family.

This bough was the key to victory. Untraceable travel through the Sidrals meant they would be able to get in and out of the Darling Palace tomorrow during the military tattoo before anyone noticed. It was the lynchpin to stealing the Heart.

Sudden screeches crested over the boat.

"Are those . . . they are!" Swappy hollered.

The boat rocked hard to port.

"Swappy!" Pavel griped, rolling his weight the opposite way to balance the boat before it tipped. "What are you doing?"

"Wyverns! And so many of them! They're so pretty! There's a pink one!"

Lexis bolted up, taking the tarp with her.

"I didn't know they had wyverns in Summer." Jack's bewildered gaze dashed from one wyvern to another, tracking them as they tested their wings performing daring figure eights. "Or that they came in so many colors. They're so small compared to Potham and Wallace!"

"Because they're babies!" Pavel fumed. "Born from our stolen eggs!"

"Stolen eggs?" Swappy asked sadly.

"My aunt told me all about a fairy called Roswen who stole

the eggs in Winter and brought them to Summer," Pavel boasted, then spat the word, "Traitor."

"That's terrible." Swappy blinked, his mer eyelids closing sideways rather than up and down.

"That's not what happened," Lexis countered. "I met her. Roswen. She's a teacher at the Academy."

"What did happen?" Jack asked.

Lexis wanted to tell Jack everything she had learned from Roswen, but she couldn't have him or any of them questioning the mission or wracked with worry the way she was about what would happen if they failed. "We don't have time to talk about it right now."

"I'll tell you what happened. Queen Kefyra punished her. Clipped her wings and banished her from Winter forever," Pavel tossed out, sounding pleased at the outcome.

Swappy belched, horrified.

Lexis let out a long, heavy sigh. Pavel was tempting fate and didn't even know it. "It wasn't her fault. None of it was her fault."

Jack gave Lexis one of his confused stares that in the past, she would have caved to, and spilled whatever information she had. But not today. She had to stay strong.

"Be careful, Lexis," Pavel warned. "You're defending a traitor. I wouldn't do that in front of my aunt."

Something had changed Pavel over the weeks they'd been separated, and not in a good way.

"You're a flyer," Lexis said to him. "What do you see when you look at them, Pavel?"

Pavel gave them less than half a second glance, and a dark one at that, but in that time he had to have seen what Lexis did. The baby wyverns circled one another, shrieking gleefully, chasing wings and tails.

Swappy raised his hand. "I know!"

"They're playing," Jack effused.

"Hey! That's what I was going to say!" Swappy groaned. "They're much healthier than Potham and Wallace."

"Because Potham and Wallace are old!" Pavel argued.

"No, Pavel, it's because this is the only place they can hatch and grow strong. The only place they can survive," Lexis explained, giving them a last look. "But . . . we really don't have time for this." She slid under, pulling the tarp over her head. "Grimes, Postal, get down. Now. Swappy, let's get a move on."

She felt Swappy's tail kick the boat onward. Pavel and Jack settled on either side of Lexis. Jack turned to face her.

"There are things you're not telling us?" It was concern she heard in his voice.

His blue eyes bore down on her so intensely she almost broke. Almost.

"Loads of things. A thousand little secrets." She smirked on the outside, but felt sick on the inside. Jack still didn't know he had two cousins, his only family, living in Summer. She mouthed *later* to him. He shrugged away, disliking that answer.

A few hours later, Swappy whistled. It was the signal that they had arrived in Summer City.

"Dock's overcrowded," the changeling whispered into a lifted edge of the tarp. "Must be a million ships out here."

Lexis had anticipated this. Overcrowded with Summerfolk tying off to stay for the Ascension.

An engine roared not far away. Lexis's heart sputtered when she heard a stern voice call, "Halt!" But Lexis anticipated this, too, hoped for it actually.

A nod from Lexis, and Jack pulled the dry cork from the dusty bottle of glamourie out with his teeth. Lexis didn't dare risk stealing another from Madame Le Deux's classroom. Jack had picked it up this morning from the contact he got the glacial flakes from, but they had no idea how long it had been sitting on their shelf. Lexis learned in Le Deux's class that this kind of camouflaging glamourie was made from oil of chameleon and that oil could go bad over time, and shouldn't be trusted past a year post brewing. From the dust on the rim, it had been at least that long.

The push and drag of Swappy's mer tail propelling the boat stopped. Jack quickly poured the potion down the sloped canvas.

Lexis heard the scrape and subsequent clunk of another boat pull alongside theirs, and felt the dead fish being moved around on top of the tarp—whoever it was, dock master or soldier, was searching through them.

"I'm delivering fish," Swappy said.

"I can see that," a deep, bothered voice retorted.

"A special gift from the mer people to the new Regent."

Paper rustled.

Swappy must have handed him the sealed documents from the "Chancellor" of the Lakelands. "Chancellor Marsh asked that it arrive in time to be served at the ball."

"The Chancellor is already at the palace. Why didn't the fish come with his entourage?"

"Um . . . well . . ." Swappy paused, thinking way too long.

Metal scraped leather, the man pulling a sword. Lexis joined Jack and Pavel, tensing, bracing for what was inevitably coming next.

"What's under those fish?"

"More fish!" Swappy said, sounding exasperated.

"Let's see about that."

The blade scuffed along Pavel's wing before diving between Lexis's legs and stabbing the hull. The tip got stuck. A hard yank and the sword retreated, leaving the boat rocking and Lexis cringing at the sting from a fresh cut on her calf.

The sword stabbed again, this time on the other side of Jack. Lexis felt him flinch and squeeze her hand hard. He was hit. Her heart sank. It took all her willpower not to throw off the tarp and blow the guard away from their boat. She had Zinger underneath her, bottles she'd taken from school, but the only way to get to it was to move which she couldn't do without jeopardizing everything. All she could do was hold on to his hand.

"You're butchering the scuttle bottom and they're supposed to be served whole!" Swappy whined.

The sword plunged again and again. Lexis had to do something. She started to move, but Jack gripped her hand harder, reminding her the stakes were too high.

A few more stabs down the other end of the boat, and Lexis heard the guard put his sword away.

"Satisfied?" Swappy shrieked.

"Round the other side. Use the last dock. There's a sign that says for palace deliveries."

Swappy shifted his tail into high gear, jerking the boat roughly to port, and Pavel, Lexis, and Jack along with it. Pavel hissed, shifting his injured wing. Jack cried out, clutching his side.

Lexis reached around him, trying to find where he was hit to put pressure on it. The back of his shirt was soaked. Jack needed help, and he needed it now.

"I have something . . ." Using her feet, Lexis clasped one of the bottles of Zinger and wiggled until she could reach it. She passed it to him. "This is a healing agent they have at the Academy."

Pavel scoffed. "If it's from the Academy, it's probably poisonous."

Jack pushed it back at her. "It's just a scrape."

"Really?" Lexis pressed on his wound, and he yelped. "It's not poisonous. I drank it every day."

"I can tell," Pavel goaded.

The fairy was grating on Lexis's last nerve and she didn't have time to argue with Jack about this either. "If you're hurt, you're of no use to me on the mission. Drink it. That's an order."

He reluctantly cracked the lid and inhaled a whiff. After a few sips, his brow creased. "Wow. I can feel it healing."

Lexis scoffed sarcastically. "Imagine that."

A few minutes later the sun dimmed, and there was a lapping sound on the side of the boat. Voices approached, and the weight shifted; Swappy getting out, Lexis presumed.

"How much longer?" Pavel warbled, scrunching to one side. "My wing has a cramp."

Lexis didn't offer him any of the Zinger, and sadly for Pavel, it was a few minutes before the fish were unloaded and the muffled voices dissipated to clomping footsteps, boots on wooden planks.

Lexis inched the tarp back and panicked at the sight of a man with cropped red hair wearing a strange navy blue uniform, a blazing Summer sun on his tunic, rushing toward them.

"Mistral . . ." Lexis whipped the wind around her hand, preparing to fire.

Blue Uniform's big yellow eyes went blazing wide and he tooted, loudly. "It's me!"

"Nil mistral." The wind settled. She climbed out of the boat first. "What is that uniform?"

"It's from a Sun Guard. Palace security. Spiffy, isn't it?" He rubbed the blazing sun. "And you'll never guess what I just saw! Queen Eislyn in the flesh! She has really pretty brown hair and—"

"Enough!" Pavel tried to sit up, but the edge of his wing got stuck under the lip of the boat. "Lexis! Jack! Get me out of here!"

"Did you hear a *please*?" Lexis asked Jack. "Because I didn't."

Pavel shifted, lowering his wing, freeing it, and shot up, knocking Jack over in the process. Jack growled.

Swappy harrumphed, demanding Lexis's attention.

"Swaps, we don't really care about the Queen."

"But she was coming out of the shrine! Coming out of Rilios! It's right at the top of that staircase! And so is the Sidral!"

"She was coming out?" Lexis felt a sudden rush of excitement. The door was open. They could move up the timeline! They could be home in less than twenty-four hours!

"There's like a thousand guards between the two. And surrounding both," Swappy added gloomily.

"That means they know about the stolen bough you're wearing already," Pavel said to Lexis using an accusatory tone that Lexis did not appreciate.

Lexis shrugged off his ire. "Of course, they do. Niall would've written to them right away."

"You say his name like he was a friend of yours," Jack commented.

"I made friends too," Swappy said.

"You met Summerfolk," Pavel corrected. "They weren't your friends, changeling. If they knew who you were they would've had you arrested."

He wasn't wrong. And if they were caught now, that would be their fate. "We don't have time for this. Rilios is open. And we're going to steal the Heart of Danu tonight."

21

THE COLLEGE OF MYSTICAL BEINGS

KELCIE AND NIALL jumped out of the Sidral in Summer City together. Giving him a ride wasn't a big deal, but it was nice to be able to do something for him for a change. He'd done so much for her last year, all through school. She'd forgotten about that with all the angst during break, and that was unfair of her.

The tree unzipped again. Expecting Brona and Zephyr, Niall groaned inpatiently when Tad Fagan exited. The Charger glowered at Kelcie, then at Niall, and stomped off shaking his head, to the back of the long line waiting to pass through security to get into Summer City.

"What is taking them so long?" Niall huffed.

Kelcie was anxious too. Ever since Lexis got away with Niall's bough, it felt like an hourglass turned over, and the sands were falling away ten granules at a time. Lexis had been at the Academy for months, waiting to strike at the right moment, the day before the Ascension, but how was that relevant to Winter? And what, if anything, did this have to do with the foreshadowing Kelcie's and Brona's mothers had showed them? Lexis was ten steps ahead, and had been for a long while. Every second counted, every grain of sand mattered, and Brona and Zephyr still weren't here.

Brona was probably trapped in the Sidral, being strangled to death by too many quiver straps. She was loaded down with three when Kelcie left and trying to add a fourth.

As they waited, Kelcie noted how the new twin swords on her back were heavier than they did yesterday, as if they somehow felt the weight of the task ahead. She leaned her head back and closed her eyes, soaking up the noonday sun. How could a place packed with this much warmth and sunshine suddenly grow abysmally cold and blindingly dark?

"We don't have time to wait," Niall fretted. "We have to get to the College of Mystical Beings as soon as possible! Let's get a place in line."

Niall believed that the Chief Druid at the College of Mystical Beings would have answers for them about the omen, or could point them in the right direction. At least it was a place to start.

Before they left, Coach Blackwell unlocked the Nether Tower for them to load up on supplies. While Brona secured jinxes to her arrows, Zephyr grabbed a shillelagh and sharpened his sword. Niall overloaded his jinx pouch and oiled the wheel on his sidewinder, both of which presently bulged under his green Adder cloak. Kelcie had only brought her obsidian swords and her father's bracelets because they were her most prized possessions besides the bough her mother gave her.

The duffel bag slung over her shoulder was light, with only a change of clothing for tomorrow. Ahead she could see classmates struggling with multiple suitcases and garment bags as if they were staying for a week rather than a single night. They were lucky. The ball was the *only* thing on their minds.

When Zephyr finally arrived, he stepped in line behind Kelcie, apologizing to the well-dressed troll family of four that he cut in front of, and who were giving him serious dagger eyes.

"Sorry. Fianna, you know? Academy rules."

"Where's Brona?" Niall snipped.

"She's coming. She had to ride by herself. Wasn't enough room for me and her arsenal."

Zephyr hefted his shillelagh and sword higher on his shoulder to pull a letter out of his pocket.

"Is it from your family?" Kelcie asked.

"Yeah. My mother says my father went all the way down to the Chancellor's office. I told him not to do it. I said tell the cousins, who will tell more of our cousins, who will tell their neighbors, and pretty soon, the whole Bountiful Plains would know anyway. But would he listen to me? No. He wasted a day going down there only to be laughed at and tossed out!"

"Excuse me! Parden me! MOVE!" Brona shouted, bumping through the line. The poor troll family was forced to duck as she squeezed between them and Zephyr.

"Is she cutting too?" one of the kids asked.

Brona swung around.

"Sorry. It's—"

"A fianna thing. So we've heard," the mother said, smoothing the waist of her silk dress. She used her fingers to comb the father's furry arm, who was growling under his breath. "It's all right, dear."

"Can I touch your bow?" the kid asked. "You did cut."

"Not unless you want to lose a hand." Brona smirked, giving Kelcie her back. One of her quivers was smoking.

"Brona, your arrows look like they're about to explode."

"Nah. Already did. Yellow jinx went off in the Sidral, but it's all good now."

At that point, the troll mother insisted on letting three other groups in front of them.

The line moved, and Kelcie got her first glimpse of Summer City, or rather the underside of it. The capital sat on its own island that was made of hexagonal black basalt columns, their smooth surfaces reflecting the sun in a way that felt both like a welcome and a warning.

A moving bridge carried visitors to and from the mainland on the biggest escalator Kelcie had ever seen. When her heels landed on the tracks, suction glued her boots to the conveyor belt.

Halfway up, Kelcie worked up the courage to look over the railing. The bay between the island and the mainland was smooth as glass, and tinted green rather than blue. She saw a bustling dock unloading cargo with hundreds of ships waiting for their turn. On the other side, the Emerald Sea lapped calmly. Using her hand to shield her eyes from the rising sun, Kelcie saw creatures circle an island in the distance. Dragonlike beasts, only with two legs rather than four, circled above them, performing barrel rolls that ended with them diving into the sea below.

"What are those?" Kelcie asked intrigued.

"Wyverns," Niall answered, leaning over the railing beside her.

"Wow. Are they friendly? Can you ride them?" she asked, rambling, but he didn't answer. He looked ill. "What's wrong?"

Casper said he and my mother are upset with me about my bough being stolen. His exact words were We need to have a conversation when you arrive. Niall rubbed his neck where Lexis had cut him when she tore off his bough. *I have a feeling there might be palace guards waiting for me at the top.*

"We'll give them the slip. With so many of us from the Academy, they'll be looking for your Adder green cloak. Swap cloaks with Zephyr and put these in your pocket!" Kelcie removed his glasses and held them out to him.

He squinted. "I won't be able to see very well."

"Do you want to get caught?"

It took a little convincing for Zephyr to agree to trade cloaks with Niall, mostly because Niall's Adder cloak only hung to his belly button, but by the time the escalator neared the looming archway in an otherwise endless wall that circled the island, Niall looked much less identifiable, at least from afar.

Ravens and Cats in panther and lion familiars patrolled the top of the wall. Other soldiers manned sleek tubular cannons resembling howitzers parked every few feet.

"Deckwinders," Niall explained. "Like massive sidewinders. They can stun a fairy out of the sky from a mile away."

Piercing cries rang out, stealing Kelcie's attention. They came from prehistoric monsters perched on the flat roof of every watchtower.

"What. Are. Those?"

"Ellén Trechend!" Zephyr exclaimed. "Wow! Never seen one up close before."

Ellen? They certainly didn't look like any Ellen Kelcie had ever met.

Twenty feet tall with long, thin, featherless bodies and leather-skin wings, they resembled pterodactyls except they had not one, but three identical vulture-shaped heads. Their hooked beaks, that were as long as Kelcie's body, were strapped closed by steel bands.

"Why are they muzzled?" Brona asked.

"Because they scare the tourists." Niall looked at Kelcie. *Fire-breathers.*

Kelcie laughed. "You say that like that's the only thing that's scary about them."

After passing through the opening, the escalator leveled out, forming a moving sidewalk that brought them into the bustling city. A sprawling metropolis, it consumed every nook and cranny of available space stopping three-quarters of the way up a huge hill. Perched at the top was a brilliant yellow structure with a tower that rose hundreds of feet into the air.

The Darling Palace, Kelcie presumed.

A squadron of Ravens in a V formation dipped over the moving sidewalk. Rising up and over the wall, they performed a synchronized U-turn, returning for a second pass.

Brona watched them closely as they zipped past again.

"I bet they're searching for Lexis." She tapped Kelcie on the shoulder. "Was she registered in Chawell Woods?"

Kelcie nodded. "They scanned her face and logged her information."

Were you? Niall asked, sounding contrite.

Kelcie nodded again.

His hand brushed against hers. *I'm sorry.*

"*You* have nothing to be sorry for," Kelcie said.

In a small park on the left, Kelcie spied two uniformed guards speaking to Roswen as she waved students over. The blazing suns adorning their blue tunics made them stick out like a sore thumb.

Kelcie subtly elbowed Niall. "Behind you. Those the palace guards?"

He gasped and put his back to them.

Yes.

AUA students hopped off in droves, leaving them exposed. Niall and Kelcie pushed Brona and Zephyr, spinning them away from the guards and Roswen to face the bustling shopping area.

From too close Kelcie heard Roswen say, "O'Shea got on with this lot."

"Move! Now!" Kelcie grabbed Niall's hand and started shuffling sideways, bumping into other riders.

"Excuse me," Kelcie said.

"Pardon me," Niall apologized.

Zephyr stepped on a man's foot.

"OW!"

Zephyr cringed. "Sorry . . ."

"You have to be kidding me! Move, people!" Brona barked.

Around the next corner, the walkway shimmied onto a street of one-size-fits-all adobe buildings made of cool white clay with colored windows and shiny red doors. Everything looked recently built, not a bit of graffiti or chipping paint anywhere.

Go! Niall jumped off the tram.

Running after him, Kelcie tripped over the raised tips of a mer man's tail, skip-hopping like a clumsy frog, about to crash-land on the pristine sidewalk, and yelped way too loudly.

"Is that them?" Roswen bellowed. "Fianna three! Chike!"

Zephyr caught her by the back scabbard. "So much for changing cloaks! Run!"

They did, like their lives depended on it, sprinting through street after street. As the streets clogged with more and more tourists, they were forced to slow down, and did their best to get properly lost in the throngs of bustling shoppers buying up tacky Ascension T-shirts with shadow drawings of the Queen.

"In here . . . quick!"

Niall hustled them into a skinny alley. He peeked out, and gasped.

They're right there!

"Niall O'Shea!" one of the palace guards shouted bitterly, and much too close for comfort.

Zephyr waved them to the end of the alley, behind a massive garbage receptacle.

"Where did he go?"

"How should I know? This one is always causing problems."

"The High Guard will have our heads if we return without him. That's what he said."

Kelcie's heart was pounding so hard she was surprised they couldn't hear it. Niall squeezed her hand, which he probably thought would help, but it only made it worse.

"I know that's what he said. I was there! That teacher probably pegged the wrong fianna. They're all trying to bust loose with a day in the city. Come on. Let's try the barracks."

Zephyr waited a count of ten before tiptoeing to the end of the alley to make sure the coast was clear.

"We're good," he said. "Let's go."

Hustling through the crowds, they crossed the street to avoid a panther bomb-sniffing bags, and gave a wide berth to a sniveling ratlike man in a dizzying pinstriped suit who was cornered by frenzied gamblers all vying to place their bets on who would be the next Regent.

"This way," Niall panted, putting his glasses back on.

He skated through several more alleys—all of them constantly checking over their shoulders—then turned on a residential street heading uphill. Sunlight beat down on them as they trudged a steep slope of never-ending townhouses stretching as far as the eye could see.

Kelcie's legs burned. Between heaving breaths, she asked, "How much farther?"

"Almost there . . ." Niall said, exchanging cloaks with Zephyr.

But they weren't almost there. He led them to another street that was more of a walkway between the houses. There was no sign of a building big enough to be a college anywhere in sight.

"It doesn't seem like we're almost there," Zephyr said, out of breath.

"Niall, how does your mother know that Regan is Regent?" Brona asked.

Niall shrugged. "I don't know."

"Have you ever been around the Stone of Destiny?" Zephyr pressed.

"No. The Shrine of Rilios, where it's housed, only opens with the reigning ruler's death or if they grant permission for a new Regent to ascend."

"Weird," Kelcie commented.

"I always thought so, but my mother has been calling her that in private for a long time. Since I was five, just after the big fire."

"Maybe the shrine was damaged and Regan got inside and touched the stone," Brona speculated.

"Possible," Niall chimed. "I don't remember too much from the days after the fire. I think I've blocked them out."

Kelcie suddenly felt ill. She was walking through the city that her father burned down nine years ago. That's why every building she'd seen looked brand new. And her father was somewhere in this beautiful city, locked in a prison cell that looked bleak in her mother's visions, a place she could never visit even if she wanted to, and she did want to, more than anything.

When Niall declared they had arrived, and Kelcie saw the pristine round limestone building housing the College of Mystical Beings, she knew it was no exception, that it too had been rebuilt after the fire.

"You think we're going to be able to find an answer to our question in a book somewhere in there? It will take years," Zephyr stressed.

He was right. It was the size of a football field.

"We'll have help."

Niall hammered the large, round knocker on the College's arched metal door. On the third try, the door cracked open. A thin old man in golden robes, with his gray hair tied off at the base of his neck, poked his head out. He had wire-framed reading glasses on the end of his nose that peered down at Kelcie first.

"Oh. Hello," he said, surprised, then his squint shifted to Niall and he smiled warmly. "Niall, my boy! It's good to see you!"

He swept Niall into a hug.

"It's good to see you too, sir."

"Look at that uniform. Your mother must be so very proud of you."

"She does love the uniform," Niall uttered. "Can we come in?"

"Why, of course!"

He greeted each of them with a nod and a merry twinkle in his soft orange eyes.

As she entered, Kelcie craned her neck, trying to take in the massive library. The domed cathedral ceiling was made entirely of gold. Sun streamed through small windows, creating checker-board patterns on the polished wooden floor.

The interior was hollow and twenty stories high. Bookshelves stretched from floor to ceiling along the walls. Others wearing the same golden robes as the old man were seated at desks on every floor. Pens halted momentarily while they inspected the new arrivals, then returned to their work, the sound of scratch-ing stick pens on parchment echoing through the voluminous chamber. Large wolfhounds napping on couches tucked against the edges of the first floor ignored them completely.

"Pathetic guard dogs if you ask me," Brona noted.

"They have no need to guard against friendly visitors," the

old man said. He opened his arms wide. "Welcome, Niall's young friends. I am Esras, the Chief Druid here at the College of Mystical Beings, a place of learning for all who want to learn. These are Summer's army of scribes. We boast the largest collection of historical documents, ancient artifacts—"

Indignant shrills raining down from all floors cut him off. Neon-colored flying insects the size of a dragonfly zoomed out from behind the many relics seated between the books. Bobbing antennae glowing like tiny headlights tilted downward—at Esras.

Wincing, Brona slapped her hands over her ears. "Make them stop!"

But they didn't stop. The chorus rose in pitch and volume as a particularly vexed one buzzed Esras's ears, landing on the bridge of his glasses over the end of his nose. The sharp barb at the end of its tail dipped in a threatening manner.

Zephyr went to swat it, but stopped short, then gave Niall a look of sheer terror. What exactly did Niall tell him?

"Don't threaten me with the Tiniest Speck!" Esras shook his fist angrily. "I show her enough respect. Now you show me mine and get back to work!"

Solid black eyes narrowed, then the teeny-tiny, yet utterly terrifying menace sped off.

"What was that thing?" Kelcie asked.

"Speck," Niall explained. "The only fairykind in Summer. They're in charge of the antiquities."

"Yes, yes. In charge, indeed," Esras rasped. He bent over and whispered, "Greedy little buggers. We used to fight with them about which of the ancient relics belonged to whom. Regrettably, my predecessor finally gave up and merged their hive with our college after the structure was rebuilt."

"Regrettably?" Zephyr asked nervously.

"Touch anything they deem theirs, and they swarm like a pack of mire wasps." He arched his back, standing tall, and rubbed on his pointy chin. "Now . . . where was I?"

"Largest collection of . . ." Scowling at the Specks, Brona stopped there.

"Yes . . . of course, and books. Largest collection of books in all of the Lands of Summer. Now, although I'm always happy to see you, Niall, and your formidable-looking fianna, I would've expected you to be busy with all the festivities going on this evening and tomorrow."

"We need to do some research."

"School project?"

"Not exactly," Niall said. "An omen."

"A bad one," Zephyr whispered.

"What *kind* of bad omen?" Esras cleaned his reading glasses with the edge of his sleeve. "A spider fall in your stew? A swan's feather tickle your ear? A hare cross your path before sunrise?"

"Worse," Kelcie droned.

"What could be worse than the ill wishes that come from an irate rabbit?"

"Our mothers came to visit us at school," Brona answered, gesturing to Kelcie.

Esras laughed heartily, returning his glasses to the tip of his nose. "I know at your age sometimes parents can feel like a bad omen—"

"Those mothers being Nemain and Macha, two of the three Morrígna," Niall clarified.

Scribes' pens on all floors stopped scribbling. That was followed by a flurry of rustling paper, along with heads tilting to listen, as if a new epic tale were about to unfold and they didn't want to miss a word of it.

Esras's mouth fell open like a codfish. "What?" His orange eyes thinned. A smile of admiration curled through blissful shock. Pressing his hands into praying palms, he bobbed them from Kelcie to Brona. "I am standing before two daughters of the Morrígna? Why didn't you tell me they were coming?" he chastised Niall, pushing him out of the way to get a better look at the girls. "Do you know what this means?"

"It means something?" Kelcie braced for the worst.

"Well, no, I mean, it's such a pleasure." He shook his head. "Or maybe not a pleasure, but at the very least a pivotal moment in time!" He drilled a finger into the air, and scribes scribbled that down. "One I will never forget—meeting you both, that is." He bellowed that last bit.

"Niall, tick-tock," Zephyr reminded.

"Right." Niall introduced them. "This is Brona Lee. Her mother is Macha, her father is Tao Lee, sometimes known as the Chameleon."

"No better finder of rare antiquities than Tao Lee." Esras shook Brona's hand erratically, moving her all over the place.

"Don't bounce her too much. Her arrows are jinx loaded," Zephyr warned.

"Ah yes, a daughter of strategy would know to do that," Esras exclaimed, cautiously releasing her hand.

"And this is her cousin, Kelcie Murphy. She is the daughter of Nemain and Draummorc."

"Draummorc?" he gasped, yanking her forward to stare into her eyes. "Oh my. That is interesting . . ."

Esras hooked his arm through Kelcie's, then Brona's, and dragged them farther into the library. The boys trailed along behind them.

"And I'm Zephyr Chike by the way, the Charger of this fianna!" Zephyr offered, but was ignored completely. "It's like we don't exist anymore," he said to Niall who shrugged in agreement.

"Do you know that there hasn't been a Danann birth in thousands of years? And for one to be Fomorian born, that is an omen of astronomical proportions in itself. Tell me, what kind of omen are you two?"

"Mostly bad," Zephyr tossed out with a chuckle.

"That's why we're here," Niall commented.

Esras stopped beside the column in the very middle of the tower and they gathered around him.

"Our mothers showed us images of the Lands of Summer in impenetrable darkness, as if the sun, moon, and stars ceased to exist," Kelcie explained.

"Every kingdom in the realm frozen over," Brona added. "Despair, and then death gripping every part of the realm."

A woman at a desk a few steps away paled and shivered, then wrote what they said down.

"Showed you? You saw them—in the flesh?" Esras aimed a firm finger at the woman. "Are you getting this down?"

"Yes, Esras! I . . . I am . . . !" She flourished her pen with wild abandon, and when she was finished, made a show of pressing it to the parchment, waiting for what came next.

"Do you have any idea of what could cause something like that to happen?" Zephyr asked.

Niall suggested, "Maybe point us to a text that might detail another time in the history of the Lands of Summer when something like that occurred?"

Esras thought for a moment, started to say something, then shook his head dismissively. The crease between his brows cratered. "I'm afraid I can't think of anything where Summer has entirely frozen over. There have been many recorded events where Winter spies have infiltrated Summer, primarily changelings and ice fairies, and have successfully dropped blizzard bombs and frost rockets."

Brona scoffed. "The damage our mothers showed us was way beyond a silly little blizzard bomb. It was game-changing. Life-ending. Completely catastrophic!"

"The darkness was all-encompassing. Do they have a weapon that can block the sun, and the moon, and the stars? So not a stitch of light can get through?" Kelcie asked.

"The sky completely?" He gave a small placating smile. "A weapon, not that I know of. Eclipses block the sun and the moon, my dear, and from a historical point of view, rather frequently."

He tapped his chin, eyes scanning the massive number of volumes overhead.

"Not to put too fine a point on it, but this could happen any second!" Zephyr emphasized. "I mean no pressure, but yeah. Any second."

Esras pursed vexed lips. "Well, then let's see what we can find."

He left them to speak to the woman sitting at a secretary-style desk, who proceeded to furiously scribble down Esras's instructions. Placing the note in the drawer, she closed it silently, as was the custom in every library Kelcie had ever been in. But as soon as the slurp of the suction tubes carried it away, chaos broke out at the College of Mystical Beings. It began with a cacophony of dings.

Scribes on all levels yanked drawers open, hopped out of their seats, then flooded the shelves, combing through the volumes. Books were rushed to the first floor, and neatly stacked on top of a nearby table with four chairs.

Niall grabbed the first one on the stack and passed it to Zephyr. "We better get started."

Kelcie took a leather-bound book that weighed half as much as she did and plopped down on a comfy brown sofa beside a wolfhound. Hearing the dog's loud snores made her miss Striker. He had had to stay at the Academy. Scáthach needed him to help watch over the school while they were gone. Brona joined Kelcie while the boys spread out at the table.

After two hours of scanning every volume in the stack, and a trunk of additional scrolls the scribes thought might contain something helpful, they found nothing. Kelcie groaned her disappointment while stretching to standing.

"My sentiments exactly." Niall closed the trunk's lid.

Zephyr and Brona passed off armfuls of books to the waiting scribes for reshelving.

Esras journeyed down from the upper floor. "Nothing?" he sighed. "Nothing at all?"

"The closest thing we could find was in the Otherworld year 2354. An eclipse blocked the sun for more than five hours. The cause was later found to be gas emissions from the obsidian mines in Dorrga Verge. But that hardly seems like it would be life-ending." He sounded as defeated as Kelcie felt.

"What do we do now?" Brona worried.

"We need to get to the barracks," Zephyr insisted. "We're long overdue."

"Not yet. We have one last possibility. The artifacts . . ." Niall looked at the Chief Druid with grim determination. "We have to consult the Tiniest Speck."

Esras sucked in a sharp breath. "You know what she's like!"

Speck antennae zapped beside the table. At first, Kelcie thought they were laughing at them, but they appeared to be transmitting to other Specks as the noise rose through the stacks, all the way to the very top, until the entire room buzzed like it had been invaded by cicadas.

The angry Speck that Esras had words with earlier returned to the bridge of Esras's glasses. Its antennae glowed in anticipation of groveling, or something much worse, judging by Esras's wringing hands. Kelcie tapped Niall on the shoulder.

"Are you saying we have to deal with those things?"

"I am."

Brona glared around the room at the Specks. "It'll be fine. I can outfly them."

"No, you can't," Esras bristled with worry.

Zephyr lifted out his shillelagh. "They come near me with those giant stingers, I'm using this."

Kelcie leaned in to listen as Esras whispered in Niall's ear.

"Do you even have anything to trade?"

Niall adjusted his falling glasses. "I'm hoping it won't come to that."

"What's he talking about, Adder?" Zephyr asked.

"The Tiniest Speck only gives information in exchange for

a relic she values so dear she cannot live without it," Niall explained. "But all of the Lands of Summer will fall to this fate. She will have to see reason. Won't she?"

Esras frowned. "I highly doubt that. More likely you four will end up with a thousand stings. I'll have to be the one to inform Scáthach you won't be coming back to school—ever!"

22

THE TINIEST SPECK

THE TINIEST SPECK lived at the very top of the College of Mystical Beings, tucked away in an attic beneath the dome of the cathedral ceilings. The climb to reach her began with a thousand steps, after which Kelcie was out of breath and her legs were screaming to stop. She scooted away from the railing on the small ramp, pressing her back against the curved wood afraid to look down. Niall ran his hand along the dirty banister, scattering dust, making Kelcie sneeze. And sneeze. And *SNEEZE*.

Zephyr reeled away from her. "Any more coming?"

Kelcie shook her head. "I always sneeze in threes."

"That's a very unlucky number," Esras mentioned.

Kelcie hocked a laugh. "How surprising."

Having flown up, Brona changed into her human form, invigorated and raring to go. "Why does the Tiniest Speck live way up here?"

"She doesn't like to be bothered by anyone, not even her own kind." Esras wheezed. "She does not take kindly to any sort of disrespect. Kneel before her. Try not to look directly at her. Ask with reverence, or risk more than just her refusal to help. She, like the rest of her hive, have quick tempers."

The Chief Druid knocked once. He paused with his ear

against the door, waiting for an invitation to enter. When none came, his hand settled on the knob and he slowly opened it.

No larger than a coat closet, the dim room was empty except for a dollhouse-sized modern mansion straight out of Hollywood. Beside it was a miniature patio with a tarnished bronze bowl for a pool. Teeny-tiny bottles cooled off in teeny-tiny coolers next to teeny-tiny flower arrangements on teeny-tiny tables. It seemed like the Tiniest Speck was having a teeny-tiny party.

The frosted glass front door swung open.

"Get down!" Esras played whack-a-mole, bonking the tops of their heads.

Kelcie's knees hit the wooden floor, but she risked a peek and wasn't disappointed. The Tiniest Speck certainly lived up to her name. No larger than Kelcie's pinkie, she wore a black silk dress with slits for her teeny-tiny wings to stick out, long strands of white pearls, and a silver crown that sat crookedly above her two glowing red eyes.

She sashayed toward them, her barbed tail swishing crossly. "You bring students from the Academy to speak to me?" With a jarringly deep voice, she sounded like she swallowed a frog. "Can you not see I'm having a party?"

"Oh, when does it start?" Kelcie asked.

The Tiniest Speck launched at her, wings whirling like a weed whacker. Kelcie's first instinct was to bat her away, but that was how she got stung the last time. Instead, she did what her old caseworker, Elliott Blizzard, had told her to do, and stood perfectly still.

"What do you mean? It's already started. It's a party for one. Now get out!"

Esras cleared his throat, garnering her attention, and a teeny-tiny glower.

"What?" she rasped.

"They bring an omen of death for the Lands of Summer, delivered by the Morrígna personally—"

"Death?" She blinked, red eyes narrowing. "What is this omen?"

"If I may?" Zephyr asked politely, bowing lower.

She flew over to him and smiled wryly. "Oh, you may . . ."

Keeping his eyes on the pool party, Zephyr launched into the story, explaining what Kelcie and Brona bore witness to, his hands clenched the entire time, and then he finished by asking a question. "Do you have any idea what could cause something like that to happen?"

"I do. And I can help you. For the right price." The Tiniest Speck floated to Kelcie, her exuberant red stare landing on Kelcie's bough. "That goes to the human world."

"It does, but . . ." Kelcie tucked it beneath her cloak. "I can't— it's all I have."

When she was in the human world, it was her link to her past. The only thing she had from before she was abandoned. That all changed when she discovered it was a key. A key to transport trees in and out of the Otherworld. But now it was so much more than that. It was the key to her Den at school. The key to get her to and from the Academy, and the key that brought her to her grandmother.

She could offer her the bracelets her grandmother gave her, but they were only worth something if you could smelt metal, and way too big for the Tiniest Speck's wrists. Then there were her swords, a prize she'd worked so hard for, and only ever used once, but if it meant saving the Lands of Summer . . .

Kelcie pulled them out, feeling her heart go with them. "What about these?"

She put on a show, spinning them at her sides, coming to a halt, crossed blades pointing up, right in front of the Speck, who wrinkled her pointy nose.

"No."

Brona offered up the new bow her father had bought her last year. "It's Troll-made."

"NO!" she croaked, sounding like a foghorn.

When that didn't work, Brona tried her mother-of-pearl-handled dagger. The teeny-tiny Queen dismissed it with a teeny-tiny wave.

"It's the bough or you can all leave."

Niall, who had been abnormally quiet, raised his hand. "We were hoping, given the dire circumstances, that you would want to help us. As you heard, the College of Mystical Beings will be in as much danger as all of Summer."

"Given the dire circumstances, so that I may have hope for a future? Is that what you offer me? Silly boy. I cannot sell hope. Or eat hope. Or drink it. I have no use for hope. Or wishes or dreams. The only thing I want is that one's bough."

This was so unfair! Why should Kelcie have to give up something that means everything to her in order to save the Lands of Summer? She had so few possessions that mattered to her, but then, she glanced at Niall, Brona, and Zephyr, all of whom were shaking their heads at her, and knew that even those things, her bough included, meant nothing to her without the people in this room. Without her grandmother and Striker. Her teachers. And her father. So she was wrong. To save all of them, to save the Lands of Summer, she would give up her most prized possession because it was where she belonged. It was home. And without knowing what would cause the impending doom, they had no way of stopping it.

Kelcie, no!

Kelcie peeled her fingers off her bough. The branches and yellow leaf to her Den left their imprint on her palm. She traced the lines, despondent, then stood up. "You can lead us to the information?"

The Tiniest Speck smirked, a victorious twinkle flashing in her eyes. "I can."

Niall's head whipped to Zephyr.

"Have to agree with O'Shea. I don't think so, Saiga. We should go." Zephyr scooted backward toward the door, grasping

Kelcie's scabbard, forcing her to back up with him. Brona and Niall followed Zephyr's lead. "Thank you for the . . . hospitality."

"I want that bough!"

The Tiniest Speck zipped behind Kelcie, screeching in her ear so loudly it felt like a needle stabbed in the eardrum. The bough strap jerked and twisted, and the next thing Kelcie knew, she was being choked by it.

Niall fired his sidewinder. The Tiniest Speck ducked, but Esras didn't. The Chief Druid's lower lip trembled, and then he fell apart, curling into a ball, sobbing like the end of Summer was already here.

Brona and Zephyr swatted at the speck, only making things worse. Kelcie's eyes bulged. She wrapped her fingers under the strap, drawing in a much needed breath, before the Speck tugged again.

"Why won't it come off?" the Tiniest Speck ground out.

"It's an unbreakable strap. Only Kelcie can take it off," Niall shouted. "Now let her go!"

The Tiniest Speck did no such thing. "I suppose you'll have to be dead then for me to get it off you." Electric pulses cracked between her antennae.

"Noooooo . . ." Esras grabbed Zephyr's shillelagh. The next thing Kelcie knew, the strap around her neck loosened, and the Tiniest Speck hurled across the teeny-tiny patio, splashing down in the pool.

Before they could make a break for it, a thousand Specks blasted through the doorway, instantly surrounding them. Stingers shifted forward, and fired without warning, spiraling in all directions. Zephyr dove for cover behind the mini-mansion, taking Brona with him.

Kelcie whipped the wind as best she could, trying to keep the Specks away from her and Niall, but her air shield wasn't wide enough and there were too many of them. It started as a tiny pinprick in her shoulder. But before she could rip out the stinger, she lost all feeling in her arm. It was completely numb! Having never sparked one-handed, Kelcie's confidence took a nosedive.

Niall yelped. His sidewinder skidded across the patio, taking down tables, spilling coolers, then went off accidentally. The teeny-tiny fairy queen barely made it out before the jinx turned the pool into a gelatinous blob.

The Tiniest Speck commanded, "Kill the Adder!"

The Specks surrounded Niall. Every stinger pointed at his heart. That many stings could very well stop it beating.

"No! Please! Stop!" Kelcie stepped in front of him untying the strap to her bough with her good hand, and dangled it before the teeny-tiny Queen. "Call them off! If you lead us to the answer we're looking for, then it's yours."

The Tiniest Speck's antennae zapped victoriously. The horde pulled back, still hovering too close for comfort.

Kelcie...

Niall whispered her name like an apology.

"I thought you'd see it my way." A clap of her teeny-tiny hands, and her Speck legion surrounded their Queen. "Make sure they don't get lost along the way..."

She zoomed out the door, leaving a long Speck trail that went all the way to the very bottom of the tower, right back where they started, but she didn't stop there. She zipped down a spiral staircase to a dank basement with low arched ceilings and countless shelves filled with dusty scrolls, stretching as far as the eye could see.

Kelcie felt Brona, Zephyr, and Niall looking at her the whole way, but she couldn't bring herself to look at them—to see them feeling sorry for what she was about to do, about to give up. Besides, there was nothing to say. Kelcie had no second thoughts. Not one. It was the right thing to do no matter how much it hurt.

Feeling came back in a rush in Kelcie's arm. The sting must have finally worn off. Esras too seemed to be coming out of the jinx hysteria, taking long double breaths from weeping so hard. At the far end of the basement, a lock clicked, then a door swung opened.

"This way!" The Tiniest Speck raised a tiny lantern. A little squeak, and the wick inside it ignited. "What you're looking for is down here."

"That's impossible," Esras roared, sniffling. "That is nothing but a dead end."

Before he finished speaking though, she was long gone. Her entourage inched closer, pressuring them to continue.

"The stairs must lead somewhere," Zephyr tossed out.

"To an old, cold cellar once used for food storage long, long ago. A remnant of the old college. It's completely empty," Esras insisted.

"Do you think it's a trap?" Niall asked him.

"It could very well be, young man."

Brona arched a conspiratorial brow. Loading her bow with an arrow that had a green jinx mounted on the head. "Charger, may I go first?"

Zephyr hooted a laugh. "If that thing does what I think it does, by all means . . ."

Confused but slightly comforted that her cousin had a plan, Kelcie traipsed after Brona, bumping down a thin set of stairs carved into the jagged stone walls. Esras wasn't wrong. The storage space was empty except for three similar lanterns to the Tiniest Speck's, lit and hanging from the ceiling. The Tiniest Speck croaked for her minions, and the Specks buzzed past them, disappearing through a four-inch crack in the corner, wasps returning to their nest.

Esras gasped. "Where did that hole come from?"

The Tiniest Speck's glowing red eyes danced with mischief from the sliver.

"Between the walls belongs to Speck, Esras. It has since we moved in."

"You moved into the walls?" Clutching his chest, Esras's agitated glare floated around the room. "That is very disconcerting."

"Handsome Charger, make use of all those pretty muscles and open the tunnel wider for you and your friends."

Zephyr crossed his arms, hugging himself. "Why do I suddenly feel exposed?"

"Because that tiny queen has a tiny crush on you." Brona winked, goading him. "She does have a nice house. A little small for all those big muscles—"

"Stop right there," Zephyr warned as he walked toward the gleaming Speck.

A half-hearted kick and a slight tug from Zephyr, and rocks scattered across the floor. Two feet high at the most, the tunnel beyond was too small for them to enter.

"Perhaps not the best plan. Wait there. We will bring it to you," the Tiniest Speck ordered.

Esras lowered to the floor, stuffing his head into the tunnel, and screeched. "These artifacts belong to the College, Speck! We merged . . . uh oh!"

Esras shot out, making way for twelve straining Specks, six on each side, lugging a six-inch-thick piece of slate toward the hole. They turned it sideways to get it out, Zephyr jumping in to lend a hand. He set it against the wall with little effort.

Kelcie lit her finger and knelt in front of the stone. Her fianna crowded around her. Niall used the end of his cloak to wipe off a thick layer of dust. The slate beneath was so blackened from age that the only thing Kelcie could make out was a sketch in the very center. Delicate feminine hands gracefully parted down the middle cradling rays of sunshine. Niall made a reverent sound beside her, as if it had some meaning to him, but didn't say anything. He traced the outside of one of the hands.

"What does that mean?" Zephyr asked him.

Before he could answer, the Tiniest Speck croaked, "It's not important. Turn it around."

Brona, still holding her loaded bough, kicked it over. On the back was a series of pictographs. Many languages in the human world were constructed with pictographs. From ancient Egyptian and Sumerian to modern Mandarin, Japanese, Hebrew, just to name a few. Kelcie had never studied any of them, but as she stared at the vertical rows, her mind auto-translated like it had in the past when she heard Fomorian. She was reading it . . .

"That's Ancient Fomorian," Esras said, confirming what Kelcie figured out. "Older than even Ogham. No one here can read that."

"I think . . . I can," Kelcie said.

"Really?" Niall asked, sounding impressed.

"*Ta erfin.* I am the heir. I think it comes with the genetics." Kelcie scooted closer.

Clutching her bough tightly in one hand, the fingers of the other tapped down a row.

"This says, *Tara vlast Alltar rask.* So much power Alltar split." She skimmed to the next row. "*Folam kirovan hapnar.* Nothingness blocked the sun, the moon, and the stars."

"Is that the Abyss?" Brona asked.

"Yes. That would make sense," Niall agreed.

"*Cheturi dan.* Four days later . . ." Kelcie read the rest in English only. "Still no sun. The lands turned too cold to walk. Bitter air. Frozen lakes, rivers, and seas."

With the next line she fell into Fomorian again without even realizing it. "*Ranhar dan. Golon. Dauoa. Ignis nan pomar.* Day seven. Famine. Death. Our Ignis elementals are too few now to help save them." She started along the edge. "It says that a Fomorian party went on a pilgrimage and returned with help. A blessing from their great *Doyen Verhosa.*" At the very bottom, Kelcie found a word she couldn't read. "Something called a *Croí na Bandia*? I don't know those words."

"Because that's in our ancient tongue," Niall gasped. "That means her heart. What does *Doyen Verhosa* mean?"

Kelcie locked eyes with Niall. "It means a supreme grandmother."

"Danu!" Zephyr exclaimed. "It must mean Danu!"

"Who is Danu?" Kelcie asked.

Brona answered. "She's the mother goddess of the Tuatha Dé Danann. Kind of like our mothers' Queen."

Kelcie filed this away under the section in her brain that always felt like an overflowing file cabinet where the drawers wouldn't close all the way. Summerfolk descended from the Tuatha Dé Danann, except Fomorians, who were an older clan, around before them, and attributed their powers as gifts from Chaos and Order, something she learned this summer in Chawell Woods. Two very different cultures, but in the end, no matter what their ancestorial deity was, they were all Summerfolk.

Zephyr swallowed hard. "So this is saying that, after the Abyss blocked out the sky completely, Danu saved the Lands of Summer by giving them . . . what?" He scratched his head.

"The *Croí na Bandia*," the Tiniest Speck sang triumphantly. "Her heart."

The word repeated phonetically through Kelcie's mind: *cree na baneeya*. It sounded beautiful.

"Danu gifted the Lands of Summer her heart. Without it, the Abyss will rise to impossible heights again. Summer will fall into unending impenetrable darkness and everyone will die."

"I know this tale," Esras insisted.

He rapped Zephyr's shoulder. "Would you mind turning that over again?"

Zephyr picked it up like it weighed nothing and set it gently back down.

Staring at the image of the cupped hands, Esras asked, "What does that look like to you, Niall?"

"Like a sketch in the *Book of Beings*? But I can't remember which one."

"Because it was the first one, and it was lost in the fire. It was from the parable called 'The Mother's Ultimate Gift.' It was a story about a mother who gives her children the one thing she cannot live without, the gift of her heart to keep theirs beating. But it said nothing of the lands freezing over or the sun never rising. It was about how boundless a mother's love for her children can be, and how mothers should never be taken for granted."

"So," Brona sighed. "What does that mean? Why is the story in the *Book of Beings* so different from the story this Fomorian stone tablet tells?"

"I don't know," Esras admitted.

"It's not!" Niall turned to Esras, brimming with conviction. "It's the same story! Think about it. Why would a parable about the goddess Danu be written on a *Fomorian* stone tablet? They don't have any connection to her. It was because *they* went on the journey to save Summer. Only *they* knew the specifics of what happened. The *Book of Beings* is a translation of this story to fit the moral needs of the time!"

"This boy is much smarter than you are, Chief Druid." Esras bristled at the Tiniest Speck's condescending tone. "That is why the Fomorians wrote specifics and the later books were watered down to a parable, a simple story to illustrate a moral."

"I don't know," Esras mumbled, disconcerted.

"What if it really happened?" Niall pressed Esras. "What if Danu's Heart *is* in the Lands of Summer?"

"It has to be!" Brona said, and took it a step farther. "That's the answer. Someone is going to steal the *Croí na Bandia*. Our mission is to stop it."

"If an omen gave you foresight, then what you saw will come to pass." The Tiniest Speck's baritone laugh echoed in the tiny space. "You cannot stop it."

"Wait a minute," Esras said. "The Abyss was created when this supposedly happened. If this is real, then how would Winter know about the Heart of Danu if the tablet is here in Summer? The details of the story hidden away by the Specks—" Esras stopped talking and glared at the Tiniest Speck.

"What?" She grinned sheepishly, rolling her eyes.

He advanced on her. "Did you sell them this information?"

She rubbed the ice-blue sapphire in the middle of her crown. "Oh, stop getting so angry. You're old and mortal and your rickety body parts can't take it."

"I can certainly last long enough to tell Queen Eislyn!"

"She wasn't even born then. It was more than five hundred years ago when I did that deal." The Tiniest Speck cackled. "And look at that, now I get paid twice for the same information."

"Get paid twice? You're a traitor!" Kelcie accused. "And this omen will fall on you and your Specks too! You live here!"

"Not for long!" Her focus dropped to Kelcie's bough.

Kelcie, the only way into Winter is through the human world! You cannot give her that bough!

Kelcie one hundred percent agreed with Niall. "No. You've already been paid for this information, by Winter. And judging by the size of that gem in your crown, more than enough to cover our bill too!"

The tiny queen's antennae zapped. A cry for backup that was immediately answered. The walls buzzed, a million Specks gathering in the shaft, ready, willing, and able to exact revenge with a snap of their double-dealing Queen's teeny-tiny fingers. "Hand over that bough, or my Specks will end you all."

Niall nudged Kelcie's elbow. *Get ready to run . . .*

"You betrayed the Lands of Summer." Brona shifted her arrow, taking aim at the tunnel, just above the opening. "And we don't bargain with traitors."

The green tip pierced the wall. Sticky syrup drained in long streaks, smothering the opening, capturing the charging Specks like flies on flypaper.

The Tiniest Speck ignored her hive's high-pitched pleas for help and raced for Kelcie's clenched fist holding the bough, but Zephyr's shillelagh was already on the move. Her crown went one way, and the cursing-mad Queen went the other. She crashed into a ceiling lantern, dropping on the dusty stone floor in an uncontrollable fit, shaking and shrieking, "H-h-how d-d-dare y-y-you!"

"Run!" Zephyr cried.

When their feet hit the stairwell, the ground beneath trembled, the raging Specks following after them in the walls. Rocks pelted their heads. Dust fell in their eyes. The cracking walls started to cave in.

The last out, Kelcie was overtaken by a wave of dust. She looked back hoping this was over, that the Specks would someday be found in the future, their little crushed bodies fossilized in the stones. Stones that would then be displayed for all of the Lands of Summer with a placard above the exhibition that said *Here lies where the last of the Specks met their dying fate.* But Kelcie never had that kind of luck.

Specks flooded the basement—the Tiniest Speck's bent antennae leading the charge.

"What kind of person are you, Saiga?" Her armies of stingers stayed behind her, waiting for her signal. "You made a bargain. A deal! A TRADE! Honor it, or you will all die."

Kelcie felt her bracelet slip down her wrist and realized she had a potential solution at her fingertips. She could try and make a replica of the branch part of her bough from the bracelet. She had no way to craft another yellow leaf like the real one had, but what were the odds the Tiniest Speck looked that closely at it? But, then, what if it didn't work? She would've wasted precious time they could be running. Kelcie swallowed the rising bile in the back of her throat. It was a risk. They would walk out of here on moveable limbs or . . .

Kelcie didn't want to think about the *or.*

"We can fight them off!" Brona's bow was locked and loaded with three jinx-enhanced arrows, the string stretched taut.

Zephyr and Niall looked less convinced.

Kelcie leaned over, turning away from the Specks, covering her face with her hands. Her back shaking, she pretended to cry, wailing loudly.

"Is she crying?" the Tiniest Speck shrieked in disgust. "What kind of soldier are you?"

"Kelcie?" Brona asked sounding concerned. "Are you okay?"

"Clearly, she's not!" Zephyr fumed.

Niall was quiet. He might've been the only one who figured it out.

The sparking word was no more than a whisper on a silent plea. After the longest second of Kelcie's life, a dollop of steel drained into her palm.

"I'm so sorry." She snorted a sniffle. "There's nothing we can do." She sobbed hysterically, stealing time to work the metal, rolling and squeezing and rolling and squeezing. She wrung her hands, pinching a tiny loop and used her pinkie nail to make a hole for her unbreakable strap to slide through.

Never a good actor, Kelcie sighed a little too dramatically as she stood up to face them, letting her real bough drop into her sleeve, catching the replica as the strap slipped through her fingers. The necklace fell only an inch before the Tiniest Speck snatched it out of the air—with her tongue.

The vile Queen wasted no time tying the unbreakable strap around her neck, the extra string draping down her back like a scarf. "You all enjoy freezing to death." She whizzed around, grinning wryly at her horde. "Pack your bags, Specks! It's moving day!"

A rousing chorus of ear-piercing shrills of joy, and the Specks sped off in all directions. Brona gaped at Kelcie like she'd lost her mind.

"How could you do that?"

"Head for the exit. Now," Kelcie harshed under her breath, rushing the spiral stairs.

"You heard the girl!" Esras pushed Niall and Zephyr. "Let's go!"

"We need to get that bough back!" Brona growled, falling behind.

They only got as far as the main floor when they heard the Tiniest Speck scream, "Liar! Cheat! Stop them!"

"What did you do?" Brona asked as her arrows exploded over the entrance to the spiral staircase, sealing it shut.

That took care of the Queen and her entourage in the basement, but some of the Specks were still in the library. And the Tiniest Speck's vacation cry message and subsequent cry to stop them must've traveled at lightning speed because teeny-tiny suitcases flew at their heads from every level.

In a mad dash for the exit, Esras stopped suddenly only halfway there and yelled, "Make ready!"

The wolfhounds woke from their long Summer naps, snarling hungry. Speck hordes descended only to be snatched midair by massive, slobbering jowls. At the same time, scribes jumped from their chairs, swapping pens for shields mounted to the sides of their desks and folded in behind them. Esras grabbed something shiny and silver from inside a drawer, but it was all a waste of time.

A few feet from the door, the army of Specks closed in. They were never going to make it. Kelcie turned to face them, planting her feet.

Before she could spark, Esras cried, "Shield wall!"

Scribes scrambled, coming together. Shields clacked, interlocking and layering, forming an impenetrable blockade. Specks collided so hard it sounded like they were standing under a metal roof in a hailstorm.

Huddled in the middle, Esras spoke to Zephyr. "Charger, we pull the shield back nearest the door, it will be the only chance to get out of here for the next few hours." By the look in his eyes, the Chief Druid planned.

Without so much as a moment's hesitation, Zephyr turned to Niall, Brona, and Kelcie, in that order. "O'Shea, you open the door. Lee, fire off a round that will give us cover from above."

In the shadow cover of the joined shields, Brona's devilish smile gleamed bright. "I've got just the thing." The red-tipped arrows piped hot as she loaded her bow.

"And Murphy," Zephyr continued, "We run. I mean, you know, take the lead."

"Come out, you cowards!" a Speck challenged.

Others continued to dive-bomb the shield wall. Needle noses broke through the wood, twitching to get to the enemy within.

Kelcie felt like a coward. "Esras, we can't leave you all in this mess. If I give her my bough—"

"What do you mean? You didn't?" Zephyr smacked his forehead. "This suddenly makes so much more sense!"

"You did the right thing," Esras insisted. "You must warn Queen Eislyn! She has more wisdom than she likes to let on. Something tells me she may know where the *Croí na Bandia* is located."

My mother? Niall's jagged groan rattled Kelcie's brain. "But Kelcie's right. We've put you in grave danger, Esras. We can't leave you."

Esras winked. "We've been waiting for this day for some time, my boy."

He and several other scribes pulled out cork-capped long-nosed cans that resembled bee smokers from beneath their robes. The cranky lady who ran the group home in Salem had kept hives in beekeeping boxes in the side yard. When bees sense smoke, they flee to the nearest cells of stored honey to quickly fill their stomachs, thus making them sluggish, and in need of a nap. Kelcie supposed it might work the exact same way on Specks. But that led to another all important question with Esras's plan.

"What do the Specks eat?" Kelcie asked him.

"They're partial to fish eggs on grumbleberry toast, a delicacy I saw the Tiniest Speck put out for her private party. A few well-placed whiffs, and a reminder of what lies in the attic," Esras instructed the scribes. "They'll gorge themselves, and wear themselves out, and then I'm going to seal over every crack in every wall! You four will go, and now, and don't look back!" He tapped the two scribes facing the door. "On three, part your shields. Adder, make ready! Show me what you've learned at the Academy! One. Two! THREE!"

As soon as the shields separated enough for Niall to launch his hand out, the door swung open. Kelcie and Zephyr and Niall ran while Brona jogged backward, firing off rounds that exploded in earth-shaking, heart-shocking flash-bangs. Blinded Specks crashed, stinging each other. The last thing Kelcie saw was Esras pop the cork on his smoke can and slam the door shut.

"Keep moving!" Zephyr ordered, leading the charge down the steep hill and through the streets, into a busier part of the city.

The whole way, Kelcie clasped the bough inside her sleeve, holding it in place, flabbergasted that she'd gotten away with tricking the Tiniest Speck for as long as she did. But worry set in for Esras and his scribes. But there was no going back now. They had to find a way to get to the Darling Palace, to Niall's mother. Hopefully, Esras was right, and she could lead them to the location of Danu's Heart.

Zephyr turned into an empty alley. Trying to catch their breaths, they never noticed the two palace guards from earlier following until their exit was blocked.

"There you are!"

Kelcie cringed, but Niall only smiled at them.

"Ah, gentlemen, just the folks we were looking for. I understand the High Guard would like to see me?"

They exchanged a confused look. "Yes. He would."

"My fianna will be going with me." Niall started to walk past them, but the shorter one stopped him.

"The High Guard didn't say anything about the others."

"But they're a fianna," the younger, taller one explained, as if it were obvious. "High Guard would expect it."

"Whatever. Fine. But get a move on! We've wasted half the day looking for you! The ball starts in less than three hours!"

23

THE HIGH GUARD

While Brona flew, Kelcie, Zephyr, and Niall rode the palace's private trolley. It wasn't long before they left behind the tightly packed homes with steeply pitched roofs for a more institutional-looking area. Kelcie got up from the fancy crushed velvet seats in the center and walked over to the railing. The prison where her father was being held was out there somewhere, and she wanted to know where.

Niall slid down the railing, bumping her elbow. "You can't see Mount Joy from here."

"That's the name of the prison? Mount Joy?" Kelcie scoffed. "Is that supposed to be funny?"

"I wish you could see him."

It was the sincerity in his voice that made Kelcie look at him. "Me too. More than anything."

Zephyr appeared beside Niall, his dimples cratering with worry. "I know I shouldn't bring up the ball at a time like this, but it's getting late, and Willow is seriously going to kill me. I left without saying anything. And we got matching outfits and everything. Maybe I could get word to her? Apologize for being late in advance, that's a good thing to do, right, Kelcie?"

"Why are you asking her?" Niall asked.

"Because she's a *girl*."

"If you're going to stand someone up, date or not, it's common courtesy to let them know in advance. Then, you're not actually standing them up," Niall rationalized.

"Doesn't mean she won't be mad at you," Kelcie added. "But maybe less mad at you."

"Oh. Great." Zephyr looked crestfallen.

Niall gestured to the guards driving the trolley. "Tell Cassuch to get her a message. He's the short one."

"And the prickly one," Zephyr groaned, but mustered his most pleasing smile and jockeyed across the moving trolley with determination.

"Don't you need to tell Delilah?" Kelcie asked.

Niall's brow creased. "Tell her, what?"

Kelcie rolled her eyes at him. "That you may be late to the ball. You're going with her, aren't you? Your name was crossed off the list."

"Oh, the *list*." He shook his head dismissively. "That's not why I was crossed off. She did ask me, Tad too, but I told them I didn't want to go with a date. I guess they removed me from contention."

Tad Fagan too? Come to think of it, Tad was paying him a lot of attention, especially at the start of school. Kelcie's knee-jerk reaction was to foolishly blurt sarcasm. "Aren't you Mr. Popular." She immediately regretted it. He looked at his shoes, shrugging. "Why didn't you want to go with a date?"

"I did, just not either of them. The person I did want to go with would've said no if I asked." He kicked his toe against the baluster.

Kelcie's heart skidded to a screeching halt. Did he want to ask her? There was no way. He hardly spoke to her these days. He couldn't even look at her now. But then, who? She wanted to know in the worst possible way, but didn't have the courage to ask.

The strained silence between them was broken by the short

guard's cackle. "Sure. I'll send it. Just as soon as the goddess declares me the next Regent."

The trolley glided to a stop, ending the conversation there, leaving it and Kelcie's heart on a cliffhanger.

Giddy, well-dressed Summerfolk paused their mingling to gawk at the gilded trolley, likely hoping to catch a glimpse of Queen Eislyn. Zephyr gave them an elaborate bow, making Kelcie laugh.

"Guests are already gathering?" Niall checked the sun's position. "I didn't realize how late it was."

Musicians struck up a lively tune from somewhere not far off as Kelcie jumped the three steps off the trolley and came face-to-face with the Darling Palace. Five hexagonal-shaped towers curved into a semicircle with the tallest in the center and descending in height in perfect symmetry from there. Every tower was capped by spiked golden domes, flags baring blazing suns snapping in the wind.

Brona landed beside Kelcie and morphed. She straightened her black cloak and smoothed flyaways, coaxing them back into her fishtail braid.

Zephyr was slack-jawed beside them. "It must take a lot of people to clean this place."

Brona wrinkled her nose. "Never been this close before. It looks more inviting from a distance. Up close, it's . . ."

"Oppressive," Niall voiced.

"I was going to say tacky."

"I think it's beautiful," Kelcie offered.

"Me too, Saiga," Zephyr agreed. He adjusted the shillelagh on his back and straightened the scabbard on his hip before giving the order. "Let's go see the High Guard."

The inside of the Darling Palace was as grand as the outside. Saffron crystal chandeliers hung from twenty-foot ceilings casting yellow haloes on the pristine white floors. Flustered staff setting out flower arrangements on every available surface couldn't get out of Niall's way fast enough as he hustled them down two more hallways. He stopped at an elevator, racing to press his hand on the golden sun in the middle of the double doors.

Inside the large elevator, which was as gilded as everything else in the palace so far, Niall poked one of only two buttons on the panel—all the way up, and all the way down—repeatedly until the doors closed.

The lift launched, rising so high so fast that Kelcie's ears popped while her stomach rode the whole way on the floor.

"Will it be just the High Guard, or will your mother be there too?" Zephyr asked Niall.

"Probably just Casper. The ball is about to start."

"You think I should just lay it on him?" Zephyr asked. "Hey, we think that someone is going to steal this thing that's going to turn the Lands of Summer into an uninhabitable frozen waste-land, but we have no idea where it is or what it looks like?"

"We know what it's called," Kelcie said.

Brona blew out a perturbed breath. "You should've brought the stone tablet, Z! You could've easily carried it."

"At the time, I was a little worried about being turned into a pincushion!"

"Well, let's say he believes us, then what?" Kelcie asked. "Es-ras said the Queen might know something about the Heart, not the High Guard."

"Right. So I segue into asking, is the Queen around for a quick confab?" Zephyr offered a charming smile, waggling his brows.

Unimpressed, Brona crossed her arms. "I think O'Shea should do the talking."

"Charger!" Zephyr declared, thumbing his chest.

"I'm with Brona on this. He's Niall's stepfather," Kelcie said.

Niall disagreed. "Casper respects process. Chargers speak for fianna."

"You see?" Zephyr harrumphed.

The elevator dinged and Niall hurried out. He paced swiftly through the short hallway. Guards lingered outside the first of two doors. Niall walked right past, stopping at the second door. Kelcie heard a baby crying inside.

"Aw, is that your new little brother?" Zephyr cooed.

Brona plugged her ears with her fingers. "Got quite the pair of lungs."

"All babies cry like that," Zephyr dismissed.

Brona's lip curled. "Then I'm not having one."

Niall knocked once.

"Come in!"

He used his telekinesis to push open the door, enjoying the guards' shocked expressions.

"Oh. You're here. Good. Come in. Aiwin is about to go down," Casper Thorn said, passing the baby off to a cooing woman Kelcie assumed was the nanny.

The High Guard looked dressed for the ball in a rust-colored tunic with five golden suns on the upturned collar, black pants, and knee-high black boots polished to a shine except for a milky-white spot on the top where it looked like Aiwin had spit up.

Niall and Aiwin looked nothing alike. Where Niall had the Queen's lavender eyes and cool pale skin, Aiwin's eyes were burgundy red and his skin light brown, like Niall's stepfather.

"Excuse us, please," the nanny said, dipping her head at Thorn, and whisked Aiwin out of the room.

Stepping behind his opulent desk, Casper frowned wistfully shifting a piece of paper from beside him to directly in front of him, as if those papers had something to do with why he wanted to see Niall. "I wasn't expecting your fianna. I think perhaps it should just be us."

"We have an urgent matter to discuss with you, sir!" Zephyr exclaimed.

"That will have to wait." A woman wearing purple robes embossed with gold hems strolled into the room and popped Niall on the back of his head. "How could you have been so stupid, little brother?"

It wasn't until she called him *little brother* that Kelcie realized it was Regan. There was no sign of the soldier Kelcie admired at the Academy last year beneath the layers of expensive fabrics, only a Regent. Her long blond hair was now brown like her mother's and draped in sculpted ringlets down her back.

"Regan, why are you here?" Niall snapped at her. "Shouldn't you be getting ready for the ball?"

Tiny gems outlining her eyebrows rose with irritated mirth. "I am ready. And I wanted to be here when Casper told you the news, to reassure you it was for the best. I thought you might take it poorly, which clearly you are."

Casper slipped uneasy hands into his pockets. "I haven't told him yet."

Niall sidestepped next to Kelcie. "Told me what?"

He held up the piece of paper in front of him, which looked like a formal document, but never got a chance to show it to Niall because Queen Eislyn swept into the room. "That you will remain here after the Ascension and will not be returning to the Academy."

Kelcie stopped breathing. Not at the sight of the Queen, who was dressed exactly like her daughter—in purple velvet robes— only she had a gold tiara on her head. The center peak was shaped into, what else, a blazing sun, and in the middle, interestingly enough, a heart-shaped amethyst. But even that reminder of the reason they were here, the Heart of Danu, vanished from her mind. Kelcie couldn't believe her ears. Niall's parents were pulling him from the school.

The Academy was everything to Niall. *She can't take that away from him!* Scáthach wouldn't let her, would she?

The High Guard waved dismissively at Regan and she reluctantly left the room. Brona and Zephyr bowed to the Queen. Kelcie caught Thorn's arched brow and fell in line beside Brona.

Niall stood defiant. "You can't."

"Oh, we can," Queen Eislyn countered.

"It's not your fault, Niall. You've been sheltered your whole life.

You're entirely too trusting. It's easy for people to take advantage of you," Thorn said, showing he didn't know Niall at all.

"That's not true!" Kelcie challenged.

"It's not, sir," Zephyr agreed.

"Oh, really? Then after more than a year of training at the Academy, explain to me how that girl could so easily lure him out of his Den before dawn and steal his bough?" Casper didn't bother to let Zephyr answer. He stood over Niall, giving him a harsh stare, and added, "Well, tell me!"

"It was . . . I thought . . ." Niall glanced at Kelcie, confusing her, then it dawned on her that Lexis must've lured him out by sending a note from Kelcie. "It was an accident. It won't happen again."

Queen Eislyn threw her hands in the air. "First you ask to see the traitor during break, and now this happens?"

"It wasn't Niall's fault!" Kelcie shouted. "Lexis tricked us all. She's a Winter spy and we think we know why she's here! Please—you have to—"

Queen Eislyn's laugh started out stifled, but refused to be contained. Casper joined in, shaking his head. This conversation was going nowhere.

"Oh yes, I received Scáthach's report. Your preceptor is as paranoid as you are after last year's assault." The Queen smirked, winking a lavender eye. "And I don't blame you, but Lexis is a child. Not a fianna of four fairies and a changeling. She is alone in the world from what I heard, a Fomorian too. I'm surprised at you, Kelcie. Fomorians are well known for their united front. But then again, you didn't grow up around them, did you?"

Brona stabbed the bottom of her bow down on the marble floors, demanding the Queen's attention. "Way to make her feel really bad, Your Majesty. Your guilt method is excellent, and should be taught at the Academy. But you're wrong. And if you and the High Guard will let someone else get a word in, we'll explain why. Because if you don't listen to us the Lands of Summer are doomed!"

Queen Eislyn glared at Brona. "Raven, your insolence is—"

"They're going to try and steal the *Croí na Bandia*!" Zephyr bellowed, letting go a huge, relieved sigh. "Sorry, ma'am, sir, just had to get it out."

The Queen's lips pursed. "The parable of the loving mother?" She sounded incredulous. "From the *Book of Beings*?"

"You do know it!" Niall exclaimed, relieved.

"I am Queen, of course I know it. That is nothing but an old story, about a mother's sacrifice to save her children. I personally believe it was written down by an ungrateful child who wanted to make his own mother feel guilty because she had to work. Oh look, this one gave up her heart so they could live, and you won't even take a day off."

"Huh, it sounded so much nicer the way Esras explained it," Zephyr commented.

Queen Eislyn adjusted her tiara. "He's a sentimental old fool."

"Why do you think it has something to do with that story?" Thorn asked.

"It all started when my mother and Brona's mother visited us at school." Kelcie explained—for the umpteenth time—what their mothers had shown them.

Zephyr took over when she was done. "At first, Niall and I thought Scáthach was right. She said most of the omens in the past have taken a while to actually happen, but then BAM!" Zephyr exclaimed with so much gusto the Queen jumped. "Niall's untraceable bough is stolen. We knew we had to start investigating right away what could cause this since we're going to have to stop it."

"You're going to stop it?" Thorn said, sounding incredulous.

"Yes," Niall said adamantly. "Because now we know what will cause it. And we know because we paid a visit to the College of Mystical Beings on our way here." He launched into the story of how the Tiniest Speck showed them the old Fomorian tablet, describing in great detail both sides. "Don't you see? Someone is going to steal the Heart of Danu!"

"*Croí na Bandia*?" Queen Eislyn repeated, her tone dripping with sarcasm as if she didn't believe him.

"Yes." Niall nervously adjusted his glasses.

"Young man, this is all a very interesting story, especially that last part, where the Tiniest Speck tried to kill you. Very exciting. A lovely fantasy tale you could write as a book one day, since you love to read them. But I hardly think your stolen bough is the beginning of anything. That story in the *Book of Beings* is just that, a story. It isn't real. And right now, your stepfather and I have more important things to do than chat about this."

Niall pleaded, "Mother . . ."

But she waved him off, padding toward the door to leave. "Niall, you will be remaining here after the Ascension."

"No! I won't!"

"What did you say?" The Queen snapped in a tone so sharp Kelcie felt the sudden urge to take cover under Thorn's desk. But not Niall. He glared at his mother, and she right back at him.

A guard knocked stiffly on the door. He entered, and held out a piece of paper to Thorn.

"Good news! The Lands of Summer are saved!" Casper declared. "Lexis turned herself in, and handed over your bough."

He showed the note to Niall.

Kelcie was relieved, but something wasn't right. "Turned herself in, where?"

The High Guard gave Kelcie a sad smile. "Here, in Summer City. Likely trying to catch back up to the school. But, in light of our conversation, I will have her held until after the Ascension, and then we will return her to Chawell Woods."

"All's well that ends well." Queen Eislyn grinned at Niall. "Now, I do hope you four won't sulk the night away up here because you're losing a fianna mate. I'm sure Scáthach will find a suitable replacement."

"No one can replace Niall," Kelcie said.

"Our Adder is one of a kind," Brona emphasized.

"I know that," Queen Eislyn fumed. "That is why I want him here!"

It was the first nice thing Kelcie ever heard Niall's mother say about him, but he didn't hear it. Niall ignored the conversation going on around him, and walked to the far side of the room to stare out the window.

Zephyr made one last plea. "Please don't do this, Your Majesty!"

"It's already done." After a quick glance at Niall, she left.

Casper crossed his arms over his chest, and spoke to Niall's back. "This is for your own good, Niall."

Thorn waited for Niall to respond but he didn't. He never turned around. After the High Guard was gone, Kelcie moved to stand beside him, expecting to find him upset, but he wasn't.

"Niall, they're saying you can't go back to school! Why are you smiling?"

"Because I know where *Croí na Bandia* is!"

24

PRISON BREAK

THE OBSIDIAN HANDCUFFS bit into Lexis's wrists. Her stomach ached so much from her powers being stifled that if the guard manning the desk didn't hurry up with the keys, she was going to vomit all over the floor.

When she first turned herself in to the guards at Mount Joy, she was dragged through glamourie detectors. Then there was the verification of her identity with the image of her face taken at the guardhouse in Chawell Woods. Being arrested was taking forever, using up time they didn't have now that they discovered Rilios was unlocked.

Lexis's mood plummeted by the second. She never counted on how miserable she'd feel in these handcuffs. It didn't help that Pavel was getting on Lexis's last nerves. He kept questioning her, first about any so-called friends she'd made over the past eight weeks at the Academy. What were their names? Did she divulge anything that might mess up the mission? Was there a possibility that they were walking into a trap? She was the leader of this fianna, not him, and she told him as much.

Swappy said he'd been grumpy the whole time. He explained that Pavel had been stuck indoors because of his obvious wings, and that his bad mood was probably because he hadn't been able to fly. Not once. Or shed any ice. Stuck in these obsidian handcuffs, Lexis was starting to feel sympathetic toward the ice fairy. The longer she was locked in them, the longer the obsidian suppressed her powers, the angrier she became.

The biggest worry Lexis had was the fake bough, but that turned out to be for naught. When the petite guard removed the fake bough, she tossed it on the desk, having barely inspected it.

"It doesn't need to be perfect," the Advisors had told Lexis. "The High Guard will be much too busy with the Ascension to go to the prison and verify its authenticity."

They had been right every step of the way. Their instructions flawless. Too flawless.

After that, a note was sent informing the High Guard their search was over.

The whole time the guard was very talkative, and Swappy too polite to hurry her up.

Almost two feet taller than his normal body, Swappy was impersonating a soldier who was a full-grown Charger, basically a walking mass of muscles, most of which were tattooed with interlocking concentric circles. He set a big, burly, comforting hand on Lexis's shoulder.

Too comforting.

Lexis would've kicked him if the guard wasn't coming up behind them with the key to open the door. Beyond that door were the cells, and the Winter fianna they needed to break out.

"You marching in the tattoo tomorrow?" the guard asked Swappy, jangling the keys.

"Yes! And I'm going to the ball tonight!" he exclaimed a little too enthusiastically.

This conversation needed to end. Lexis stepped on his foot.

Swappy flashed Lexis a quick grin as if to say, *What? It's all going so well*, which only made her more anxious.

"You soldiers have it the best. I always wanted to go to the Academy, but I never got past the Bridge of Leaping." She frowned at Lexis and said, her tone dripping with sincere disbe-lief, "And to think you gave it all up for a bough."

"To think," Lexis repeated, trying not to think about any-thing but getting through that door.

Some twenty guards filed past the desk on their way out for the shift change. Swappy had spent hours watching the prison last week. Replacement guards entered one at a time, clocking in with the facial recognition camera. According to Swappy's calculations, it would take five minutes for all of them to get through.

Five minutes of the prison having few to no guards on the individual cell floors. Five minutes to break the Winter fianna out, and make their escape. Lexis's leg twitched, raring to go.

Once through the door, the guard told Swappy, "I'll take her from here. Go enjoy the ball."

Lexis held her breath, hoping Swappy could handle this next part on his own. If she looked back, the guard would know something was up. If she looked back, she would see that look on Swappy's face. The one she saw on the way to the prison when a hairy woman with a twitch rodent's nose and curly whiskers gave him a sweet cake and he accidentally changed to his own green-haired, green-eyed, pale-skinned self. The same one when he told her he thought Summerfolk were nice, and wondered why Summer and Winter were at war to begin with. The one that meant he wasn't strong enough to finish this mission. But then again, Swappy had never let her down.

Lexis heard a subtle thwack and turned around in time to see the guard crumple into Swappy's waiting arms, sound asleep, making little purring noises.

"I hope that doesn't leave a lump," Swappy apologized as he picked her up without so much as a grunt, and stuffed her in a closet filled with green prison garb. He shut the door, bending the handle, making it that much more difficult to get open.

Swappy returned to Lexis's side, a whole new person. Well, not entirely new. He was a mirror image of the petite guard:

brown hair in a tight bun, sunken cheeks, while winking a droopy brown eye at her. He jingled the key rings. "Easy peasy."

Passing through the next heavier door, Lexis gasped at the sight and smell of the cavernous dungeon, a tomb carved into the middle of the dark basalt island Summer City sat on. Every floor another ring of cells where prisoners were caged. To call the place dismal was being nice. A creaky metal stairwell clung to the black cylindrical walls, spiraling downward, pausing on landings that circled the cells—balconies really—with a deadly fall beyond the railings. No windows at all, the only light came from crystals in sconces fashioned between the cells.

The still air reeked of urine, sweat, and mold. From the stench and her stifled powers, Lexis's stomach started to roll again. She couldn't take these handcuffs anymore.

"Take these off *now* . . . please."

"On it!" Swappy flipped through the key ring to a small section of obsidian keys, trying each in the locking mechanism until . . . *click.*

When the last shackle fell off, Lexis's hands heated, desperate to burn. She poured all of her strength into keeping that from happening. Walking through the prison with her hands on fire would draw unwanted attention. But it was hard. A terrible bitter-tasting, dizzying rush, and she never wanted to feel that way again.

"Second floor," Swappy said.

With staggering breaths, Lexis took the steps slowly, regaining her balance and not wanting to stir the prisoners before they reached the ones they were here for.

Still, she was curious, and glanced in the cells they passed. An old troll playing solitaire, a leering pixie, then two cells that were empty. In the last was a Fomorian, sleeping on his cot. Four obsidian chains stretched from him to the walls, one locked to every limb.

Though he was facing away from Lexis, she saw ringed horns longer than any she had ever seen before, and red hair—like

Kelcie's. Unopened letters were neatly stacked like precious keepsakes on a nightstand made from a crate turned on its side. It had to be Kelcie's father, Draummorc.

Lexis's parents had never answered her letters when she left for Braverwil. They were filled with all the exciting things she was doing, how hard she was working, and how sorry she was for leaving the way she did. She only ever wanted Braverwil. Only ever wanted to be the best Winter soldier ever. She wanted them to be proud of her and her accomplishments, but they never answered. And it hurt.

"You should answer your daughter's letters."

"What?" His voice was softer than Lexis expected. "Who?" He sounded confused. He shifted in his bed, lowering his legs to the floor. "You know my daughter?"

The obsidian chains kept him a good foot away from the bars. She couldn't imagine what it felt like to be wrapped in that much obsidian, to have your powers caged for years. It must be excruciating.

Hunched over, his face was hidden behind a scruffy red beard, but his eyes, like Kelcie's, twinkled with fervent relief, then fell, narrowing, concerned.

"You're a child. Why are you here?"

"We need to get a move on!" Swappy-the-guard nudged her shoulder.

Lexis nodded, answering Swappy, but her determined stare never left Kelcie's father. "Just answer her letters, okay? Because there's nothing worse than feeling like you don't matter, especially to your own parents."

She heard him say, "Wait! Please. Come back! Is she okay?"

It was that last question that made Lexis pause and glance over her shoulder at him. "Funny, that's all she wants to know about you too."

She didn't wait for him to answer. Whatever he said, it didn't matter. Lexis knew from Kelcie that Summer was never going to let him out of prison. Letters were all Kelcie was ever going to receive from her father. What more was there to say?

She jogged after Swappy, who, having grown impatient, was taking the next flight of stairs two at a time. On the next landing, Swappy sprinted around to the other side, to a cell with no bars to keep the inmate inside, but rather a see-through material Lexis suspected wasn't plain old glass. Behind it stood Achila Grimes wearing one of the dull green prison outfits that looked like an oversized onesie on her. Her shock white hair had turned yellowish. Her wings, twice the size of Pavel's, lay flat against her back to keep from bumping the ceiling. Her lip ticked just enough to show off her fangs.

"You're early. What's wrong? And where's my nephew?"

Swappy beamed a big smile at her, flashing the guard's perfect teeth.

"He's fine."

"That's not what I asked you, fool!"

His smile fell, and he farted—loudly, distinctly—then hid behind Lexis, dragging the stench along, and forcing Lexis to deal with her. Lexis had met Achila Grimes only twice before, when she came to school to visit Pavel. She was scary, snappish, rude, but a hero of Winter, a hero now fallen, locked away, but not forgotten. The Advisors were very specific. She and the others in her fianna too had a part to play in stealing the Heart of Danu.

"The shrine is already open," Lexis explained, trying to keep her voice steady, to show no fear, but it wasn't easy with Grimes's snarling fangs so near the glass. "Pavel is getting word to our contact in the human world. The ball begins in less than an hour and will provide better cover than the tattoo. It's time to go."

"This change does not come from the Advisors or our Queen. How do we know Pavel's word will get there in time? You can't just change orders! Who made this decision?" Grimes hissed, frost billowing through her flaring nostrils.

"I did." Doubt snuck in and Lexis suddenly questioned her own decision. Maybe they should have waited until tomorrow. But there was no going back now. "And we're wasting time."

The guards' footsteps tapped on the rickety floor above. Any second, the new shift would be down here. Lexis had anticipated a fight to get out, but it would be a whole lot easier if they were already out of the cells. She should never have stopped to talk to Draummorc. "We have to go! We have to go right now!"

Identical twins materialized out of thin air in the cell beside Achila. Small wings and orange hair, these were the creeper fairies Nevver and Latchkey. The Advisors described them perfectly.

Swappy immediately went to work on the lock on their cell door.

Lexis checked the sides of Achila's, trying to find how it opened, but there was no button or keyhole.

Once the twins were out, Swaps kept going. He released Pethia, the dark-haired changeling, and she immediately transformed into the twin of the guard Swappy was impersonating so that there were two of them.

"Get Achila out and let's go!" Nevver or Latchkey snapped.

"Hey!" a weak voice called from a few cells down.

"Who is that?" Lexis asked.

Swappy shrugged. "Orders from the Advisors only included these four."

"He's nobody," Pethia hissed.

"How dare you, Pethia? If it weren't for me—"

"We wouldn't have rotted in these cells for six months!"

Then it dawned on Lexis who the other prisoner was: Elliott Blizzard, Kelcie's . . . what did she call him? Her caseworker in the human world, the one who was secretly a Winter spy. He was with Achila's fianna on the mission to destroy the Academy for the Unbreakable Arts with King Balor's evil eye. The mission that failed and landed them here. The Advisors never mentioned him.

"Are you saying he's from Winter too?" Swaps lifted the keys. "If he's one of us, why didn't the Advisors want us to get him too?"

"Because he failed! The botched mission at the Academy was all his fault. Him, and that wretched girl!" Achila seethed. "Even the Advisors no longer count him as missing. He's dead to them. And dead to us!" Her grating cackle warbled, bouncing off the glass. "Queen Kefyra told him when we left to come back with the eye, the erfin, and the end of the Academy, or don't come back at all. If the Advisors left Blizzard off the list, then he stays here. We never disobey our queen, do we, gasbag boy?"

"His name is Swappy," Lexis told her. "And no, we don't."

"But Lexis, he's one of us," Swappy fretted.

Swappy was wrong. Elliott wasn't one of them, not anymore, because the Queen would never let him be. And if he did go with them back to Winter, Blizzard would likely end up like Roswen, with his wings clipped.

Boots scuffed on the stairs. Guards were coming.

"Get me out, Pulse!" Achila barked.

Knowing she was going to regret this, Lexis pressed her palms on the glass-like material, sensing abnormally fast vibrations. It felt like an unexploded bomb and Lexis was about to light the fuse.

"Hey! What are you doing?"

A guard called, jumping the rest of the stairs. His feet barely touched the landing before the explosion knocked him and the three behind him off their feet. Achila Grimes stepped out of her cell, her white eyes glowing, firing an unending supply of ice from her hands, freezing the guards in place.

She ogled her handiwork. "That felt good. Who's next?"

She didn't have to wait long. The crystal sconces flashed. Sirens WHOOOOPed. Footsteps pounded above, more guards descending. Achila let out a screech of pure joy, as she stretched her wings to their full height, then flew to the first floor, heading straight for the bulk of the guards. Lexis heard the WHOOSH and leaned out to see Achila freezing them too. Pretty soon, there was going to be a mountain of ice blocking their way and they wouldn't be able to get out themselves!

Nevver and Latchkey vanished. Pethia play-acted like she was a guard chasing after Grimes. None of them bothered to worry about Swappy or Lexis—like they didn't matter anymore, like Elliott Blizzard didn't matter anymore—only getting Danu's Heart did. The war was everything. Lexis believed that, only maybe not as much as she used to.

"Lexis . . ." Swappy worried, pointing an errant finger at Elliott.

"We can't let him out, Swappy." She took the set of keys from him. Crestfallen, his lower lip quivered, nodding, stopping when she added, "Catch up to the others. I'll be right behind you." She didn't want to tell him what she was going to do, because if Grimes or the others saw her, when they returned to Winter they would tell the Advisors or the Queen, and if anyone was going to get in trouble it was going to be her, and her alone. She was their Tol, their leader. Every move they made was her responsibility.

Swappy never disobeyed or questioned, but she saw him look back, a hint of a smile crossing his lips, before he left. Lexis ran to Elliott Blizzard's cell. She could just make out his outline standing beside a cot as she removed the obsidian keys from the ring and dropped them on the ground.

"I just want to go home," he said.

"Yeah." A strong gust of wind blew the ring through the bars, scraping to a stop at Elliott's feet. "Me too."

Skating, sliding, and leaping her way over the frozen guards, Lexis made it to the first floor. She saw Swappy, still looking like the guard, holding open the exit door, waiting for her.

Draummorc was standing as close to the bars as the chains would allow when Lexis sprinted by his cell. She had no time to stop, and didn't, but, out of the corner of her eye, she glimpsed his shocked expression when she tossed him the obsidian keys.

25

DANU'S HEART

R ILIOS," NIALL WHISPERED, tapping on the window.

Kelcie crouched so Brona and Zephyr could see too.

Fifty feet below, in a grassy field packed with soldiers, the sun dipped below a round, windowless shrine ringed with staked torches yet to be lit. From the top of the Darling Palace, Rilios's silver roof and the milky white stone walls looked lonely and quiet, waiting for what tomorrow would bring.

"The Stone of Destiny is in there, right?" Zephyr asked. "You think Danu's Heart is too?"

"I think the *Croí na Bandia* is inside the Stone of Destiny."

Brona's silver gaze ignited with intrigue. "The Stone of Destiny sings when touched by the Regent. It knows the will of Danu. O'Shea, you're brilliant!"

Zephyr muttered, counting by fives. "The good news is that there is an entire platoon in that field, fifty soldiers."

Two dozen of which were posted between the torches, protecting Rilios itself. Ravens soared from the top of the Darling Palace, barrel-rolling through the airspace above the shrine. Nothing was going to get near it unnoticed.

Across the field, Kelcie saw lions pacing figure eights around a hawthorn tree. She knew it by the red berries and thorny branches.

"Why is that tree guarded?" she asked Niall.

"That's our private Sidral." Niall's hand lifted to his neck, patting, searching. "My bough! That's why Lexis stole my bough! Only mine or my mother's, Regan's, or Casper's would work on that Sidral! We have to tell Casper! They're going to steal the Heart of Danu and escape through that Sidral!"

"But Lexis turned your bough in," Zephyr retorted.

Kelcie gasped. "That doesn't mean it was actually Niall's bough!" Her adrenaline spiked as a chilled breeze raised the hair off the back of her neck as Kelcie lifted her bough out of her pocket. "Lexis is a pulse elemental. I saw her wield fire when I chased her to the Sidral at school! That means she can control all four of the elements like I can. And if I could make something that looks a little bit like my bough in seconds—"

"Lexis had weeks to copy Niall's bough," Brona finished for Kelcie. "Wow. Winter is good."

"That's not helpful." Zephyr frowned at her. "And we don't even know if this is true. This is all speculation. We should go to the prison, and see the bough for ourselves. How far is it?"

"That's strange." Niall leaned so far out the window Kelcie fisted the back of his cloak, worried he was going to fall.

"Careful!"

"Do you see that?" Niall declared, hoisting his arm. "The shrine!"

A bobbing light shone through the silver roof, and moved. Someone was walking inside with a torch or lantern.

"Do you see that? My mother is the only one who can open the entrance to the shrine. It's supposed to happen right before the Ascension. But if there's lights inside—"

"The shrine must be open!" Zephyr screeched.

Orange spots flashed in and out of Kelcie's peripheral vision, caching her attention. Her breath caught at two familiar orange-haired fairies appearing out of nowhere beside the Sidral.

Brona saw them too. "Look!"

"What? Oh gads! It's those creeper fairies! I thought they were in prison?" Zephyr fretted.

Niall groaned. "Seems Lexis being arrested was all part of Winter's plan."

Brona slid an arrow out of her quiver and nocked it in her bow, but never got a chance to take the shot.

The Sidral's trunk split open. Large gray monsters vaulted out.

"Bodachs!" Niall howled.

"In the flesh!" Brona gaped a wicked smile curling her lips.

Boogeymen. Bringers of nightmares. Dreamers of death. They plowed through ten soldiers at a time. The creeper fairies manned the Sidral, opening and closing it like it was an elevator from hell, unloading carload after carload of bodachs.

Bedlam erupted on the field between the Sidral and Rilios.

Raven squadrons on their way to the Sidral altered course, heading after the bodachs that had broken through Summer's lines and were likely now attending the Queen's ball.

"The bodachs are a distraction," Niall surmised.

Brona fixed on the shrine. "I'm going—"

"No, you're not!" Zephyr yelled so loudly it hurt Kelcie's ears. "Do you remember what happened on our overnight? Those selkies blowing darts through your leg should've taught you that fiannas stick TOGETHER!"

Kelcie pulled her twin swords. She twirled them, loosening her wrists. "Then what are we waiting for?"

Niall rolled out the door, his sidewinder in hand.

In the hallway, Kelcie heard Aiwin laughing.

Niall glowered at the guards posted on either side of the door. "The palace is under attack! Get inside my mother's chambers, and bolt the door!"

"What are you—"

Communicators on their belts sounded a blaring alarm, then Casper's angry voice boomed. "Sun Guards at the Queen's chambers. Lockdown! Lockdown now!"

Niall slapped his hand down on the sunny spot between the elevator doors repeatedly, as if that were going to make them open sooner. When the *DING* finally came and the doors parted,

Niall started to rush inside, only to hop backward, trying to get away from a decomposing corpse stumbling out. It tossed an empty champagne flute over its shoulder and belched.

Kelcie had never seen anything so frightening in her life. Rotting leather skin over taut muscle. Tentacles for hair. A face more skull than flesh baring inch-long teeth. Niall immediately launched his hand out, attempting his scream defense. It seemed to have no effect, because the bodach charged at Kelcie in a wild fit of rage.

Before she could react, tentacles snapped like a whip, wrapping around her throat, heaving her off the ground. Kelcie's swords slipped from her grip. Painful doesn't begin to describe how much it hurt. Her head felt like it was about to snap off her neck. She kicked, flailing, trying to squeak out a sparking word, but nothing could get past the bodach's grip, not even air.

Her vision tunneled. She saw only the bodach's skeletal nose and the thousands of cockroaches pouring out. Scurrying across the stretched tentacles, they flooded her neck, crawling over her face. Lips pressed, she thrashed, seeing every overcrowded bedroom in the group homes Kelcie lived with in the human world, all infested with cockroaches. So many nights, hearing their little legs clicking on the floor, feeling them when they reached her bare arms. But Kelcie wasn't in the human world anymore. She smacked her cheek, and felt only the painful sting of her own hand. This wasn't real! None of it, except the tentacles choking the life out of her.

"Let her go!" Brona's arrows struck the bodach where its heart should be, but they passed right through its skeletal body, thumping off the elevator.

Niall rapid-fired a rainbow of jinxes that had no effect. Only Zephyr's sword proved useful, cutting through the tentacles.

The cockroaches vanished on the way to Kelcie landing on her knees. She wheezed precious air into her lungs, retrieving her swords, and sparked.

"Ignis!"

Fire broke from her palms, funneling through the twin obsidian swords. Smokey black blazed sinister red. Scorching heat exploded from the curved tips, straight into the bodach's concave chest. Two blinks later, there was nothing left of the nightmare but a pile of ash, and a charred shadow outline burned into the marble. She heard Niall gasp, and then flinch.

Shock turned to horror as she realized her hands, and thus her swords, were still blazing fire. Kelcie cried, "Nil ignis!"

The swords returned to their normal shadowy color, yet still smoked from sharing Kelcie's power and amplifying it. Kelcie stared at them, dumfounded. She had never used her powers when practicing with these swords, and it was a good thing, or Coach Blackwell and his new Nether Tower might never have survived. It was terrifying, but then again the Darling Palace was still standing. She controlled the fire, just like she controlled the swords. And if she did it once, maybe she could do it again.

Scrambling for the elevator, Brona touched the edge of one of the blades, wincing. "That was amazing!"

"Did you know those swords would do that?" Niall asked as the doors slid open.

"No." Kelcie lowered the swords by her side, astonished.

"Let's be glad they did because there are going to be a whole lot more of those things between us and the shrine!" Zephyr let out an anxious shrill exhaling.

Inside the elevator, a light on the ceiling spun, a speaker beside it continuously stating the obvious.

"Intruder alert! Intruder alert! Intruder alert! Intruder alert!"

"My gel arrows were completely ineffective!" Brona changed out the arrows in her bow for ones loaded with red jinxes. "FIRE! FIRE! The reading never said anything about FIRE! Madame Le Deux needs to update her textbooks!"

As the monotonous voice droned on, repeating "Intruder alert!" Zephyr came up with a plan to get them from the elevator to the shrine.

"Niall, lead us the fastest way out of the palace to Rilios.

Kelcie, you're his wingman. Or should it be wingwoman? Let's go with wingperson! You see one of those things coming for our Adder, burn it to dust. Brona, fly. Keep a lookout for anything we're going to miss coming our way. The goal is to get to Rilios! And speaking of winged people, if those creeper fairies broke out of prison, we can expect the others to be with them, and that includes a very surly, very dangerous ice fairy."

"Achila Grimes," Kelcie spat her name.

Zephyr continued talking fast. "Conserve ammunition at all costs. Our fight is in the shrine. Let the soldiers deal with the bodachs."

"What about you?" Brona asked.

"I may not be able to get rid of them with this," Zephyr pulled his shillelagh from its holster on his back, "but I can knock 'em out of play."

"Arrived," the elevator crooned, and the doors parted.

Kelcie's swords felt ten times heavier as they rushed into the hallway and found the palace in complete mayhem. Bodachs swung from chandeliers by their tentacled heads, swiping at staff who reached for anything and everything to fend them off. Flower vases did little to help, but toppled dessert trays and tables of champagne flutes proved irresistible, and feasting bodachs made for easy targets.

By Niall's side, as the bodachs lunged for him, Kelcie gripped the swords the same way she did in the hallway upstairs, calling for fire, lighting up one bodach after another.

Some bodachs burst into dust. Others ended with a much more shocking demise. Those who'd recently eaten imploded—skin falling off, bones cracking in half, and half again—while vomiting undigested souls. It was beyond digusting.

Kelcie did her best to keep up with Niall, but it wasn't easy. He was faster, much faster, and wasn't slowing down no matter how many times she called his name.

As they passed through the main hall, the doors to the court-yard flung wide. Kelcie saw ball guests running for their lives.

Tentacles snatched a fleeing sprite right out of the night sky. Her classmate Marta Louisa took a flying leap, transforming into a jaguar midair, biting the sprite free, but many were not so lucky.

A troll shrieked past with her blue dress hiked above her knees, trying to get to an overflowing trolley, but never made it. The only thing that made it on the transport was her white stilettos when the bodach spit them out.

Casper Thorn was trapped with a team of palace guards surrounding Queen Eislyn and Regan. Kelcie hesitated continuing on, but Scáthach sprinted into the fray, hurling her flaming spear at the same time unmuzzled Ellén Trechend soared over the garden flame broiling large swaths of bodachs at a time.

Out of nowhere, Tad Fagan crab-crawled through the open palace door in a failing attempt to get away from a bodach. Tentacles launched at Fagan's throat. Too close to Tad to use fire, Kelcie got between them, swords thrusting, the hooked tips catching nothing but rib bones. The bodach used this to its advantage, pulling Kelcie closer, its nails digging into her back. Brona's arrow hit the bodach right between the eyes.

Gray muck rained down as Kelcie bounced off Fagan's rock-hard abs and fell on the floor beside him. Fagan staggered to his feet, coughing, his black suit covered in ash, looking surprisingly appreciative.

"Thanks."

Brona croaked-a-you're-welcome overhead.

"Kelcie! Brona! Hurry up!" Niall hollered.

Kelcie saw him and Zephyr take a hard right. When she caught up to them, they had gone into an elegant sitting room. Built-in bookshelves on every wall, deep sofas and chairs spread out, giving readers loads of peaceful, comfy spots to sink into and get lost in a book for hours. With a place like this in his house, it was no wonder Niall spent so much time reading.

A sofa had been moved away from the wall, and Niall and Zephyr were kneeling next to a three-foot-wide grate in the floor. Brona landed beside Kelcie, shaking bodach dust off her feathers, remaining in her familiar form.

"This is an old sewer tunnel. It leads to an exit hidden by bushes in the garden behind the palace, about twenty feet from the shrine's entrance," Niall said in a rush, loading jinxes into his sidewinder. "It's the only way we'll get there in time, unless of course the bodachs found the way into the tunnel from the other side, which we won't know until we're down there."

"Really? You had to say that, didn't you?" Zephyr grumbled, lifting out the polished brass grate. Without a moment's hesitation, Niall jumped in. Kelcie heard a hard thud, but no yelp.

"Come on! It's only about five or six feet down."

Brona flew down, shifting and loading her bow upon landing. Putting her swords in her scabbard, Kelcie was more than happy to let Zephyr be chivalrous, and accepted his offer to help lower her to the ground, alleviating the distinct possibility that she would twist an ankle.

Her swords were immediately back in her hands. Only a couple feet across, the secret passage was stiflingly small, and very, very dark. It was quiet though, and hopefully that meant the bodachs hadn't discovered it yet.

"Give us light, Saiga," Zephyr ordered.

Kelcie reluctantly put away one of her swords to cup her palm for her flame, and felt a sudden strange loss—a tug on her heart like when she had to say goodbye to Brona at Chawell Woods. But this was a sword, not a person. *Ridiculous.* She tried to bury it, but the sadness was still there, a hundred yards and three turns later, when the tunnel slipped into a steady decline.

A combination of stale urine and rotten eggs assaulted Kelcie's nostrils, leaving a horrid taste in her mouth. She stopped breathing through her nose.

"What is that smell?" Brona asked.

"Old sewers," Zephyr answered. "I really don't want to think about what we're stepping on right now."

"It's fine. I sneak out this way all the time," Niall dismissed.

The ground dipped steeply at the exit—a loose grate as tall as Kelcie—and they heard grunting, shrieking, and roaring, the sounds of the battle still raging. Kelcie took that as a good sign, that there were still plenty of forces securing the shrine, but as Zephyr shifted the grate a foot, enough for them to take turns climbing out, Kelcie saw a very different reality.

Summer's forces were nowhere near Rilios. Flaming spears and arrows streaked across the field at the Sidral where a steady flow of bodachs were *still* coming out.

There was no time to waste.

Niall duck-walked to avoid drawing attention. Brona and Zephyr followed, while Kelcie brought up the rear, extinguishing her palm and taking out her second sword, relieved to have it back in her hand.

Niall tucked against Rilios's smooth walls. As they moved around to the other side, Kelcie saw the shrine was made from a single piece of moonstone, its milky luster like an unyielding cloudy day.

Niall stopped short at the entrance—an arched opening—which appeared to be magical, because there was no actual door.

"Useless! Help her, gassy boy!"

The shrill voice coming from inside the shrine was unmistakably that of Achila Grimes. *Oh joy* . . . Kelcie really hated that fairy. She hated even more that there was no time to stop and plan. With an unending supply of nightmares exiting the Sidral, no help was coming. Kelcie's and Brona's mothers were right. It really was up to them.

Brona loaded her bow. Niall check his sidewinder. Zephyr pulled his sword.

Kelcie did some quick math: assuming the Orange Crush twins were working the Sidral, that left Grimes, Blizzard, Pethia, and Lexis. Four against four. The odds were even. But then, who was gassy *boy*? Kelcie gripped her swords tighter.

Niall looked back. *I'll go first and take Grimes out with the scream.*

Zephyr nodded his agreement, spinning the grip of his sword once in his hand before trailing after him.

The narrow passageway wound in a spiral. Kelcie's anxiety rose with every unconscious Summer soldier they found captured in frozen webs. The temperature dropped dramatically, the uneven ground icy and slick. Kelcie's hands started shaking. The grips of her swords warmed as if in response.

Skating around the next bend, Kelcie felt pins and needles all over like she'd passed through a static electricity force field. Niall's hair on one side reached for the ceiling. Then, the passageway ended.

Her heart thundering, she got only a second to take in the space. Round, like the outside of the shrine, but the inside was unexpectedly large. There was a stone—seven feet tall and about four feet thick—set in the center. Lexis was crouched beside it, her palms flat on the surface, her curly hair falling out of its ponytail, sweat pouring from her brow. She leaned her forehead on the stone, looking exhausted. And she wasn't alone. An exact replica of her was doing the exact same thing.

There were *three* others: two hovering behind her—a black-haired boy, another boy who was bald and armed in ice with a set of fairy wings, and, standing over Lexis, the only one Kelcie recognized.

Achila Grimes. Her wings fanned out with a *thwack*.

The ice fairy held a torch higher, growling in Lexis's ear. "You're not even trying."

"Really? Why don't you try and open it, then?" Lexis snapped.

Or maybe it was the twin.

Changeling, Niall corrected, or said . . .

Too many times Kelcie thought Niall could read her mind, but didn't want her to know. She didn't want to know either.

"If you fail, your fianna will take the blame!" Grimes shrieked.

Maybe it was the swords giving her confidence or the fear she saw in Lexis's eyes, a fear that reminded her of how she felt last year when that same fairy tricked her into the Ta Erfin challenge, forcing her into a fight against her own father for something she never wanted, with an evil spirit making her do things she would never have done on her own. Things she didn't want to do.

Kelcie pushed Niall aside.

"What are you doing?" Zephyr whispered harshly. "Saiga!"

Kelcie heard Brona's bowstring draw to give her cover.

Lexis leaned on the stone, wincing, closing her eyes. A move Kelcie did when she needed to draw more power. "Ther—"

"No! Stop! Lexis, don't!" Kelcie pleaded, stepping out. "If you do this, if you take the Heart of Danu, everyone in Summer will *die*!"

The second Lexis belched a gasp. "Die?" Her hands fell off the Stone of Destiny.

"That's exactly what they said you'd say!" the boy ice fairy boomed.

"Pavel, what do you mean? What did they tell you?" Lexis asked like it was an order. When he didn't answer, her mismatched, conflicted stare fell on Kelcie.

It dawned on Kelcie that she and Lexis weren't just Summer or Winter, they were Fomorian. The one thing that connected them now and forever. The words on the stone tablet came back to Kelcie, and she hoped Lexis would understand them too. *"Tara vlast Alltar rask."*

Lexis's mouth fell open, and she said, "So much power Alltar split."

Kelcie's heart sang. She understood! *"Folam kirovan hapnar."*

Lexis stood up. "Nothingness blocked the sun, the moon, and the stars."

"Shut up!" Achila Grimes growled, lobbing a storm of ice at Kelcie, which Lexis's twin melted before it could get to her.

"She's telling the truth," Niall exclaimed, coming to stand beside Kelcie.

He raised his sidewinder at the roof, proving he meant no harm. "Please. Listen to us. If you take the *Croí na Bandia*, the

Heart of Danu, the nothingness, the *Abyss* will block the sun and the moon and the stars. In a short time, everyone and everything in Summer will die!"

"Everyone? What about the wyverns we saw? What about all the nice people we met?" Lexis's twin asked her.

"What about the people who died in Volga, Swappy?" Pavel hissed through his iced fangs. "They're lying to us! I'm telling you this is exactly what the Advisors told me they would say!"

Lexis looked at the dark-haired boy who had remained quiet. He simply shrugged, leaving the final decision to her. A final glance at Grimes whose lip curled, and Lexis folded.

Although she said, "They're lying, Swaps," what Kelcie really heard was, "We don't have a choice."

A snow-white stripe raced down the black-haired boy's head on his way to turning into a saber-toothed tiger (which Kelcie had to admit was incredibly cool). Then he lunged at Kelcie.

Brona rushed to Kelcie's defense, shifting on the fly, scraping talons down his back. The tiger reared. His dagger-length canines caught her wing on the updraft and he hurled her to the ground.

Brona morphed to her human form, her arm deeply scratched and bleeding, but she still managed to fire off three arrows at once. Anticipating, he scaled the wall, moving out of the way a second before they struck, and circled back. Equally gifted, Brona had met her Winter match!

Niall glared at Grimes, arm extended, brow furrowing deeper than Kelcie had ever seen before.

"Argh! You evil . . . OW!" The evil fairy grabbed the sides of her head. Her wings and knees buckled at the same time, and she fell over, writhing in pain.

"Hey! That's my aunt!" Pavel flew at Niall, throwing razor-sharp snowflakes, forcing him to run and lose his grip on Achila.

Zephyr went after her, running up the wall, jumping into the air, his shillelagh making contact with Achila's leg. The shock overtook her all at once. Her wings skittered to a halt and she dropped to the ground yet again, this time a twitching mess.

"Y-y-y-y-ou wr-r-r-r-etch!"

Diving backward, Niall unloaded every jinx in his sidewinder at Pavel, keeping him busy. Brona and Zephyr charged at the saber-toothed tiger, pinning him against the wall, giving Kelcie a shot at getting to Lexis. She saw Kelcie coming and slammed her hands on the Stone of Destiny.

The other Lexis changed into a skinny boy, green hair falling in his face. He rushed Kelcie, startling her with a hug. A second later, Kelcie was staring at her own freckled face.

In the mad scramble to get to Lexis, Kelcie had foolishly lost sight of Achila Grimes. The shillelagh's effect must've worn off because the next thing Kelcie knew ice knives cut across the backs of her hands. She dropped her swords and was hog-tied by frigid webs, spinning up and over her mouth, making it impossible for her to speak.

"Do it now!" Grimes barked at Lexis and the changeling.

The others grappled and exchanged fire, and all Kelcie could do was watch in horror as her doppelgänger joined Lexis, pressing palms to the Stone of Destiny, about to use Kelcie's stolen powers. Maybe *stolen* wasn't the right word exactly, but it felt like she'd been robbed.

Together they called, "Theran!"

Together, the shred of space between their hands and the stone glowed.

And together, they strained, pressing as hard as they could.

Fissures crackled, then all at once the giant stone splintered and fell in two perfect halves. Lexis reached inside, retrieving a sculpture no longer than Kelcie's arm, two hands parted down the middle, cradling rays of sunshine. The carving on the front of the tablet.

Danu's Heart! she heard Niall say with awe. His breath seized all at once, and he winced.

Light flooded the chamber, so bright Kelcie was forced to close her eyes. She strained against the bitter cold webs, realizing they were no match for the power of the Heart. A hand grabbed Kelcie's and she knew it was Niall.

Kelcie . . . can you hear that?

"No!"

There was a loud *clank* and the light shut off. Everything went possibly dark. The ground started quaking and didn't stop. Kelcie heard rumbling and groaning.

Kelcie lit her free hand and found Lexis staring back at her through the darkness, a metal box with thick straps like a backpack in her hands—the perfect size to hold the Heart. Though Kelcie expected to see a triumphant, arrogant smile on Lexis's face, she found her looking conflicted.

The fractured walls and splintered ceiling creaked, about to fall on top of their heads. Then the roof caved in.

26

BLIZZARD

ET OFF ME!" Brona yelled.

"I was trying to save your life!" Zephyr bellowed.

"You did. Thanks. Now get off! You're crushing my quivers and they're loaded with jinxes!"

Zephyr gasped and rubble shifted. Kelcie reached for Niall and found his hand reaching for her too. His fingers collapsed around hers, and she sighed, relieved. They were all alive, at least for the moment.

For half a second, as the moonstone glistened with the last remnants of light and life, wishful doubt set in. The shrine was gone. The field around them plainly visible. The Sidral quiet, only a few bodachs were left, and were being chased by Ravens. Lexis and the others her age, Achila Grimes, the creeper fairies on Sidral duty, all of them were gone, the Heart of Danu with them.

Maybe what Nemain and Macha showed them was wrong. Maybe the Fomorian tablet was wrong. Maybe Summer was going to be the same as it always had been, blissfully filled with warmth, and flowers, and birds, with life.

The last dying ember in the moonstone drifted toward Niall's feet and went out. The change was immediate. Darkness rolled in like a blanket of unmoving storm clouds, dimming the moon and stars right before Kelcie's eyes. It was that fast, and then the skies were so black even the smothering darkness was invisible to the naked eye.

Kelcie had never seen the Abyss, but imagined it like the stone tablet had described, rising to such heights the sun and moon couldn't reach Summer. They couldn't reach her grandmother, or Striker. Couldn't reach her school, or Summer City, or the Bountiful Plains, where Zephyr's family was, or Binary Gulch, where Brona's father Tao docked his ship to watch the Ascension from his favorite pub. Or her father trapped in a cell, already cold from dankness and despair. Her mind scrolled through the images of the stone.

Seven days was all they had to get it back.

Day one. Six days left, Niall corrected, sounding as distraught as Kelcie felt.

Niall must've said that to Brona and Zephyr too. Kelcie's cousin rushed for her quivers that had somehow ended up inside the broken Stone of Destiny. Zephyr's jaw set, eyes filled with grim determination. Kelcie reached for her swords, only to find her scabbard empty. Frantically searching the rubble for her twin swords, Kelcie couldn't find them anywhere.

"Where are they?"

Zephyr cleared his throat loudly, demanding her attention. He heaved a slab of moonstone bigger than Kelcie, pointing to her swords that were buried underneath. As soon as they were back in her hands, Kelcie felt like she could take a deep breath again. It was so strange.

On the way to the Sidral, Chargers on horseback surrounded them.

"You!" One aimed his sword at Kelcie. "I saw you get into the Sidral!"

"It was a changeling." Brona shook her head at him. "Really, why don't you think before you speak?"

A few Chargers around him laughed, but not Regan.

"Raven, show some respect," she ordered, dismounting.

Her shredded purple robes fanned out behind her as she went straight for Niall. "What were you thinking?"

"*We* were thinking that if we didn't stop them from stealing Danu's Heart that we were all going to die!"

"Thanks for the include. That was very thoughtful of you," Zephyr said to him.

"What is Danu's Heart?"

Kelcie and Brona groaned.

"And why is it getting so cold?" Regan shivered along with the soldiers around her.

Casper Thorn galloped his horse around the Sidral, halting to dismount, and picked something up. He padded directly to Niall, holding out his missing bough. Niall's lips parted in shock as he took it.

"Thank—"

"Ah. Nope. I talk. You listen." Casper Thorn was angry. "You and your fianna are to return to your room in the palace and remain there."

"Until when? They're getting away!" Brona exclaimed.

"Until after I have visited the College of Mystical Beings and have seen that tablet for myself."

"What tablet?" Regan cried, hugging herself. "Do you know why it's getting so cold?"

"It's only going to get colder," Kelcie said, then looked at Thorn. "There are more Ignis elementals in Chawell Woods. I know if asked they would help, you know, keep fires burning."

Thorn frowned at her, nodding slightly, and if Kelcie wasn't mistaken, seemed almost grateful for the suggestion, before turning to Regan, who was still whining about the dropping temperatures.

"Regan, gather up any soldiers not occupied by the remaining bodachs. I'll need backup dealing with the Tiniest Speck." He pinned Niall with a stern stare. "To your room. Now." Then at Brona. "All of you are with him."

Niall didn't say a word.

Zephyr nodded. "Yes, sir, we're with him. One hundred percent. For sure. We will be sticking together . . ." Under his breath he added, muttering in dismay, ". . . all the way to the Lands of Winter."

As soon as Casper was gone, Niall handed his bough to Kelcie to help him tie the unbreakable strap around his neck. Once secured, he picked it up, staring at it sadly before tucking it under his shirt.

"Why do you think they left it?" Zephyr asked.

Brona huffed, exasperated. "Because they didn't need it anymore. They had what they came for. If anything, it was a liability, a way for the Heart to be returned." She tapped her foot impatiently. "How long are we going to stand here? They're getting away!"

"I know, but where are we going?" Zephyr whispered. "How are we going to get to Winter?"

Kelcie had never thought about it before but . . . "Elliott was from Winter. He came to Massachusetts to check on me and move me all the time so—"

"So there must also be a way to Winter in Massachusetts," Niall finished for Kelcie.

"My bough will take us to Boston," Kelcie whispered back. "So we go to Boston, and we figure out how to get to Winter from there."

"Figure out?" Zephyr worried.

"We don't always have all the answers!" Brona snapped, too loud.

Niall's sister cast a glare in their direction—like all this mess was somehow their fault—before mounting her horse.

"Didn't Casper tell you to go to your room?" Regan blurted.

"Didn't he tell you to go round up soldiers?" Niall retorted.

That got rid of her. Unfortunately, she left five soldiers stationed at the tree, making their departure a little more difficult.

"We need a distraction to get to the Sidral," Zephyr said, speaking out of the side of his mouth.

"I got this." Brona ran over to the soldiers, bursting through their huddled ranks, and declared, "We have a situation! There's another fairy in the shrine's wreckage!"

It was a good idea. If they followed her, that would get them a good fifty yards away, but her heralded news was met with disbelieving smirks and chuckling.

One of the soldiers swatted the guy beside him. "Give it a ch-check. Then walk them to the-the-the palace. B-be sure they do as the High Guard said. And get me a blanket on your way back. And a cup of hot t-t-tea!"

"F-F-F-FIVE of them!" another chimed, hopping up and down, trying to stay warm.

"This way! Hurry!" Brona waved at the soldier to follow. She led him around the far side of the rubble, where they were hidden from view.

"What is she doing?" Zephyr jogged in place, blowing into his cupped palms.

Kelcie smirked, knowing full well what Brona was doing. She would never forget the sight of Tad Fagan clucking like a chicken after Gavin Puce used a special Raven technique called the Bird-brain. She wasn't the least bit surprised when a minute later the soldier came running back into view. Brona had learned from a master.

"We got a cold one!" he yelled, retreating back into the rubble. "Hurry! He's waking up!"

Brona crossed paths with the other soldiers sprinting as fast as they could to the shrine's rubble as she raced across the grass, heading straight to the Sidral.

"Go!" Zephyr whispered.

Starting in an awkward tip-toed crane walk, they hot-footed it after Brona. Coming around the far side of the prickly hawthorn tree, Kelcie stumbled when she came face-to-face with her past.

Elliott Blizzard.

His back plastered against the trunk, he was standing between them and their only chance to get away. Unshaven, his beard was more gray than black. His dark hair was chopped off at odd lengths like he'd cut it with a dull knife, and he looked so uncharacteristically baggy in his saggy green prison clothes. The Elliott Blizzard Kelcie knew in Massachusetts only wore tailored suits and drove a Porsche 911. He would never have been caught dead in that outfit. Kelcie, on the other hand, thought it looked comfortable.

Come to think of it, in hindsight, his expensive things should've been her first clue that he wasn't really working for the Department of Social Services. She glared at him, realizing that she knew nothing about the real Elliott Blizzard, the nimble fairy and spy for Winter, and never did. Everything he told her her whole life had been a lie.

Kelcie's windblast spun around him, capturing him, although he didn't put up a fight. His tiny wings sputtered to a stop, but he said nothing, only gave her a sentimental smile that turned her stomach.

"I guess you missed your only way out of here!" she said to Elliott. "Fianna, our ticket to Winter just arrived by bullet train."

Niall wasted no time setting his bough against the bark.

Boots crunched on frozen grass. Kelcie heard one of the soldiers yell, "Hey! Get away from there!" They were out of time. It was now or never.

In a mad scramble into the Sidral, Kelcie released the air rope on Blizzard, expecting to have to fight to get Elliott inside, but he willingly jumped, and then, to her utter confusion, made sure the others got safely in too.

THEY HAD TO change trees because only Kelcie's bough could open the Sidral to get to the human world. A quick stop at the Academy gave her all of five seconds to see Striker and send him to Chawell Woods to wait for her with Kelcie's grandmother. Knowing they would be together made it easier for Kelcie to leave.

An ancient hum greeted them at their next stop, in Boston, where all of this began for Kelcie—over the bridge in the park not far from the Boston Museum of Fine Arts. Expecting an ambush, Kelcie was surprised to find the magically hidden area empty, and the park fairy-free.

Zephyr gripped Elliott's wings in the Sidral and refused to let go as he hopped out.

"I'm not going to run away," Elliott complained. They were the first words he'd spoken, and they grated on Kelcie's last nerve.

"Why would we believe you?" she asked.

He sighed, sounding utterly broken. "Never mind."

"So, where's your bough? And how do we get to Winter?" Brona demanded. "We need to go now!"

Elliott stopped, his bare feet unbothered by the three inches of fresh snow on the ground. "A. I don't have it on me. And B. I will take you to the Winter Sidral, but you cannot go into Winter looking like a bag of Skittles. You'll stand out like the Academy cadets you are. Braverwil doesn't wear color-coded uniforms. Aífe prefers everyone to blend in."

"Who's Aífe?" asked Zephyr.

Niall scratched his head. "Scáthach's sister. She runs Winter's school."

Confused, Kelcie frowned. Why would two sisters be on opposite sides of the war?

"I will take you to my house," Elliott offered.

"So we can walk right into another trap like the one you set for me at the museum? How stupid do you think I am?" Kelcie yelled. "Where is the bough? And where is the Winter Sidral, Elliott?"

"I'm taking you to it! I promise you that this is not a trap."

"We have no choice but to go with him," Zephyr said, clasping Elliott's wings so hard the fairy whimpered. "We need the bough and the location of the Sidral, but we also need more information about Winter and what we're getting into. And he's going to tell us everything."

"Fine. We'll go with you," Kelcie agreed, but wasn't happy

about it. "But know if you're lying to me, Elliott Blizzard, I'll let my cousin shoot one of her jinx-loaded arrows right up your nose."

As they trudged toward the road, Brona leveled an arrow at Elliott's side and Zephyr held on to his wings.

"Maybe this is a good time to explain to your scout troop that there are laws against walking around with weapons pointed at people, in Massachusetts anyway." Blizzard smirked. "And since you are still technically a minor, Kelcie, and I am still listed as your caseworker, they might want to treat me with some respect and let go of my wings!"

Kelcie shook her head. "I don't think so. But Brona, he's right about the weapons. Put that away. And if anyone asks, we're going to a costume party."

Snow fell, another inch accumulating on the road by the time they crossed it to get to the front of the museum. Along the way, they passed the repaired window Achila Grimes broke last year.

She glared at Elliott, fresh anger rising. All the years that he'd kept secrets from her. The worst, that he knew who Kelcie's parents were and never told her. But as much as she wanted to hate Elliott, she couldn't, and that made her feel weak.

"What?" Elliott asked, catching her staring.

"You're a monster."

"I did a bad thing."

"Stop talking to her," Niall warned him.

"She talked to me first!" Elliott gave Niall a curious look, shaking his head, his shoulder blades twitching. Kelcie could have sworn he was laughing.

A look at the dimming skies told Kelcie it was a little earlier in Boston, but not by much. They climbed in a cab parked out front of the museum. Elliott gave the driver directions, an address in a place called Beacon Hill.

During the short drive, Zephyr, Brona, and Niall hung their

heads out the window, bellowing, "What's that?" every five seconds.

Cars, buses, traffic lights, helicopters, airplanes, Christmas lights that had yet to be taken down, Dunkin Donuts (Kelcie begged to stop, but Elliott flatly refused) . . . and on and on until the yellow hatchback pulled over in front of a palatial townhouse in the most expensive part of Boston. Kelcie couldn't believe Elliott had dumped her off in group homes where she sometimes slept thirty to a room, had barely any heat in freezing winters and never any air conditioning in hot summers. Places where most days she only got one good meal which was served by a free lunch program at school. And he went home to sleep here.

He must've noticed her jaw drop because he leaned over the front seat to say something, but never got the chance.

A frantic man burst out of the house, taking the four front steps two at a time. "Elliott! Is that you?"

Wavy blond hair standing on end, he wore a navy-blue suit, a wrinkled white button-down shirt, and a loosened tacky tie with rain clouds on it.

Brona tapped Kelcie on the shoulder and pointed out the back window of the cab to a billboard. Looming twenty-five feet above was a giant picture of the guy: perfect smile, in a similar suit, advertising for a local news station with the slogan: *All the latest weather news, tune in to our weather authority, Oliver Sprinkle!*

Elliott tried to get out of the cab, but the driver grabbed his arm. "Where do you think you're going? You have to pay me first."

"I have to get money. They'll stay here as collateral. If I don't come back, you can keep them."

"Oh, no. Not letting you out of my sight," Zephyr said, hustling after him.

Kelcie watched through the window as Oliver Sprinkle threw his arms around Elliott. "I've been so worried!" Pulling back to give him a once-over, he cupped his cheek. "You look terrible.

Are you hurt? Where have you been? What in Otherworld are you wearing? And why are you in a cab with four children? Are they from Summer? Elliott!"

Kelcie gawked at Elliott's five-story colonial townhouse. Planter boxes weighed down by six inches of snow, and snarling gargoyles on the roof. It looked well-groomed, yet creepy. A lot like Elliott.

Keep watch, Niall warned. *Those things could be spelled to come to life.*

"Spelled?" Kelcie gaped at the gargoyles.

Niall must've been speaking to all of them because Brona smooshed Kelcie into him, trying to get a better look at the statues. "There are witches in Winter. For all we know, that Oliver Sprinkle is one of them."

"I think he's a weatherman," Kelcie corrected.

"Right. Exactly. A witch who can manipulate *the weather,*" Brona retorted.

"I'll explain inside. Will you please pay the cab?" Elliott said to Oliver.

Oliver eyed them warily through the cab's window. "My wallet's on the dresser upstairs."

Elliott walked at a fast clip, a snail's pace for a nimble fairy, into the house.

Zephyr chased after him, which left Oliver conflicted about staying or going, but not Kelcie.

Ignoring the driver's protests, Kelcie hustled after Zephyr, who had entered the house. Brona and Niall were right behind her.

The house was as posh on the inside as it was on the outside, and a nightmare to keep clean. Everything in the room was white—the walls, sofa, chairs, Formica coffee table—the only exceptions being red crushed velvet drapes and parquet wood floors.

Kelcie cleared her throat soundly. "Mr. Sprinkle, exactly how much do weather people make?"

"That is a very personal question."

"I want my money!" the driver called from the stoop. He clunked the knocker. "I'm going to call the police!"

Niall was all over the bookshelf beside the fireplace and Zephyr was on the staircase, heading upstairs, his shillelagh in hand, looking for Blizzard.

"A fire!" Brona declared.

Oliver caught her cloak before she got away. "OKAY! THAT'S IT! You, stop touching my books!" he shouted. Niall set the book back. "And you with the stick of doom, Elliott will be down—"

A blur whizzed by Zephyr, knocking him into the railing, and suddenly Elliott was walking out the front door and slamming it shut behind him.

Oliver seized the moment of silence. "Listen to me! All of you, get back here." He pointed to his socked feet. "We have a no shoe and no weapons policy in this house. Park them here, right where I'm standing. Otherwise, you can wait for Elliott outside!"

"Fine," Brona conceded. "You can have my shoes but I never go anywhere without my weapons, not even to bed."

"Well, then, you know where the door is . . ." He tapped his foot impatiently. "I'm counting . . . one . . . two—"

"Before we agree to this, what *are* you?" Zephyr plonked down the stairs, his shillelagh resting on his shoulder.

"What am I?" His bushy blond brows creased. "Oh." He laughed. His teeth were so bleached they looked fake. "I'm mortal, your standard everyday Winterfolk. I don't have powers. I didn't go to *Braverwil*." He said that like Braverwil was some kind of elite school. "Do all Summerfolk have powers?" he asked curiously.

"No."

"You see, then, I'm like the rest of Summerfolk, who just have your everyday average jobs. Only nine years ago, Elliott had to move here for work, and I came with him."

"That was a very long answer to a short question." Brona

scowled. She cornered him against the orderly coats hanging from hooks on a tree behind him.

Elliott opened the door and snarled, his lip twitching. "Leave him alone!" He closed the door and threw the bolt. "Shoes and weapons here!" Unclipping Kelcie's cloak, Blizzard hung it on its own hook, then put a hand out, snapping for her scabbard.

She begrudgingly passed it to him. The others then acquiesced, discarding their boots, bows, swords, sidewinders, and shillelaghs, and moved to the fireplace, where they jockeyed for the warmest spot in front of the fire.

"So where's your Winter bough, Elliott?" Kelcie plopped down on the sofa, resting her feet on the coffee table.

Sprinkle cast them off. "Who in the world raised you?"

"I guess you could say he did." Kelcie flashed a sarcastic smile at Elliott.

"What?" The weatherman grimaced at Elliott, waiting for an explanation.

"Oliver Sprinkle, meet Kelcie Murphy. My assignment for the past nine years. Kelcie, Oliver is my husband."

Kelcie's jaw dropped. "You're married?"

"Your assignment?" Oliver gasped.

"What's this for?" Brona frowned, holding up a glass snowflake coaster.

Oliver took it from her. "It's a coaster. You put a glass on it. And it stays here."

Elliott trudged to the stairs, running a hand through his filthy hair.

"Where are you going?" Oliver squeaked.

"Look at me!" Elliott paused on the bottom step. "I need a shower and a drink, not necessarily in that order."

"Well, how long will your assignment and her friends be staying?" Oliver asked, smiling through gritted teeth.

"Just one night, Oliver."

"Night?" Kelcie lit her hand on fire.

Oliver screamed, backing away. "Elliott! Do they all do that?"

"We are not staying here! You said you'd get us the bough and show us where the Sidral is!" Brona fumed.

The next thing Kelcie knew, Elliott was standing in front of her, inches from her flames. "Listen to me. You can hate me all you want for what I did to you, but it will never be an ounce of the regret I feel in my heart for having done it. Give me this one chance to help you. Please. I may have been a useless caseworker, but I am a good spy."

Elliott's face was covered in sweat from being so close to the flames on her hand, but still he didn't move. Kelcie wanted to believe that he was telling her the truth, that he really cared. That this wasn't some kind of a trap. But only time would tell, and time was something that was in very short supply. The clock to Summer's demise was ticking. Every second counted.

"I hate that I can't tell if you're lying."

"I'm not. I'm a very good spy." He smirked.

Kelcie cracked a smile. She closed her fist, extinguishing her hand.

"So, good spy, what do you think we need to do first?" Zephyr asked.

"You need to eat, to plan, and to sleep, in that order."

He's right, Kelcie.

She looked back at Niall, stunned and slightly miffed to hear him agree with Elliott. Zephyr was nodding too.

Brona crossed her arms, smirking. "They have to sleep sometime too, Kelcie. They try anything . . ." She slid a finger accross her neck.

"Lovely." Elliott zoomed back to the stairs. "Now that that's settled, please order them pizza, Oliver."

"Fine."

"Three cheese, and one pepperoni for the scamp, because she doesn't like to share food." Elliott winked at her.

"If we're staying the night I want Fanta too," Kelcie countered. "Please."

"Fanta?" Oliver convulsed.

Blizzard shrugged. "She did say please . . ."

As he disappeared, Oliver sized up each of them while picking up his cell phone. "We'll order eight. I don't like to share food either."

True to his word, a minute after the pizza arrived, Elliott returned, smelling spring fresh, hair wet and slicked back, cleanly shaven, and dressed in jeans and a T-shirt. On the way to the kitchen, he grabbed something from a drawer in a credenza, then made another stop for a bottle of wine from a refrigerator Kelcie didn't realize was there. It was camouflaged behind white cabinets, like they didn't want anyone to know the kitchen was a kitchen.

Claiming the empty chair next to Oliver, Blizzard set a map down in front of Kelcie. On the top, written in rigid font, were the words *Lands of Winter*.

Her fianna got up and came around the table to examine it over her shoulders.

"Is it real?" Brona asked, skeptical.

"I think so. It matches what I've seen in my mother's war room," Niall answered.

Zephyr picked it up to take a closer look.

"It's real," Elliott insisted.

Oliver poured him a drink.

Zephyr used his greasy index finger to guide the map in front of Elliott. "Where did they take Danu's Heart?"

He arched a thin, dark brow. "I don't know."

"He's lying," Brona grumbled, taking two more slices of pizza, including one of Kelcie's pepperoni, on her way back to her seat.

Elliott took offense. "I'm not lying. I've been in prison. I had nothing to do with this."

"Prison?" Oliver blurted. "Oh, honey. That's what that smell was? Please tell me you're done with that job. I can't take another six months—"

"I'm done. Very done," Elliott promised.

Zephyr closed his empty pizza box and took another. "I don't get it. Why did the others leave you at the Sidral?"

Elliott looked at Oliver. "They left me at the prison. Queen Eislyn blamed me for our loss last year at the school."

"What?" Oliver groaned.

"And Grimes refused to come to my defense. They didn't bother to take me with them when they left, or help me escape. They just left me there."

"I hate that fairy," Oliver spat.

"Couldn't agree more." Kelcie chomped down on her plate of crust. She always saved the best part for last.

"How did you escape?" Niall asked.

"The girl who came to break them out . . . she took pity on me for some reason and tossed me the keys as they left."

"Lexis?" Kelcie asked.

"Curly dark hair. I didn't get her name."

It had to be her. Why would she do that? Why would she waste precious seconds during a prison break to help him? They clearly didn't know each other. But that wasn't entirely true. Lexis did know who Elliott was. Kelcie told her about him that first night in the Saiga Den when Lexis wanted to know the story of how Kelcie's fianna battled King Balor's evil eye at the school last year. Was it possible Lexis helped Elliott because of *her*?

Lexis had asked her if she hated Elliott. Kelcie's response danced through her mind now as she stared at him. Her exact words were *I could never hate him*.

"Then you waited for me," Kelcie said, tearing off another piece of crust with her teeth.

"I originally followed them, thinking I could beg my way back into Grimes's graces to take me home, but then if I did, she would know the girl let me out. She risked everything to help me. Seemed like a poor choice for me to pay her back that way. And then I saw it. The Abyss rising . . ." Elliott mused, spinning his wine.

"You saw that? It happened so fast!" Kelcie exclaimed.

"Nimble fairy." He winked, smirking. "Keener vision. Otherwise I would bump into things. Summer is in real trouble. And I will get you into Winter." He lifted a thin silver chain over his head and held it out to her, staring at Oliver. "You can keep it. I have no use for it anymore."

Oliver smiled, nodding. "Good. I like it here."

Rather than branches and leaves, the Winter's bough resembled the roots of a tree, snake-like and twisted. Kelcie took the bough her mother gave her out of her pocket, placed it on the chain beside Elliott's, and then put it on before Elliott changed his mind.

"Now the question is, where to begin the search?" Zephyr asked.

"I have an idea." Kelcie smiled at Elliott. "Where is Braverwil, exactly?"

IN THE EARLY hours of the morning, under the cloak of darkness, Elliott Blizzard drove them to a graveyard on the outskirts of Boston. He pulled over beside a rusty cemetery gate. Mist squeezed between slanted tombstones, and mausoleums were buried in snowdrifts. Somehow a graveyard seemed a much less inviting station to the Otherworld than the bridge over the pond in a park by the museum. It was telling.

"This is it," Elliott said, looking everywhere but at them. "Keep alert."

"For what?" Niall asked.

Elliot glanced over his shoulder at him. "A trap. This is the only Sidral into Winter in the Northern Hemisphere, and Kelcie's bough returns to the human world from Summer in Boston. Grimes knows I was left behind, thus likely to have been found by Kelcie, and after being betrayed, gave her my bough. This is the only place Kelcie and all of you would enter Winter. Don't you think Grimes would've thought of that?"

Niall ground his teeth. "Yes. That is an excellent point."

Elliott had done more than just give Kelcie his bough. While they slept, he and Oliver searched through an attic full of boxes, and in the last one they found all of his old Braverwil uniforms. They started younger than at the Academy. Kelcie and Brona fit in his early years. Niall was easy because Elliott was skinny like him when he was the same age. In fact, Elliott was still pretty skinny. Oliver was forced to break out his sewing machine to let out the chest to accommodate for Zephyr's big muscles.

Climbing out of the car, into below-freezing temperatures, Kelcie was warm, almost too warm. The suits had some kind of magical insulation that, according to Elliott, would keep them from dying of frostbite in the Lands of Winter, at least during the daylight hours. But it also was the perfect disguise, something he thought of when Kelcie said Lexis had posed as an Academy student since the start of the school year.

"Thank you," Kelcie said, trudging after Elliott through the crunching snow. "For everything."

"It's almost like you want us to succeed," Zephyr crooned.

"Yeah. Maybe you secretly want Summer to win this war," Brona added, settling her bow over her shoulder.

"I wouldn't go that far." Elliott winked at Kelcie.

They trekked through standing graves dating back to the 1600s, up a hill, then another, heading toward a stone archway that looked as old as the stone crypt underneath Haven Hall. A howling wind stirred snow and leafless branches. A strange ticking—the sound a clacking tongue makes—came from behind them. Elliott paused. His subsequent *uh-oh* left Kelcie waiting, breathless, looking everywhere but at him.

Something flew over them so close Kelcie felt the downdraft on her neck. Something sharp snagged her hair as she dropped to the frozen ground. Kelcie wheeled over, lighting her hand like a torch to see what it was, and wished she hadn't.

Before Kelcie could ask what it was, fanged owls spiraled up and over the archway with a murderous glint in their solid white eyes. Elliott stepped out in front of them, letting out a tiny wail.

"Vampire owls! Of course! Grimes knows how much I hate the sight of blood. Especially my own!"

Before Kelcie knew what he was doing, Elliott had used a knife drawn from his boot to cut his forearm. Kelcie never knew owls could sniff, but these did, audibly and with zeal.

"I'll distract them! The Sidral is just through the archway!" Elliott declared, his normal baritone voice rising three octaves to a trembling vibrato as his entire being started vibrating. "Run! All of you! Now! And don't look back!"

The frenzied birds chased after him. The others raced ahead, but Kelcie felt conflicted. How could she leave him like this? If they caught him . . . a big if. He was a nimble fairy. Niall came sprinting back.

He said to run! He grabbed Kelcie's hand, making the decision for her.

Under the archway, they joined Zephyr and Brona, stumbling over a sea of bulbous roots, some topping a couple feet high, on their way to the fattest tree stump Kelcie had ever seen. The top half was cut on a jagged slant as if this tree once went to another place, maybe Summer, and the route was abruptly canceled.

The owls' screeching headed back their direction. Kelcie fumbled Elliott's Winter bough against the bark. When it didn't work, she slapped it on the top. When that didn't work, she freaked.

"Where does this thing go?"

Brona climbed on top of the stump and started jumping up and down.

"Open!"

Niall and Zephyr helped Brona, adding their weight, while Kelcie tried different parts of the stump—sliding it into every nook and cranny—but nothing happened.

Kelcie looked at the charm and realized what she had to do.

She lunged for the biggest root. On contact, a hole in the middle of the stump opened. Her fianna fell in.

"Kelcie!" Brona yelled, her cousin's voice growing farther and farther away by the second.

The murderous owls whipped through the archway, eyes narrowing in on Kelcie, and pivoted downward, their long sharp claws on their way to turning her into a pincushion. Where was Elliott? What if he was hurt? Or worse . . . A moment's hesitation and the hole started to close. It was now or never . . .

Run. Elliott told her to run, and that's what she was going to do.

Kelcie scrambled over the roots. The vampire owls swooped, fangs extended, rasping like rattlesnakes right next to her ears. There was no time to fight them off. She felt their claws tear the back of her new Braverwil uniform as she dived through the closing hole headfirst.

27

A HERO'S WELCOME

THE LAST TIME Lexis and her fianna visited the Boreal Citadel they had entered through an underground tunnel and never saw another soul except the Queen's Advisors. Today, they were marched through the grand twenty-foot sapphire doors, up the main spiral staircase, and presented to the Queen during a thrown together reception for the conquering heroes with all the noble families in the Lands of Winter in attendance. The applause was unending, their grateful smiles as bright as the gems they wore. Lexis was the hero she always wanted to be, and had never felt worse in her life.

The procession began at the Sidral in Galanta, the bustling city nearest the citadel where Jack had grown up.

The Advisors were there when they arrived. Still wearing the same blue and black tabards as the many guards with them, they had changed one thing about their appearance. Gone were their expressionless polished silver masks, traded in for ones painted slate-blue with harrowing permanent smiles and dia-mond-tipped fairy fangs. They didn't bother to see if Lexis and her fianna still had all their fingers and toes. They only cared about the box containing their prize.

Achila led the way, but Lexis carried the Heart of Danu. The ice fairy's hands were still blistered from touching the box in the shrine. The heat emanating from the Heart was unbearable for most, but as a Fomorian with fire powers, Lexis was able to tolerate it for a time, time that was running out. Her stomach queasy, her arms burned raw, she couldn't wait to be rid of it.

During the march to the citadel, Achila spoke in hushed tones to the Advisors. The changeling, Pethia, and the creeper twins, Nevver and Latchkey, folded in single file behind the ice fairy, as was protocol, but it made it impossible for Lexis to hear what Grimes was saying. She was positive the ice fairy filled them in on everything, including Lexis having second thoughts. She likely took full credit for stealing the Heart too.

Seeing as how half of them were dressed in Summer prison clothes and the others wore thin linens in Winter, it wasn't surprising that people on the street stopped and stared. Jack and Pavel smiled at all the looky-loos. Jack even boasted about having been on a mission in Summer to a couple of the kids from town who recognized him, until Lexis shut him up.

The mission was top secret. Period. The end. They were never allowed to talk about any of it, not what happened before they left, during the time they were gone, or what would come next for the *Croí na Bandia*.

As uncharacteristically giddy as Jack and Pavel were, Swappy was the opposite. He didn't crack a single joke, belch out an overzealous hello at the town's admirers, or break wind when they were greeted at the surprise reception at the citadel. Every time Lexis looked back at him, he was staring at what Lexis carried in her hands, his brow creased, and Lexis knew why.

He was worried. She was too. She wanted to believe Kelcie was lying like Pavel said. But what if she wasn't? Lexis was shocked when Kelcie spoke to her in the ancient Fomorian language. Few Fomorians in Winter knew that language, and Kelcie had grown up in the human world. When would she have learned it? And the words sounded stilted, like they'd come from one of the old tablets in the Mezron temple, what the clan used to document important events before paper. What if all of the Summerfolk *were* going to die because the *Croí na Bandia* was stolen? The

Advisors had warned Pavel that someone in Summer would say that very thing, which meant that it had to be true. Lexis's stomach churned so hard she almost dropped the precious box she carried.

The farther they padded into the reception, the hotter the box grew. Lexis swung the strap on her shoulder, carrying it on her back, giving her hands a break.

The blue radiating from the sapphire walls made everyone turning to greet at them look anemic. Waitstaff passed around trays of yellow sparkling wine, a color not randomly selected, only adding more evidence that what Lexis carried on her back was Summer's stolen sun. Swappy gasped, and broke formation when he saw two people, one with green hair, both with big smiles, the woman's matching his. Lexis assumed these were his parents.

The white lace train of Queen Kefyra's dramatic dress rustled along with her dragging wings as she approached.

"Our heroes are home!" She raised her glass. "The saviors of all of Winter!"

As the guests repeated the Queen's toast, and glasses clinked, Lexis lifted the strap off her shoulder and held the box out to Achila so she could be the one to give it to the Queen.

"This is your triumph." Achila smiled sardonically, stepping aside, "and I would never take that away from you."

Carrying the box against her chest, Lexis felt the *Croí na Bandia* thrumming shakily, slowing and skipping beats, a clock winding down. A memory jolted her. Her at maybe three, sitting on her mother's lap. Her mother's cascade of luscious brown curls falling into Lexis's face as she pressed an ear to her mother's chest to listen to her beating heart. It was such a wondrous sound.

Hearts are just ticking clocks. That's what her mother had said. *When it stops beating, our time is over. That is why every moment is precious. Every action important. Because we never know how long we have, so we must make every moment count.*

Lexis suddenly felt much older than twelve, and a part of her resented it. She had wanted to be a soldier. Wanted to join the fight between Winter and Summer, but never thought about what that fight represented. Braverwil's library was filled with books, detailing skirmishes, missions, and battles between the Lands of Winter and the Lands of Summer that date back thousands of years. Winter sent Achila and her fianna to destroy the Academy for the Unbreakable Arts, and in retribution, Summer sent giants that tore down homes and ended lives in a village Lexis loved. A cycle of devastating actions and reactions, like Roswen had said, perpetuating hate. It needed to end. And now, Winter had stolen this all-important magical beating heart from Summer. And if Kelcie was telling the truth, which deep down Lexis knew she was, it was a blow that would end the war once and for all. But everyone would die. And that was unacceptable to Lexis. Was it possible the Queen didn't know? That the Advisors had hidden it from her too? What about the nobles gathered to celebrate? Did they realize what stealing this Heart might do to Summer?

In silent answer, Queen Kefyra ripped the box from her hands by the strap. The guards shifted as she passed it off to one of her Advisors, then closed the gap, keeping Lexis from seeing which way the Heart went.

Lexis's own heart thundered. Queen Kefyra knew, and had this crowd here for a reason. She wanted nothing, not even her own soldier's questioning, to come between her and victory. Winning the war really was everything to her.

Exhausted and emotionally depleted, Lexis wanted to go home to Braverwil.

"Your Majesty," Swappy asked, "will you open negotiations with the Lands of Summer to end the war?"

Her wings lowered, folding together, and she laughed sarcastically, giving Swappy a placating smile. "That is not for you to worry about. You and your fianna will return to school now." She winked at Swappy's parents, who added another set of grins aimed at Swappy, these ones condescending.

"What? We can't stay for the party?" Jack asked, drooling at the buffet trays being set out on the tables in the back of the room. "We're hungry."

"Starved actually," Pavel added, but stepped back when he saw his aunt's narrowed glare.

"Your service and loyalty have been appreciated and noted, but I cannot be responsible for keeping you from your studies."

Queen Kefyra clapped. Several of her guards filed in behind them. "Escort them to the Sidral."

"Lexis?" Swappy looked up at her with such sadness in his eyes she didn't know what to do.

Nothing she was going to say was going to change anything, but it might get them into terrible trouble. Swappy included. She shrugged, hoping he would understand.

Swappy stormed out of the room, leaving Lexis wishing she had done it first.

28

WINTER NOT—SO—WONDERLAND

TEN SECONDS INTO a terrifying free fall, Kelcie halted midair. Sap poured in, gluing her legs together, then her arms, and continued until it was up to her neck. All she could do was scream as the ride started again, and she plunged through narrowing roots, the Sidral's veins stiffening from plummeting temperatures.

What if she ended up in a different place than her fianna?

Her frantic breath misted as an icicle grew on the tip of Kelcie's nose and drooped her eyelashes. Her racing pulse beat in her eardrums, counting every second Kelcie was separated from them.

Tick-Thump. Tick-Thump. Tick-Thump.

What if by the time she got there, they were captured? Or worse . . .

Tick. Tick. Tick-THUMP!

A harsh pivot snagged her braid painfully while ejecting her from the Sidral. She landed spread-eagled on something cold and hard, wet, and extremely slippery.

Ice!

Kelcie tensed, rising to hands and knees before assessing her surroundings. Through crinkling frozen eyelashes, she figured out she was in the middle of a frozen lake. Muted daylight cast a gray pallor over everything. Pine trees along the banks filled the crisp air with a delicious spicy mint flavor. Weighed down by generations of ice, they sagged, fatigued.

"Everybody all right?"

Relief flooded her at the sound of Zephyr's bellow. Kelcie found him and Brona waving at her from the bank.

"Yes! Kelcie's here too!" Niall shouted.

Kelcie grabbed her chest, startled, and laughed. Niall was only a few feet from her, his hand stretching to reach hers. At least they had all made it to the same place, even if it was so cold she couldn't feel her face anymore, and after only seconds in the Lands of Winter. Niall tugged, gliding her closer, his hand so warm she didn't want to let go but was forced to as he sat on his knees, taking in the pristine landscape.

"I wasn't expecting this kind of beauty in Winter," Niall mused.

"Hurry up, you two!" Zephyr called.

"I'll give you a ride." Kelcie smirked, threading her fingers through his. "Hold on tight. Mistral . . ."

They made it halfway there when a pointed fin broke through the surface, splintering the ice, breaking Kelcie and Niall apart.

Arms as thick as tree trunks shot out of the water, snatching Niall and hoisting him into the air. Rising another five feet, a hulking mass of muscle with bumpy crocodile skin started squeezing the life out of him.

Help!

"Niall!" Kelcie leaped, trying to grab his foot, but missed badly. She crashed down, her feet coming out from underneath her, and fell into an uncontrollable spin, gliding away from him.

Zephyr beat the bank, breaking off ice chunks to pitch at the monster. His first was a fastball strike to an arm that sank beneath the surface only to be replaced by another!

Kelcie came to a stop. Beneath the ice, staring back at her, was a gawped mouth full of teeth, and a scaly head with no eyes; it was the ugliest thing Kelcie had ever seen!

The creature roared at Kelcie, and Niall suddenly cried out. A red spot spread along his Braverwil uniform where a dagger-length nail punctured his side. Brona's arrow loaded with a sleep jinx pierced its shoulder. The creature rocked.

"Heads up! It's going down!" she called.

Niall fell out of the monster's grasp, crashing on the ice and barreling into Kelcie. Things were looking up until the monster fell under the surface, the wake turning the ice Kelcie and Niall clung to on end. It took every last ounce of strength Kelcie had to keep Niall from slipping off as it came crashing down.

Niall clutched his side, wincing, his breath seizing along with Kelcie's at the sight of something else moving beneath the ice.

"There's more of them!" Kelcie warned.

She needed time to get Niall to the bank. There was only one thing she could think to do, but had no idea if it would work. With one hand clutching Niall's, she used her other to pull one of the swords from her scabbard, placing the tip in the water.

"Caenum!" Kelcie called. Once the water shivered at attention, she sparked again. "Theran . . ."

The surge was different, radiating, slowing, turning liquid to solid. The surface around them refroze. Putting the sword away, she grabbed Niall around the waist, feeling him flinch when she accidentally touched the nail still in his side. Panic rising into her throat, she blasted a tailwind that sent them speeding across the frozen lake, and careening into the bank.

On impact, Niall cried out and Kelcie felt horrible.

"I'm so sorry!"

It's not . . . gah! . . . your fault.

Zephyr turned green when he saw Niall's wound. "Gads! Uh, that's . . . I can't even . . ." He closed his eyes briefly, Adam's apple bobbing from repeated swallowing.

Brona wrinkled her nose. "That thing has to come out. Want me to do it?"

"No!" Niall handed Kelcie his glasses to hold. The sound that came out of Niall when he pulled it out was guttural and angry, the yelp as it fell to the ground filled with raw anguish.

Niall leaned his back against a trunk and let her use her palm to put pressure on the wound. When the bleeding didn't stop, she pressed harder. Wincing, his eyes closed. His mouth dried and cracked from the cold, then his lips yellowed, something that was very worrisome.

"What was that thing?" Zephyr asked.

"*Afanc*," Brona answered.

Hair-raising cracks echoed across the lake.

"We need to go." Kelcie tugged Zephyr over to Niall, wrapping one of Niall's arms over the Charger's shoulder, and taking the other. They dragged him upright. "There were more of them beneath the surface."

"More? How many more?" Brona asked, loading her bow.

The ice shattered.

"Too many!" Zephyr cried, backing up. "Go! Now!"

Baby afancs the size of full-grown crocodiles broke through the surface, clawing each other to take the ice first, which they did five at a time. Their nails worked better than crampons, making running on ice as easy as running on land.

Within seconds of reaching solid ground, the babies were nipping at their heels. With Niall injured, there was no way they were going to outrun them. Kelcie let go of Niall's arm, and pulled her swords.

Spinning the blades at her sides, Kelcie sparked air and thrust. The twister plowed through the baby afancs, scooping them into the air, carrying them across the broken ice, but showed no signs of stopping.

Before Kelcie realized what was happening, the tornado drove into the Sidral, tearing it, roots and all, from the ground.

Kelcie ended the tornado, but the damage was done. The entire tree sank, along with the baby afancs, to the bottom of the lake.

"I guess we're not taking that Sidral home." Niall's breaths were shallow, and he cringed in pain. "Hate to say it, but I think I need help. I can't feel my side." His face crumpled. "It feels so strange."

Kelcie carefully lifted his cloak and shirt to check the wound. The bleeding had lessened, but there was a distressing blue ring around the puncture.

"That's not good." Zephyr hefted Niall higher, trying to keep him on his feet. "Birdie, show off those navigator skills of yours. Which way do we go?"

Brona scanned the sky, which was mostly a blanket of white clouds. Kelcie had no idea what she was looking for until her cousin's finger pointed at a drifting gray patch.

"That way. We follow the smoke."

TRUDGING THROUGH THE Woods, Kelcie kept her swords in hand, waiting for the next monster to jump out at them, but it was surprisingly peaceful—a winter wonderland.

Hearty pines like those by the lake were shrouded in ice and snow. Every so often a pop of color would appear: a cluster of yellow-leafed bushes, a lonely bulbous orange fruit, and barren stalks draped in red berries to name a few. Nosy little rodents with long twitchy rabbit ears and sweeping bushy squirrel tails peeked out from holes in the trees as they passed. For a short while, a curious blue fox trailed after them, never coming close enough to make Kelcie too nervous. What struck Kelcie the most was the inviting silence. A gloomy quiet that was undeniably winter.

Half an hour later, it was getting dark out, and Niall was in so much pain he couldn't keep pace. Zephyr picked him up and started carrying him. They needed to find help for Niall, and soon.

They were nearing the smoke when the forest ended abruptly at the top of a hill. The trees were cracked in half as if hands had pried them apart.

At the bottom of the hill was a town, or what was left of it. Every building lay in ruins and the place looked deserted. They followed enormous footprints down a broken street, and found the most unexpected thing, a giant made of rocks frozen in a block of ice.

"That's a cewr. Those giants are in Summer too, high up in the mountains of Chawell Woods," Brona said, knocking on the ice. "Did you see them, Kelcie?"

"No. It was too dangerous to leave the paths."

Niall lifted his head and motioned for Zephyr to put him down. His knees weak, Niall leaned on the ice, taking a good look at the giant, then at the destruction behind them. "Never heard of them doing this before. They're docile, sleep . . ." He paused to wince, making Kelcie's stomach tighten with worry. ". . . most of the time." He set his forehead on the ice like his head hurt. *When I was little . . . my father took me camping on them.*

"They weren't sleeping when they did this!" A little boy half their age lugged a piece of metal across the road, coming toward them in a hurry. "Hey! Did you say in Summer?" His big gray eyes shifted between them, scrutinizing. Kelcie did the same to him. Pointy ears poking through a wool cap. Tiny wings fluttering out the hole in the back of his purple sweater; he was a fairy, but what kind?

"Are you the ones who saved Winter?" He gestured to their Braverwil uniforms. "The ones who went undercover? I cannot believe my luck! Right here in the Volga wreckage! Are you here to help with cleanup? No. That's silly. You're heroes. The Queen wouldn't make you do that."

Heroes? Kelcie wanted to tell him exactly what she thought of his heroes, but it was their turn to play a part, their turn to go undercover. Kelcie put her swords in her back scabbard so as not to frighten him.

"Yeah. That's us." She gave him a cocky smile.

"It was in all the periodicals this morning! Which one of you is Jack Postal?"

Zephyr raised his hand, grinning.

"Can you shift for me?" The metal bar clanked to the ground. The little fairy's wings quivered with glee. "Oh, please?"

Niall deftly changed the subject. "This one giant did all of this?"

His ears shifted down. "No. There were more. Five or six here. Some in other cities too, from what I heard."

"Where did they come from?" Kelcie asked.

"What do you mean, where? Summer sent them." The boy backflipped for no particular reason.

"How could Summer send giants here?" Brona asked, like it was the most ridiculous thing she'd ever heard.

Niall, however, looked at Kelcie, haunted.

When I went to the war room to ask my mother about your father, this is what she was talking about. A map of Winter was lit up in three places. Volga was one of them.

Could Queen Eislyn really be capable of inflicting this kind of damage? Innocent families probably lived here.

But was Winter any better? They attacked the Academy last year and now they'd stolen Danu's Heart.

"Don't know, but they did." The boy's mouth fell open at the sight of Niall's bleeding side. "That's an afanc's nail mark! Oooh, shouldn't use that Sidral. Lake is full of 'em."

Niall's knees buckled. Zephyr scooped him up.

"Helpful, really. But what would be more helpful," Brona advanced on the poor kid, "would be for you to take us to someone who can help him."

"The Aria! He needs the Aria! She's this way!" he said, backing away from her.

Wings flittering, the boy's feet barely touched the snow as he sped off, leaving very little trail for them to follow. The few times they thought they'd lost him, he backpedaled, leaping into the air to catch their attention, then kept going.

Zippy led them past a row of recently built log cabins and into a small village wedged between two tall, snowcapped mountains.

Fairies of all shapes, sizes, and colors lined up outside a brick building. Kelcie scanned for soldiers but everyone was dressed like the boy, in simple tattered wool clothes. She heard Zippy bellowing that the heroes who stole the Heart of Danu and ended the war were coming through, one of them injured, and to get out of the way!

They exited the village a few minutes later, taking a well-trodden path, but to where? Niall was pale, his breathing labored. Kelcie set a hand on his forehead, and gasped. "How much longer?" she barked at the boy, beginning to think this was some kind of a trap.

"Almost there!"

Around the next bend, the wind changed direction, brushing past Kelcie's ears with whisperings as if it carried secrets, or warnings, or both, on its way to blowing open the gate on a white picket fence. In the small yard, miniature suns the size of basketballs shined down on garden beds blooming with herbs, vegetables, and fruits that seemed impervious to the cold and snow.

Beyond that was a homey wheat-colored brick home. With round steamy windows, a pointy roof too tall for snow to stick to, and three chimneys spewing smoke, it looked inviting, too inviting. The door abruptly opened. A pale woman in a white duster coat rushed out, sniffing the air. Brona stepped in front of Zephyr and Niall, lifting a dagger out of her boot. She lowered the fur-lined hood, her wavy blond hair falling down her back. The vertical, black pupils in her yellow cat eyes fell on Niall.

"You brought them here?" she thundered.

Fairy boy froze, his wings sputtering to a stop. He tugged on the pointy part of his ear, nervous. "They're from Braverwil! They're—"

"I know who they are!" The little boy squeaked at her deadly tone and ran away so fast he left snowdrifts in his wake.

She knows . . . Niall's voice was barely audible in Kelcie's head. *She knows we're not Lexis's fianna. She knows we're from Summer.*

Kelcie exchanged a wary glance with Brona and Zephyr. They were all thinking the same thing. If this Aria person knew they were from Summer, she was going to turn them in. A silent argument broke out between them, heads jerking, foreheads creasing, eyebrows reaching for the sky. Niall ceased, gasping for breath, ending it.

The aria cursed under her breath, rushing at Zephyr. She placed her hand over Niall's heart. "Well? What are you waiting for? Inside! Now! His life force is slipping!"

29

THE ARIA

ZEPHYR STUMBLED OVER the threshold, barely able to hold on to Niall because he was thrashing so much. Brona panned the surroundings and the skies one last time before entering. The Aria watched as Kelcie stopped to pick up Niall's glasses which had fallen into a pile of snow. Kelcie carefully folded the temples and placed them in her pocket, because Niall was going to be fine and he would need his glasses soon. She said as much in a silent prayer to anyone who was listening.

The house creaked and moaned, almost warily. On the left of the room was a kitchen, but for more than food. The far wall reminded Kelcie of Madame Le Deux's classroom, only most of the contents were alive and moving. Shelves were packed with glass jars containing all sorts of bugs, spiders, and worms, big and small, in dirt, cocooned or crawling all over each other. On the top, plants swayed to a beat only they heard, with various shades of flowers—laughing yellows, squealing oranges, smoking reds, and snarling blues—baring tiny, corkscrew teeth.

The round windows in the kitchen cranked open on their own, letting the cold air in, easing the tremendous heat coming from three blazing fires in the hearths. Cauldrons hanging over the flames from swing-arms gave off conflicting smells, some sweet, some musky, and a combination that was nauseating. There were three sinks too, three butcher-block islands, and three mortars and pestles. Kelcie remembered the Chief Bard at the College of Mystical Beings saying things happening in threes, like Kelcie's sneezes, meant bad luck. She really hoped Esras was wrong because everything in the house was in threes.

The Aria dropped her coat on a chair. Beneath she wore a plain yellow dress with red stains down the front and caked mud on the cuffs.

"Set him on the last table there," she ordered, hustling about, snatching items from her shelves.

Zephyr put Niall down on the last of a row of three shiny metal tables. Niall moaned with his eyes tightly closed, his body twisting and turning, writhing in pain.

Brona stayed close to the door, guarding the entrance, and shook off the outside chill like a bird after a cold rain.

"He was stabbed by an afanc's nail," Kelcie explained, trying to be useful.

"That much, I can smell."

The Aria returned, pausing a second to scrutinize Brona, Zephyr, and finally Kelcie on her way to setting cloth and a blue bottle on the table next to Niall. Kelcie got as close to Niall as she could without getting in the Aria's way. He was trembling from fear or from cold. Kelcie couldn't do much about the cold, but she didn't want him to be afraid. She grabbed his hand, squeezing gently. His eyes opened, met hers, then rolled as his body tensed all over.

His legs and arms twitched uncontrollably.

"Hold him down!" the Aria shouted.

Zephyr pinned his legs as Kelcie held on to one arm, while Brona clasped the other.

The Aria produced a pair of small scissors from her pocket that she used to clip a snapping blue flower, then set it down beside Niall's head, where it yapped and shook like an irritated Chihuahua. Using her fingers, the Aria pried apart the fabric around Niall's wound. It was worse; much more swollen, and violent blue. She carefully picked up the flower by its stem, and hovered it over the wound. It sniffed, then all at once the flowers launched, gawped jaws spreading over the wound, sticky filaments latching onto either side. The stigma stretched, plunging directly into the cut.

Niall stiffened, arching his back. Zephyr cried out like he was in pain. Brona stared deep into the wound, fascinated. Kelcie gripped his hand and braced his arm against her.

"You have to hold still, Niall," Kelcie whispered.

His head flipped toward the sound of her voice. His eyes rolled up, and stayed there for too long. *Kelcie* . . .

"What are you doing to him?" Kelcie asked, anger spilling over into her tone.

"This will remove the toxins out of his blood."

"Good. That's good," Zephyr said, wrestling with Niall's kicking legs.

The stigma started slurping blue goop from Niall's wound. That was apparently all Zephyr could stomach. He closed his eyes, gagging.

The Aria's brow creased deeper with worry by the second. Niall's breathing slowed so much Kelcie couldn't see his chest moving. "Why isn't it helping?"

The woman ignored her, adding another blue flower. "How long was the claw in him?"

"A few seconds?" Kelcie guessed.

"More like a minute," Brona corrected.

"Well, this isn't good. Glowering hazel usually works quickly."

"It's not working?" Zephyr bellowed, heaving breaths. "Do not tell me he's going to die! That is not an option!"

"Please!" Kelcie begged. "Do something! Please!"

Brona let go of Niall to examine bottles on the Aria's shelves. "There must be something else you can try!"

A glimpse at Niall's snow-white face and the Aria barked, loudly and with authority. "That blasted oath will be the end of me!"

A herd of orange-spotted lynxes poured in through the open window over the sink, flooding the kitchen. Zephyr stepped back as they circled the table, but Kelcie refused to move no matter how much they hissed, spit, or yawled. She squeezed Niall's hand, threading her fingers through his—an unbreakable lock.

"Ladies! We have an emergency!" the Aria declared.

Without hesitation, the lynxes reared, their front paws landing on Niall. Kelcie had heard of animal therapy for sick patients in hospitals, where dogs like golden retrievers visited kids so they could pet them. It made them feel better, the way Kelcie loved to pet Striker when she was upset. The strange thing was that these lynxes were petting *Niall*.

The Aria placed her palms over his wound, fingers spread like an arched spider, giving the flowers plenty of room beneath to work.

"Charger! Raven! Saiga!" Her vertical pupils widened. Her yellow eyes dimmed until they were the color of the night's sky, and glistening with stars. "I want you to call to him with your mind, something an Adder can sense deep in his bones. He won't understand the words, but that is the draw. He will need to return in order to find out what you're saying to him."

Return? He couldn't hear them? If this didn't work, was she saying that Niall was going to die? Or was she saying . . . he was dead already? Distraught, Kelcie couldn't breathe. She couldn't think. But she had to! What could Kelcie say to him that was so important he would do anything to hear it? *Please don't go. We need you!* He knew that. She needed something else. Something from deep down. A truth she would never have the nerve to say to him if he were awake. She closed her eyes, and imagined them at the ball. Wearing fancy clothes, Niall's charming shy smile looking down at Kelcie's hand as she led him onto the dance floor. *I–I want to dance with you, Niall. One dance. When this is all over. When we save Summer. Just one dance at the ball.*

The Aria started chanting in a language Kelcie didn't understand. The lynxes joined her, their paws beating a rhythm on his legs and arms, their voices sounding more like needles scraping concrete than music. Kelcie's eardrums throbbed in protest, demanding to be plugged by her fingers, but she wasn't letting go of Niall's hand, no matter what. She opened her eyes.

The woman's long thin fingers bent upward over his wound unnaturally, in the wrong direction. The louder she sang, the more her jaw tensed as if she were fighting a force only she could see. For a brief moment, it looked like the Aria was losing, her fingers rising to a point where they might break off. Kelcie heard Zephyr scream and Brona gasp—from either the disheartening sight of Niall's stillness or from bleeding ears. The lynxes' cries on the third time through the chant reached a pitch that nearly drove Kelcie to her knees.

The Aria's fingers lowered. Kelcie crushed Niall's hand, refusing to believe this was the end, refusing to let him go.

Niall woke with a start, his intense purple gaze wide and afraid.

"He's awake!" Kelcie cried, her eyes watering from tears she didn't realize were there.

"There you are." The Aria blew out an exhausted breath. She wiped her brow with her sleeve, tossing a look of satisfaction to the coven of lynxes. "Well done."

As quickly as they came, the cats left, single file, through the window, the last rubbing against Zephyr before dashing away. Zephyr and Brona flanked the table, their expressions softening, relieved.

The Aria set a hand on Niall's forehead. "That was very close, young man." She checked the glowering hazel, now plump and sagging on his belly.

Niall suddenly threw his head back, banging it on the table. "It hurts. Whatever those things are doing! Please take them off!"

"I thought Summer soldiers were tougher than that," she said. Niall was right all along. She did know they were from Summer, and yet she had helped them. "A few more sips . . ."

"Listen to her, Adder," Zephyr ordered, staring everywhere but at the slurping flower.

"She saved your life, O'Shea," added Brona.

"Squeeze my hand as hard as it hurts." Kelcie wiggled her fingers.

He was strong enough to crush her fingers, rubbing bones together.

"Ow." She laughed.

His breathing didn't return to normal until the glowering hazels were removed. The Aria placed the swollen flowers in separate jars, then set them on the cluttered shelves beside a vat of hairy pink spiders.

"Thank you . . ." Kelcie paused, realizing she didn't know her name.

"Ingrid."

"Thank you, Ingrid."

"I don't understand," Brona blurted. "If you know we're from Summer, why did you help us?"

"Because I'm bound by the supreme law that all witchkind are bound. We treat the patient, no matter who they are or where they came from. The patient right in front of us is all that matters. Life over death. It is a game Arias don't like to lose." She glowered at Brona. "But that doesn't mean I'm always happy about it . . ."

"We call your kind Healers in Summer," Zephyr said. "Only they don't have any kind of magic or animal covens . . ."

"I'm going to clean and dress this young man's wound." She waved her hand. The door on the other side of the room creaked open. "Go in there. Give me some space to work. I was about to indulge in a tray of brumble biscuits and mint tea." She looked put out. "I suppose you can have it. Tea is likely cold by now though."

Zephyr and Brona moved into the other room. Kelcie started to leave, but Niall refused to let go of her hand.

Ingrid arched a censoring brow at him. "The worst part is over."

Niall squeezed Kelcie's hand tighter.

Please stay.

The fear in Niall's voice made it impossible to leave. "If you don't mind, I'd like to stay with him. I won't get in your way."

Ingrid shrugged. "Suit yourself." She began the laborious task of cleaning off Niall's side, pouring liquid from the blue bottle onto one of five white cloths that it would take to stop the bleeding.

"How did you know Zephyr was a Charger, and Brona a Raven, and Niall an Adder?" Kelcie asked.

"He was carrying someone of a similar size with ease." Ingrid retrieved a jar labeled *Saveur Milk Jam*. "The girl with the black hair, she had a talon morphed when you arrived. And this young man," she smoothed a dollop over the wound, "I heard him speaking in my mind. Powers got away from him, like the Raven." She glanced at Kelcie, then back at the wound. "You were the only surprise, Fomorian."

"Because there are Fomorians in Winter."

"That's not what I mean. I was told that the Summer Queen locked away their Fomorians, yet here you are."

Kelcie frowned, not wanting to talk about that in front of Niall, or with someone she didn't know—in Winter.

"Here I am."

Niall gripped her hand tighter. Kelcie wasn't sure why. He didn't look in pain anymore.

Ingrid picked up a knife with a dull blade and ran the face along the wound's broken skin. It magically smoothed together, healing to a thin seam. "Why are you here?"

Don't tell her. We can't trust her. He saw the mutiny in her frown and added, *We thought we could trust Lexis, and look at what happened.*

The reminder wasn't lost on her. She gave him a small nod. "It's a very long story, and I'm not sure I'm allowed to tell it."

"You don't trust me? If anyone found out you're here, I'd be marked as a traitor for helping you, oath or not."

"We won't tell anyone," Kelcie promised.

"I will have to trust you then, I suppose." Ingrid helped Niall sit up, but he fell back down. "Ah, well. My hopes of being rid of you quickly are officially dashed. He's not going anywhere for a while."

A blink later, Niall's breathing smoothed to slow and steady. He was asleep.

Ingrid lifted her hand, flicking her fingers at the windows. The panes slammed shut and the tattered curtains closed. "I guess there is nothing to be done. You'll have to stay here tonight."

"Are you sure?" Kelcie asked.

Zephyr and Brona poked their heads through the door.

"We don't want you to get into trouble for us," Zephyr said, armed with two cookies, one in each hand.

"We were told to seek shelter at night." Brona looked as conflicted as Kelcie felt. If they stayed, time would be lost, time they couldn't get back. The six days they had to retrieve Danu's Heart and return it to Summer would be down to five. But what choice did they have?

"It's settled, then. You'll stay in the other room," Ingrid said. "I don't want to find you wandering around my house."

"Yes, ma'am," the three chimed together.

Ingrid laughed sadly. "Tiny soldiers."

An hour later they were hunkered around a fireplace in Ingrid's living room, sitting on big pillows, eating from a vat of soup and scarfing down a loaf of crumbly bread. After, Kelcie sank into the thick shaggy green rug, happy to be warm, dry, and full.

Ingrid joined them an hour later, sipping a hot cup of something that smelled sour. Niall followed on wobbly legs and plopped down next to Kelcie. He drank several glasses of water and filled a bowl of soup, his spoon wasting no time diving in. Kelcie was glad to see him eating. He caught her smiling at him and smiled back. She immediately turned to look at the fire, hoping the heat would explain her reddening cheeks.

"I helped you, and believe I deserve to know why you're here." Ingrid began her interrogation.

"Will you make us leave if we don't tell you?" Niall asked.

"Don't you think I've given enough without receiving anything in return?" Ingrid countered. Her elbows fell on her knees as she leaned forward, rolling the cup between her palms. "I will have to offer something to the Queen's soldiers when they no doubt show up at my door."

"Soldiers," Kelcie gasped. "Elliott's bough was probably traceable. She's right. It's likely only a matter of time." She glanced around, trying to remember where she'd left her shoes.

Zephyr set his bowl down. "I hadn't thought of that. I got lulled by the warmth in here. I guess we should be going now."

Brona stood up. Niall only made it to his knees before Ingrid pushed him down.

"You will be safe until morning. They too will be deterred by the cold of night. I can make you tell me, you know, especially after what you've just eaten."

Niall set his bowl down.

"If you don't know, then you don't have to lie to them," Kelcie tried.

Ingrid stood up to leave the room. "Why would I lie to them? What are you and Summer planning now? I have been treating patients from Volga for weeks. Do you know how many were injured? How many were lost?"

"We're not here to hurt anyone. We're trying to retrieve something very important that was stolen from the Lands of Summer," Brona answered. "And if soldiers show up, they will already be well aware of why we're here."

Brona was right, and brilliant. Ingrid stormed out, the interrogation over.

The warmth, full bellies, and soft pillows left them all yawning. They fell asleep side by side, in a strange place, in a foreign land, without a lick of hope to save everyone they cared about, everyone they'd left behind, knowing tomorrow would be another day of fighting to survive, but at least they had each other.

30

CROSSROADS

SOMEWHERE BETWEEN ASLEEP and awake, Kelcie felt her skin prickle, like putting on a sweater made of thorns. She heard a deep, gravelly, recognizable voice speak.

King Balor.

Her pulse racing, she tried to run, but couldn't get away from him. His words traveled swiftly, like a train on a collision course with her, sounding spiteful and growing more intense, saying the same thing over and over.

Vlast mian!

The power is mine.

Vlast mian!

The power is mine.

Vlast mian!

The power is mine.

"NO!" Kelcie screamed.

Wake up, Kelcie . . . she heard Niall say, a whisper in the darkness. Her arm shook, and shook, and Niall's voice grew louder, overpowering the nightmare, overpowering King Balor's roar. *You're having a nightmare. WAKE UP!*

Kelcie bolted upright, gasping, and hugged the scabbard holding her twin swords.

"That was some nightmare." Niall squinted, patting the rug,

searching for his glasses. His hair was flattened and his cheek puffy from sleeping on his side. "What was it about?"

"Sorry . . ." Kelcie spotted the glasses on the edge of the fireplace and passed them to him. She didn't want to talk about King Balor because those conversations always led back to her father, and she didn't want to talk about him, especially not with Niall.

"Oh, um . . . wow. I can't remember."

He held up his glasses, examining the cracks. Shrugging, he put them on anyway. "Seeing through broken vision is better than not seeing at all."

His eyes still closed, Zephyr grabbed Niall's leg. "Oh no, you don't!" Niall flew five feet across the room, crashing into a cone-shaped lamp.

"Zephyr!" Kelcie yelled, rushing to help Niall.

"I am so sorry, Adder! I was having the weirdest dream."

Brona jumped up with a loaded bow in her hands, string stretching to the point of no return. "What's happening?"

Kelcie was glad it wasn't just her. Everyone was on edge.

Niall clutched his stomach, trying to speak with the breath knocked out of him, and wheezed instead.

Footsteps padded through the kitchen. Zephyr pulled his shillelagh out from beneath the folded up blanket he'd used as a pillow and handed Niall his sidewinder from the floor.

All four of them tiptoed to the closed door and listened. Kelcie peeked through a hole in the doorknob. Lynxes paraded between the butcher-block islands, carrying baskets of plants and berries, but also the occasional dead rodent in their mouths, all of which they left on the floor. The Aria picked through the bounty, thrumming with disappointment.

"Why are there no spider-trow infants? I specifically—"

A purple lynx with blue-tipped ears jumped through the kitchen window, mewing and whining.

"Soldiers, where?" Ingrid glanced through the window, waving, then rushed the front door. Plastering a big grin on her face, she yanked it open. "Oh! Hello. How can I help you?"

"The Sidral was activated late yesterday by a bough that belongs to someone known to be in Summer's prison. We can only assume it's been stolen, and are asking everyone to keep an eye out—"

"Let's discuss this outside, shall we?" Ingrid walked out, closing the door behind her.

Whenever Kelcie heard teachers or foster parents use that phrase, it only meant one thing.

"She's ratting us out! We have to leave now!" Kelcie whispered harshly.

The next few moments passed in a panicked mad scramble to find a way out. There were three other doors in the room. After a quick check, Zephyr ushered them through the only one that didn't lead to a set of stairs.

Kelcie heard the soldiers in the kitchen as she skip-hopped down the hallway racing after her fianna, yanking up her boots.

Zephyr made a wise choice. The hallway led to a rear door that exited the house into sparse woods, giving them plenty of places to run, but few to hide. Fresh snowfall blanketed the ground, hiding tree roots. Kelcie managed to find every one, stumbling and tripping, straining to keep upright.

Four soldiers in all-white uniforms, similar to the Kevlar unitards Roswen always wore, chased after them, shouting for them to stop.

Two nimble fairies zoomed past, getting in Zephyr's way. Twice the size of him, they were still no match for his strength. He lowered his shoulders and barreled right through them.

Airballs hissed, missing Brona, Niall, and Zephyr, but nailed Kelcie in the back. She fell, eating snow.

In the second it took for Kelcie to roll over, the soldier fell to his knees, reaching for his head.

"Ah!"

Niall was at Kelcie's side, his glare concentrating on the soldier who thrashed ringed horns and winced blue and brown eyes. Arms out, he was trying to spark air, the word *Mistral* forming on his lips, but Niall's scream was too much for him.

"Above you!" Brona's warning came too late. Kelcie looked up at the same time ice daggers rained down.

"Mistral!"

Before her air shield manifested, Kelcie felt the sting of a sharp tip scrape her shoulder, cutting right through her Braverwil uniform.

Niall changed his focus, forcing the ice fairy out of the sky, leaving the Fomorian free to attack.

He rose to a whopping seven feet tall, towering over Kelcie. Nostrils spewing visible breaths, the fury in his two-colored eyes sent chills down Kelcie's spine. Around her the fight continued. Niall and the ice fairy. Brona and Zephyr embroiled with the nimble fairies. But as Kelcie pulled her swords, everything happening around her fell away. There was nothing but Kelcie, her swords, and her opponent. A sudden rush of confidence rolled her shoulders. She spun the swords once. Twice. When she did it again, her opponent lifted out his own pair of twin swords.

"I can play that game too."

He mirrored her moves, spinning, then performed a synchronized move across his body, and thrust.

Kelcie blocked, and was already on the move by the time he lunged. She could hear Coach Blackwell yelling, "Move your feet. Never stop moving! Short blades mean you have to get in close!"

Kelcie did, but he was quick, and she took an infuriating pommel to the chin that landed her flat on her back. But there was no time to think about that. No time to worry over the taste of blood in her mouth. She scrambled to her feet, barely blocking his jabs.

She retreated, spreading her stance, planting her feet. Putting her strong arm forward, and the rear hand back, to use one sword for attacking and the other for defending, Kelcie sank deep into the pit of her stomach, where her powers churned.

"Mistral!" he called.

Kelcie sparked air at the same time. His wind gust headed straight for her, but on instinct, she swiped the blades around her body the way she did with the steel ones from training, only these were made of obsidian. Her swords stole control of his wind and her return blast sent him careening into a tree.

Niall's sidewinder clicked. A black jinx exploded on the Fomorian soldier's forehead. His eyes rolled up and he fell, snoring louder than Ollie.

"Thank you," Kelcie exhaled, exhausted.

By the time Kelcie turned around to find her cousin and Zephyr, Brona had fired a ring of arrows into the ground, surrounding the two nimble fairies. The fletchings exchanged electric charges, creating a force field that shocked them every time they tried to escape.

"You evil little bird!" one of them called.

"You'll pay for this!" the other sniveled.

The ice fairy sobbed hysterically, clinging to a tree to stay upright. "You'll never . . ." she hiccupped a breath, ". . . get away!"

Brona grabbed Niall's sidewinder out of his hand.

"What are you doing?" Niall exclaimed.

She spun the wheel, then fired off three black jinxes, putting them all to sleep. "We need time to escape!"

"But those were all the sleep jinxes we have left! I only have three more shots, period, and they're all zappers!"

"I saw," Brona droned. "But you have a whole bag of ammunition—"

"That is in the witch's house! It was in the kitchen!"

The Fomorian snorted in his sleep. Brona loaded an arrow, just in case.

"We can go back for it," Kelcie offered.

"No," Zephyr said. "Who knows how many soldiers are there by now? O'Shea, where's the map?"

He patted his pockets. "Probably next to the ammunition bag."

"Great!" Zephyr kicked a tree, leaving a dent.

"Then we move on. Plan stays the same. We find Lexis and get her to tell us where Danu's Heart is," Kelcie said.

"You really believe she's going to do that?" Brona asked, skeptical.

Kelcie shook her head, annoyed. "I can't have this argument with you again."

Last night, as they plotted their first moves in Winter, Brona had wanted to find Grimes's fianna's weakest links, the creeper fairies Nevver and Latchkey, at the base where Elliott told them they were stationed. Her plan was to capture them, and torture them into divulging where the Heart was, but there were too many ways that could go wrong.

First of all, even if by some miracle they could capture two fairies who could turn invisible, Kelcie didn't want to torture anyone, not ever. And she was pretty sure Brona didn't want to either. Second, with their luck, the twins wouldn't even be there. Elliott was only guessing.

Lexis would've gone back to school. Kelcie knew that for sure, because that's exactly what Kelcie would've done.

"Elliott said that Braverwil was located inside the tallest mountain of the Eternal Peaks," Kelcie said. She panned the skies, but the mountains weren't visible. "Any clue which way to go?"

"They should be west of here, based on what I remember from the map," Niall said.

"And which way is west?" Zephyr asked.

Brona pointed left. "That way. Want me to scout?"

"No. It's too dangerous. I have yet to see a raven in Winter, and an oversized one would be too visible." Zephyr smiled. "But this is good. We have a direction. We go that way."

The ice fairy asleep against the tree mumbled a curse. Icicles grew from her fingernails, stabbing the trunk.

Zephyr tiptoed away from her. "How long will they sleep, Adder?"

"The ice fairy and Fomorian, two hours, but harder to guess with the nimble fairies. They have very high metabolisms," Niall answered.

Zephyr nodded, already on the move. "Let's walk really fast and no talking. Never know who or what is lurking in these woods."

They hiked in apprehensive silence for a good hour. As they neared the end of the forest, Niall rubbed the spot where the claw had been in his side, frowning.

"Does it still hurt?" Kelcie whispered.

He shook his head. *Feels numb, actually.*

"Then why are you making that face?"

What face?

"Like it hurts you," she laughed softly.

He stared at the ground. *I was just thinking that Fagan always calls you a bad omen, but I think I'm the one who's a curse.*

Kelcie had never heard him sound so down on himself before. "Why would you say that?"

Because this is all my fault. All of it. My bough gets stolen. Not Regan's. It wasn't like they didn't know where she was all the time too. And of course I'm the one who gets stabbed and needs help, making it easy for the Winter soldiers to find us. Oh, and as we're escaping, what happens? I forget two of the most important things for our mission to succeed!

"You almost died, Niall!"

Zephyr shushed her.

That's no excuse. I really think I'm cursed. He kicked snow. *Maybe my mother's right. I am a liability. If we somehow miraculously get the Croí na Bandia back, maybe it's a good thing I won't be allowed to return to the Academy.*

"It wasn't your fault. It was your mother's fault for not listening to us when we tried to tell her what was going to happen." Niall didn't look convinced. "Fine. If you want someone to blame, blame me. I'm the one who encouraged Lexis to test for the Academy."

I could never blame you. That was you being nice to someone who you thought was in a bad situation.

Like Niall was nice to her last year when she was in a bad situation. That was their problem. They were both too nice. The old Kelcie, Boston Kelcie, had her guard up all the time. She would've sniffed out Lexis's plan long before she could put it into action. Expecting soldiers, she would've stayed up all night at the Aria's house to leave before dawn. Kelcie needed to let her old self, her distrusting self, back out if they were going to survive Winter.

His brow creased. *Do you think Lexis will tell us where the Heart is?*

"I don't know. But if she doesn't, we press onward and find the creeper fairies the way Brona wanted to in the first place. We have four days left, Niall, and we're the only chance Summer has to survive."

UNABLE TO SLEEP, Lexis had gotten up before dawn and forced Jack to come climbing with her. Pavel never liked to rock climb. Since he could fly, he felt like it was beneath him. Not to mention he'd been acting mad at her since they returned from Summer. And Swappy never stopped talking. Lexis needed to think, and with Jack, she never needed to talk.

"North face or south?" he had asked as they exited his Den in a hurry, hoping to get out before anyone woke up and started asking questions.

No matter where they went, classmates stared at them as if they were some kind of heroes, and peppered them with questions they weren't allowed to answer. The story was everywhere thanks to Jack opening his mouth in Galanta. It'd only been forty-eight hours, and the press had already started running articles speculating that a Braverwil fianna had gone on a daring undercover mission and returned from Summer with a grand prize that would end the war. Lexis knew because one of her

Den mates left a stack of them on her bed that must have been delivered in the middle of the night. In one, Achila Grimes was quoted (although she was called an anonymous source) singing Lexis's praises as the Tol of the fianna, saying she was the reason the mission succeeded. Reading it made Lexis feel sick.

"South," Lexis said.

"Oh, looking for a grueling workout this morning? Maybe I should've stayed in bed," Jack replied as they passed through the empty halls. "Aífe's week off of class was for a job well done, to rest and recuperate from all those miserable sweltering weeks in Summer."

Guilt slowed her pace. "They weren't all miserable."

Stepping into the chute, Jack stared at her with those challenging blue eyes, but refrained from commenting. Was the whole time in Summer that bad for him? Was she foolish for even caring about the people she met? Her fianna was home, safe and sound, and the mission, a huge success. That was all that mattered. Winter was all that mattered, at least that's what her steadfast head kept muttering to her rueful heart.

The mountain face lowered, leaving a small platform for them to stand on. They were a hundred feet up and about to go much higher.

"Race you to the top!" Jack morphed hands and feet, and launched for the first deep pocket. With his synchronized movements, and a permanent crimp to his claws, Jack was a fast climber. Really fast. To catch up, she would need the wind at her back. Lexis took a deep inhale.

"Mistral . . ."

She launched upward, stretching for a ledge, her gale keeping her safely pressed against the mountain. But after an initial burst of energy, Lexis fell behind, her mind wandering back to her Saiga Den at the Academy and the glorious pool, then to the beautiful flowers on that campus—so many colors. She could still feel the tickle of Striker's nose nuzzles and hear the cry of the baby wyvern hidden in the Fringe.

The Summerfolk were not what she had expected. She'd always imagined them as hateful and evil, uncaring and arrogant, but they weren't. Most of them anyway. They were just normal folk, like folk in Winter. And all of them would die if what Kelcie said was true. Kelcie's sweet grandmother, her Fomorian Den mates, the fianna she was assigned to, whose names, Sophia, Malakai, and Paulie, she suddenly could never forget. And Roswen. She really liked Roswen.

Lexis's wind died and she slipped three feet before catching an edge.

Jack smirked at her from a ledge halfway to the top.

"You're making it way too easy for me, Lexi!"

He only ever called her that when they were alone, but it made her cheeks burn. Regrouping, she pushed on, climbing to him, letting him help her over the lip.

She sat down, catching her breath and taking in the view, then turned, her eyes lifting to his black hair. There had never been any secrets between her and her fianna before the mission. She wanted to go back to the way things were, and to do that, Lexis needed to tell Jack about Kelcie and Brona. "Those two girls from the Academy . . ."

"Which girls?" Jack sat beside her, dangling his paws over the ledge.

"The ones in the shrine . . ."

"The redhead?"

"And the black-haired girl who looked a little like you. They're your first cousins."

Jack didn't move. His breath came fast and furious, whistling through his nose. "That's impossible. My father would've told me if I had family before he died, Lexis. Pavel's right," he spat. "Everything they told you was a lie."

"No. It wasn't. Not that side of your family," she explained. "They're the daughters of Nemain and Macha."

"What? No way!" he immediately dismissed, angry. "I mean . . . I suppose . . ." Quiet for too long, when he looked at her again, he asked, "You think they were telling you the truth? That their mothers and mine are, you know, sisters?"

"I know they were. The whole school knew it."

"I have *family*? In Summer?" Jack sounded as confused as Lexis felt, then his face fell into a glower. "Why didn't you tell me when we were there?"

"Because I was at the school! And then we had, what, one day together before—"

"I get it. Nothing could distract from the mission," he said bitterly, back to angry. "Are there other things you didn't tell us?"

Lexis hugged her knees.

"Lexi, you haven't been acting like yourself at all. Meeting two girls who are my cousins, that's not what's wrong."

Lexis didn't want to burden him, but she needed to tell someone. More than telling him about his cousins, it was the real reason she'd wanted to go climbing with Jack, wasn't it? "When I was in Chawell Woods, Swappy brought me a note from Queen Kefyra."

"I know." His brow furrowed. "I was the one who gave it to him to give to you."

"Right." Lexis's half-smile faded. "Well, in it, Queen Kefyra said that failure was unacceptable, that there would be consequences. She threatened all of us, not just me. And it was all I could think about."

"You really think if the mission didn't succeed that she would've punished us somehow?"

"Yes. Without a shadow of a doubt. Remember the teacher Pavel and I got into an argument about when we were in the boat to Summer City? Roswen?"

Jack nodded, and listened keenly as Lexis told him Roswen's sad story.

After, he stared out over the frozen tundra. "Do you think she was lying to you?"

"No. I don't. That's just it. No one in Summer was lying. They didn't know I was an outsider. They were nice and caring and tried to help me fit in. But those Advisors, and the Queen, they purposely didn't tell us what taking the Heart of Danu would do. What if what Kelcie said was true? What if all of the people in the Lands of Summer are going to die because we took the *Croí na Bandia*?"

"I—" Jack stopped himself. "Why would the Queen lie?"

"A lie of omission isn't technically a lie. And because if she told us the truth, we wouldn't have gone." Lexis looked at him, her stomach cinching. "Would we?"

Jack shook his head. "No. We wouldn't."

"And now there's nothing we can do about it, even if we wanted to." Lexis didn't feel like climbing anymore.

A couple hundred feet below, four Braverwil cadets ambled halfway up the mountain pass, stopping to gawk at the Abyss.

"Shouldn't they be heading to class?" Lexis asked.

"Where?"

She pointed them out.

Jack morphed to see through his tiger eyes, to get a better look. He mewed, then transformed back to his tall, lanky self, laughing.

"It's them! I can't believe it. They're coming after the Heart!" Jack smiled bigger than Lexis had ever seen him smile before. But then it was gone, replaced by a concerned frown. "What do you want to do, Lexi? Stop them, or help them?"

Though she was relieved at first, the closer they came, fear seeped in. If Lexis and her fianna helped them, their lives in Winter would be over. They'd be imprisoned for life, or worse. But this was Lexis's chance to right the wrong. Was she not going to take it?

"I don't know. But let's get Swappy and Pavel. Whatever we're going to do, we have to do it together."

31

ELLÉN TRECHEND!

THE WIND WHIPPED snow into Kelcie's face, blurring her vision as they hiked around the mountain, trying to find a way into Braverwil. Elliott had told them where it was, but he neglected to mention the location of the door. It never occurred to Kelcie to ask. What kind of building doesn't have a visible door? A place that doesn't want unwanted visitors—like Haven Hall.

Four figures walked through the knee-high snow drifts, heading straight for them.

"Is that who I think it is?" Brona seized an arrow from her quiver, nocked it in her bow, and drew the string.

Kelcie wiped her watering eyes with her sleeve. "Should we take this as a good sign or bad sign?"

"Bad. Definitely bad," Zephyr said, lifting out his shillelagh.

Not taking any chances, Niall raised his arm and his sidewinder.

Pavel lifted off the ground, flying ahead of the others, smugly bobbing and weaving, making it impossible for Niall to get a scream-lock on him or Brona to get off a proper shot.

Zephyr raised his hand. "We're not here to fight. We want to speak to your Charger."

"You mean my Tol," Pavel said. "Fiannas at Braverwil are led by those chosen by Aífe, those she deems worthy, not by their big muscles."

"You're kinda arrogant," Brona noticed.

"And you're out of your league. Go home." Pavel fired off an ice knife that Kelcie batted away with an air shield.

She steeled her nerves and tugged out her swords. "As Zephyr said, we'd like to speak to Lexis."

"So speak," Lexis said, approaching.

The shifter with the intense blue eyes and the changeling with the mop of green hair flanked her. It was strange to see Lexis in a Braverwil uniform, yet it fit her better. She had a confident swagger Kelcie had never seen before.

Niall shifted his arm in Lexis's direction. "That's close enough."

"Especially you, Burpy!" Zephyr leveled his shillelagh at the changeling. "Don't you come anywhere near us!"

"His name is Swappy, Zephyr," Kelcie corrected.

"You remember me." Swappy smiled a big grin.

"You're hard to forget," she mused, twirling her swords, trying to keep her wrists from tightening up in the cold.

"Niall O'Shea, Zephyr Chike, Brona Lee, allow me to introduce you to the rest of my fianna. That's Pavel Grimes." Lexis jerked her chin at the ice fairy.

"Sorry about your aunt," Zephyr said.

"You mean because she went to prison?" Pavel growled.

"No. Because she's your aunt, and she's so awful," Brona answered for him.

Pavel raised a fist but Lexis shook her head. "Stand down," she ordered. A censoring brow arched at Brona. "Not helpful." Lexis then looked at the shifter. "And that is Jack, Jack Postal."

Jack stared a little too intensely at Brona and then at Kelcie.

"The Heart isn't here," Lexis said.

"We figured," Zephyr said.

"Where is it?" Niall asked politely.

Pavel moved to hover over Lexis. "We're not telling you anything."

Niall spoke to Pavel, but took a challenging step at Lexis. "You just said fiannas at Braverwil are led by those chosen by Aífe, those she deems worthy. If Aífe is anything like her twin sister, Scáthach, then Lexis was chosen because of what's in her heart as much as her head. And someone with a good heart would help save countless lives by sharing information."

Lexis's face crumpled.

"Please, Lexis," Kelcie added, hoping it would help.

"We only want to know where it is," Brona insisted.

Ear-piercing screeches came from the direction of the Abyss, shaking Kelcie to her core. From too many sides of the mountains, poles lifted into the sky, blaring sirens that made it sound like an army of the dead was about to march on them.

Zephyr was the first to ask, "What's happening?"

"You mean what has his mother sent now?" Lexis glared at Niall.

"My mother?" Niall gaped. "My mother," he ground out, stunned.

Like Kelcie, he was probably remembering the giant in Volga, the town in rubble, the marks on the map in Queen Eislyn's war room. Were they saying those sirens meant Summer was attacking again?

Featherless wings rose over the woods, heading in their direction. Vulture-like heads, three to a creature, cocked hooked beaks, and breathed fire, melting everything in their path.

They were the most terrifying creatures Kelcie had yet to find in the Otherworld. It took her several painful heart-stopping beats to realize she'd seen them before!

"Ellén Trechend?"

These were twice the size of the ones she'd seen in Summer City.

"But that's impossible!" Niall fumbled his glasses, losing them in the snow.

Pavel dropped out of the air, stomping on them, pulverizing what was left of the lenses.

"Hey!" Zephyr shoved the ice fairy off, sending him crashing into the snow. "That was not cool!"

Pavel got in Lexis's face. "And you wanted to help *them*?"

"Back off, Pavel!" Jack stepped between them.

Niall squinted. "How could we send an army of Ellén Trechend to the Lands of Winter?"

"That's so weird. I was just going to ask you that!" Swappy exclaimed.

"Call them off!" Lexis snapped at Niall.

He stared at Lexis, his lips parted, but nothing came out. It was like he was in a state of shock or something.

"What? Do you think he's carrying around a special whistle? He can't call them off!" Kelcie argued. "If Queen Eislyn sent them, she's the only one who can."

The Ellén Trechend shifted in unison, dipping over the vast frozen tundra, setting their sights on the tallest peak that they all happened to be standing at the base of.

Sections of the mountain's face slid down. Teams of ice fairies rocketed out. Pavel launched into the air, joining them. All at once, the fairies' ice met the Ellén Trechend's fire directly over the mountain.

A huge wyvern dipped into the heart of the fight. Red hair flowing behind her, the woman on its back carried flaming spears, one in each hand. This had to be Scáthach's sister, the preceptor of Braverwil.

A squat in the stirrups, and she jumped, landing on the wyvern's back, standing as if she were riding a surfboard. She hurled one spear, then another, never missing. Two Ellén Trechend turned to stone, and fell out of the sky on a collision course with the hard, frozen ground. The crash sent shock waves beneath their feet.

Brona met Kelcie's stare. She could tell her cousin was thinking the same thing Kelcie was—that they should join the fight.

The launch bays opened again. Elementals as young as ten and as old as sixteen fought from the platforms, whipping wind, holding back the beasts, until one broke through.

Students ran for cover only seconds before the raging three-headed monster slammed into the launch bay head first. A loud explosion rocked the side of the mountain. Two students fell off the platform. Kelcie's frantic legs were moving before her mind came up with a plan.

Brona and Pavel were way ahead of her though. Her cousin morphed, and took off, getting there first. Brona's talons wrapping around the wrist of a boy of maybe eleven, slowing his descent while Pavel hurled an ice shelf, stabbing it into the side of the mountain beneath the other student, stopping his fall.

An Ellén Trechend rounded on Pavel. Inhaling a huge breath, its dull gray chest glowed fire-breathing red. Beaks cocked.

Kelcie found Lexis standing on both sides of her. It took her a second longer than she had to realize one was Swappy, but she couldn't tell which. Their fireballs exploded on the monster's side, but it didn't even flinch.

"Fire won't work on them!" Niall yelled. "They have fire running through their veins!"

The next fire flume missed badly, singeing Pavel's wing.

"Owa!" Pavel growled.

"Swappy! Fire won't work!" Lexis on the left yelled.

Swappy changed into himself, embarrassed. "Sorry! Forgot the other sparking words."

Zephyr pushed Swappy out of the way to get a clear shot. His shillelagh pelted Ellén Trechend in the neck, sending a shocking jolt through its body, driving its spewing flames off course—toward the ice shelf where the boy had his back plastered against the mountain.

There was only one thing Kelcie could think to do.

"Mistral!"

Her hands shook as she threw the most important wind slice of her life. The air disc spun like a buzz saw, ricocheting off the mountain, cutting straight through the monster's necks.

Brona dropped Zephyr's shillelagh at his feet, then landed and morphed. "We've got more incoming!"

Pavel crashed down beside Lexis, the upper portion of his wing singed and smoking. "I-I can't fly."

A fresh round of screeches came from behind them. Kelcie glanced over her shoulder, cringing. Two Ellén Trechend were nearly on top of them, and unlike the first wave that had their sights set on the school, their heads were dipped, solid black eyes looking straight at them.

There was no way to outrun them. No way to escape the three heads spewing fire like water cannons. The only choice was to stand their ground.

"Lexis!" Kelcie shouted over the screeching. "I don't want to be barbecued and eaten today, do you?"

She shook her head. "Not really!"

"Then we work together?"

"Agreed. On three! One . . ."

"They're getting closer!" Swappy shrieked.

Kelcie took a few steps foward, creating enough of a gap between herself and Lexis for the others.

"Get between us!" Lexis yelled, raising her hands over her head.

It sounded like a gas pipe burst. Fire struck the ground only a few feet away.

"Two!" Lexis bellowed.

The heat coming off the flames was sweltering.

"Three!" Zephyr ordered.

"Mistral!" Kelcie and Lexis cried together.

Their air streams blended from the start, forming into a huge funnel cloud that mushroomed, shielding and deflecting the firestorm raining down from above in huge sweeping gusts. The flames never stopped, not for the Ellén Trechend to breathe or to land, and not when they stabbed talon-tipped elbows into the ground and leaned in. So much heat bore down it felt like they were standing in a broiler. The fire got closer and closer, and stronger and stronger. Kelcie's arms and knees shook under the mounting pressure. Sweat poured into her eyes, so hot it stung.

"I can't hold this much longer!"

Yes! You can! Niall implored. *Or we're all going to die!*

The air was so hot taking a deep breath did nothing to help. She growled through the pain, desperate to hold on but her knees gave another inch. Kelcie heard Zephyr and Swappy both whimper.

"How angry are you that we stole Danu's Heart?" Lexis hollered over the flames.

"You want to talk about that *now*?"

"I want you to channel all that anger, driving it right back at their big black eyes! A simultaneous sweep and follow through! Can you do that?"

No! She couldn't! Kelcie could barely make out the monster's beaks through all the flames! How was she going to find three pairs of moving eyes?

Brona shifted closer to Kelcie. "I got you, cousin!"

Kelcie had no idea what she was talking about. It felt like the only one who had her right now was the gigantic fire-breathing vultures!

Brona pinned three arrows and stretched her bow.

"What are you doing, Brona?" Jack shouted at her.

"You worry about your Saiga. Let me worry about ours!"

"You can do this! Saiga! Saiga!" Zephyr cheered. "I'll count!"

"No! I will!" Lexis's voice was a tense, uncompromising growl. At least she was feeling the pressure too.

"Then start counting!" Kelcie yelled, her arms nearly breaking.

"No counting. NOW, KELCIE!"

Using a forward-sweeping motion with one arm, Kelcie's other hand plowed through the center, putting everything she had left into pushing the wind and fire back. Three of Brona's arrows went along for the ride. Consecutive *SHUNK*s were followed by a huge explosion. Hardened Ellén Trechend chunks fell on top of them.

"Owa!" Swappy wailed.

Meanwhile Lexis's monster let out visceral, ear-piercing shrieks. Eyes scorched, it took off, flying blind, and crashed into the mountainside over and over, trying to find open air.

"Did I say fire any arrows?" Lexis snapped at Brona.

"What's your problem?" Brona hissed, getting nose-to-nose with Lexis.

"That's her problem!" Jack roared.

Kelcie followed Jack's finger, pointing at the sky, where three more Elléns headed for them!

"It seems like every time we kill one, more head our way!" Jack growled.

Swappy let a ripper go. "That's bad! That's very bad!"

"Well, if you had said that sooner!" Brona spat.

"We need cover!" Zephyr said.

Niall added to that request. "The kind that doesn't burn!"

32

SANCTUARY OF THE DAMNED

THE THREE-HEADED VULTURES were literally hot on their heels as Lexis led the way, serpentining through the open tundra. She leaped the last few feet into a densely packed pine grove. A WHOOSH overhead and the trees erupted in flames. Kelcie darted from trunk to trunk, bringing up the rear.

Run faster! Niall cried in her head.

Like that was going to help.

"Sanctuary of the Damned?" Lexis called.

"It's locked!" Pavel dismissed.

"Yeah, and we've got a Charger who can open it!" Lexis laughed, a deranged laugh like Brona let out during sparring, like she was actually enjoying the thrill of battle.

Kelcie wasn't enjoying the thrill, and leaving the grove felt like a really bad idea, but Lexis did it anyway. She ran across an unpaved road, and underneath an aging archway, into a snow-covered courtyard. On the other side was a tarnished metal building with gabled roofs, and seven stained-glass windows depicting seven dead ivory swans, blood dripping down their fronts. Lexis thought they would be safer inside there?

Zephyr yanked on a heavy metal door, jerking it open a crack. Flames tickled Kelcie's heels as Niall's phantom hands tore the door open wide. Kelcie dove in last and Zephyr slammed the door shut, cutting off the fire, and slid the bolt, locking them inside. Catching their breath, no one spoke. Kelcie looked around, frowning. With pews in rows paying homage to a silver dais, it looked like a place of worship, but worshipping what?

Pavel reached over his head, rubbing the singed part of his wing. "This is why Queen Kefyra ordered us to take the Heart, Lexis! Because she wanted these attacks to end!"

"Don't you think I know that?" Lexis fired back.

She was stepping up on the dais, but Jack stopped her. He whispered something in her ear. She reluctantly nodded, making Kelcie fear the worst.

Jack made a rumbling sound in the back of his throat, the kind a cat makes right before it scratches your leg. "We don't have the Heart. Queen Kefyra is the only one who can help you now."

"Not that she will," Pavel sniggered. "Not after yet another attack! You're a bunch of pathetic fools. Coming to Winter like this was a huge mistake."

Zephyr inched farther into the place. "I agree with you that coming to Winter was a mistake."

"What?" Niall gasped.

Zephyr shook his head at Niall, ordering him to stop talking, and continued. "Or I did—"

"No or. No buts. Just get out," Pavel barked.

When no one moved, ice covered his shoulders, making him look ten times bigger, like a football player in shoulder pads. An ice spear grew from his clenched fist, a spear he pointed at Zephyr.

"I said GET OUT! Face what your Summer's Queen has sent all on your own."

"No!" Swappy belched so loud the glass windows vibrated. "Pavel, let the man speak! He's making a calm, collected speech, or at least trying to, and you're turning into a bully. That was Jack's job in this fianna! You used to be nicer than him!"

"Jack's gone soft," Pavel sneered at him. "And I don't have to be nice to them. In case you forgot, they're the *enemy*!"

Kelcie started at that word. *Enemy.* It was an ugly word. "I don't want to be your enemy."

"Well, that's too bad because you're from Summer," Pavel grumbled.

"Technically, I'm from the human world." She clutched her boughs. "With the keys to all three worlds now. And since I didn't grow up with this fighting, I just have one question and then we'll leave."

"Charger was talking, Saiga," Zephyr groaned.

Kelcie pleaded with her eyes, to which Zephyr rolled his.

"What's your question?" Lexis asked.

"How did this war start? Why have the Lands of Summer and the Lands of Winter been fighting for so long? Answer me that, and we'll go."

"Hey! That's a really great question!" Swappy smiled. "I want to know that too! Why are we fighting?"

Pavel looked at Lexis, who shrugged. "Don't look at me. I don't know."

"Your parents are abbots. How can you not know? Aren't there like a thousand books that they made you read about this stuff?" Pavel snapped. "You know this! You don't want to answer because you don't want them to leave. You want to help them. You've changed, Lexis."

"No, I haven't!" She stormed at him.

"Jack, do you know?" Swappy asked. "I mean, your mother is Babd. She was there when the war broke out, wasn't she?"

That name, pronounced *Bev*, was very familiar to Kelcie.

"Your mother is Babd?" Brona asked Jack with disbelief. "Kelcie, his mother is Babd. That makes him—"

"Your first cousin," Lexis chimed in.

"Oh! Yay!" Swappy teared up, lower lip trembling, beaming at Kelcie's and Brona's newfound cousin. "Jack, you do have family!"

Jack didn't say anything. He stared at Kelcie and Brona as if he were seeing ghosts. Kelcie saw the resemblance Jack had to Brona right away. The black hair and the shape of their eyes, it was so similar. Kelcie was the odd cousin out.

"Why don't you already know the answer, then, Kelcie? Why don't any of you three know?" Swappy asked sincerely.

"Because no one knows," Niall interjected. "Because no one seems to care anymore."

"Yeah. They just want to keep fighting," Swappy moaned.

A loud *WHOOSH* crashed into the windows, making everyone dive for cover. Blazing light shined through, but the stained-glass swans came to life. Their wings spread, creating a shelter from the firestorm. The pressure mounting, they seemed to be holding.

Niall's shoulder bumped hers and stayed. Normally, Kelcie would've been self-conscious with him this close to her. But right now, it was comforting. Everyone got up cautiously keeping an eye on the windows.

Zephyr padded toward Pavel, who lowered his spear, keeping him back. "All of Summer will die if we don't get Danu's Heart back."

"Lexis? It's true, isn't it?" Swappy asked.

"Why would they come all this way if they weren't telling the truth?" Jack answered.

Lexis crossed her arms, chewing on her bottom lip. "I think the Queen and the Advisors know everyone and everything in Summer will die without the Heart of Danu, and they're fine with that."

"But you're not, is that what you're saying?" Pavel pressed.

"And you are?" Jack countered.

"Maybe this is what had to happen to drive both sides to talk?" Niall stepped toward them. "If we bring the Heart back, I will speak to my mother, and make sure she calls off these attacks, and then maybe we can get Queen Kefyra and Queen Eislyn to sit down and speak to each other. We orchestrate a diplomatic mission, instead of a military one."

"In Boston!" Kelcie suggested. "The human world is Switzerland. It won't take a side. And Elliott Blizzard's husband is uber rich. We'll make him order like twenty pizzas," she added. "Nothing bad can ever come out of a meeting with pizza."

"She's right about that," Brona said from the other side of the room. She'd quietly made her way to a spot that gave her the perfect angle to line up a shot—just in case.

"I don't know what it is, but pizza sounds good!" Swaps interjected, a sharp cracker adding a definitive exclamation point. "Excuse me."

A closed door across the pews flew open.

"You're not excused! You people are making enough noise to wake the dead!" A woman with delicate features and a warm smile climbed the last two steps from the basement, and stopped at the threshold. She finger-combed her glossy chestnut mane, dragging it forward so it hung to the waist of her shimmering black dress. "And now that you have, we're very, very hungry!"

"Did you all know that there were ghosts in here?" Kelcie asked.

"She's not a ghost. She's a banshee! Her touch comes with an omen of death." Lexis ignited her hands.

As if Kelcie didn't have enough omens in her life!

Jack morphed, and bravely paced in front of his fianna.

"Never know who you're going to find when you enter abandoned buildings. You shouldn't have come in here," the banshee scolded. "But now that you did, let's have a party! Who wants to dance?" Soot flaked from her batting eyelashes, leaving streaks down her cheeks.

"We have to get out of here!" Niall exclaimed.

Brona ran on top of the pews, catching up to Zephyr, who had made a mad dash to the door. He threw the bolt and swung it open. But on the other side, he was greeted by an Ellén Trechend.

Niall's invisible hands slammed the door before Zephyr lost his eyebrows. "Can't go out that way."

"There is no way out," the banshee sang.

She stepped aside for seven half-dead people– made of nothing but skin and bones—to skip-hop into the room in a walking-dead conga line. As soon as their bony feet touched the floor, they began shedding their skin, molting like snakes into overly made-up teenagers wearing bejeweled bright-colored gowns and dizzying pin-striped suits.

Kelcie pulled her twin swords, spinning her wrists twice as the rest of the teenage banshees fanned out around the room, surrounding them. With battle-axes in their manicured hands, they drove the two fiannas into a back-to-back huddle.

"They're dead," Brona explained. She fired off a round of arrows that struck a blond-haired one in the chest, ruining her blue dress.

Blondie ripped the arrows out with a look of disgust and dropped them on the floor.

"Which makes them very hard to kill," Zephyr worried.

"I read that if you chop their heads off, they'll turn to stone like the Ellén Trechend did," Niall offered.

Blue Dress lunged at Brona. Zephyr took a mad swing that left her blond head rolling across the floor. The rest of the body crackled, turning to stone. "And that is why we love our Adder!"

Lexis stared at Kelcie's twin swords. "You need two?"

Kelcie hesitated. What if she stole it like she did Niall's bough? How could Kelcie trust her with one of her most prized possessions? But then Kelcie realized that maybe, just maybe, if she showed her that she trusted her, Lexis might change her mind, and help them get the Heart back.

Kelcie tossed her one of her swords with a caveat: "I want it back."

"If you live, I'll give it back. If you don't, I'll keep both. How's that sound?"

"Exactly what I'd expect from you," Kelcie mumbled.

"I don't want to chop their heads off," Swappy said. "That's mean."

"They're already dead!" Brona pulled a long dagger from her boot and passed it to Swappy. "But if you feel really bad, just apologize after you decapitate them."

"Will you all shut up?" another banshee in a red gown screeched. "We're going to *sing*!" And she did. She sang that last word, carrying the note for what seemed like forever, snapping Kelcie to attention, making it impossible to turn away from the show.

Humming in mismatched minor keys as if trying to find the perfect one, their voices rose, cresting in blended harmony.

At that point, Kelcie lost sight of the others, unable to take her eyes off a dark-haired hunk heading straight for her, singing only for *her*. She swooned, her grip on her sword loosening. Thought escaped her. Momentary pain blinded her, waking her up. She felt Niall's arm touching her hand.

Prince Charming's face flash-framed like an X-ray, skull and teeth and that axe lifted above his head, about to take hers off. Kelcie gasped, jumping backward. The blade got stuck in the pew, and Kelcie set his sleeve on fire.

Kelcie heard Niall shriek, and turned to see his invisible hands lifting a sword to stop the redhead's axe from splitting his skull in two. Then they were sparring.

"You ruined my dinner jacket!"

Prince Charming leaped over three pews, landing in front of Kelcie, swinging his axe across and down. Kelcie blocked and pivoted, dipping behind his back, matching his moves, right and left, batting away strike after strike.

He fell back, catching his breath, then smiled smugly. "You know you want a kiss . . ."

"Ew! No. I really, really don't!" Kelcie faked a retreat, then spun, using both hands, taking a wild swing.

Prince Charming's smug smile crashed on the ground, breaking into a million tiny pieces.

Weapons crossed, the red-haired beauty leaned in to whisper something to Niall, but never got the chance. His sword spun, twisting the axe out of her hand. Her head went one way while her body crumpled, turning to stone at Niall's feet.

Swappy stared longingly into the eyes of a seven-foot-tall woman in a pink taffeta dress. Pavel was faring even worse with two guys wearing twin polka-dotted ties vying for his attention.

Niall ran through the aisles, using the scream to break them from their trances. He got to Pavel first. The ice fairy lifted off the ground at the same time the banshees swung their axes, turning one another to stone. Swappy was next. He blinked repeatedly, in shock and then utter dismay, shrieking at the top of his lungs. Kelcie threw her sword at him. He made an impressive mad-grab, catching the grip, taking a closed-eyed, wild swing at Pink Taffeta. Her head bounced off a puffed sleeve and rolled under the pew.

Zephyr stared at the auburn beauty dancing especially for him. She blew him a kiss before her axe swung down.

Niall squinted. Zephyr cried out, reaching for his head, changing course at the sight of his impending doom.

Zephyr caught the shaft just below the heavy blade and kicked the banshee, sending her crashing into the wall where the bow sash around her waist got caught on a hook. Axe still in her hands, she leaped off the hook, snarling and frothing. Niall slid Zephyr's sword across the floor, where Zephyr caught it, and delivered the final blow.

By the time Kelcie caught up to Brona, her cousin had the blond banshee pinned to the wall by arrows. "For the last time, I don't want to dance with you!" Kelcie wasn't sure if Brona was entranced or not, but as soon as she tossed her her sword, there was only one left in the room.

The beauty with the curly brown hair had Jack trapped on the silver dais, purring like a good kitty. Sitting tall, his tail wagged gleefully as she raised her axe with one hand and bent to pet him with the other. "Pretty saber-toothed kitty."

Zephyr jumped out from behind a curtain and lopped her head clean off. Jack half-lunged at Zephyr. His claws an inch from Zephyr's throat, when he stopped suddenly, and roared at Niall. Jack morphed, blinking at the stone curls at his feet, and punted it, sending it flying over the pews for an extra point.

Kelcie counted . . . seven banshees. Someone was missing.

"Where's Lexis?"

A scream ripped through the stairwell the banshees had come from.

The basement was as cold as death. Torch-lit sconces spanned the circular room, illuminating seven mausoleums set in a row.

The blond bombshell who started this all had Lexis in her arms, a dagger against her throat. Kelcie's sword was on the ground, out of Lexis's reach.

"You can all get out! I only need one!"

"We're not leaving without her." Kelcie ignited her hand.

Bombshell sniggered. "Then you can all die with her."

33

SEVEN DEADLY SEERS

WHAT DO YOU want from her?" Kelcie asked.

"A blood donation to wake a legacy from our ancient past." The banshee smirked, tapping Lexis's neck again. "I've waited a long time for mortals to cross the threshold of the Sanctuary of the Damned. None of my sisters or brothers had a drop of blood left or I would've carved them up a long time ago. Always so annoying. Always whining about who had the better hair or biggest hand. But that's all over with now. Thank you for making me an only child. And now, for the offering."

Before Bombshell could act, Swappy sucked in a harsh breath, catching everyone's attention. "Vampire Trolls? There are Vampire Trolls in those tombs?"

"They're no ordinary Vampire Trolls," the banshee cackled.

"The Seven Deadly Seers," Pavel gasped.

"Very good. Someone is studying hard at Braverwil! Locked a stone's throw away by Queen Kefyra herself. She doesn't wish the future to be foretold. She believes the future of Winter is what she makes of it."

"And what would you ask the seers?" Niall questioned.

"That's for me to know and you to find out, should you want to stick around." The banshee turned the knife so the blade was against Lexis's throat.

"Lexis?" Jack shouted.

Lexis didn't answer. She didn't struggle. She wasn't moving at all. Niall could wake her up, but with the sharp edge touching her neck, it was too dangerous. Lexis might be startled and move, cutting herself by accident.

"She can't hear you right now. She only has eyes for *me*," the banshee sang.

The THWACK surprised everyone, including Lexis. The tip of an arrow stuck out of one side of the banshee's head, the fletching out the other.

The banshee's lip curled at Brona, offended. "How dare you ruin my hair? It has to be perfect! Today of all days! You evil—"

Lexis grabbed Bombshell's arm, twisting the knife out of her hand. Whipping the wind, Lexis used a gust to push the banshee into the wall, and swung Kelcie's sword.

Unlike the others, this banshee turned to dust.

"Thank you," Lexis said to Brona, rubbing the gash on her neck. She passed Kelcie her sword. "And thanks for the loan."

A bit of banshee hair was stuck to the tip of the blade.

"Couldn't clean it off first."

Lexis shrugged. "Thought you'd want a souvenir from your trip to the Lands of Winter."

"We should get out of here before something else wakes up," Pavel said. "And they need to be going."

"Wait," Brona said. She tapped her dagger on her chin in a way that made Kelcie very nervous. "Kelcie wanted to know what started the war. And none of us know. Why don't we ask a seer?"

"They see the future, not the past," Lexis explained.

"Then let's ask them what ends it," Niall suggested.

"What will knowing that change?" Jack asked.

"Maybe nothing, but we're here. And it kinda feels like maybe we were all meant to be here, together, doesn't it?" Zephyr asked.

"I'm leaving." Pavel started to walk out. "I'd rather face the monsters outside than listen to this anymore."

"That's insubordination, fairy!" Lexis shouted in his wake, but he was gone.

"Well, if we're gonna do this . . ." Zephyr borrowed Brona's dagger on his way to picking up a small bowl from in front of the first of the seven mausoleums. Setting it down, he closed his eyes before slicing his palm, not wanting to watch his blood drip into the bowl. Then he carried it to Lexis.

"I think it should be from both Winter and Summer. Tol and Charger."

"You can take my blood!" Swappy volunteered.

"No," Lexis said. "He's right. It should be mine."

Jack took the blade from Zephyr and wiped it off on his uniform, then held it out to Lexis.

After her blood joined Zephyr's, they walked together and Lexis set the bowl back down where Zephyr found it.

All seven mausoleums' doors lifted the exact same time, making Kelcie jump. Skeletons draped in black robes rushed the exit, but were blown back inside by some kind of invisible force. They returned more tentatively, as if realizing the iron bars laid at the thresholds were there to keep them from crossing. Arms shot through the bars, stretching to the point of no return in a desperate fit to reach the bowl.

"I think you have to give it to one of them," Brona prompted.

Zephyr picked up the bowl with shaking hands, passing it to Lexis. "I'm fine if you want to do it."

She smirked. "They can't get out."

"I'm fine if you want to do it," he repeated, flashing dimples.

Lexis approached the one in the middle, leaning out, keeping her distance. He snatched the bowl from her hands and drank it down. A tongue licked lips that weren't there before. A three-foot body filled out beneath the loose robe. The vampire looked trollish, like the ones Kelcie met in Summer, except for a bald head, the long fangs, and a tattoo on his forehead of three connected spirals.

The slate doors closed on the other mausoleums.

"Oh, to have a little more." The vampire licked the bottom of the bowl. Beady red eyes fell on Lexis, then Zephyr, then the others watching intently. "What is your question?"

Kelcie inched closer to hear better.

"See, the Lands of Winter and the Lands of Summer are still at war after thousands of years," Zephyr started.

"Tell me something I don't know . . ." He shrugged.

"A Vampire Troll with a sarcastic sense of humor. I may be warming to Winter." Brona smirked.

"Legendary seer, tell us. When will the war between Summer and Winter end?" Lexis asked reverently.

"When the Lands are no longer split, Daughter of Abbots, and Alltar is reborn. That is when the war will finally end."

Kelcie was confused and frustrated by that answer. It was impossibly vague. From the looks on everyone else's faces, they were equally as annoyed.

"Not the stealing of *Croí na Bandia*?" Jack asked.

"Did I say stealing the Heart of Danu? No. I said what I said," the seer scoffed, irritated. "When the Lands are no longer split, and Alltar is reborn, the war will finally end. That is the answer. Now, eating always makes me tired." The troll tossed the bowl on the ground, yawning, and strolled into the shadows of his mausoleum.

The door fell, gaveling the session over.

"What do you suppose the banshee wanted to ask him?" Swappy contemplated.

Brona laughed. "I don't really care."

Jack laughed under his breath.

Swappy wrinkled his little nose. "You two are definitely related."

"You heard the seer. Stealing the Heart won't end the war," Niall said.

Lexis climbed the stairs, marching toward the sanctuary's door that Pavel had shut behind him. Jack and Swappy kept tight on her heels, as did Kelcie and her fianna.

"Stop! Please!" Kelcie called. Lexis looked back over her shoulder, her hand on the door handle. "We need your help, Lexis. Help us return the Heart to Summer."

"We can't. If I help you, if anyone in my fianna helps you, we will lose everything. Lose our place at Braverwil. Lose—"

"The songs that are being written in your honor," Brona finished for her. "Is that it? Honor and glory? Because I get those things. I live for those things. Nothing is more important than the mission."

"But sometimes that mission changes," Swappy chimed. "Right, Lexis? If we tell all of this to the Queen then maybe she'll hand it over because she wants to end the war too. Then we can all work together and figure out how to get rid of the Abyss!"

Lexis smiled sadly at him. "She'll laugh in our faces, Swaps, right before she locks us in prison for treason." She exchanged a look Kelcie didn't understand with Jack. After a deep inhale, she turned back to the door to leave, but paused. "The Heart is at the Boreal Palace. Or at least, that's where we left it. That's all I can tell you."

"That's something. Thank you. And I'm sorry for what my mother's done. I'm sorry about the giants and the Ellén Trechend. I'm sorry innocent Winterfolk were hurt," Niall said, sounding exhausted.

Lexis nodded and walked out the door. Swappy gave Kelcie a hug, which made her laugh. He left her with a final request. "Please save the wyverns."

Jack saluted Brona and Kelcie, as if to say, *It was strange to meet you, but cool all the same.* The feeling was entirely mutual.

With no immediate signs of the Elléns when they walked outside the Sanctuary of the Damned, Lexis, Jack, and Swappy ran away as fast as they could to make it look like they were being chased. Pavel Grimes was likely lurking. Kelcie should've known that anyone with the name Grimes would never listen to reason. After all, his aunt did threaten to kill Kelcie last year—a couple of times. Life with Auntie Achila probably wasn't easy.

No one spoke much as they continued on, leaving Braverwil behind, heading north in the direction of the Boreal Citadel, which gave Kelcie time to think.

"It's not an excuse, but my guess is that Lexis was left with little option," Roswen had told Kelcie the night Lexis stole Niall's bough, and now Kelcie understood why. Because Roswen knew what it was like to face the wrath of their angry queen. The Winter's Queen had her wings clipped.

The farther they walked, the more she wished Lexis and Jack and Swappy were here. She would never want them to get in trouble, but the mission ahead felt—impossible.

The nearest Sidral was a two-day walk through harsh snowdrifts. If they made it that far, that only left them two days. One to break into the Boreal Citadel and steal back Danu's Heart, which was probably guarded by a thousand soldiers. And another, if they even made it that far, to get through the human world, and home.

As the sun wound down, frozen, aching feet led to a lot of complaining. With little choice, Zephyr let Brona scout for a place to rest for the night.

"I found a cave and it was warm inside. Must be radiating from inside the mountain. But it's a climb."

No one argued when Zephyr said, "Let's do it."

But Brona wasn't kidding when she said it was a climb. The snowy trail to get to the cave was steep and slippery and difficult to see at dusk. A sharp drop-off promised a painful death if you didn't dig your heels in with every step. Leaning into the headwind helped them move slightly faster than a turtle, but not by much.

"This was a terrible idea!" Niall fretted from the lead position.

"We're almost there!" Brona snapped.

Kelcie planted her feet. "How far is almost?"

A quaking rumbled from the top of the mountain. Snow avalanched so quickly, there wasn't time to scream.

Kelcie felt arms on both sides sweep her against the face of the mountain, crushing her into Brona and Niall.

"Hold on!" Zephyr cried.

But there was nothing to hold on to except each other. The sound of thunder rolling down the mountain lasted only a second, but when it was over, and Niall and Brona let go, Zephyr was gone.

"What are we going to do? Where did he go? Charger! Where are you?" Kelcie bellowed.

"Gang!" he called.

They looked over the edge. Zephyr clung to a thick branch sticking out of the mountain.

"Found the cave, and I can feel warmth coming out of it. I'm going to check it out." He swung like a gymnast around the high bar three times and released, vanishing, hopefully into the cave.

"Did he make it?" Niall worried.

Brona flew down, her voice echoing a few seconds later. "Yeah! And it's really warm!"

Niall went next, dropping onto the branch in a crouch and diving into the cave. Kelcie mimicked Niall's technique, but slipped off and ended hanging from the branch for a solid minute before she could manifest enough wind to push her through the opening. When her feet hit sturdy ground, Niall caught her and pulled her away from the edge.

"Thanks."

This cave was warm, likely venting something inside the mountain, something volcanic. That thought dropped her stomach into her shoes.

There was a sticky sheen slicking the walls in the rear of the cave that was disgusting.

"Looks like lichen," Brona said.

Lichen or not, Kelcie wasn't sitting on it.

She padded closer to the entrance and sat down, feeling a bulge in her pocket. She'd completely forgotten Elliott stuck a pack of Sour Patch Kids in there. The contents felt a little squished and warm when she tore open the package, but it was food and she was starving. She poured them into her hand and started sorting them by color.

"What are those?" Niall asked.

"Candy. You eat 'em."

Brona and Zephyr leaned over Niall to see what Kelcie had.

"Why are you doing that?" Zephyr asked. "Just pass them out so we can all have some."

"I like to mix certain colors together." She popped a blue one and a green one into her mouth at the same time.

"That's two from your share. Now start divvying them up fair and square. I'm counting with you." Brona scooted closer, putting her grubby fingers all over Kelcie's candy.

A minute later Kelcie's palm was sadly empty.

"That went fast," she pouted, turning over the bag to make sure she didn't miss any.

Zephyr stuck out his tongue. "Why does my tongue hurt?"

"The acid in the sugars on the candy is eating the flesh off your tongue," Kelcie explained. "It'll be fine in a few minutes."

"I'm thirsty," Brona complained.

Kelcie scooped a handful of snow from just outside the cave and handed it to Brona.

"What am I supposed to do with this, Saiga?"

"Eat it. It's just frozen water."

Brona tentatively licked some into her mouth. "Water tastes even better this way!"

"So that guy, Jack Postal, he's your cousin," Niall said to Kelcie.

"Guess so. The few times I've seen my mother she's only ever been with Brona's mother."

"Maybe his mother sided with Winter in the war and ours with Summer," Brona speculated. "Like Scáthach and her sister. That was strange seeing Aífe fighting today. I thought it was Scáthach."

"Me too." Zephyr leaned the back of his head against the wall, folding his arms over his chest. "I have to sleep." His eyelids dipped, a weighted curtain with no hopes of going up.

"How's your side?" Kelcie asked Niall.

"It's fine. A little sore." He yawned, but shook his head, refusing to give in to exhaustion. "It's weird to think this time last year we'd all just met, isn't it?"

"And now here we are, trapped in the Lands of Winter in a moldy cave, eating candy that is eating away our flesh." Brona grinned, resting her head on Zephyr's arm. "Good times."

Kelcie used Niall's shoulder as a pillow. "Is this okay?"

"Sure." He scooted closer to her. "How do you think anyone could ever get rid of the Abyss?"

Kelcie yawned. She thought about saying, *One problem at a time, Adder.* One day at a time too, because every day since they had arrived in Winter had been one fight for their lives after another. But instead, she said the one thing she knew to be true.

"You're the genius. You'll figure it out."

34

THE LIBRARY

THAT NIGHT, LEXIS snuck down to the library. Jack met her there, along with Swappy. She didn't invite Pavel. The ice fairy wasn't in the fairy hive when she returned. He wasn't in the commissary eating, or with the cleanup crew working on the lost launch bay. Lexis found Pavel in the last place she looked, hoping he wouldn't be there: Aífe's office.

She listened outside the door long enough to hear him tell Aífe what had transpired in the Sanctuary of the Damned, every detail of the conversations with the Summer fianna—the flat rat.

If he told Aífe, then he likely had told his aunt too. Hearing the betrayal hurt like nothing Lexis had ever felt before. Since she was ten, Jack, Swappy, and Pavel had been her best friends. It was Pavel's family's stature in the armies that made Lexis's appointment as Tol stand out. Pavel never argued about it, he took it like a good soldier, even though she knew his aunt was disappointed with him. Maybe she should've expected this. She didn't have the heart for this war anymore. She wanted it over.

Lexis didn't bother to stay long enough to hear Aífe's response. Whatever it was, even if Aífe didn't report the incident to Queen Kefyra's Advisors, Achila Grimes would, and likely get her nephew Lexis's position as Tol in a new fianna.

As she walked away, she remembered that day Aífe called her

name. Being a Tol was the greatest honor that could be bestowed upon a first year. When Aífe chose her, Lexis knew she had made the right decision coming to Braverwil, even though it meant disappointing her parents. But now, after a long mission where she worried about her fianna, her friends, as much if not more than the mission itself, she wasn't entirely sure she was cut out to lead them. Being Tol was a heavy burden. She was responsible for her team, and she was letting them down. Full of anguish, all she could think about was that at this very moment the people she met in Summer were suffering, and it was all her fault.

On the long walk back to school, past the rock piles that once were Ellén Trechend, Swappy begged Lexis to let them help the Summer fianna get the Heart. She wanted to, but how could she put Swappy and Jack in harm's way like that? And she was no help to the Summer fianna on her own. Jack suggested the best way to help Summer, short of committing full-on treason, was to do a little research. If the war was going to end when the Abyss was gone, then they first needed to figure out what originally caused it. It was a good idea, so they sneaked out of bed after curfew and headed to the only place they could think of that might have answers.

Tucked away on the other side of the mountain, the library was Lexis's favorite place in the school. Trees grew inside the cavernous space. Moonlight flooded a window normally occupied by sunlight during the daytime. She padded through the stacks, methodically scanning titles with her lit finger.

A few feet away, Swappy swung his lantern, excited. "This one says Life and Times of someone called Lugh. That's old enough for sure!"

"Too old. Lugh is a god of light, the grandson of King Balor who survived his wrath, and in turn killed him. That is before our people came into the Otherworld."

"For someone who hates her parents being abbots, a lot of it sunk in," Jack commented.

"I don't hate it. I just didn't agree with them, at least not when I was ten."

"And now?"

The lights flickered on.

"Out of bed after curfew . . . ?" the preceptor asked. "That's unlike you three."

Startled, Lexis dropped the book she was holding on Jack's toe.

"Owa . . ."

Swappy belched Aífe's name with such gravitas that Lexis felt a breeze.

She wanted to die! Aífe had to have heard what she'd said.

Nervous fingers crossed as Lexis stood at attention with her arms stick straight at her side.

"Sorry, ma'am." Lexis scrambled for an excuse. "We missed a lot of work and were hoping to do a little studying while it was quiet in here."

"It's a library. It's always quiet in here, Lexis."

Lexis's stomach sank. She hated lying, mostly because she was terrible at it. But she also never thought she'd ever have to lie to the one person she admired the most.

Aífe was still in her uniform, still covered in dust from the afternoon's exhausting events. Her hair was braided out of the way, a change for her, as if she were expecting more surprise attacks, and soon.

She gestured for them to sit at the tables beneath the big oak tree in the middle of the library. Lexis was stunned when she joined them, taking a seat, rather than standing over them, her usual style when she doled out punishments to cadets.

Aífe folded her hands together and set them on the table. "Lexis, I asked you a question. And now?"

"And now . . . ?" Lexis's heart hammered.

"When I walked in. You said you didn't agree with your parents about the war when you were ten. I'd like to hear the answer to Postal's question. And now? Have those sentiments changed?"

"Yes," Lexis admitted, relieved and terrified to say it out loud. "I thought being a soldier was about glory and honor. That to be the best fighter, the best leader, the best at everything, was all that mattered."

"Then the giants came," Jack mumbled. "And we all wanted Summer to pay for what they did."

"But then we went to Summer." Swappy swallowed, trying to stop his voice from shaking, but it was a tide that would not be held back. He was a bundle of love for everyone and everything, and by the sadness in his eyes, Lexis knew he was about to say what she didn't have the courage to. "And it was full of Summerfolk, who were just like Winterfolk, who have nothing to do with the war. They're just people and families and friends and wyverns. Then we took their Heart, and well . . ." He sniffled. Tears fell, and his lower lip trembled. "Kelcie said that if they don't get it back they're all going to die. Is that true?"

Aífe's hands fisted. "It was the *Croí na Bandia* you stole?"

"Yes, ma'am," they said in dismal unison.

"I assume this Kelcie is from Summer." Aífe stared over their heads, conflicted. "Long before you or your parents were ever born, a Speck tried to sell me a Fomorian scroll that explained how the Heart of Danu came to be in Summer. If that is what was taken, then I can confirm it is true. In a short time, the lands will grow uninhabitable. Queen Kefyra's predecessors came into that knowledge as well. They purchased the scroll. Until her, though, no one had the nerve to act on the information in it."

"Your sister is in Summer," Swappy pressed. "Don't you care?"

"My sister and I have long fought on opposite sides. How this all ends will not change that. Nothing will." She sighed, resigned.

Swappy hugged his knees, rocking in his chair. "And then there's that stuff that Vampire Troll seer said."

Aífe perked up. "One of the Seven Deadly Seers? Were you in the Sanctuary of the Damned?"

"Yes, ma'am," they admitted.

"You managed to get by the banshees?"

"We had help. Pavel told you about the Summer fianna here in Winter," Lexis said. "I was listening outside the door."

"Then you know he did. I'm more interested in what the seer had to say," Aífe retorted.

"That the war between the Lands of Summer and the Lands of Winter will end when they are no longer split, and Alltar is reborn," Jack explained. "We were hoping to figure out how the Abyss came to be, but the answer doesn't seem to be in here."

"It isn't. I don't know myself, and I've read every book in here many times over."

"So what should we do, Aífe?" Lexis asked.

The preceptor stood up. "In life we all have choices to make, some bigger than others. I like to call those defining moments."

"I know." Lexis grimaced. It was one of the first lectures Aífe gave first years. "But . . ."

"We want to help them," Jack confessed.

Aífe set a hand on his shoulder. "One thing I've learned in my immortal life is that we only regret the chances we don't take."

"Are you saying we should go?" Swappy asked, hopeful.

"I'm saying that this is a defining moment." Aífe rocked on her heels. "And there will be consequences with whatever you decide. I'm now going to turn in, so that if you decide to go, I will have no knowledge of that. And if you decide to stay, well then, I'll see you in the morning."

As soon as they heard Aífe shut the door to the library, Swappy clucked his tongue. "We're going, aren't we?"

Jack nodded. "I'm in."

Lexis's shoulders slumped. Their stern stares felt like they weighed a thousand pounds. Whatever decision she made, Lexis knew they would go along with—one leading them down the path to treason, and the other tucking them safely back into their beds.

A defining moment for sure: Lexis had to follow her heart no matter how loud her head was screaming.

"We're going. We just have one stop to make on our way out."

35

A RIDE TO GALANTA

ELCIE FELT A disconcerting poke on her cheek, then something stabbed her hand. Her eyes flew open. Looking back
at her were triangular blue eyes belonging to a baseball-
sized tarantula with pointy ears, wires for hair, and a mouth full
of jagged teeth that bit down on the end of her nose.

"Ow!" Kelcie pushed it off, only to feel another set of teeth
sink into her leg. "Gah!"

"Who bit me?" Zephyr whined. "You better stop! Ow! Brona?"

"It's not me!" Brona hopped up beside him, stomping. "They're
biting me too!"

Kelcie tripped over Niall, and gasped, distraught. Sunlight
poured into the cave opening. It was morning. They had slept
all night.

And the walls were crawling with spiders.

Niall mumbled, somehow still sleeping through this nightmare.

"Niall! Get up!"

He rubbed his eyes, and put on his busted glasses like nothing
was wrong. "What's all the—" He jumped to his feet. "Gads! Baby
spider-trows in the flesh!"

"Eggs!" Zephyr freaked. "I WAS SLEEPING ON EGGS!"

The hundreds of yellow bumps on the floor, ceiling, and walls
of the cave weren't bumps at all. They were clusters of eggs,

most of them now hatched. Kelcie kicked and flicked, hopped and danced, trying to keep them from biting her, but there were too many of them.

A gargantuan shadow fell over her. A seismic whistle shattered eardrums. All eyes turned toward the entrance where a much, much larger spider-trow blocked the entire mouth of the cave. A grateful smile spread, crinkling much larger blue triangular eyes.

"Hello, breakfast," she cackled. "Why don't you four lie back down? Make things easy on yourself. My babies are hungry."

"That spider is talking!" Zephyr exclaimed.

"More pressing I think is that she wants to feed us to her children!" Brona argued.

"Use your shillelagh!" Niall yelled to Zephyr.

"I can't shillelagh somebody's mother!"

"Wonderful! You go first!" Mama Spider-Trow advanced, pointed legs stilting over broken shells, heading straight for Zephyr, slimy drool spouting from every orifice.

Niall didn't hesitate. He fired off a round from his sidewinder, one of his last three jinxes hitting her right between the eyes.

"Th-th-that's n-n-n-not n-n-nice . . . Ah . . . AH . . . CHOOOOO!" Mama Spider-Trow sneezed, hurling snot that smothered the flames on Kelcie's hand she was using to keep the babies away.

Hundreds of babies crawled under their mother who was still sneezing and sneezing. There was nothing left to do.

"We have to get out of here!" Kelcie cried.

Brona took off first, leading the way, only she was heading farther into the cave. Kelcie let the boys usher by her, then pulled her swords to buy them some time. A flip and thrust, sparking a mighty wind, the legion of spider-trow babies barreled into their still-sneezing mother, pelting her hard enough she slipped on her own snot and slid out of the cave.

Running to catch up, Kelcie was forced to hunch as the tunnel grew skinnier, and darker, and wetter. She slipped, and was caught off guard by a sharp decline. Plunging straight down, she crashed into Zephyr, who crashed into Niall, who barreled into Brona, leaving them sliding flat on their backs until the tunnel ended on a pile of four-eyed, six-finned, rotten, stinking fish.

A forked tongue stabbed and slurped. A mouth like a dragon's polished off five in three bites. In a whirlwind of panic, the four leaped to their feet, stunned at the sight of a wyvern lapping up the nasty fish like it hadn't eaten in days.

Zephyr's eyes grew wide. "That's a wyvern!"

It was a wyvern, one that looked exactly like the one Kelcie had seen flying over Braverwil. So big, it completely filled the cavernous space. Between its legs, Kelcie saw daylight. They'd found an exit, only they had to get past this extremely menacing, utterly terrifying beast.

"I've got this," Brona said, loading her bow with three red-tipped arrows.

The wide-eyed wyvern coughed up a half-eaten fish, screeching. Rather than backing away, it bounded forward, shaking its head, and mewing as if it were trying to speak. Then, Kelcie smelled something much worse than the fish.

"Swappy?"

"Oh, yeah, it sure smells like him." Zephyr pinched his nose.

The wyvern gave Kelcie a sheepish grin, and lifted a leg toward her. A rolled-up piece of paper was tied to him.

He giggled like it tickled when she took it off.

"How did he find us?" Niall asked.

"Probably pretty easily with the prints we left in the snow," Brona answered.

The wyvern nodded.

"Why don't you just morph back so we can talk to you, Swappy?" Zephyr asked.

Swappy shook his head.

"Changelings can't return to their stolen identity once they've changed back," Niall explained.

Swappy licked the side of Niall's face to say thank you. From the look on Niall's face, he really wished Swappy hadn't.

"Ick. Fish breath. What's the note say?" Niall asked, wiping his cheek on his shoulder.

Brona yanked it out of Kelcie's hands before she had a chance to read it.

"'Swappy is here to give you a ride. Will meet you in Galanta. Jack and I went ahead to get provisions. There's a bag with bread tied to his other leg in case you're hungry, that is if Swappy didn't eat it. Burn this note. Lexis.'"

Zephyr checked Swappy's other leg. "You ate the bread, huh, Swappy?"

Swappy burped. He stomped his foot, shaking the cave, as if saying, *Yes!* and *Hop on.*

"How do we know this isn't some trap?" Brona asked skeptically, waving the note in Swappy's face.

"Birdie has a point." Zephyr arched a high brow at the changeling, whose expression dipped into a deep frown.

She did have a point. Lexis had had plenty of chances to change her mind, before, during, and after she stole the Heart. Why would she suddenly change her mind now? Then again, maybe it wasn't a sudden change. Maybe, she wanted to right the wrong. There was only one way to find out. "I guess that if this war is ever going to end, we're going to have to trust one another," Kelcie said, burning the note.

Niall tentatively set his palm on the flat surface of Swappy's nose and closed his eyes. Swappy didn't move or flinch. His big black eyes crossed, trying to look at Niall's hand.

Niall looked over at Zephyr. "What do you say, Charger? Shall we go for a ride?"

Kelcie was excited right up until the point where Swappy dove out of the gaping hole, plummeting straight down. She closed her eyes, trying not to scream, squeezing Zephyr's waist for dear life. Niall's grip on Kelcie's stomach was just as tight, making it impossible to breathe.

It was a long flight—almost eight hours—but with it came a bird's-eye view of the Lands of Winter. Swappy dipped low over pristine frozen tundra, his claws playfully brushing snowdrifts, then rose to thin-aired altitudes over a forest of petrified trees, leaving Kelcie and her fianna shivering, yet awed. Next up was another forest, the most beautiful Kelcie had ever seen in her life, with orange crystal-leafed trees that softly clinked like wind chimes in their wake.

Following a rise in the terrain into a snow-covered clearing, Kelcie saw a building of clustered colorful towers that looked like a temple. When they flew over it, the spark in her belly where her powers lingered warmed. She felt a triggering rush, as if this was some kind of focal point of elemental energy. She wished they could stop, but there wasn't time. Swappy dipped, soaring above a herd of antelope with ringed horns and droopy jowls.

"Saiga!" Niall cried, pointing.

Real. Alive. In the flesh. Did they once roam Summer? Would they again if the continent was whole one day?

When they passed over a busy city, Kelcie only got a split second to glimpse the Boreal Citadel surrounded by a massive wall at the very end of a peninsula before Swappy descended quickly, taking Kelcie's stomach with him. He soared out over a vast, choppy ocean before circling back, and dropping lower, into a rolling fog that provided cover for them to land on a snowy field beside a barn.

Hopping off their ride, Swappy changed back to his normal self, stooped over from exhaustion. He stretched, groaning, but said nothing as if worried about being overheard.

A saber-tooth tiger Kelcie assumed was Jack trotted out of the barn, jerking his head repeatedly, indicating they should follow, and fast.

The barn was only half full of horses; the other stalls were caged and occupied by those dreadful screeching vampire owls. Kelcie glared as they passed, her thoughts racing back to Elliott. Jack morphed mid-step, hurrying into a tackle room where Lexis was hunched over a table with only one chair and a drawing that looked like a sort of crude map of lines and arrows.

"We found only one way in, but you're not going to like it."

"It's nice to see you too." Kelcie smiled at her.

She smirked. "I bet it is. Look, Pavel probably knows we're gone by now and ratted us out to his aunt. So that means this is likely a suicide mission."

"Good. The more dangerous the better," Brona boasted.

Jack exchanged a fist bump with her. "My sentiments exactly."

"How are you for weapons?" Lexis asked.

"I'm out of ammunition for my sidewinder, so basically, it's pretty useless." Niall set it on the table. "Except," he lifted out a black marble, "I found one more nighty-night jinx."

"So you've got only the basics: swords, shillelagh, bow and arrows, and one jinx," Lexis hummed. "Jack procured a few frost bombs." She kicked a basket of smoking snow globes. "And purchased a handful of nicker-twisters from the jester's shop around the corner."

She tossed Kelcie a spiked silver object that reminded her of the metal jacks she used to play with when she was little.

"Nicker-twisters?" Niall asked.

"Worst wedgies ever!" Swappy wrinkled his nose.

Poor kid sounded like he spoke from experience. Kelcie set it down carefully.

Lexis slid the sketch over and sighed. "Okay. So here's what we've learned so far . . ."

What Lexis and Jack had learned wasn't much. They had a way into the citadel, a steam tunnel, but had no idea where it came out. And the location of Danu's Heart was still a complete mystery.

"We can only hope it's still in the reception hall where we last saw it," Lexis finished.

"So basically, we are walking into a trap," Niall concluded.

"Like I said . . ." Lexis agreed. "Kelcie, the Heart can only be held by you or me. The others might be able to carry the lysterium case by the straps, but only for a few minutes. It's that hot.

Achila kept replacing the melting ice on her back around the case, and still ended up with a pretty bad burn. That was after holding it for only a few minutes. Then she had to give it to me."

"I carry it. Got it," Kelcie affirmed.

"And hopefully, it's still in there. If not, then we're doomed," Lexis hummed, likely contemplating their demise.

Jack reached into a cardboard box beside the table and passed out white uniforms to Kelcie, Brona, Niall, and Swappy. Lexis and Jack already had them on.

Swappy held his up. The bottoms hung a foot past his ankles. "It's a little big."

"Hopefully you can find someone to change into pretty quickly, Swaps," Lexis said. "The rest of you shorties will have to roll them up." She winked at Kelcie, who would have taken offense, but she *was* short.

"Hold on. You three are coming with us? Into the citadel?" Kelcie asked, concerned. She glanced at Jack and Swappy, seeing them nodding. "You can't! If you're caught—"

"We started this. We're going to finish it," Lexis said adamantly.

"We'll be fine, so long as we don't get caught," Swappy blurted.

"And now you just cursed the mission!" Jack snapped. "Why do you do that? Why must you always state the obvious?"

Swappy answered with a long, loud toot.

Zephyr pinched his nose. "Oh, for d'at, Swappy, and fo' eating da bread, go fin' us something to eat!"

Swappy hopped to it right away.

"You could all take a lesson from d'at changeling," Zephyr said. "He may be gassy but he does exactly what you tell him ta do, when you tell him ta do it. Maybe he should come back to Summer with us."

Niall, who had been abnormally quiet during the planning stage, scooted around Jack to speak to Lexis. "I have a better idea about how we should proceed, if you're open to it," he said.

"One that might make you heroes of Winter again instead of traitors."

T HEY WAITED AN hour, letting night fall before venturing out of the barn. Walking in two single-file lines, the traditional way for fiannas in the Winter army to move from place to place, Lexis led the way through the streets of Galanta that were lit up like any big city. Bundled-up Winterfolk hurried past, rushing to get indoors after dark, except for several restaurants with outdoor tables serving fairy families who appeared less bothered by the cold.

As they came to the end of a block, Jack said in hushed tones to Lexis, "Right here."

She turned into an alley that led to a flight of stairs, then another that spilled onto the rocky banks of a windy bay. Kelcie's cheeks, raw and chapped from riding Swappy all the way here, stung miserably. Her eyes were dry and yet they wouldn't stop watering, making it hard to see.

Niall's idea was brilliant. Lexis, Jack, and Swappy would enter the citadel and raise the alarm that a Summer fianna was on their way to break into the citadel and steal the Heart of Danu back. The Queen would check on it, thereby revealing its true location. The rest was a series of complicated signals and logistics with a dash of what-ifs that left Kelcie confused. Thankfully, her job was to carry the Heart of Danu. That much, she could do.

Trudging across the slippery rocks, the path led to a steep climb up an embankment onto the peninsula, at the end of which was the sapphire-blue palace. Lexis stayed close to the wall that shielded them from the wind as they trekked through three feet of snow, to the promised steaming vent.

"You're sure about this?" Lexis asked Niall, handing him the map.

Niall took it. "Very."

Jack waved Kelcie and Brona over. "I don't have a lot of family. Well, none, actually. So I just wanted to say it was really cool to meet you both. I don't hate you or anything, just because you live in Summer." He winced. "Yeah, that sounded a whole lot better in my head."

"And we don't hate you because you live in Winter," Brona answered.

"That was pathetic," Kelcie said, elbowing her.

"What? I don't hate him. In fact, if we spend a lot more time around him, I may come to like him more than you."

"Nice." Kelcie scowled at her. "Look. I'm horrible at goodbyes, Jack. So how about we say that if we don't die today and Summer is still around after tomorrow, that we plan a family reunion?"

He half smiled. "Yeah. Good. That sounds good."

Kelcie gave him a hug, feeling him tense. "Take care of yourself."

That was it. All the time they had. It felt way too short. Lexis, Swappy, and Jack left. Kelcie knew she would be seeing them soon, but by then, they would be trying to kill her and her fianna too.

36

BOREAL CITADEL

ZEPHYR DID THE honors on the grate, replacing it once they were inside the small vent. Cramped and hot, Kelcie couldn't see anything through the steam as she crawled up the sharp incline. The nicker-twisters in her pocket kept getting wedged into her groin, which necessitated momentary pauses and careful extraction or Kelcie would end up in a most embarrassing situation, and Niall was behind her.

"I see a light," Zephyr whispered.

Kelcie wasn't sure if that was good or bad, but at least their time in this claustrophobic steam room was almost at an end. She didn't dare think about what her hair looked like. Not that it mattered, especially when she was about to enter a battle that would determine the fate of the Lands of Summer, and that included her grandmother, Striker, and her father.

The light was bright enough for Kelcie to see Zephyr had his ear against the vent. He carefully and quietly removed it, and set it down below, then somersaulted out.

Kelcie followed, mimicking his move, and dropped the last few feet to the ground below. Lexis explained that this part of the citadel was supervised by the Queen's Advisors. Underground, there were shafts that peeled off in different directions with both private rooms, and prison cells. But it was Swappy who knew the most important information. He said that if they found the hot spring (which he snuck into when they were here) then they'd find the citadel's Sidral—their only way out once they got Danu's Heart. It was in a room beside it.

Kelcie smelled rotten eggs as they neared the end of the tunnel. She looked out, finding a cavern that was as large as a gymnasium. Columns formed from stalagmites and stalactites growing together surrounded a steaming, bubbling geothermic hot spring. For the first time in Kelcie's life, luck was on their side! The vent was for the hot spring!

The Sidral wasn't visible from where they were, only the soldiers standing guard in front of the archway.

All that was reassuring, but first they had to get upstairs. Lexis said they would find a way to get the Queen into the reception room. That was where she, Jack, and Swappy would be with Danu's Heart, ready to pass it off.

"There!" Brona whispered. She pointed to a set of stairs on the other side of the hot spring. But, sadly, the spring was occupied by none other than the two orange-haired fairies that forever seemed to pop up at the worst possible times. And here Kelcie would've expected them to be tired of hot temperatures after all their time stuck in Summer.

"We're going to have to cut across. Whatever you do, stay down," Zephyr whispered. "I'll bring up the rear."

That meant Kelcie had to go first. She dropped to all fours, crawling stalagmite to stalagmite as fast as she could, biting down hard on her lip to keep from yelping at all the sharp points breaking off on her kneecaps.

The twins didn't notice her at all, or Brona or Niall, but Zephyr wasn't so lucky. Being a foot taller than the rest of them, he had a much harder time hiding behind the columns. He was only halfway across when Kelcie heard Nevver or Latchkey call him.

"Hey! You there! Can you do me a favor?"

Kelcie held her breath. Niall inched down the stairs to get a better look. Brona leaned on his back. Kelcie leaned on hers, but she couldn't see much with all the steam.

Zephyr carefully lifted out his shillelagh and sword, and left them behind the column before he walked toward the bubbling hot spring, nervously pursing his lip, cratering his dimples. "Of course."

"Move the towels closer."

"Not a problem." Zephyr glanced in Kelcie's direction, flashing wide eyes, on his way to a stack of pink towels.

He returned, placing them on the edge. "Here you go."

As he turned to leave, the nearest fairy twin grabbed his arm. "You look familiar. Where have I seen you before?"

"I don't think we've met. I'm on a new assignment here. But it's a pleasure to meet you. Duty calls!" He wrenched his hand free.

Marching swiftly around the column, he grabbed his weapons on the way to the stairs, ignoring their demands for him to get back there.

"We should use the frost bomb on them," Brona whispered, lifting it out of her satchel.

Zephyr snatched it from her and returned it to the bag, mouthing, "Go!"

At the top of the stairs was a wooden door. Kelcie listened and when she didn't hear anything, she gave Niall a thumbs-up, and pulled her swords.

The door opened into a hallway. Blue sapphire walls cast everything in confusing shadows. Sadly, this was where the map ended too. The way to the Queen's reception hall, where Lexis last saw the *Croí na Bandia*, was up a spiral staircase, but where those stairs were, they didn't know.

The next three turns led to more empty hallways filled with silence, and painting after painting of the same woman at different ages. White hair combed in a perfect bob around her face, skin so pale it was see-through, always in a dress made of snowflake-patterned white lace. Even without the diadem across her brow, Kelcie knew immediately who she was: Queen Kefyra. Every painting void of color, she looked the very definition of winter.

Through a set of double doors, they entered a sculpture garden, and found the spiral staircase.

"This has been way too easy," Brona noted. "Where are the guards that should be searching for us?"

"Maybe the Queen's out of town? And Lexis is waiting there to hand over the Heart?" Zephyr enthused.

Do you hear that? Niall asked.

"I don't hear anything," Kelcie whispered.

Creeping slowly up the spiral stairs, as they neared the top, they ducked down. Kelcie peeked over the edge several times, catching glimpses of too many soldiers in white, the Queen beside a pedestal, and on the last look, the case she'd seen in the shrine in Summer City, the one containing Danu's Heart. What she didn't see was Lexis, Jack, or Swappy. Her stomach back-flipped. Their plan was doomed. There was no way they were going to get through them all to take the Heart.

Kelcie inched down to deliver the bad news when Niall abruptly did an about-face and spider-crawled down the stairs—all the way to the bottom.

"Where's he going?" Zephyr whispered harshly.

I hear something.

Following after him, Kelcie listened. Tapping of footsteps—heels on glass, babbling water fountains at the other end of the garden, mumbling from the reception room at the top of the stairs.

"What do you mean, specifically?" Kelcie asked in hushed tones when she caught up to him.

Singing. Like when we were in Rilios.

Kelcie, Brona, and Zephyr exchanged shrugs, shaking their heads.

Brona gasped. "Are you *hearing* the Heart?"

I-I think I am. It's not coming from that room.

"But I saw the case up there. On a pedestal right next to the Queen," Kelcie insisted.

I believe you. But she could have two boxes.

At the bottom of the stairs, they entered the sculpture garden, tiptoeing around the Bearded Fairy of Unusual Size, and past a tribute to the Seven Deadly Seers before blood donation that were disturbingly good likenesses. Next came a quiet banquet hall filled with long tables and chairs. Another set of stairs came next—Niall was running at this point, making way too much noise.

"Slow down!" Zephyr hissed, but Niall didn't. He sped up, rushing up more stairs that must go to a different part of the citadel. The others trailing behind him, Niall took three steps at a time, passing the first and second floors. Each floor looked like an apartment building, like these were residences or bedrooms. But why would the Heart be here?

Halfway up the third flight, Niall stopped and looked back. *It's on this floor . . .*

Zephyr grabbed Niall before he could get away and whispered, "Single file, remember? That's what Lexis said. Single file. You can lead the way, but slow down!"

"Right." Niall nodded.

They lined up and came down the stairs walking as a Winter fianna. Unlike on the other floors, there were only two doors on the hall, one at either end. Outside one were three women in plain white dresses, carrying stacks of towels and linens. But sadly, Niall headed to the other door, which was guarded by a guy twice the size of Zephyr, holding a metal staff across his body.

"I didn't call for reinforcements," the guard grunted.

"No. Her Majesty has asked us to retrieve something," Niall tried.

The guard's deep belly laugh made it all the way down the hallway, catching the attention of the ladies in white.

"Could you possibly bend down so I can explain in confidence?" Brona cast a glance at the servants. "You know how they gossip."

He smirked, leaning toward her. "What?"

The look of surprise on his face when Brona's nose grew into a black beak and jabbed him on the forehead was priceless. His eyes grew wide with anticipation.

"Open the door," Brona instructed. "The Queen has asked us to bring her the *Croí na Bandia*. I'll hold that baby for you." She took the staff out of his hands, nearly dropping it. "Ooh. Heavy. Bet it packs a punch."

Deadpan, the guard lifted out a key—three connected snowflakes—and held it to the door. Kelcie's heart had never pounded so hard in her life.

One of the three servants headed their way, hugging her linens, with a serious look of concern on her round face.

"What do you think you're doing? You heard the Queen. That door is never to be opened." Letting the sheets fall to the floor, she produced a loaded crossbow.

Kelcie's nicker-twister stuck in her forehead. Black smoke twirled like DNA. The woman lost the weapon, making a desperate attempt to dig her underwear out of her backside.

"Ugh!"

The door hissed open. Niall went straight in, ignoring how useful his scream would've been at that moment. And of course, Zephyr followed Niall.

Wedgie Woman danced, screeching, "Stop them!" She groaned. "Hit the alarm!"

Linens hit the ground. Both women reached for a flat panel behind them, but Kelcie got there first, or at least her airball did.

"Mistral!"

The gust blasted them all the way to the other end of the hallway, but that wasn't going to keep them away for long!

"I got 'em," Brona said with iron nerves.

Her arrow bounced off the sapphire wall. The tip burst, smothering the women in laughing gas. They slumped on top of the moaning Wedgie Woman, clutching their sides, laughing so hard they couldn't get up.

Kelcie and Brona rushed after Niall and Zephyr. The room

was as large as the entire Saiga Den. Glass shelves and silver pedestals displayed jewels.

The soldier was curled into the fetal position, rubbing the retreating red mark from Brona's Birdbrain. Zephyr stood over him with his shillelagh at the ready for when the magical hypnotism wore off.

Niall was standing beside a case that was an exact replica of the one Kelcie saw in the reception room, and in the shrine in the Lands of Summer, Rilios.

"That's the real one?" Kelcie asked.

Yes! Niall tried to pick it up, and ripped his hand away. *Owa! It's blistering hot!*

The alarm went off, blaring so loudly it felt like someone was taking a baseball bat to Kelcie's eardrums. She shifted her scabbard to her side, making room for the box.

"I got it."

Kelcie picked it up and set it straight back down. It was way hotter than Lexis said it would be. Blisters bubbled on her hands, and she'd barely touched it. Maybe it was because the Heart had been out of the Stone of Destiny for so long. She saw Brona's and Zephyr's panicked stares and knew Niall was speaking to her in her head, something about finding another way to carry it. Pedestals toppled. Arguing broke out between them. Kelcie heard none of it. What she did hear was her mother's voice telling her to be strong, and felt the swords in her scabbard radiate a power, feeding her own.

The strap settled across her body and the full heat of the *Croí na Bandia* hit her back. She winced and coughed, gasping.

"You okay?" Niall asked.

"It's hot. Like really, really hot."

Boom.

Ba-boom.

Boom.

Danu's Heart was beating, like Kelcie's own heart.

Boom.

Ba-boom.

Silence.

Boom.

A beat that was slowing down.

She took her swords out of her scabbard, feeling a rush of confidence that helped her steel against the pain. They had the Heart, and were now only one step away from heading home.

"We need to get to the Sidral fast."

They only made it as far as the hallway when soldiers flooded from every direction. Ice fairies skipped the stairs, flying at them from above and below. But there was no need for them to fire off a single ice knife. They had them surrounded in seconds.

Achila Grimes hovered above the soldiers gliding in their direction. Pavel was by her side. Kelcie wished she was surprised by that, but she wasn't.

"Look at what we have here," Achila snorted. "Pavel, you have done well."

Pavel smirked. "It is curious that they knew where to find the true Heart. I wonder, Aunt Achila, is there a spy here in the citadel?"

Soldiers flinched.

Kelcie took a deep angry breath, feeling her power surging through her veins into the swords. Her breath turned hot, her stomach churned. A fire like the kind she used on the bodachs would melt their precious sapphire walls, and bring this place down on top of their heads. She could do it . . . she wanted to do it. This was her mother's fury, unshakable, unbreakable, unstoppable. She could taste victory . . . but victory at what cost?

All of these people would get hurt, and two wrongs don't make a right. She loosed a breath, stemming the rising tide. There had to be another way to get out of here.

Lexis and Jack pushed their way through the soldiers. Their stern expressions were trying to tell her something, but it didn't matter what it was—Kelcie put the swords away.

"That is not the true Heart. This is."

Heads lowered at the snap of a cold, rich voice. The soldiers parted for the glacial woman from the paintings as she padded down the hallway, holding the case from the reception hall, an exact replica of the one in Kelcie's possession, carrying it by the straps. Her wings spread to their fullest, greatest height as she reached Lexis and handed her the case.

Achila Grimes sniveled, "Your Majesty, we were coming—"

"Not fast enough. Saiga, put that back in the safe."

Lexis gripped the case gingerly, confusing Kelcie. Was it possible the box Kelcie had was so hot because it was a fake? Maybe Niall was wrong. Should she try and make a switch? She stared at Lexis to catch her attention as she passed by with the other box on the way to the safe, but she was looking everywhere but at Kelcie.

You've got the real one, Niall insisted.

How could he be so sure?

Lexis returned, and Queen Kefyra wrinkled her pointy nose.

"With only twenty-four hours left until Summer is finished forever, all but four of you—Lexis, Jack Postal, and Achila and Pavel Grimes—shall remain here, in the safe, guarding the Heart. Go!"

No one argued. In a single-file line, the soldiers marched into the vault until they were all inside.

Queen Kefyra smirked in Kelcie's direction. "Lexis, escort this fianna to my—"

The Queen farted. It was the longest toot Kelcie had ever heard!

Soldiers, not knowing that it was really Swappy posing as the Queen, turned away so the Queen wouldn't see them laughing.

Jack cursed. Lexis groaned.

Pavel yelled, "That's not the Queen!"

Soldiers in the vault rushed the door. Niall used his invisible hands to try and close it, but there were too many pushing on the other side. Zephyr shouldered the door, then shifted, placing his back against it. Niall added his weight, but it was a losing battle. It was only a matter of seconds before they busted out.

Meanwhile, Achila and Pavel took turns dive-bombing, alternating between rounds of ice knives and frosty flumes. Lexis whipped an air shield, but the ice and snow started building up around them. Jack morphed, roaring and raring to get in the fight, but they were trapped between the fairies and the soldiers who were about to break free.

Kelcie retrieved her swords.

On Achila's next pass, Kelcie sidestepped outside of the range of Lexis's shield, sliding her swords across her body.

"Caenum . . ." she sparked, swinging in a circle, drawing the ice flume with her, and sending it straight back where it came from.

Achila fled, but the frozen wave caught up with her, freezing her wings together mid-flap. Brona hit her too, with a nicker-twister. Squirming on the ground in a fit of rage, Grimes's solid-white eyes looked like they were about to pop out of her head.

"Charger!" Brona called with a frost bomb in her hand.

She lobbed it to him, only to have Pavel intercept the pass.

The fairy snarled at Swappy, who stayed in character, face reddening with outrage. "How dare you—"

Brona clapped her hands over her head, making a huge show of morphing and chased Pavel up and down the hallway.

Seeing her gawped beak, Kelcie realized Brona had a knicker-twister in her mouth. She barrel-rolled, rising above Pavel, and spit Jack onto his back.

Pavel whinged, reaching for his backside, losing the frost bomb to Jack who leaped, catching it midair and tossing it to Zephyr.

Jack, who had been running beneath Pavel, leaped, catching the frost bomb with gentle ease before it hit the ground. Jack landed on top of Achila Grimes. Still suffering from the nicker-twister, she managed to grab on to Jack's ankle, freezing and twisting it so hard Kelcie heard the sound of bones breaking. Jack transformed back to his two-legged self, crying out in pain but unable to get away from her.

"NO!" Lexis blasted Achila away from Jack.

The ice fairy barreled into her nephew at the same time Zephyr popped the frost bomb up and over the top of the door and into the vault for two points.

The bomb triggered with an explosive hiss. Solid ice expanded in all directions, freezing the soldiers from the waist down, but it didn't stop there. Zephyr scooped up Jack and ran down the stairs with Kelcie, Lexis, Brona, and Niall following, barely making it out of the hallway before the entire floor was caked in four feet of ice.

On the way downstairs, Kelcie heard Swappy yelling in the Queen's voice, calling for more guards to help the Braverwil fianna stop the intruders. They rushed through the empty dining hall and into the sculpture garden. Jack wrestled out of Zephyr's arms, forcing everyone to stop.

"Go! I'm only going to slow you down!"

"No," Kelcie refused.

"Heck no!" Brona sniffed. "We don't leave family or friends behind."

"Jack's right," Lexis challenged. "We'll get them to the Sidral and be back for you."

"I'm counting on it." He winced, hobbling behind a fountain.

Pandemonium erupted. A sea of white uniforms rushed into the room, trampling the Seven Deadly Seers. The real Queen Kefyra appeared on the spiral stairs that led to the reception room, her diadem on crooked, digging sleep out of her eyes while screaming, "Seize them!"

Running for their lives, Zephyr led the way through the basement door and down the stairs that took them into the cavern, where the creeper fairies were no longer in the hot spring. They were standing in front of the archway to the Sidral, and they weren't alone.

37

A VOICE FOR THE AGES

BRINGING UP THE rear, Lexis dropped out of the stairwell, talking to Zephyr when she should've read the room.

"I melted the doorknob, buying a few seconds at be—"

She started at the sight of the two Advisors standing beside Nevver and Latchkey. She really wished she'd left those annoying twins in Summer. The masks shielding the Advisors' identities were painted with triangles and circles in confusing geometric patterns, haunting and terrifying all at the same time. Lexis knew things were going very, very wrong when she saw Kelcie dip down from the stairs leading to the reception hall and never return.

Niall's plan would've have worked had the Queen's Advisors not been ten steps ahead of them, per usual. The fact that they'd made it this far was a miracle. But now Lexis's, Jack's, and Swappy's covers were blown, and everyone in the citadel would soon know they were helping the Summer fianna retrieve Danu's Heart. There was nothing she could do about that now. But she could swallow the fear that threatened to immobilize her, and help Kelcie get the *Croí na Bandia* back where it belonged in time to save Summer.

"What do you think you're doing, Lexis?" one of the Advisors asked, soldiers pounding on the door to get into the basement punctuating every word.

"The Heart of Danu has to go back to the Lands of Summer."

Kelcie looked ill. Her mouth was cracked and dry, her heaving breaths visible. Carrying the Heart was a heavy burden, and she wasn't going to be much good in this fight.

The creeper fairies vanished and reappeared beside Kelcie, trying to take the Heart from her. But the Saiga wasn't having it. She thrashed right and left, the straps stretching to the breaking point. Zephyr's shillelagh connected with Nevver or Latchkey, and Niall's scream drove the other to their knees.

The banging on the door was relentless.

"Lexis?" Queen Kefyra peeked out from the stairwell, and tentatively came down the stairs—barefoot.

The Advisors were so surprised at the sight of her, they didn't see Lexis mouth "Go" to Zephyr. They didn't realize Kelcie, Brona, Zephyr, and Niall were on the move until they were through the archway.

The Advisors rushed to stop them but didn't get far. Lexis sparked Caenum, drawing from the hot spring, putting to use the water whip she and Ollie had practiced in Rapshider Hall for the past two months. She launched the Advisors into the very middle of the pool.

As Lexis heard the rasp of the Sidral closing, the soldiers broke through the door. She fell on her knees, relieved. The Heart was on its way home, and hopefully one day, she would get to see that baby wyvern, Striker, Roswen, and Kelcie again.

Swappy transformed into his green-haired self with a big smile on his face.

"Why are you looking so happy? You've just committed treason!" Pavel snapped.

"I'm smiling because the nice people I met in Summer and the wyverns that live there will be saved."

"Not yet they won't," Queen Kefyra hissed.

Achila Grimes and several other soldiers ran between

Lexis and Swappy, heading for the archway with vengeance in their eyes.

Dᴜʀɪɴɢ ᴛʜᴇ ʀɪᴅᴇ in the Sidral, Kelcie concentrated on not throwing up all over Brona.

Boom.

Ba . . .

Boom.

Silence.

Ba . . .

Boom.

The beat of Danu's Heart was slow—too slow.

"We have to hurry."

Her side where the Heart rested screamed in agony when she climbed down gingerly off the stump in the graveyard. She stared at the sky, seeing the sun above the horizon, but not by much.

Zephyr panned the trees. "We have to get out of this graveyard before those fanged owls show up and make this exit much more exciting."

Niall set a comforting hand on Kelcie's shoulder as they exited the archway and started walking around the headstones.

"You're burning up!"

"It's the Heart. I'm okay." Kelcie trudged on, feeling like there were weights in her shoes.

I wish I could carry that.

"I'm okay. I'm okay," Kelcie repeated.

Then why do you keep saying that?

Kelcie laughed, aching all over. "Because if I say it enough, maybe it will be true."

The graveyard looked different when the sun was up. From the shape of the moss-covered headstones and overgrown weeds, no one had been buried here in a long time.

Every step felt like one too many. How did the old Fomorians travel from the Isle of Youth all the way back to the Lands of Summer carrying this? Then again, Kelcie had no concept of how far that was. Maybe Danu snapped her fingers and they returned to where they started. Her mother said their island home had moved into another world. If they could move a whole island, they should be able to make a wish and have it happen, right?

Kelcie closed her eyes, picturing Rilios, and made a wish to Danu. When that didn't work, she tried her mother and Brona's mother and Jack's mother (feeling like the whole trifecta might help). The wish was always the same. *Please help me. Please take me home.* Because the Lands of Summer was her home and if the Heart didn't make it in time, if the fragile beating she felt on her shoulder stopped altogether, everything would be lost.

One step at a time, Kelcie plodded a course between two angled vine-covered headstones, then around the first of three mausoleums.

And then she heard the Sidral hiss behind her and the shrill voice of Achila Grimes.

"Fan out! They can't have gone far!"

Quick-thinking Zephyr jumped into action, easing open the door to a mausoleum. Kelcie was the last to step into the musty, dark tomb. The Charger almost had the door closed when Pavel came into view.

"There's no one here!"

"We don't need to catch them here. There is only one way for them to get to the Lands of Summer. We just have to get there first," one of the Orange Crush twins said.

"What's that?" someone asked.

"Excuse me! You! Over there with the wings!"

Kelcie had to be dreaming. She swore she had heard the voice of Elliott's husband.

"I'm Oliver Sprinkles, local weatherman with WVB Channel One, Boston's news leader, and we would love to talk to you about your frosty condition. Are you responsible for the un-expected *blizzard*?"

It was Oliver. How did he know they were here?

Did you hear that? Oliver said "unexpected blizzard." I think he means Elliott is here!

Elliott was here. That was good. But how did he know? Kelcie leaned her forehead on the cool stone, ignoring the centuries of dirt rubbing off. Her head was so hot it felt like her brain was on fire.

Police sirens wheeled into the graveyard, one after another, a steady parade of cop cars coming to a screeching halt. Doors opened and Kelcie heard Boston's finest shouting.

"Wheeuh do you think you're going? This is private propahty! Take youh cawstume pahty, oh cawsplay event, oh whatevah you call it out of heeuh."

"You hearhd the Sarhge! Vacate now!"

"But, Officer, my interview. How about I give you nice folks a ride?" Oliver offered, his voice quivering on the words *nice* and *folks*.

"That would be very accommodating of you," Achila said smoothly.

Kelcie took long, deep breaths, trying to stand still.

They'll be gone soon. Hang on, Kelcie. She felt Niall's hand brush hers.

The thirty seconds it took for the cars to drive away felt like a lifetime. As soon as Zephyr pushed open the door, a familiar car's headlights flashed from the road.

"Elliott." Kelcie winced a smile, trudging toward the car. "Shotgun . . ."

"Where?" Brona ducked.

"What kind of gun?" Zephyr asked.

"She means you lot get in the back! She's riding up here with me," Elliott said through the open window, gunning the engine.

Before Zephyr could get the rear door closed, Elliott slammed on the gas. The tires spun on ice, screaming with delight but hardly moving until they scraped asphalt. Then he peeled out, speeding out of the cemetery.

"Oliver is in a van with Achila Grimes," Kelcie worried.

"He volunteered, and I told him she's as frosty as they get, but he thought you were worth the risk. And quite frankly, he was hoping for a chance to get back at her after she left me in Summer like that, and so was I." Elliott's expression turned grim. "He's got help in there with him. Don't worry. Fairy nets and starving vampire owls will leave Achila wishing she never left Winter to come after you."

Kelcie saw bite marks on his hands and cheeks from the last time they encountered those owls. His steely blue eyes were ringed with dark circles like he hadn't slept in weeks.

"You've been planning for our return," Niall chimed in. "How did you know we would be here today?"

"I didn't. We've been staking out the graveyard since you've been gone." Elliott winked at Kelcie, then frowned. "You look terrible."

"So do you." Kelcie laughed, then cringed.

"Let's get you and that thing home." He jammed the pedal all the way to the floor.

EYES CAST THEIR way as they moved swiftly through the busy park toward the Summer Sidral.

Kelcie stopped before the bridge. "You need your bough back." She struggled with the knot on the string.

Elliott shook his head. "You keep it. It's more of a liability for me since it's traceable. Oliver and me, we may have to leave Boston for a while."

Niall interrupted. "We have to go, Kelcie."

Not for the first time when Kelcie said goodbye to Elliott Blizzard, she choked up. In the past, it was generally because he was leaving her somewhere she knew would be miserable.

This time, it was because she didn't think she would ever see him again.

"She's coming." Elliott pushed Kelcie onto the bridge.

"But what if I need you? How will I find you?"

Elliott patted her cheek, something he did when she was little, but hadn't for a long, long time. "Go to Mr. Dooley's. Seven-seven Broad Street. Ask for Jökull Leak. He'll know where to find me, always."

THE SIDRAL'S BRANCHES hung low. Piles of leaves scattered with the cold breeze coming from inside the trunk as it opened for Kelcie's bough. Everyone tensed, climbing in.

Boom.

Silence.

Boom.

Silence. Silence.

Boom.

It took three beats of Danu's Heart in the case before the veins flickered, lighting.

Niall let out a heavy breath like he'd been holding it. Moving at a much slower rate than normal, they held hands the whole ride, worrying about what they'd find when they got home.

Kelcie's bough brought them to the Academy for the Unbreakable Arts. When the Sidral unzipped, they got their first look at the devastation caused by the Heart's absence.

Pitch dark, the air was too cold to breathe. The colorful greens and fragrant smells from Befelts Garden were gone. Not a single bird chirped or squirrel scampered. Not a single leaf remained on any of the forest's trees, not even on the Sidral's branches above them. There was nothing but death and emptiness.

And no one was there to greet them. Niall reached out and set his bough on the hardened bark. For too long the Sidral sat idle. For too many shallow breaths. Niall pressed his palm flat over the bough and closed his eyes. Kelcie imagined him using his silent voice to speak to the Sidral, to will it to give them one last ride. The bark closed, this time to take them to the Darling Palace.

Boom.

Kelcie's brain fuzzed, hearing only that single heartbeat, and it was getting even softer. She didn't know what to do. It had to keep beating! They were almost there!

When the Sidral opened, Kelcie was so dizzy she fell out.

"Kelcie!"

Niall tried to take the case off her and cried out. His hand blistered before her eyes. Kelcie started coughing furiously. It was so hard to breathe.

"Loo-ook!" Brona coughed.

But Kelcie couldn't look. She was too dizzy to focus on anything. Zephyr picked her up, and then he was running. They all were, toward something. Through the haze, Kelcie saw Rilios was gone. The moonstone floor was all that was left, and the Stone of Destiny—still split in two—sat waiting for its Heart.

A light appeared in the darkness. No, not a light. A hand on fire, and it was moving toward them too.

More emerged from the palace. All Ignis—Fomorians from Chawell Woods, here in Summer City.

Falling off Kelcie's shoulders, the case clanked on the ground. She could no longer hear the Heart beating. Panicked, Kelcie wrestled out of Zephyr's hold and stumbled to help.

"I got it!" Markkus said, grabbing the case. But Kelcie couldn't stop, not until the Heart was back where it belonged.

"Anuyen!" Doyen's arms wrapped around her. "Let us do it. You've done enough."

Kelcie heard Striker's yip behind her, then felt his tail feathers brush her leg. Her vision swimming, Kelcie wasn't entirely sure she trusted any of this was real. What if they never left the Sidral and this was all a dream?

But then the case opened, and the light was so bright Kelcie had to look away. As she heard the others set the *Croí na Bandia* into the Stone of Destiny, and placed the two halves together, the light and her grandmother's arms fell away. Niall and Brona and Zephyr clutched her, all four of them watching together as Doyen sealed the two halves of the Stone of Destiny together, making it whole.

"You have to stand it!" Niall coughed, speaking frantically, ". . . in the middle! On the spot! That's where it was!"

"Quickly!" someone yelled.

Rock scraped rock. There was a loud *SHUNK*. A beam pulsed to life. Light sprang from the top of the Stone of Destiny into the sky. The black mantle peeled downward, the Abyss retreating from the power of Danu, and the sun appeared at high noon, raining warmth, and comfort, and life.

The ground lit in spirals. The Lands of Summer woke up from a deep sleep with a *BANG*. The earth terraformed before their eyes. Grass grew beneath their feet. Decaying bushes were shoved aside by new growth. Bulbs burst through petrified flowers, adding splashes of pinks, yellows, blues, and oranges in the burgeoning sea of green. The Sidral breathed a deep rejuvenating breath.

Life growing from lifelessness—happening in only seconds. Kelcie smiled, taking a deep breath of her own, and then promptly passed out.

38

A STUNNING STAR

OVER THE NEXT few days Kelcie and her fianna stayed in Summer City in the barracks with the rest of the students from the Academy for the Unbreakable Arts, except for Niall.

No one had seen him since the day they returned. Brona said that after Kelcie passed out, palace guards escorted him into the Darling Palace and he never returned. Not even when Scáthach came to get them.

Their preceptor had chosen to keep everyone together in the city to help the residents in whatever way they could, but also to keep the students' spirits up. While they were gone, Coach Blackwell had been working with Ollie, making sure every last Fomorian in Chawell Woods was accounted for and dispersed throughout the realm. Now Kelcie, her grand-mother, and her clan waited to hear from the Queen on whether they could remain free or would be forced to return to the Woods.

Doyen received a surprise invitation to stay at an old friend's home in Summer City, but her grandmother decided to use her skills as a Theran and treat them to a vacation they would never forget. She crafted some pretty impressive diamonds, sold to the rat-faced bookie in town, and reserved rooms for herself and her friend at Summer City's most expensive hotel while waiting out the Queen's decision.

The first day after the Heart's return, during her fianna's report to the High Guard, Kelcie had asked whether the Queen had determined her clan's fate, but Thorn put off the answer, deftly changing the subject to someone else that was constantly on Kelcie's mind: Lexis.

"So you're saying that the fianna from Winter who spent weeks here infiltrating Summer on a covert operation to steal the Heart of Danu suddenly had a what?"

"A change of heart?" Zephyr offered.

Brona went straight for the jugular, taking no prisoners—as always.

"Sir, with all due respect, we saw what our giants did to a village, and were there when the Ellén Trechend you sent attacked. If the roles were reversed, if Summer had the chance to stop those things from happening to our people, would Queen Eislyn not take it?"

Casper turned red with irritation. "I believe she would, especially now!"

"But isn't that the problem, sir? When does the fighting end and the talking begin?" Zephyr asked.

Casper Thorn didn't answer that question either.

"Now, Murphy, you're going to have to turn over that Winter bough," Thorn said, almost as an afterthought.

"No, sir."

"Excuse me?"

"I can't, sir." Kelcie was grateful for the new unbreakable leather strap Scáthach had given her before the questioning began. She must've known this was coming. "You see, if I give this bough to you, and it is used to carry out something terrible on the Lands of Winter, then I would be responsible for that."

"The person who gave you that bough tried to destroy your school last year. A horrible act against Summer."

"An act he regrets and for which he is sorry."

Thorn didn't press the issue any further, but Kelcie got the impression from his arched brow and beard stroke that the conversation wasn't over.

Kelcie spent the rest of those days thinking about Lexis, and Jack Postal and Swappy Toots. What would Queen Kefyra do to them? How could Kelcie find out if Lexis was in trouble? They weren't enemies anymore. They were friends. Friends stuck on opposite sides of a war that would only end when the Abyss was gone.

There had been no word about or from Kelcie's father. She wasn't sure asking to see him in prison would be a good thing to do while waiting for the Queen to decide the fate of her clan, since he was the reason they were all locked away in the first place. In fact, she thought it best not to bring up his name at all.

Kelcie was at breakfast in a makeshift mess tent set up outside for AUA students when Scáthach announced that today would be their last day in Summer City.

"The Queen has decided to hold off on the Ascension, and thus the tattoo is canceled. With the war escalating, she doesn't believe a change of leadership is the right thing for the Lands of Summer at this time."

"Regan must be so annoyed," Brona giggled in her ear.

But as her cousin said it, and Kelcie thought about how the next Regent was chosen, she couldn't help but wonder if Queen Eislyn was wrong about Regan. The Stone of Destiny sings when touched by the next rightful heir. Niall heard the Heart singing. Kelcie had a sinking feeling that when the next Ascension was called for, that the Heart inside the Stone of Destiny wouldn't sing for anyone but him. She didn't tell Brona. Or Zephyr. But she was pretty sure Niall, as smart as he was, had figured that out too. She missed him, and didn't want to think about the fact that he might not be returning to school.

"However," Scáthach continued. "The Queen does believe celebrations are in order. The ball she had originally planned to accompany the ceremony will be held this evening."

Her hooded gray eyes reached for the sky as everyone jumped

out of their seats, cheering their fool heads off. Kelcie didn't jump out of her chair, but she didn't hate the idea of a ball.

Brona elbowed her. "It won't be so bad. We can dance together."

"Promise?"

She hooked Kelcie's pinkie. "Promise."

"AND . . ." Scáthach shouted, demanding silence. "There is another reason for us all to celebrate. A proclamation went out today to all of the Lands of Summer that the Fomorian clan will no longer be required to call Chawell Woods their home."

The entire student body erupted in applause.

"We get to go home over break!" Brona squealed, stamping her feet and hugging Kelcie.

Kelcie could only cry.

The rest of the morning was filled with smiles and hugs. The Saiga Den met up in the park, along with the Fomorians in the city. There were toasts and promises, food aplenty and then goodbyes. Markkus, Ollie, Dollin, and Payton had gone back to the barracks by the time Kelcie got her last hug from Doyen.

"I'll see you in Moon Bay as soon as break begins. No going on Tao's boat this year. And you tell Brona I'll expect her too. Tao can come and stay with us, like he used to as well."

Kelcie held off asking about Draummorc as long as she could, but she couldn't let her grandmother leave without knowing. "Have you heard from my father, Doyen?"

"No. I did try to see him, but High Command refused my request. Give it time, Kelcie."

Kelcie hated that answer, but it was better than the last time she and her grandmother talked about Draummorc, when Doyen told Kelcie to let him go. Kelcie closed her eyes to the warm sun and wished harder than she ever had before, willing her father to hear her, telling him that she was close by and thinking about him.

W HEN KELCIE GOT back, Brona rushed up, shaking two dresses.

"They're from Regan. They're pretty, right?"

Brona held the black silk dress with feathers for straps up to herself. "This one was definitely meant for me."

She tossed Kelcie the other, emerald green and made of soft velvet.

She wondered if Niall was going to the ball. With no word from him, Kelcie vowed to find him tonight, even if she had to storm the palace. Her fingers brushed the soft green velvet, and she smiled. If she had to go to a ball, it was nice to have something pretty to wear.

An hour later, Kelcie was trapped in teenage hell. Willow and Brona forced makeup on her, then left her with Marta Louisa and Payton, who used a hot rod to curl her hair into pretentious ringlets. Not her normal style, but she didn't hate it.

As she climbed on the transport, she saw Brona in the black gown. "You look like a goddess."

She leaned her head on Kelcie's shoulder. "So do you."

The trolley glided through the shopping district, ticking up the giant hill, passing the College of Mystical Beings. Kelcie had heard that after an intervention from the High Guard, the Speck hive was relocated to a building on the other side of the city, as far away from the College as possible, taking their artifacts with them of course.

The sky exploded halfway to the palace. Kelcie went for her swords only to remember that Marta Louisa had told her they didn't go with her dress, and made her leave them in the barracks.

"It's just fireworks," Zephyr said, resting his arm on the railing next to her. He looked dapper in his silver suit and black tie, which did in fact match Willow's dress perfectly.

There were fireworks, but not like any fireworks Kelcie had ever seen before. They went on and on. For fifteen minutes, a million colors rained down from the night's sky over the entire city.

A shooting star stopped, changing course, dropping to a hundred feet overhead, and spun like a disco ball. Lights swirled into a moving picture.

"What's that?"

Zephyr craned his neck. "I don't know."

Brona shrugged. She didn't know either.

"A stunning star," Willow effused, taking Zephyr's hand. "Probably fallen above all the kingdoms so everyone can watch the ball. The Queen does it for all the big events."

Pixel by pixel, row by row, column by column, a glorious scene appeared. Flowers and twinkling lights dangled over a dance floor before a gilded stage where musicians tuned instruments. A round of applause started and spread to every part of the trolley. It was way better than watching it on a tiny screen.

Roswen wove her way through Kelcie's classmates to speak to Kelcie, looking like an elegant dove in her long white satin gown. Her pink hair was coiled into a seashell bun, and her eyebrows were decorated with sparkling white gems.

"I understand that the events of what happened over the past seven days are classified. And I would never ask you . . . you know what, never mind." She turned to go, but Kelcie stopped her.

"Roswen, you were right about Lexis. We could never have saved Summer without her."

The music started playing as the transport came to a stop at the Darling Palace. Roswen smiled, giving Kelcie a gentle squeeze on her arm, and then continued to the front of the trolley.

"AUA students, we will meet back here on this very trolley the minute the ball ends. Any of you not here will get a month's detention! Got me?"

"Yes, ma'am," they chorused.

Roswen hopped off, joining Scáthach, Coach Blackwell, and Madame Le Deux as they walked into the courtyard. It was weird seeing her teachers dressed up in fancy clothes. Le Deux in blue lace. Coach Blackwell in a clean white shirt and kilt, and Scáthach in her dress Academy uniform that included a cloak made up of every Den color.

Excited, Kelcie's classmates rushed the courtyard. But Kelcie took her time, taking in the twinkling lights shaped like raindrops magically suspended in the air, and the blooming purple roses and lavender sprigs that had regrown in the past forty-eight hours. She tasted food from every passing tray while scanning faces, hoping to find Niall, but after ten minutes of eating, he still didn't make an appearance.

She made her way to the dance floor to see who had the courage to go out there first. It was Zephyr and Willow, of course. After that, it was like a dam broke and the rest of the student body joined them. It was just Kelcie and Brona still standing awkwardly on the side when Marta Louisa asked Brona for a dance. Kelcie had never seen her cousin blush like that before. They asked Kelcie to come with them, and she did for a song, but when she still didn't see Niall, she decided it was time to find him.

A woman carrying a tray of champagne flutes smiled at her as she entered the Darling Palace.

"Have you seen Niall?" Kelcie asked.

"I believe he's in the sitting room."

"Thank you."

Kelcie walked a little more slowly. Why didn't he come outside? Her stomach tightened with the only logical answer. He wasn't coming back to school. But was he just not going to say anything? Was he going to let them leave tomorrow and not even say goodbye?

The room was quieter, but she could still hear the music outside. She found Niall by a window, staring out. A big grin broke on his face when he saw her.

"Hi!" He was in his formal school uniform. His hair was cut shorter, making him look older, and he had a new pair of glasses on.

"Is that uniform a good sign? Is your mom letting you come back to school?"

"How could she say no?" he laughed.

Kelcie laughed too. "Then why are you in here and not outside with everyone?"

"I, um . . ." He pushed his glasses up his nose even though they weren't falling and took a seismic breath. "I was trying to work up the courage to ask you to . . . um . . . dance."

Kelcie's jaw dropped.

"You look really nice, by the way."

Nodding, she momentarily lost her ability to speak. When she found it, she returned the compliment. "You do too. Was that it? Did you ask me, I mean . . ." The butterflies in her stomach lodged in her throat. "Yes. I would like to dance with you if that was you asking me."

He stepped closer. "Really?"

Kelcie let go of her held-back smile. "I do."

Niall held his hand out. "Can I hold your hand while we walk out to the dance floor?"

Kelcie nodded again.

Hands are weird, she thought walking out of the Darling Palace with him. Everyone has them, but no two persons' ever feel the same. Brona's were really strong from drawing her bow all the time, and gave Kelcie strength whenever she snagged her pinkie. Zephyr's hands were big, but always warm, gentle, and filled with compassion, just like him. Niall's hand was something else entirely. When he clasped her hand, it made Kelcie so happy she got scared. If Madame Le Deux could bottle that feeling, she'd make millions.

THE NEXT MORNING Kelcie readied to return to school. The emerald dress fit nicely into her backpack. Even if she never had another occasion to wear it, she was going to keep it forever to remember her first ball, her first dance, and her first kiss. She placed her twin swords into the scabbard on her back, thinking not about the ball, but about Lexis. Kelcie, Brona, Niall, and

Zephyr had talked about her and her fianna last night, about how they might've stolen the Heart but if it weren't for them, Kelcie and her fianna would never have retrieved it.

"So do we owe her or not? I feel like it kinda cancels each other out," Brona calculated.

"With everything she did for us, we owe her" was Zephyr's response.

"I just hope she's okay," Niall said. "I asked my mother to stop the attacks on Winter."

"What'd she say?" Kelcie asked.

"She laughed. Told me that I didn't know what I was talking about."

"What does that mean?"

"I think it means that the Vampire Troll Seer was right. This war isn't going to be over until the Abyss is gone and the two lands have to literally face each other across a battlefield."

39

A NEW MISSION

L EXIS?" SWAPPY SANG from the cell beside hers. "How long are they going to keep us here?"

"Forever," Jack answered from the other side of her. "They are never letting us out. Never! Ever!"

Jack was having a really bad day. Swappy whimpered.

"But the food is terrible. If I eat another bowl of festor worms—"

"What? You're going to continue to break wind at a record-breaking rate, punishing us even more than having to eat festor worms for every meal?"

Lexis bonked her head on the bars. Jack was having a really, really bad day.

Hearing a door creak, Lexis's stomach tightened, and not from the festor worms. Queen Kefyra had yet to pass a sentence on them. It had been over a month. But according to the Advisors who came to see them yesterday, the Queen was wrapping up her interviews with witnesses this morning, and once done, she would decide what to do with Lexis, Jack, and Swappy, which Lexis translated as whether they should live or die.

Steps rounded the corner. Lexis stood at attention, hearing Jack and Swappy get up.

Queen Kefyra paced before them in a long white lace gown, her hands clasped, her face pinched, looking properly miffed. To Lexis's surprise, Aífe was with her, her arms folded over her chest, looking annoyed. The Advisors moved to stand behind their Queen, staring over Lexis's head, wearing masks with unreadable expressions.

"A month of conversations, all leading to the same conclusion we had at the start. A monumental waste of time. Why we need to bother with due diligence is beyond me."

"It is your law, Your Majesty," one of the Advisors uttered.

"I know that, fool! But laws can be changed!"

Queen Kefyra was in as bad a mood as Jack.

Lexis gripped the bars, feeling nauseous from the obsidian cuffs on her wrists.

"Your Majesty, please know that what we did, we only did because we didn't want to be responsible for people dying," Lexis said.

"Well, you are responsible! The next time Summer sends another army of monsters it will be on your heads!" she shrieked.

"Your Majesty, you expected too much from these children," Aífe commented. Lexis started at the insult. How could she call Lexis a child? After three years of training and being at the top of her class, didn't that mean anything? Didn't her opinions matter?

Aífe winked at Lexis.

A game was afoot. Their preceptor was up to something.

"Yes. Seems I did. And as much as I would like you all to pay the ultimate price, you have parents who would miss you. At least the gaseous one does. Been in my chambers for the past four weeks begging for their little pooky goblin to live."

"Really?" Swappy burped.

"And as cold-hearted as I am, killing children is one step too far, even for me."

Lexis's shoulders fell below her ears for the first time since they'd locked her in the cell.

"Yes, Your Majesty," Aífe agreed.

The Advisors remained mute.

Lexis sighed with relief.

"So we're to be locked up in here forever?" Jack asked in a snippy tone that made Lexis want to shake him.

Aífe's ruddy eyebrows shot straight up as she shook her head.

"Perhaps you would like to pay the ultimate price instead?" Queen Kefyra sneered at him. "No one would miss *you*, Jack Postal."

An Advisor cleared his throat. "But then again, we don't wish to bring down the wrath of a Morrígna on Winter either, do we, Your Majesty?"

"No. I wouldn't." She clapped her hands. "So, the three of you are summarily dismissed from Braverwil. You are not permitted to step foot in the school."

Lexis should've been prepared for it. Being expelled from school was the least the Queen could do under the circumstances. But hearing her say the words felt like a punch to the stomach. All Lexis had worked so hard for over the past three years was finished. The future she had dreamed of for so long, gone.

Aífe shrugged sadly, nodding. There was nothing she could do.

The Queen continued. "Swappy Toots will be remanded to his parents and on house arrest for the foreseeable future."

Swappy gasped. "You mean I can't leave the house at all? They'll be stuck with me at home all day, every day?"

"Yes," she spit, annoyed.

"They're going to be so mad," he whimpered.

"Somehow that makes me rather happy." Queen Kefyra clapped once more, sharply. "Jack Postal, you will be placed in a workhouse in Galanta to serve the time you earned for theft before going to Braverwil."

Jack made a grumbling noise but held his tongue.

"And you, daughter of abbots who never wanted to be like her parents, who only wanted to serve and protect the Lands of Winter, you will return to Mezron, to the temple you so despised. A failure, and also under house arrest. You will not train. If I find out you are training for any reason, I will lock you away again. Is that understood?"

Hope swelled. "Yes, ma'am."

Lexis had no plans to train. She was going home, to the one place she might be able to find answers about the Abyss. She had a new mission. A better mission. A much more important mission. She was going to figure out how to get rid of the Abyss once and for all. And she knew she was going to need help to do it.

"A defining moment for sure," Aífe said, as if reading her thoughts.

Lexis nodded, doing her best to look dismayed. "Yes, ma'am."

Queen Kefyra turned on her three-inch heels and clomped out. Aífe followed without looking back. The Advisors opened the doors to the cells and lined Jack, Lexis, and Swappy up in single file. The order didn't matter anymore, but Jack padded around Lexis to stand behind her.

The Advisors escorted them out of the citadel, through the long tunnel, and into blinding daylight. When her vision cleared, she saw that Jack looked taller. She had been in the cell next to him for a month, but hadn't been able to see him. And Swappy looked thin, too thin.

One of the Advisors removed Lexis's obsidian bindings. As they clanked in his hands, Lexis felt her powers surge, and her stomach ease.

Plodding toward the open gates at the bottom of the hill, Lexis saw Swappy's parents first, scowling in his direction. The Advisors must've told them he wasn't allowed out of the house. Lexis's parents were there as well, waiting for her.

Her heart leaped at seeing them. Tears threatened, and she was desperate to hug them, to tell them she missed them, and that maybe they were right about this war. Never-ending and futile. It was pointless. But first, she needed to prepare Jack and Swappy.

But as she leaned over to Swappy, he knew what she was going to say. Swappy spoke out of the side of his mouth. "We're going on the other mission, right?"

Lexis gagged. His breath smelled like undigested festor worms.

"Will you shut it?" Jack growled at him. His intense blue gaze darted to her, but only for a second so no one would see. "We'll be ready when you are."

Lexis held back her smile. "Good."

40

A LETTER FROM DAD

A MONTH BEFORE BREAK, Kelcie was at her desk, studying for her final in Madame Le Deux's class long after lights-out. Since returning to school, Kelcie and her fianna had been peppered nonstop with questions about where they were and what they were doing when the sun disappeared, none of which they were allowed to answer. Instead they were told to lie.

The only time they could speak the truth of it was during a visit to the Chief Druid, Esras. Niall had arranged for them to remain behind the day after the ball to visit with him before they left Summer City. It took over three hours for the scribes to write down the story of what happened so that it could be added to the *Book of Beings*, something Brona was ecstatic about.

"To have our names recorded in the history books for the Lands of Summer is something soldiers hope for their entire lives! And we've achieved it at thirteen!"

But then the books were ordered locked away, not for public consumption. Casper Thorn stormed in with the Queen's order. None of them were permitted to discuss being in Winter. Summerfolk were told that it was the bodach attack that had caused the darkness and the cold, that in the end, High Command repaired the damage—all of which was basically true through Queen Eislyn's distorted view. That left the story vague and open to a lot of interpretation, like the story of the Loving

Mother that was supposed to be about the Heart of Danu, except for one thing: that it was blamed on Winter.

It *was* Winter, but without knowing what Summer did to them in the recent past, it looked like they attacked for no reason. Summerfolk spoke of revenge. The cycle of violence would continue if something or someone didn't stop it.

The High Guard decided there was no reason for Niall's identity as the Queen's son to remain secret since Lexis knew who he was, and that Kelcie and her fianna, should anyone ask about their whereabouts over the dark week, explain they had been locked in Niall's chambers inside the Darling Palace when the bodachs attacked, and thereafter. Kelcie thought it made them sound like cowards.

Ultimately when their classmates asked, Niall lied and said his parents were servants at the palace, like he was embarrassed to be the Queen's son.

Oddly enough, it was Tad Fagan, the Charger who constantly picked at Kelcie and the other Fomorians at school, who started to question the official story.

"The sun doesn't vanish in every part of the realm because bodachs attack Summer City. It didn't happen when Draummorc burned down the place. Why now? And Kelcie and Brona tried to warn us!"

"Are you saying High Command is lying?" Willow had asked, shocked.

"I'm saying we should listen next time. Pay more attention. Try to be a help." He'd actually looked at Kelcie with respect when he said it too. Maybe it was because she'd saved him from a bodach during the attack at the Darling Palace, or maybe he finally got it through his thick skull that he and Kelcie were on the same side. Kelcie hoped it was the latter.

The words on the open page of Kelcie's *Unexpected Interloper* textbook blurred. She was only halfway through the chapter on water goblins when sleep came over her like a tidal wave. She sank into an empty black sea. This was a safe place. A happy place. A void where neither dreams nor nightmares could reach her. The silence felt dense and impenetrable, like being submerged deep underwater.

His voice came on like a loudspeaker experiencing uncontrollable feedback. Ear-blasting, mind-stabbing pain radiated, but still she didn't wake up.

Erfin! You cannot hide from ME forever!

If Kelcie could cower, she would, but she couldn't feel her body. This wasn't real. It was a nightmare banging on her subconscious, trying to get in. Like the cauchemar banging all night on Doyen's door, Kelcie would stay in this darkness, never letting Balor in!

Kelcie . . .

Her name floated, a pebble caught in a slow-moving current, as if he were drifting farther and farther away. But that voice wasn't Balor's, it belonged to her father. Kelcie started to go after Draummorc, desperate to find him, but only floated through the nothingness—swimming hard and going nowhere.

Kelcie . . .

Dad!

Her father was here, with her, tangled in this nightmare with Balor. But that was impossible. This wasn't real! Yet even if it was only her subconscious playing tricks on her, she needed to believe that he still cared about her enough to call to her in his dreams and nightmares. If this was the only place she would hear him say her name, then she would stay, no matter how scared she became.

Kelcie . . .

Her name zoomed by again. It was so dark. Impenetrably dark. She could light a fire. A little one. Just enough to be a beacon for her father. But what if Balor found her? What would happen then? *This isn't real.* She was sitting at her desk, probably asleep on top of her book at the Academy, safe and sound.

Wasn't she?

"Ignis." The word left her mouth and a tiny flame ignited on her finger.

For several long, arduous, painstaking seconds there was nothing but the still flame and dense silence not even the sound of her own heartbeat could pierce.

Balor's laugh was low and dangerous. Before Kelcie could blow out her finger, he spoke.

I can see you now . . .

KELCIE BOLTED UPRIGHT. Drool trailed from her bottom lip to her book, smudging the word *deadly*. Her heart hammering, hands shaking, she looked up at the sea glass. The full moon bathed her in cool calming moonlight. She was in her room. She was at her desk. It was only a dream—or a nightmare—both intertwined, because her father was there with her.

The drawer *DING*ed.

Kelcie winced, checking Payton, hoping Niall hadn't woken her up. He'd sent her a note an hour ago saying he was still studying. They planned to check on each other every hour to see how it was going.

Relieved to hear Payton's soft snores rumbling on, she carefully opened the drawer, trying not to make any noise, and brought out the delivery.

But it wasn't one of Niall's normal white cards with his Adder snake on top. It was an envelope she'd sent her father, only his name was crossed out, and hers was written above the scratch marks.

It was from her father.

Kelcie's hands started shaking. She couldn't believe it. He'd written her back!

"Finally!"

She slid the paper out and unfolded it. He'd written on the back of one of her letters. They must not give him any paper to use, or a pen, because his words looked messy and hard-fought for, like they'd been written with an old piece of charcoal, the same way it looked last year—the first time he'd written.

> Kelcie, I'm sorry I didn't write you back. I read your letters, every one, and wanted to, but my worry for your safety kept me from doing it.
>
> Parents aren't perfect. We make mistakes. And I have made grave mistakes with repercussions I will never forgive myself for, one that put your life in jeopardy, and to my dismay, continues to do so. But I believe I can rectify it.
>
> Balor has been haunting me, calling for me. I thought it would stop after you bravely destroyed his eye, but it's only gotten worse. More demanding. His will is something I cannot deny, and I fear he wants to use me to get to you. Just writing you a letter gives him an opening.
>
> I don't know what he wants with you, but I won't let him hurt you again.
>
> I hope this isn't goodbye. But if it is I want you to know that my love for you goes beyond anything I could've ever imagined. It began before you took your first breath and has never, and will never falter. You have always been the best part of me and your mother. I wish I could go back and do things differently, but wallowing in the past won't do you any good. I have to live in the present in order to look out for your future, and I can't do that from a cell.
>
> Stay safe.
>
> Your father, Draummore

"What?" Kelcie shouted, disbelieving what she was reading. "That's impossible!"

She got up and paced. How could Balor's spirit be haunting her father? And why couldn't her father refuse his will? Balor was dead—nothing but a ghost—but he had been dead for thousands of years when he controlled her and her father with his evil eye. A terrifying chill ran up and back down her spine.

Payton made annoyed noises, rolling over. "What are you yelling about? I have finals too, you know!"

Kelcie sat down at her desk, ignoring her. She was too frantic. On the one hand, she should tell someone, because her father could, at this very moment, be breaking out of prison. But on the other hand, he was her father, and if her father was right, then he was only going to leave prison because Kelcie's life might depend on it.

This was a moral quandary of epic proportions. She should wake up Niall and Zephyr and Brona, but didn't. Instead, she reread her father's letter again. And again.

He was right. He couldn't do anything to help her or himself from inside a prison cell. Kelcie folded up the letter and tucked it in her duffel bag, the one she would take home with her over break. She slid the drawer as quietly as possible, shutting it.

Then she closed her book and climbed into bed, sending another wish out to the universal granter of all wishes.

Please let my father be okay.

GLOSSARY

INSPIRED FROM LEGEND

AFANC (AH-VANC)

From Welsh mythology, afancs were water monsters who preyed upon those who entered their lakes. Typically found in the Lands of Winter in the Otherworld, they still don't take kindly to strangers in their lakes.

AÍFE (EE-FAH)

In Irish mythology, Aífe was Scáthach's twin sister, and a legendary martial artist as well. They were also enemies. They had a falling-out over Scáthach's star pupil, Cú Chulainn, romance coming between them. In the Otherworld, they're on opposite sides of the Never-Ending War, running schools, training warriors.

BANSHEES

In Irish mythology, Banshees are typically pictured as old hags. They are considered to be harbingers of death and doom.

CAUCHEMAR

From various European mythologies, Cauchemar are creatures that mess with your sleep. If they gain access to your home, they will torment sleepers, inflicting pain, feeding off dreams, turning them into nightmares.

CEWRI, GIANTS OF WALES

Both King Arthur and Gwalchmai fab Gwyar were giant-slayers in Welsh mythology.

CÚ CHULAINN (COO CU-LLEN)

Legendary hero of Ireland, Cú Chulainn was Scáthach's most famous student. His real name was Setanta. When he was a child, he was attacked by a dangerous dog and killed it, but the dog's owner, Culann, was very upset. Setanta took the dog's place as Culann's protector and the name Cú Chulainn. A son of the god of light, Lugh, he jumped the Bridge of Leaping in one leap, so Scáthach agreed to train him. It is said that in battle he could kill eight men with each stroke of his sword.

CÚ SITH (SUE-SITH)

A mythical hound in Scottish folklore. In the Lands of Summer, they are extremely rare and fiercely loyal. Impossibly fast, magical enchantments don't work on them. In order to capture them they must be physically restrained.

DULLAHAN

A headless horseman from Irish mythology. Generally, Dullahan is depicted riding on a black horse, and carries his own head.

ELLÉN TRECHEND

From Irish mythology, the Ellén Trechend is a three-headed monster said to have wreaked havoc on Ireland during the Battle of Mag Mucrama until it was finally slain by the hero poet Amergin.

FIANNA

Fiannas were small, semi-independent warrior bands in Irish mythology. This name carries on in the Lands of Summer and the Lands of Winter.

FOMORIANS

A magical race noted in Irish legend, said to wield the destructive forces of nature. They lived in Ireland, both before and during the same time as the people of the goddess Danu.

GOSSAMER QUARTZ

An invasive crystal-weed that grows two shoots when you cut off one.

GRAPPLER EELS

Eels are technically fish but look like snakes. Unlike ordinary eels, grappler eels have been fortunate to dine on enchanted tadpoles in the frigid lake on the far side of the Moaning Mountains in the Lands of Winter. Those magical frog babies give the grappler eels the power to both elongate to ten times their normal size and multiply when attacked. However, all clones must be swallowed as soon as the fighting is over.

GRINDYLOW (GRINDYLOWS, PL.)

Originally from English folklore, grindylows live in ponds waiting for children to come near so they can drag them under the water. In the Lands of Summer, they are frequently added to stew.

HOFFESCUS STONES

Only found at the bottom of Morrow Lake on the grounds of the Academy for the Unbreakable Arts, they are vital components of all glamourie potions.

ISLAND OF THE ETERNAL YOUTH

A floating island the gods and goddesses of the Tuatha Dé Danann call home in the Otherworld. It is unreachable by Summer- or Winterfolk.

KING BALOR AND HIS EVIL EYE (BAY-LOR)

A giant with a cyclopic eye, King Balor once ruled over the Fomorians in Ireland. Dark-hearted, he tried to murder his own grandsons to prevent the prophecy of his demise from coming true. Even severed from his head, his eye wreaks destruction when opened.

LUGH (LEW)

Lugh is the only surviving son of Cian and Ethniu, Ethniu being the daughter of the Fomorian tyrant King Balor. In battle with the Fomorians, Lugh used sorcery and magical weapons like his spear Gáe Assail, which always hit its target and returned to his hand on command. The spear was said to be so dangerous that it had to be kept in a cauldron of water to keep it from setting everything around it on fire. At the Battle of Mag Tuired Lugh lead his father's people, the Tuatha Dé Danann, to victory against the Fomorians when he killed Balor. Lugh's son is the Irish hero Cú Chulainn.

MEMORY BEETLES

From Mount Echo in the Lands of Summer, heat their bellies and these beetles will mimic sound or speech.

OLLIPHÉIST

From Irish mythology, the Oilliphéist is a sea serpent believed to inhabit many lakes and rivers in Ireland. It currently resides in Chawell Woods in the Lands of Summer in the Otherworld.

RED CAPS

Red Caps are murderous little folk, sometimes referred to as goblins in Celtic mythology. They get the name *Red Caps* because they dip their hats into the blood of their victims. Residing in Chawell Woods, they never give the other inhabitants a moment of peace.

SALMON OF KNOWLEDGE

From Irish mythology, the druids believed that these particular salmon ate several nuts from a magical hazel tree that had grown near the river. Once the nuts began to digest in the fish's belly, the wisdom of the world was given to it, and a person who ate the salmon would gain its knowledge. Thousands of years later, they're living in various parts of the Lands of Summer. Although they have kept their powers of speech, their supreme intellect didn't survive evolution.

SCÁTHACH (SKAH-HAWK)

Her name translates to *the shadowy one.* In Celtic mythology, she was a legendary teacher of warriors whom many heroes owed their prowess to. Her original school was located on the Isle of Skye.

SELKIES

Found in both Celtic and Nordic mythology, these sea people can shift from seal to human form. In the Lands of Winter, selkies inhabit the Gracelan Archipelago. They are inhospitable and feed intruders to their brethren sharks.

SEVEN DEADLY SEERS

Ancient Vampire Trolls seers who, for a blood donation, will answer a question about the future.

SPRIGGAN (SPRIGGANS, PL.)

Woodland creatures in Cornish mythology. Those at the Academy are a unique breed that grow no taller than an action figure, can zap latent powers out of their dormant state, and whose sap has healing powers.

SYLPH

A devious shape-shifting air spirit.

THREE MORRÍGNA

Sister war goddesses in the Tuatha Dé Danann, Macha (MAKH-uh) strategy, Nemain (NEY-van) fury, Badb (BEV) vengeance.

TROLLS

Trolls are found in many European and Nordic mythologies. In the Lands of Summer, they call the Boline islands home. They are renowned architects and clothing designers.

TUATHA DÉ DANANN (THOO-A DAY DU-NON)

From Irish mythology, the People of the Goddess Danu were a supernatural race inhabiting Ireland before the arrival of the Milesians, the ancestors of the modern Irish. Legends say they descended to Ireland riding on a cloud of mist. They are thought to have left Ireland for the Otherworld.

VAMPIRE OWLS

In Celtic mythology, the owl was a sign of the underworld. A creature of keen sight in darkness, and a silent and swift hunter, the owl is often a guide to and through the Underworld. In the Lands of Winter, the vampire owls have been bred by the Winter Queen, and set free in the petrified forest where they hunt anything with a pulse. They've also been sighted in the human world when called upon to do the Queen's bidding.

WOOD GOBLINS

Goblins are found in many European mythologies. In the Lands of Winter, wood goblins live in trenches beneath the Dauour Forest, eating everything they can catch.

WYVERN

From Welsh mythology, they are dragon-like, but have two legs rather than four.

NOMENCLATURE SPECIFIC TO THE OTHERWORLD

ALLTAR

The name of the original united continent that was split in two by war.

CROÍ NA BANDIA

Translated from Irish, it means *heart of the goddess,* but it is not the heart of any goddess, but Danu, the mother goddess to Irish mythology. She gave it to her people to save them when the Abyss formed and blocked the sun.

SIDRAL(S)

Sidrals are the common Otherworldly name for saplings of the Tree of Life, which grows on the Island of Eternal Youth. Tree travel is the only way to enter the Otherworld from the human world and cannot be done without a silver bough. Within the Lands of Summer, Sidral travel is the most desired and fastest way to get from place to place. In the Lands of Winter, most inhabitants avoid it at all costs. Bouncing around in tree veins has been known to break off fairy wings, and the roots freeze and must be flushed at least once a year.

SILVER BOUGH

Keys that open the portals to Otherworldly travel. In the Lands of Summer, silver boughs are clipped branches from saplings of the Tree of Life, while in the Lands of Winter, silver boughs are grafted from the roots.

THE ABYSS

How the Abyss was created is still a mystery to Summer- and Winterfolk. The only ones who know are the gods and goddesses, who will never willingly divulge the events of that darkest night when the waters of the largest river were turned into an unending jail between the continents, a vortex of nothing.

THE NEVER-ENDING WAR

Should you be gifted a silver bough, note that the two kingdoms—the Lands of Winter and the Lands of Summer—are in an unending war. Because their continents are split by the Abyss, they no longer march massive armies against each other, instead fighting a more devious game of cloak and dagger, infiltrating, and terrorizing.

ACADEMY FOR THE UNBREAKABLE ARTS TERMINOLOGY

ALPHA

Each of the five Dens has a designated leader who is both in charge of their Dens and tasked with helping new students learn to use their powers.

DEN

During the entrance test, when a prospective student's powers are unlocked by the spriggans' zap, they are designated a Den. It is where they will be lodged during their time at school so that they may interact with others who have similar abilities, and learn from their peers.

FIANNA

A fianna is the unit a student is assigned to by Scáthach. Typically, there are four members in AUA fiannas.

THE DENS

ADDERS (GREEN)

Adders' abilities vary the most. All are typically telepathic.

While some add telekinesis to their arsenals, others turn empathic.

CATS (RED)

Cats can shape-shift into any feline form.

CHARGERS (BLUE)

Chargers are gifted with incredible strength and a strong connection to horses. A rare few can develop the ability to communicate with animals.

RAVENS (BLACK)

Ravens can transform into ravens. Some can throw their voices, a technique known as bird braining.

SAIGAS (YELLOW)

Fomorians spark one elemental power (Air, Water, Fire, or Earth) and, if fostered, it will grow. If it isn't, the spark dies. A pulse elemental can spark all four elements, but those are very rare, generally no more than one in a generation.

ELEMENTAL POWER SPARKING WORDS

Caenum (CAY-num)	*Water*
Theran (THER-an)	*Earth*
Mistral (MIS-tral)	*Air*
Ignis (IGH-nis)	*Fire*

BRAVERWIL ACADEMY

THE DENS

The Dens do not wear specific colors to differentiate them. The entire school wears the exact same uniform, along with its preceptor.

CHANGELINGS

Changelings have the power to shift into any animate object they touch, and in doing so can mimic everything about them, including their powers. However, once they shift back, they cannot return to the form without another touch.

FAIRY

Although all fairies have wings, not all can fly. Below is a list of different kinds of fairies at Braverwil.

ICE FAIRY

The ice coursing through ice fairies' veins is so charged they can freeze their enemies without ever tiring. Their oversized butterfly-shaped wings are strong enough to fly them into high altitudes where oxygen thins.

NIMBLE FAIRY

A nimble fairy can, if in shape, reach the speed of sound. Although they have wings, they are small, and they cannot fly.

CREEPER FAIRY

Creeper fairies are gifted with the power of invisibility. If born with an identical twin, life becomes much more challenging because if one turns invisible, the other will as well, and vice versa.

SABER-TOOTHED TIGER

These deadly shifters can only take on one form of cat: the saber-toothed tiger.

SAIGA

The Saiga Den is made up of Fomorians who spark one elemental power, or on the rare occasion, can wield all four—the pulse elemental.

TOL

The leader of a fianna. At Braverwil the leaders are not specific to a Den, but rather are chosen by Aífe, their preceptor, at the start of the first year. The Tols then go on to pick the members of their fiannas from the rest of the class.

ANCIENT FOMORIAN

A language as old as time in the Otherworld, but rarely spoken anymore in Fomorian families.

TA ERFIN (TA ERFEEN)

I am the heir.

VLAST MIAN (VLAST MEE-AN)

The power is mine.

VAS (VAS)

One

DVAN (DV-AN)

Two

TRISAN (TRIS-AN)

Three

CHETURI (CHEH-TUR-EE)

Four

DOYEN(DO-YEN)

Grandmother

DOYAN(DO-YAN)
Grandfather

MAYA(MY-YA)
Mother

TEVAN(THE-VAN)
Father

ANUYEN (AH-NU-YEN)
Granddaughter, but also apple

TO NAMMASA(TOW NAMASSA)
I love you

TARA VLAST ALLTAR RASK (TAR-AH VLAST ALL-TAR RASK)
So much power Alltar split

FOLAM KIROVAN HAPNAR (FOW-LAM KEER-O-VAN HAP-NAR)
Nothingness blocked the sun, the moon, and the stars.

CHETURI DAN
Four days later

RANHAR DAN
Day seven

GOLON
Famine

DAUOA
Death

IGNAS NON POMAR (IGH-NAS NON POW-MAR)

Our ignis elementals are too few to help save them.

DOYEN VERHOSA (ANUE-MAYA VER-OW-SA)

Supreme grandmother, a goddess

ACKNOWLEDGMENTS

THIS BOOK COULD never have come together without my editor, Bess McAllister. Long calls, last-minute changes butting up against looming deadlines. I cannot thank you enough for your unfailing and unending support.

And to everyone at Starscape, Devi Pillai, Claire Eddy, Sanaa Ali-Virani, Anthony Parisi, Isa Caban, Eileen Lawrence, Saraciea Fennell, and Ashley Spruill, a big thank-you for all that you've done and continue to do for this series. It is an absolute pleasure working with you.

Also, a very, very special thanks to Anah Tillar, whose insights into the authenticity of the characters were invaluable!

Lastly, to my dog, Bailey. I'm so sorry I neglected your walks, and gave you cookies to trick you into skipping playtime. You deserved better. It won't happen with book three.

I promise.